Fenwick Travers
and the

PANAMA
CANAL

Fenwick Travers
and the
PANAMA
CANAL

An Entertainment

RAYMOND M. SAUNDERS

LYFORD
Books

This edition printed 1996

LYFORD Books
Published by Presidio Press
505 B San Marin Dr., Suite 300
Novato, CA 94945-1340

Library of Congress Cataloging-in-Publication Data

Saunders, Raymond M., 1949—
   Fenwick Travers and the Panama Canal / Raymond M. Saunders.
      p. cm.
   ISBN 0-89141-607-2 (paperback)
   ISBN 0-89141-481-9 (hardcover)
   1. Panama Canal (Panama)—History—Fiction. 2. Title.
PS3569.A7938F456   1994
   813' . 54—dc20   95-18194
                                                       CIP

Printed in the United States of America

To my wife, Mia, a true friend and partner. Also, I would like to extend my thanks to Mary Talercio and Richard Edleman who assisted me by proofreading this manuscript.

I think proper to say, therefore, that no one connected with this Government had any part in preparing, inciting, or encouraging the late revolution on the Isthmus of Panama, and that save for the reports from our military officers . . . no one connected with this Government had any previous knowledge of the revolution except such as was accessible to any person of ordinary intelligence who reads the newspaper. . . .

> Theodore Roosevelt
> January 4, 1904

I took the Isthmus, started the canal and then left Congress not to debate the canal, but to debate me.

> Theodore Roosevelt
> March 23, 1911

Oh, Mr. President, do not let so great an achievement suffer from any taint of legality.

> Attorney General Knox to President Roosevelt upon being asked to construct a legal justification for the revolution in Panama

You have shown that you were accused of seduction and you have conclusively proved that you were guilty of rape.

> Secretary of War Elihu Root after listening to President Roosevelt's protestations of noninvolvement in the Panamanian revolution

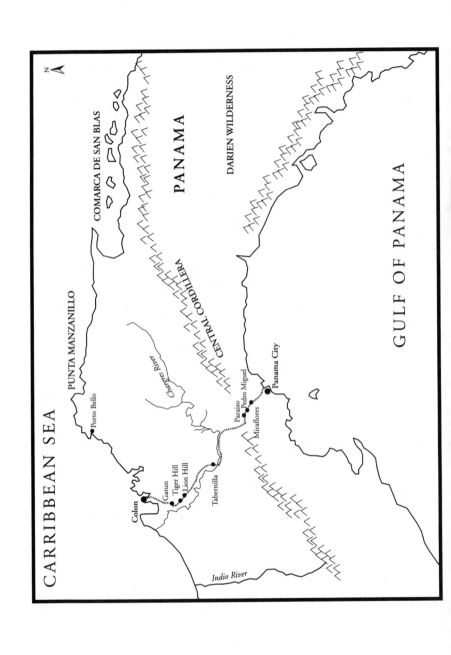

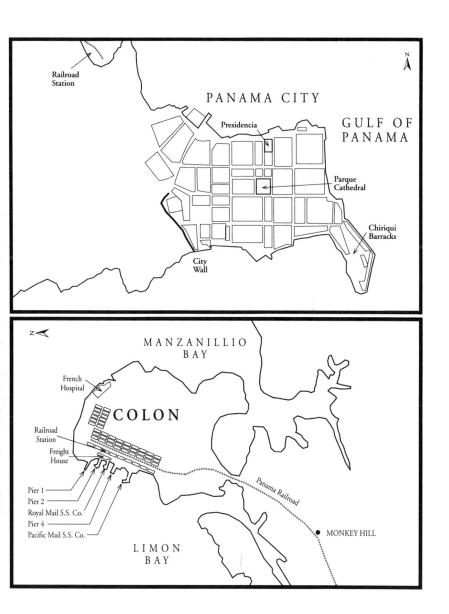

Prologue

The enclosed papers constitute the memoirs of Maj. Gen. Fenwick Travers, United States Army (Retired). His memoirs were first brought to light in 1948 when MSgt. Willie Dutton, a rum-soaked veteran of two world wars, offered to sell them to the curator of the United States Army Museum at West Point, New York. Before this unusual transaction could be consummated, Sergeant Dutton encounterted legal difficulties. Specifically he was court-martialed for black marketeering activities in which he had engaged during his recently concluded tour of duty in Trieste, Italy. Sergeant Dutton unwisely elected to act as his own attorney at his trial. He argued unconvincingly that a mule kick to the head, which he suffered during the 1939 Louisiana maneuvers, had left him incapacitated and not responsible for his conduct. Following his conviction and subsequent transfer to Fort Leavenworth, the mists of time once more enshrouded both Sergeant Dutton and the memoirs.

By happenstance the memoirs surfaced once more, in 1955, when an abandoned footlocker stored in a musty Government warehouse in Fort Monroe, Virginia, was inadvertently opened. The papers were found under carefully wrapped packages of occupation scrip from both world wars, two antique Japanese swords, numerous pairs of women's nylons, and an armed German hand grenade of 1915 vintage. The army historical section in the Pentagon was contacted, and that office made a concerted attempt to locate General Travers's family to return the documents. Unfortunately, the general's spouse was deceased, and apparently there had been no issue of the marriage. Rumor at the bar at the Army-Navy Club in Washington, D.C., had it, however, that the general had been quite fecund and had sired a dozen or more illegitimate offspring around the world during his colorful, albeit checkered, career. Frustrated in its attempts to locate any Travers heirs, the army consigned the memoirs to a cavernous archive in Arlington, Virginia.

There matters stood for thirty-five years, until the papers came into my hands. Feeling the need to share General Travers's rollicking and often-bawdy story with the world—and also feeling the need to earn a living—I compiled his collective works into a series of volumes, the third of which follows. General Travers, it turns out, is one of the most enigmatic figures in recent American history. Although virtually unknown to the general public, he was notoriously prominent within the small regular army of his day.

After years of painstakingly corroborating the general's papers with published histories of the United States Army, I gradually became aware showing that General Travers, although of flexible moral character and seemingly possessed of an insatiable appetite for female companionship, was one of this nation's most influential military figures in the first half of the twentieth century. Rising from the lowly rank of private, Travers eventually became a major general and along the way participated in campaigns from the Spanish-American War to World War II. A born swashbuckler and an adept social manipulator, General Travers also managed to thrust himself into intimate acquaintance with an astonishingly large number of heads of state, captains of industry, and underworld bosses of his day.

The story, long and rich, has been partly told in my previous volumes regarding General Travers's adventures in Cuba, China, and the Philippines. This volume resumes the tale retrieved from that footlocker in Fort Monroe many years ago.

1

Saratoga, New York
18 July 1903

"Here he comes, Fenny!" cried Jim Brady. Yes, the famed Diamond Jim who was the toast of Saratoga Spa and Manhattan. "My Lord, look at how he makes the clods fly!"

"Oh, he's a beauty," I agreed, lifting my binoculars to watch the chestnut yearling flash into the far curve. As the rider held the reins taut, the yearling rounded the curve smartly and thundered home to complete his morning workout.

"Look at that, Fenny. He's ready, I tell you," crowed Brady as the lathered colt slowed to a nervous canter. "Did you see how the exercise boy hardly lifted his crop to that horse? Chickamauga was born to win races. We can't lose, I say. I can just feel it!"

"Well, Jim, I hope you're right," I said carefully. A man would have to be blind not to see that this horse was something truly special. His lines were perfect, and the fire in his liquid eyes hinted that within his chest beat the heart of a champion. If Chickamauga ever reached his full potential—and from my perspective, that was a big if—he would make money for a few fortunate people. Since I had been befriended by Jim Brady, the reigning king of America's horse tracks, I just might be among them.

A windfall was something I desperately needed, you see, since I was embarrassingly short of funds at the moment. Oh, I had returned from the Philippines quite flush, all right. Thanks to the unpredictable and savage Moros who had taken an unexpected fancy to me, I had sailed from the islands with a tidy little sum in gold and jewels. That grubstake, however, which would have lasted a prudent fellow for years, had melted away at the various gaming tables and horse tracks I'd frequented during the first few months after my return. Now, as my long-awaited wedding to the beautiful Alice Brenoble loomed on the horizon, my funds were sadly depleted. Brady, however, serenely confident in Chickamauga's promise, proclaimed loudly and repeatedly that the colt was the answer to my woes.

1

"Fenny, that horse will be the hottest animal on the track this season or my name's not Diamond Jim." He laughed with glee at the prospect of the easy money to be made from the yearling, and as he did his great girth shook, making the diamond stickpin in his silk cravat sparkle crazily.

"Well, Jim," I replied, "I sure hope so. My money"—whatever was left of it, that is—"will be on Chickamauga. Nonetheless—well, there's something about that horse that troubles me."

"Oh?"

"Don't get me wrong, Jim. Your yearling looks magnificent. He's got the lines, and he seems to have excellent track instincts. Yes, Chickamauga appears to have every innate advantage a champion Thoroughbred can possess. That's why it's such a shame that he's so damned . . . slow."

"Slow?" rumbled Brady.

I raised my hand to stave off what promised to be a counterblast of outrage. "Jim, if I didn't like you, I wouldn't bother to give this to you straight. Now hear me out. Chickamauga's just not showing the speed needed to win the Saratoga Special. If he runs like this tomorrow, he'll finish back in the pack for sure."

To my surprise, Brady took my words calmly—in fact, almost serenely. He cocked his massive head and said, "Fenny, you've got to bet with your head. Look beyond appearances. You can see that every fiber in that animal's body says it's a champion. Put your money on Chickamauga. You won't be sorry, mark my words. You can't lose with that horse."

That, coming from Diamond Jim, should have been as good as money in the bank. Hell, not only did he know the odds on the nags, he helped make them. Jim had his pudgy fingers into other big-stakes games of chance besides horses, mind you, and being under his wing afforded me access to them on damned favorable terms. In the few weeks since he and I had become bosom pals, my battered fortunes had stabilized; and I hoped that by the time of my marriage to Alice in two days, my ledger would show a healthy balance once more. Still, seeing was believing, and what I had just witnessed left me feeling decidedly cool toward Chickamauga.

In retrospect, all the signs of impending disaster had been evident. I should have read them, but I had grown too damned complacent in the year or so following my return from the Philippines. You see, I had been assigned to the War Department and put to work as a glorified clerk in the office of the quartermaster general. To some, duty in the War Department might be considered rather plush garrison duty. After all, it was just the place for a sharp young fellow to become noticed as a diligent plugger, one who could whip out masterful reports to dazzle and amaze his elders.

I was hardly the ambitious type, though, and I found the place stultifying. Why, I'd become a damned office-bound drone, capering about at the beck and call of anyone who wore more gold braid than I did. True, it was preferable to crossing blades with opium-crazed Moros in the wilds of Mindanao, but Lord, it was a dreadful existence. My days were spent pushing mounds of paper back and forth across my desk until quitting time. About the only amusement I got was when, sorting through the mountains of correspondence before me, I chanced upon particularly urgent requisitions. These I would stamp "Denied" in bold red letters and post right back to their senders.

Mild diversions like these, though, were hardly enough to occupy me, and in a fit of ennui I decided to actually take a stab at learning the quartermaster business. I suggested to my immediate superior, one Major Reynolds, a superannuated fogy who had been ensconced in the War Department since the Indian Wars, that he might want to turn me loose a bit and let me try my hand at letting a contract or two. To my amazement, Reynolds did exactly that. He detailed me to purchase a thousand bridles for the cavalry. That seemed an attainable goal, and although the paperwork was tiresome, things went reasonably well. I paid no more than retail plus a handsome commission to a dealer in Cincinnati. The perhaps too-generous draft I authorized against the Treasury raised Reynolds's eyebrows, but he was an amiable old fellow and wrote it all off to inexperience.

Next he entrusted me with acquiring beef cattle for the Department of Texas. Warming to the task, I penned a contract with a factor in San Antonio for five hundred head of longhorns. The price was excellent, well below the going market rate. Why, I thought, here was an opportunity to redeem myself for paying a premium for those damned bridles. I suppose it might have been prudent of me to have arranged for an inspection of the critters before taking delivery. That might have involved a few extra hours in the office, though, so I figured, why bother? After all, cows were cows, right? If they had four legs and a set of horns each, they would pass muster, and I felt quite safe in assuming that such was the case. What was more, it wasn't as though I was spending my own money. No, the transaction was on Uncle Sam's account, not mine, and that knowledge gave me the assurance I needed to expedite matters. I signed a payment voucher for the herd sight unseen and arranged to have the lot of them shipped by rail to

Fort Bliss, Texas. My haste was understandable, you see. I had to snap up this bargain before the factor tried to back out of what was obviously a losing proposition for him.

The deal being done, I was feeling quite good about my business acumen until the first troubling telegram clattered in from Texas. It seemed that a few of the longhorns had been found to be deceased upon arrival. That was damned unfortunate but hardly unusual. Perhaps someone had failed to water the beasts during their sojourn. Or perhaps they had succumbed to parasites. Such things happened, I knew, so I shrugged the whole thing off and went about my business.

Try as I might to put the matter out of my thoughts, though, the telegrams kept coming in, each one more alarming than the last. Now the longhorns were expiring all over Fort Bliss. Their carcasses littered the rail yard, the post corral, and the streets of nearby El Paso. The air was filled with clouds of buzzing flies. Ominously, the post's herd of cavalry mounts was beginning to act in a damned peculiar manner. The post surgeon, the telegrams informed us, was working frantically to uncover the cause of the strange malady.

A tense knot of officers was gathered around the telegraph by the time the surgeon's diagnosis came across the wire. There could be no doubt about it, he averred: it was anthrax!

"Good God, Travers!" gasped Major Reynolds. "You bought diseased livestock!"

"But, but, sir," I stammered in my own defense, "at the price I paid, that herd was an exceptional value. Yes, indeed, a rare bargain."

"An exceptional value? Why, you dolt, those cattle are absolutely worthless. Don't you understand that the government has been defrauded?"

If I didn't then, I certainly did by the following day, which was when the investigation started. I was suspended indefinitely from any purchasing activities and advised informally that, pending the outcome of the investigation, I might do well to consider alternate pursuits—such as civilian life. I was under a black cloud, you see, and when I requested a month's leave, permission was readily granted. The War Department wanted me out of sight, and the sooner the better.

More than a bit put out by the ungracious handling I'd received, I flew to sweet Alice Brenoble for solace. This was a bit ironic, since it had been Alice who over the years had trailed me around the globe, trying as best she could to tie the matrimonial knot. The poor, lovesick girl had even followed me to the wild Philippine Islands, only to fall into the clutches of the savage Moro pirates of the Sulu Sea. Alice's near brush with a life of degrading servitude, though, had done nothing to cool her ardor for me— and in truth the feeling was mutual, for Alice was a rare beauty. That was why I had allowed myself to become affianced to her, although I was not prepared to submit to wedlock until I had worked out a suitable financial arrangement with her miserly uncle, George Duncan. Uncle George, perhaps fortunately for me, had proven to be tighter than a newly caulked ship, and without financial inducements dangled before me, I had managed to forestall a binding union with dear Alice and thereby keep my freedom over the years.

Now, however, it was I who needed her, and with the tables turned I found myself damnably vulnerable. Alice gave me the succor I sought and then some. In fact, I got such sweet consolation that before I quite knew it I had lost my head and actually let Alice talk me into setting a date for our long-delayed nuptials. All of this explained why I was in Saratoga Spa in upstate New York; it was the site my betrothed had selected to end my bachelorhood. Here Alice had passed the most treasured moments of her childhood, and it was here that she intended to drag me to the altar at long last.

As I waited stoically to pass through the grim portal into matrimony, I assumed that my swashbuckling days were behind me. To all appearances my army career was over, and if that proved to be the case I would just accept the fact and make my stay in Saratoga as memorable as possible. That was why, as I leaned against a rail watching the horses at their morning exercise, I had but one goal in the world, and that was the single-minded pursuit of dissolute bliss for the duration of the short period of freedom that remained to me.

Brady's voice interrupted my reveries. "Are you up for some breakfast, Fenny? These early morning workouts stir up the appetite something fierce, eh?"

He patted his ample girth in anticipation of a feeding. Brady was three hundred pounds if he was an ounce, you see, and his meals were rituals he observed with the single-minded devotion of a saved sinner at a camp meeting revival.

"Sounds like just the thing," I seconded, hearing the now familiar sound of his stomach growling. Together we headed for the tables set by the track clubhouse where, with a great show of deference and fussing, the headwaiter showed Jim to his usual spot near the rail. Trackside breakfast was a tradition at the Spa, as Saratoga was known to habitués. Like Jim and me, many high rollers appeared at dawn to check on the condition of their horseflesh. To accommodate this gaming elite, the track management laid out a breakfast spread in the summer months—"the season" as it was called hereabouts.

Once settled in, Brady surveyed the menu as the waiter hovered nearby. He eyed the thing like a savvy investor going over a prospectus, for he was all business and missed nothing. "Bring me an alderman in chains," he ordered, pointing out the roast turkey swathed in links of pork sausage.

I looked at him agog—an entire roast turkey for breakfast? The waiter, however, used to Jim's gargantuan and eclectic appetite, didn't blink an eye. "Right away, Mr. Brady."

"And get me some appetizers while I wait, son. I swear I'll expire from hunger if I don't get something under my belt pronto." Seeing my amazement, Brady assured me, "It's a small bird, Fenny, not much larger than a chicken."

The appetizers arrived, scrambled eggs and thick slices of ham. Brady set to, showing me how he had earned his reputation as America's foremost trencherman. He shoveled this forage into his maw, his fat jowls quivering as he masticated the vittles into smithereens. He grabbed a frosty glass of freshly crushed orange juice, his favorite beverage, and washed his food down in a flood of the pulpy liquid.

Then, able to speak again, he gasped, "Five hours to track time, Fenny. Want to turn over a few cards at Canfield's 'til then?"

Canfield's Clubhouse was the premier gambling establishment at the Spa, and Brady was one of its most honored clients. He was welcome at any hour of the day. "I can't, Jim," I answered. "Alice is due at the station in an hour. She's been down in New York with her uncle, seeing to some last-minute wedding details. I promised to meet her when she arrives."

"Good idea. Make 'em happy at the very beginning and keep 'em that way forever after," advised Brady, jabbing a fork in my direction for emphasis. "It's the secret to a long marriage, Fenny."

Brady, as far as I knew, had never been married a day in his life. "Right, Jim."

Brady gave a grunt and went back to his food, making short work of the rest of the fare laid before him. Just in time, too, for then his turkey arrived and he ripped into it like a starved marten in a henhouse. Bones and skin flew everywhere, and before my eye the once majestic bird was reduced to a skeleton. In an astonishingly short time, Jim had cleared the table of every morsel in front of him.

He gulped down a further half gallon of orange juice, belched, and then broke wind loud enough to start a regatta. Satisfied at last, he said, "Let's be on our way, Fenny. There's money to be made, I tell you."

He called for his phaeton, which was promptly rolled around, pulled by two matched grays. A gaggle of track boys and grooms appeared to help Jim into his equipage, a procedure roughly akin to hefting a grand piano through a second-story window. After much pushing and wheezing, Jim was aboard, I was at his side, and we were off.

"Seegar?" asked Jim as we rolled along, handing over an elegant black Havana. I thanked him, put it in my mouth, struck a match on my boot, and did the honors for both of us. We sat in silence for a while enjoying our cigars. The rich smoke wafted up around us and then slipped out the coach windows to mingle with the heavy mist that was just now burning off the verdant foliage. Ah, Saratoga in the summer; there might be prettier places in the world, but at the moment I couldn't think of any.

As if reading my thoughts, Brady rumbled, "It's a great life, Fenny." He took a deep pull on his Havana and then exhaled slowly. "You know, I expect to live off the winnings of that horse for a few years."

"Chickamauga, you mean?"

"Yep. Today he's an unknown. The odds will be heavily against him. All the big money in the Saratoga Special will be on Calcutta, the favorite. You and I will buck those odds, naturally, and we'll clean up. Then, later in the season, when Chickamauga is better known, the odds won't be as favorable, but his speed will produce a nice steady income nonetheless. It'll be like having gold-backed certificates in the bank."

I saw no point in repeating the obvious. Unless Chickamauga ran tomorrow like a horse possessed, Jim would lose a bundle, and the rest of my cash would evaporate at the same time, for I couldn't offend Jim by betting against his nag. I could only hope that Brady would see the light at the last minute.

"Well, the way you talk it certainly sounds that way, Jim. Why, if I listen to you much longer, I'll decide to resign my commission and become a professional gambler myself."

This was more than just idle blather, you see. I was toying with the notion of taking up the cards in earnest, now that my military career was in ruins. Brady, though, would not hear of this. "That would be a mistake, Fenny, take my word for it. Professional gamblers are a desperate lot. They try too hard and many of them wind up on the rocks. No, I'd never become a professional if I were you."

"But Jim," I protested, confused, "you're a professional, aren't you? And you're doing just dandy, right?"

Brady gave a good-natured shake of his head at my denseness. "Fenny, Fenny, it's like I told you earlier. You've got to see through appearances. Now, I may look like a gambler, and I gamble all the time, of course, but I wouldn't call myself a professional."

"Jim, you've lost me."

"Hell, Fenny, my line of work is selling. Games of chance to me are an avocation, a mere sideline."

I was incredulous. "The great Diamond Jim Brady is a salesman?"

"Oh, ho, my young friend, not just a salesman. No, I am the drummer of the age, the man who makes more money on sales commissions in a year than most good-sized cities collect in taxes."

"Then what is it you sell?"

"Railroad cars, Fenny, and parts. Wheels, seats, undercarriages, that sort of thing. If it can be bolted, welded, or strapped to a train, I sell it."

"But to whom, and for whom?"

"I'm the leading agent for the railroad car combination, the cartel that controls the manufacture of locomotives, coalers, cars, cabooses—the whole shebang. I sell to the high rollers I rub shoulders with, the railroad men. They come to me because they know me and they trust me. I don't cheat at the tables or at the track, at least as a general rule, and they respect that. So while I'm making money from the ponies and the dice, I'm setting up the contacts I need for my next sale. There's a wonderful symmetry to the thing, Fenny."

Now *there* was a little-known tale, I thought, nodding my head appreciatively. Brady was a businessman first and a swell about town second.

The mention of my commission, though, had piqued his interest, and he mused, "You know, I've been watching you, Fenny. You're smart, and smooth to boot. You'd make a hell of a salesman yourself if you put your mind to it. How long have you been in the army now?"

"Six years, more or less." Much less, if you counted only the period of my honorable service.

"Six years," whistled Brady. "My, my. And all that time spent fighting in one corner of the world or another. Why, I remember your name being in the papers when you returned from China. All of New York was there to greet you at the dockside, yours truly included."

I nodded in fond remembrance. "China was grand, Jim. I marched all the way to Peking, you know." And plundered the place upon my arrival, I recalled with silent satisfaction.

"That would have been enough adventure for any one man," Brady went on, "but then you ran off for a few years to fight those Moros in the Philippines." Here he gave a shudder and confided, "You know, the thought of them little brown savages with their swords and spears makes my skin creep."

"You're not the only one, Jim," I assured him affably, causing Brady to give out a great guffaw that rocked the carriage on its springs.

"Quit pulling my leg, Fenny. I'll bet a thousand to one that those Muslim fanatics never caused you to lose a moment's sleep."

"If you can get me odds like that, Jim, then I'll swear you're right," I replied, giving him a clap on his well-upholstered shoulder. If Brady wanted to make me out to be an icon of martial virtue, I figured, let him. All that mattered was that my reputation as a stalwart soldier had gained me entrance into his circle and that there was profit to be made in that association.

Maybe it was the breakfast in his gullet, or maybe the lingering exhilaration from watching his colt run, but whatever the reason, Brady was in an expansive mood. "Fenny, I'll let you in on a little secret. Rubbing elbows with you for the past week has made me feel, well, damned patriotic. Now that's a feeling I don't get too often." He slammed his massive thigh and laughed once more, feeling in fine fettle and enjoying himself to the nines. He genuinely liked chumming around with a war hero; he liked it damned fine.

I could have lapped up his adoration for hours, but long experience had taught me that folks like their heroes humble, so I turned and protested, "That's kind of you to say, Jim, but I think I'm getting the best of the bargain. After all, with the tips you've given me on the ponies, I've made my annual salary and then some. What's more, all of that's before Chickamauga has even been led to the gate at the Saratoga Special. If you're right about your horse, my friend, that should be a payday to be savored for a lifetime."

"It will be, Fenny," he vowed confidently. "The odds against Chickamauga will be close to thirty to one, maybe more at post time. If we play this right, it'll be a bloodbath for the bookies and pure gold for you and me." He added with an avuncular twinkle in his eye, "Think of this as my wedding present to you, Fenny. If things go as planned, you'll be fixed for a few years. That way you won't have to depend on that tightwad future father-in-law of yours for handouts."

"Ah, I see you've made the acquaintance of the famous George Duncan."

Brady nodded. "That I have. He's been coming to the Spa ever since he struck it big in copper out in Arizona. He plays the roulette wheel, rarely the faro tables. But he's not a good gambler; he almost always leaves a loser. The thing that marks George Duncan, though, is *how* he loses. He always claims he was cheated or, worse yet, tries to change his bet after the wheel stops spinning."

None of this was a revelation to me, of course, having had personal experience with Duncan's miserly ways. "That sounds like the George Duncan I've come to know and love."

"If it ain't one thing with Duncan, it's another, and getting him to cover his checks, well, that's a whole story in itself," continued Brady. "As rich as he is, he'll stiff you until December on a check drawn in July. Eventually he pays, whining and cussing the whole time, of course. Duncan's smart enough to know that if he were to welsh he'd never see the inside of a Saratoga gaming house again, but it's a trial for all concerned." Brady shook his head in consternation, evidently recalling some personal transaction with George Duncan.

One thing puzzled me, however, and I said so. "Tell me, Jim, if Duncan's so infernally aggravating, why don't the gambling clubs just close their doors to him? I mean, there's plenty of other business besides his, isn't there?"

"They'd like to, Fenny, believe me. The trouble is, though, they can't afford to. George Duncan simply loses too much and too often to be turned away. I've seen him leave a hundred thousand dollars on the table at one sitting. I guess you could say his antics are just a cost of doing business up here. He's a burr under everyone's saddle, but all the same he's a first-class meal ticket."

The carriage turned into the crushed gravel drive that led up to the portico of the Anaconda Hotel, one of Saratoga's oldest and finest. Liveried footmen materialized to haul Brady down from the phaeton. The Anaconda was quiet, for most of its guests would not be stirring for several hours yet. Together we stepped into the lobby. There, on the floor at the foot of an ornate spiral staircase, was an intricately tiled mosaic of a powerful racehorse, its head raised as though it sensed a challenge in the air.

"That's Tammany," explained Brady. "He was one of the finest colts to ever set foot on a track. I made a few bucks off old Tammany myself, God bless him."

"He must have been an exceptional horse to get his likeness memorialized on the floor of the Anaconda."

"Oh, Tammany was good, all right, but nothing like Chickamauga will be. No, Tammany's claim to fame was that he belonged to Marcus Daly, a copper baron like George Duncan. Daly just happens to own this place, so he can damn well stick the image of his colt on the floor for all to see. Just be grateful he wasn't partial to beagles, or we'd be standing on a pack of 'em instead of this lovely creature."

The smell of breakfast being served drifted out from the dining salon, causing Brady to smack his lips and move in that direction. "Care to join me for a small repast, Fenny?"

"What? Eat again? Why, Jim, you just demolished a roasted bird and so many sausages that if you laid 'em end to end, they'd stretch from here all the way to New York City. Surely you must be joking."

The hunger in Brady's eyes, though, was unmistakable. "Why, that turkey merely whetted my appetite, Fenny, nothing more. The ride back from the track always sets me in a mood for a proper breakfast. I'm a man who needs to keep his innards conditioned, and if they're not kept properly primed, well, I can't think clearly. I guess I just burn off my feedings faster than the next fellow." Judging from his girth, I rather doubted Brady ever burned off anything, but I didn't want to offend him so I held my tongue. He waddled into the nearly deserted dining room and we were shown to an exquisitely set table by a window. A squad of waiters appeared to take what promised to be an extensive order from Jim. A chilled pitcher of orange juice was set before him while I sipped a cup of java and sat back to enjoy the view.

Before me spread Saratoga, the mecca of the finest families of New York, Boston, and Philadelphia. Here flocked the Vanderbilts, the Whitneys, the Belmonts, and the Astors. At Saratoga they gambled, took the waters, and promenaded about with their wives and paramours. Later today, the restaurants would be thronged with the haute monde, and the gaming houses would ring with laughter and curses until well after the sun set beyond Great Sacandaga Lake. In short, the place was awash with loose money and beautiful women, the two commodities that I happen to find absolutely irresistible.

As I sipped and dreamed, a second breakfast arrived and Brady set to with grim determination, and it was only after he had swallowed enough provender to choke a hog that he became sociable once again. He gave out a great belch, dabbed with his napkin at the maple syrup smeared over his surprisingly dainty pink lips, and inquired lightly, "When's the wedding, Fenny?"

"The day after tomorrow. We're to be hitched at the Episcopal Church."

"And the honeymoon?"

"Newport. Duncan's giving us his place on the beach for a few weeks. His gift to the newlyweds, you see."

Brady snorted. "Anything except cash. Well, Duncan's too old a dog to change his ways, I suppose. Overall, though, it sounds like everything's set. The timing's perfect too, you know, what with the Saratoga Special scheduled for tomorrow. You'll be able to get all your wagering out of the way so the future Mrs. Travers will have your undivided attention, eh?" He laughed slyly and gave me a great wink.

"That's the way I see it, Jim."

"And then?" he asked. "It's back to the army for you, I suppose?"

"I suppose," I replied vaguely. "I've arranged for quarters at Fort Myer in Arlington, so Alice and I will be fairly comfortable." I didn't mention that I expected our stay in those new digs to be a short one.

"Comfortable? On the pay of a captain?" Brady challenged me with an arched eyebrow. "Surely the niece of George Duncan might find herself just a mite pinched living the life of an army wife."

"I've made that very point to Alice, Jim, but she insists that the wedding go on." I didn't add that I expected her to bring along enough of a dowry to allow me to rise to her level rather than have her descend to mine.

"Loyalty," grunted Brady. "That's what matters, Fenny, loyalty. Money comes and money goes, believe me. Loyalty, however, abides."

Loyalty wouldn't buy a shot of cheap whiskey in a post exchange, of course, yet Brady seemed to actually mean what he was saying. He was a strange bird, all right, which was probably why I had taken such a cotton to him. "You know, Jim, I've never properly thanked you for the swell time you've shown me. Why, you've put me up here and treated me like a long lost brother, and even set a chair for me at some of the biggest games in town."

"Games at which, I might note, you manage to hold your own," he observed approvingly.

"Well, Jim, I admit that games of chance have always held a certain fascination for me." What I meant was that I'd shirked official duties for years to spend countless hours hunkered down in flea-bitten cantinas from Havana to Manila where I gambled away my pay, usually months before it had been earned. After an existence like that, it was no mystery why I knew a thing or two about wagering.

"Your fascination shows," he replied.

Deciding to take that for a compliment, I returned to my point. "Well, anyway, I just wanted you to know that I'm overwhelmed by the way you've taken me in. I mean, all I did was send you a wire that I'd be up here to get hitched and that I'd like to make your acquaintance at the same time. Before I knew it, you were at the station to greet me, and the red carpet has been rolled out for me ever since. I really appreciate all of this, Jim. Really."

Who wouldn't, though? Brady wouldn't let me pick up a tab, and he insisted on staking me to all the card games I attended under his sponsorship. I was in vagabond heaven, and I only wished that I'd had the foresight to send that telegram years earlier.

"Ah, nuts," Jim said with a bashful wave of a bejeweled hand. "It's not all that big a deal, Fenny. And besides, the way I see things, it's you who's doing me the favor."

"Me?" I asked, genuinely puzzled. "How do you figure that, Jim?"

"It's like this, Fenny. When I make a big sale, it's not so much the commission that matters as the thrill of the deal. As for gambling, although I like money as much as the next fella, it's not so much the cash I crave as the thrill of the bet—you know, that split second before you know the outcome and when your entire stake might be swept away in the blink of an eye. That's what I crave, Fenny, and whether I win or lose is only secondary. I need to be at the rail when the horses run, whether my pony shows or not. It's the feeling, Fenny, not the payoff. I'd rather gamble with style and grace and lose a million than whine and hedge and end up winning two million. That's what makes me different from the other plungers hereabouts."

"Like George Duncan?" I asked with a grin.

"Duncan? A plunger?" snorted Brady. "No, he's merely a cash cow for the locals. Definitely a dyed-in-the-wool contributor. No, I was talking about the big sports, the ones who actually win at the tables. Like Bet-a-Million Gates, for instance."

"That's a familiar name," I said.

"It ought to be. John Gates has been a fixture in this town for years. He started like me, you know. Yep, he was a lowly drummer. His line was barbed wire, though. Got into that business back in Chicago at just the right time and made a fortune. All the cattle ranchers wanted the stuff and they snapped it up as quickly as the factories could churn it out. Gates made a killing, and soon he moved from barbed wire to Wall Street to really make his mark. Right now he's got two big passions. One is to create a steel combine from coast to coast."

"You mean a trust, like the one J. P. Morgan's trying to put together for steel?"

"Gates and Morgan are in that scheme together, Fenny, thicker than thieves, in fact. Old J. P. needs Gates's mills to make a go of the thing, and Gates needs Morgan if he's ever going to leave the stigma of his drummer days behind."

"And Gates's other passion?"

"Gambling."

"That's a bit odd for a fellow who has all the cash he can possibly use, don't you think?"

Brady shook his head. "Not for Gates, Fenny. The more he has, the more he wants. Why, he'll give you odds that the sun won't rise in the east, and he's not above fixing a race or causing a stock run as long as the end result is to line his pockets. That's what makes him so . . . interesting."

"Sounds like a gent I'd like to meet."

Brady eyed me, a crafty expression on his wide face. "You will, Fenny, and right soon. In the meantime, all you need to know is that Gates is addicted to gambling. To him winning at the tables—or in business—is the only goal, and style be dashed. If he loses, instead of taking his lumps like a man he throws a tantrum that's heard all over Saratoga. Now, I like winning as much as the next fella, like I said, but I like to do it with a certain flair. If you've got style, I say, the world will sit up and take notice. Yessirree. I make it a point to do all my gaming in style. That's what I call being a sportsman, you see. I do everything Gates does, but with class. Yep, that's me. James Brady, sportsman."

"Be that as it may, Jim, none of what you've said explains why you'd want to befriend a rather ordinary captain of infantry."

"Ordinary? You? Who are you kidding, Fenny? You're the Tiger of Palanan, the fellow who collared that outlaw Aguinaldo."

"Now, Jim, don't pour it on too thick."

"Too thick, hell. Why, you're on first name terms with that jackass in the White House."

"True enough. That jacka—er, President Roosevelt and I are acquainted."

"That's my point, man. As a sportsman, I need to be seen with the bluebloods and the shakers who flock to Saratoga. They may be rascals to a man, but they're the people who matter in this country. And I happen to count you among that select group, my friend."

"Er, thanks, I guess."

Oblivious to his left-handed compliment, Brady rattled merrily along. "Oh, don't thank me. You're a genuine hero, Fenny. My God, man, you plucked Peking from the Manchus and helped take the Philippines for Uncle Sam. Next to you, the high rollers at Canfield's Clubhouse are pikers. So don't sit there thanking me for letting you pal around with me, Fenny. It's you who's doing me the honor."

About then a waiter appeared with the tab, a collection of paper the size of a small ledger. "Well, Jim," I said, "since you put things like that, why don't you get this tab like all the others you've gotten, and then throw in my room bill to boot? It's the least you can do."

"Haw, haw!" exploded Brady. "That's what I mean, Fenny. That's style!"

Brady's laughter died suddenly in his throat as a sinister voice from behind me sneered, "Oh, we're jolly today, ain't we, Brady?"

I turned to see a squat, heavily muscled fellow in a loud plaid suit standing with his hands on his hips. The wad of tobacco in his jaw and the mud on his shoes told me his status—racetrack trash. The bulge under his coat told me something else: this lout was packing a shooting iron.

Brady recovered his aplomb with a visible effort. "Morning, Crawley. I see your owner let you out for a morning run. Well, be on your way, and mind that you don't spoil the carpet."

Crawley reddened at this; he looked like he'd rise to the bait but then thought better of it and growled instead, "Blow all you want, Brady. Mr. Rothstein'll let his money do the talking at the track. Then we'll see how sassy you are."

Crawley turned to me, gave me a quick once-over, and sneered, "So, Brady, you've decided to bring some muscle up to keep you company for the season, have you?"

"To protect me from what, Crawley? Certainly not the likes of you. No, this is Captain Travers of the United States Army."

Under the circumstances, I felt no need to rise and extend a hand. I merely sat back and studied Crawley coldly, and he returned the favor. Then, apparently having fitted me into some pigeonhole in his little mind, Crawley did an abrupt about-face, marched over to a corner table, and joined a sallow young man with the demented look of a rabid rodent. This, I took it, was Mr. Rothstein. Together Crawley and his master glowered in our direction as Brady resumed his meal.

"Friends of yours?"

"Naw. Crawley's the creature of Arnold Rothstein over there, who in turn is a vicious little bookie from New York."

"Rothstein, eh? Never heard of him." I eyed Rothstein as I spoke and was rewarded with a snarl from across the room.

"You're not missing anything," Brady assured me. "Rothstein is one of the slickest fixers in the country. Don't get me wrong, Fenny. Everybody indulges in a little fixing now and then, even me. People with style, though, show a certain moderation in such matters. But Rothstein's different. He's so crooked he can't operate without a fix being in. What's more, it's all a big joke to him. So what if the little suckers get crushed along the way? In fact, the more of them that are swept away in his swindles, the more he seems to enjoy it. But if the shoe is on the other foot and Rothstein thinks the fix is in against him, well, look out. He doesn't like that one bit, and he's not shy about letting the world know."

"That's where Mr. Crawley comes in, I suppose."

Brady smiled tightly. "Yes, Crawley's job is to get the message to one and all that it don't pay to play games with Mr. Rothstein's money. If you fix a bet against him, Crawley fixes you."

"I take it that you and Mr. Rothstein have a, er, history?"

"Oh, we've crossed swords at many a game table, and the more I see of Rothstein, the less I like him. He uses people up and throws 'em away. He's poison, and I steer clear of him if I'm able. The only good news about Rothstein is that he sticks to the ponies and his cards. Seems that baseball and prizefighting bore him. His big delight is the all-night poker games in the back room of Canfield's."

"All that seems harmless," I ventured.

"So far it has been. I know enough about Rothstein, though, to be wary of him. He wants to be the cock of the walk here in the Spa, and to do that he needs to push his way past me and the other high rollers. Sooner or later, he'll start in on that pushing."

I pulled out my timepiece. "Where has the morning gone? I'm due at the station to fetch Alice. Jim, I've got to run. I'll catch up with you this evening. Where will you be?"

"Canfield's club. Look for me after eight."

"I'll see you there," I promised and made to rise, but Brady stayed me with a hand on my arm.

"Fenny, when we were back at the track, do you remember what I said about appearances?"

I thought a second. "Why, yes. You told me to bet with my head and to look beyond appearances."

"Good. Yes, very good," he said approvingly. "When Chickamauga was rounding the track today, did you notice anything about the way the exercise boy held the reins?"

I cogitated mightily. "They were tight. High and tight."

"Meaning what, Fenny?"

Then it struck me. The exercise boy had deliberately held Chickamauga back, just as he had done each day since I'd been at the Spa. Why, Brady must be trying to say that he had ordered that the colt be kept from showing its speed! No wonder he was so confident of making a killing. He had taken careful pains to gull all the watchers at the track, me included, and now the stage was set for a major upset.

As Brady watched the light of understanding begin to gleam in my eyes, he sat back and sighed expansively. "See you tonight, Fenny. Eight o'clock sharp."

2

I galloped into view of the station just as the heavy pall from the approaching locomotive appeared over the tree line to the south of town. Soon the train was screeching to a halt at the siding in a dense cloud of billowing steam. As the vapors cleared I could see Alice standing on the platform of the first car in line. She wore a fetching gown of primrose batiste cotton all trimmed with white Alençon lace that outlined her lithe form to perfection. From beneath her wide-brimmed *peau de soie* hat, an ornate affair festooned with ribbons and feathers, her green eyes searched the station. She saw me, smiled radiantly, and threw me a happy kiss. Lifting her hem, she flew down the steps and into my arms. "Fenny, dearest! Oh, how I've missed you!"

"Alice, my love," I laughed and then gave her a deep kiss full on the lips as a stream of carefree vacationers, following close behind Alice, veered left and right to make their way around us. When I released her, Alice took my arm and led me to where the carriage sent out from Sycamore, the estate of George Duncan, stood waiting.

"Everything's coming together nicely, Fenny," she bubbled as we walked. "The Van Pelts will arrive tonight and the Grosworts later today. The last of the RSVPs have come back, and I expect nearly three hundred guests on my side. Thank goodness Uncle George has been a dear and lent me his private secretary to help with all the arrangements. The ceremony will be at eleven and then the reception at the United States Hotel at one sharp. Oh, here I am prattling on about the arrangements and I've completely forgotten to give you this."

She reached into her handbag and produced a plain envelope postmarked from Elm Grove, Illinois. I knew what it was at a glance: the reply from my uncle, Judge Enoch Sheffield. At Alice's insistence I had sent him a wedding invitation. I took the letter from her, opened it, and scanned the contents.

"Well?" queried Alice anxiously.

I folded the letter and thrust it deep into my pocket. "The judge and Aunt Hannah send their regrets. The hogs are sick and this is an inopportune time for either of them to leave Black Hawk County."

"But I don't understand, Fenny," said Alice, crestfallen. "I thought they would surely want to be here for your wedding, especially after the way they had hastened to your side upon your return from China. I thought you had reconciled all your differences with them."

"Well, evidently their affections have cooled somewhat." I didn't bother to add that my attempt to borrow a thousand dollars from Uncle Enoch without any security had undoubtedly been a major splash of cold water upon our warming relationship. So there it was. Three hundred guests were streaming into Saratoga to see the wedding of George Duncan's beloved niece, and not one of them would sit on the groom's side of the church. I saw Alice's heartache for me and had to smile, for I was used to being on my own and, frankly, I was more than glad that I would not have to endure the judge's overbearing company.

"There, there," I comforted her. "I'll tell you what. Put the Grosworts on my side of the aisle. There's about, what, two platoons of 'em, wouldn't you say? That ought to balance out the playing field somewhat, eh?"

Cheered by this, Alice gripped my arm tighter and gave me a little peck on the cheek. "That's what I love about you, Fenny. You never let your pain show if you think I might be hurt."

"There's no point in bawling out loud about it, now is there? Uncle

Enoch would be here if he could, and I know his absence will grieve him as much as it does me."

This last part was true enough, but I knew that Alice would never catch my meaning. No, dear Alice was so good-hearted that she earnestly believed others were similarly inclined. That, I suppose, was why she had nothing but adoration for me and the deepest affection for her devious uncle, George Duncan.

The carriage driver opened the door with a practiced flourish, then helped Alice up while I tied my mount to the rear of the rig. Soon we were under way, with Alice chirping happily by my side and me hugging her close and trying furtively to grope her creamy thighs through her silky flowing skirts.

"Now, Fenny," she said with a laugh. "You'll have enough of me after the wedding. Can't you just be still for a while?"

"Impossible," I replied straightforwardly, giving her soft cheek a kiss and letting my hand roam over the contours of her hips.

"Fenny, please! I'll be all mussed when we arrive, and Uncle George will know exactly what you've been up to."

This slowed me a bit. "Oh? George has come up already? I rather thought he was planning on staying down in the city until tomorrow. Didn't you say he had business there?"

She nodded. "He had told me he needed to see his solicitor. He spoke to me yesterday, though, and told me he decided to come up a bit earlier than expected. It has to do with some matters he wanted to raise with you. Do you have any idea what they might be?"

"No, I can't say that I do," I replied warily. All this was news to me, you see. Other than Alice, George Duncan and I had absolutely nothing in common. In fact, the two of us had spent hardly a moment in each other's company since my arrival back from China nearly three years ago, when he had begged me to throw over my army career in favor of becoming a poorly paid strikebreaker for him. What the dickens could he want to talk to me about now? Alice's comment about the solicitor, moreover, touched a raw nerve. Why was Duncan palavering with lawyers just days before the nuptials of his only niece?

It was all exceedingly odd, but I didn't have long to ponder the matter, for soon we were at Sycamore and Alice was down and running through the front door crying, "Uncle George! Uncle George!"

At the sound of her voice, Duncan appeared. He looked as fit as ever, all decked out in a riding jacket and glistening boots.

As he kissed his niece I asked, "Been out riding to the hounds, have we George?"

"Not exactly," he replied crisply. "I've been busy running off some varmints that took up lodgings in the stables during the winter. I find that one has to keep after such creatures or they'll move right in on you. Oh, that reminds me. Has Alice mentioned that I'd like a word with you?"

George Duncan always could get straight to the point when it suited his purposes. "Why, yes she has. Nothing's amiss, I hope."

"Nothing we two can't straighten out," he replied pointedly.

I gave him a damned sharp look at this, but Alice was too delighted to notice. "I'm almost giddy at having the two men who matter most to me under the same roof," she declared rapturously. Looping arms through ours, she held us together for an instant, which was evidently pure bliss for her. "Oh, I could stay like this forever, but the wedding details are driving me to distraction. There's so much to do." She dropped our arms and bustled away, saying, "It's all so wonderful, and the best is yet to come. Now Uncle George, don't weary my darling with any dull business advice. I know you mean well, but I want Fenny's mind to be clear for the wedding. Now promise me, won't you?"

"Alice, I'll promise only that I'll be mercifully brief."

Alice sighed, knowing her stubborn uncle. "If that's the best I can get, I suppose I'll just have to take it. Fenny, feel free to run screaming from the house if at any time you can stand no more of Uncle George's company."

I smiled broadly. "Oh, I don't think things will come to that."

I was wrong, as it turned out. Duncan steered me to a study off the main corridor and drew the doors shut. Then he turned and laid his monstrous proposition before me. "I'll be frank with you, Travers," he began. "I never thought this wedding would come about."

I said nothing, for I was fully aware of Duncan's strenuous efforts over the years to extinguish Alice's love for me. He had intercepted letters, rebuffed me when I came calling, and done everything he could short of bundling Alice off to a nunnery.

"I finally gave in when you returned from China. It was then that Alice made it clear to me that she would have you and no other. Why you, when there were so many more eminently suitable beaux vying for her attention, well, I just have never grasped . . ." He let that thought die and returned to the point. "When you went out to the Philippine Islands, Travers, it was my last hope that whatever was between you and Alice would die a natural death. To my astonishment, however, Alice went there after you.

When I heard about the pirates and the kidnapping, well, it was about all I could bear. Finally, when the two of you returned last year, I decided to throw in the towel at last."

I clapped him hard on the shoulder. "That's just grand, George. I'm really so glad we had this little talk. I feel ever so much better," I assured him and headed for the door.

"Wait," he snapped. "There's more."

I stopped in my tracks. "Oh?"

He went to the desk, a handsome rosewood affair inlaid with ebony, and took a portfolio from the top drawer. "Travers, you undoubtedly know that Alice is quite well off."

"That's no secret, George," I said carefully, peering at the portfolio with curiosity. I hadn't exactly analyzed Alice's wealth, you see, but I certainly was aware of it. Other than Alice's exquisite feminine charms, it was the thing that drew me to her like a moth to a flame. In fact, without the lure of easy lucre, I wouldn't be contemplating matrimony at all.

"You might not know that several years ago I created a certain trust for her. It's this trust that provides the income upon which she lives. It's generously endowed, and I think that protecting it would be in the best interests of both Alice and you."

I wasn't quite following Duncan, so I murmured noncommittally, "I'm generally in favor of protection, George."

"Good. I take it, then, that you will have no qualms about executing this document."

He pulled a thick sheaf of legal-sized papers from the portfolio and laid them on the desk. Then, plucking a quill from its stand, he dipped it into the inkwell on the desk and held it out for me.

I stared at the pen like it was a hissing rattler. "Just what the blazes are you trying to foist on me here?"

"Foist? I don't like that word, Travers." Duncan's tone was suddenly cold and hard. "I'm Alice's trustee, and it's my legal duty to protect her interests. This document will do exactly that."

"Oh?" I retorted angrily. "Well, why don't I just look it over a bit, eh?"

I snatched the papers from the desk and drew back a few steps as though the pen was a weapon that could be suddenly plunged into my vitals. Hastily, I plowed through paragraph after paragraph of "whereas" this and "whereas" that, until I got to a large black "therefore." I carefully studied the language that followed. Many of the words were Latin, and even the English ones were arcane, but I quickly got the gist of the thing.

"My God, you want me to sign a quitclaim to Alice's trust!"

Duncan beamed. "Remarkable. My solicitor wagered me that you would never penetrate that language. Well, he was wrong and now he owes me ten dollars. Yes, you're exactly right, Travers, although in the legal profession I think this document is called a prenuptial agreement."

"Well, I call it pure thievery," I thundered, "and I'll not sign this infamous thing!"

I intended to wed Alice in relatively good faith, but in the event something untoward ever happened to her, I aimed to collect my just deserts, trust and all. I wished Alice no harm, mind you, but if the worse ever did come to pass, I believed firmly in the time-honored maxim that the winner takes all.

"Oh, quit your hysterics, Travers," demanded Duncan. "This is nothing more than a prudent business precaution."

"Call it what you want, but to me it's pure thievery. I intend to share all I have with Alice, and I expect the same in return."

"Don't make me laugh," scoffed Duncan. "What have you got to share with Alice other than the few coppers that might be jingling about in your trousers pocket?"

I tried to bluster out some sort of answer, but in fact the only property I owned was my .45 Colt, the few gold coins stashed under my bed at the Anaconda Hotel, and a bank account that was but a shadow of its former self. Galled beyond endurance, I blurted defiantly, "Well, it's the thought that counts!"

Duncan sneered at this flapdoodle. "It's as I surmised. You're just a few short steps from the poorhouse, aren't you?"

"Maybe that's so, Duncan, but at least I still possess the brains I was born with, damn you. I won't sign your blasted scrap of paper."

"Then you won't wed Alice." He stood there with his arms folded, glaring at me triumphantly as though he'd just delivered the coup de grâce.

I sneered in his face, for I knew a thing or two about Alice. "You're bluffing, Duncan. I'll wed her with or without your consent, and you damn well know it."

Duncan didn't flinch a whit at this retort. "I don't want to do this, Travers, but if you force my hand, I'll have no choice."

Something in his tone warned me to proceed with caution. "You'll have no choice about what?"

"I'm both the grantor and the trustee of Alice's trust. The trust principal doesn't become payable to Alice until her thirtieth birthday, or upon her marriage, whichever first occurs. Before then I can, as grantor, revoke the trust. Unless you either sign this agreement, or call off the wedding, I'll take steps at once to undo the trust, and Alice will come to you penniless."

"You wouldn't dare!"

Undaunted, Duncan shot right back, "Just try me, Travers. Oh, Alice wouldn't suffer, for I'd make sure she received a tidy allowance. That's all it would be, though. An allowance, a loving gift. It certainly would not be anything she could bequeath, or worse yet, liquidate, under your rapacious influence."

"Damn you, Duncan! You've hated me from the first time you laid eyes on me back in Arizona. How could you think of anything as tawdry as money on the day before your niece's wedding?"

"Oh, spare me your feigned indignation, Travers. I'm raising these matters because I know they're at the front of your feral little mind. Don't deny it. You've wanted to worm your way into my fortune for as long as I've known you. Well, you weren't successful with me, and now I'm bound and determined to keep Alice's assets out of your grasp as well. You're nothing but an opportunist, sir. An opportunist and a filibuster."

"And you're nothing but a pompous little tightwad," I fired right back. It was clear that we understood each other's character perfectly and might have gone on to elaborate at length on each other's myriad shortcomings had we not been interrupted by Alice's cry of alarm.

"Uncle George? Fenny? Is everything all right in there?"

At the sound of her voice, Duncan composed himself with a visible effort. "Yes, Alice, everything's just fine. Now you run along and let us men finish with our business."

As the sound of her footfalls receded in the distance, Duncan turned on me once more and rasped, "Sign the agreement, Travers, or I'll revoke the trust."

I had learned long ago that the only way to handle Duncan was to seize the initiative and then hold on for dear life. Accordingly, I lashed out, "I'm not signing, damn you, Duncan. What's more, unless you guarantee that you won't fiddle with a single detail of that trust, I'll go to Alice this instant and tell her the wedding is off."

Duncan paled, for he had never expected this turnabout. If I got to Alice first, I was sure to paint him as an archvillain who didn't give a fig for her happiness. "You wouldn't!" he exclaimed.

"Just try me," I vowed, throwing his own arrogant words back at him. "I'll tell Alice the whole thing is off, and to send the Grosworts back to Jersey City or wherever it is they hail from. I'm sure she would be very interested to know that the reason for my change of heart is you and your skinflint ways. She just might throw your precious trust and your allowances right back in your face and remove herself from your household entirely. You'll be alone, my friend, and all because of your miserly attempt to squeeze me this day."

I watched Duncan closely as he pondered my words in silence. He had no wife and no children; for all his money, his only source of human companionship was Alice. If he lost her because of me, he would lose everything. Despite his vulnerability, though, Duncan didn't fold easily, especially in matters involving money. He could sniff out a bluff a mile away. After he recovered from his initial shock at my bold tactic, his remarkable instincts reasserted themselves.

"You're not fooling me, Travers." He almost laughed. "You'd rather hack off your own right hand than walk out on Alice. No, you can't play that card, my greedy friend, and I know it. I've got you spitted proper, and I'll be damned if I'll let you go."

I stood there red-faced and furious, not knowing whether to go to Alice and lay this shameful matter at her feet as I had promised or to leap across the room and throttle the life out of my tormentor. In the end, I did neither.

"Damn your miserable hide, Duncan!" I screamed and stormed from the room, flinging the agreement into the air as I went. I was out on the front steps heading for my horse when Alice caught up with me.

"Fenny! What is it? What happened?"

I pulled the reins from the hitching post and mounted in a fury. "It's nothing, darling, nothing. Your uncle and I had a, er, a political discussion, nothing more. Seems he's a fiscal conservative while I'm what you might call a free silver man. You must forgive me if I run off now, dear, but I'm afraid it's necessary."

Alice was frantic with anxiety. "The wedding, Fenny. Has anything happened? Has anything . . . changed?"

I shook my head, trying to clear the mist that shrouded my numbed brain. "I, I don't know. Come to me tonight at the Anaconda. We'll talk then."

"When, dearest?"

"After midnight. Promise me you'll come."

"I promise, my love. Oh, I promise."

Then I was pounding down the drive, leaving Alice sobbing behind me.

3

The crowd at Canfield's Clubhouse was boisterous. Swells in dinner jackets and white ties crowded about tables stacked high with chips, and there was a heightened sense of excitement in the air beyond that normally found in a room packed with gamblers. Perhaps it was the fact that the Saratoga Special would be run in the morn. Or perhaps there were other high-stakes games under way about which I was ignorant.

I eyed the clientele appreciatively. At a green baize–covered faro table was Senator McCarren, the hard-drinking solon from Brooklyn who was a Saratoga fixture during the congressional recess. Arrayed about him like chicks around an old hen were a clutch of young Vanderbilts and a few Whitneys, all plunging as deep as the senator. In a far corner at a roulette table was Bet-a-Million Gates, a black cigar gripped in one hand and a half-drained glass of good Scotch in the other. He was betting hundred-dollar chips, I noted with envy. At Gates's elbow was Jim Brady, resplendent in a canary yellow suit and a lime green waistcoat of brocaded silk. The huge diamond stickpin on Brady's pale blue cravat glowed like a lighthouse beacon on a treacherous coast. Here, I knew, was a place where I could forget the woes that Duncan had thrust upon me.

"Evening, Jim," I greeted Brady. Out of the corner of my eye I noted the malevolent visage of Rothstein at an adjacent wheel. Rothstein was betting conservatively; he seemed to be biding his time rather than doing any serious gambling. Crawley, I knew, would not be too far away.

"Fenny, this here's John Gates. I've been telling him all about you."

Gates was rich, and that fact entitled him to a fawning greeting from me. "This is a genuine pleasure for me, sir. I'm truly overwhelmed."

Gates, a heavy, coarse-looking gent with a shaggy thatch of hair and an unkempt walrus mustache, didn't look my way as the roulette wheel turned. Judging from the grease on his vest where he had evidently wiped his hands after dinner, I was thankful that he dispensed with the conventional hearty handshake.

"Glad to meet you, Travers," he rumbled, intent on his game. "Heard about your doings out in the Philippines. Nice work. I would'na bet a thousand to one that anybody would have taken that rascal Aguinaldo alive—sonofabitch!"

Gates had put his money on red, and the wheel clattered to a stop on black. As the croupier scooped up Gates's chips, Gates lambasted the fellow as a scallywag and a thief. The table was fixed, by God, and Canfield was in on the scheme.

When his outburst subsided, I continued carefully, "You flatter me, Mr. Gates, but the plain truth of the matter is that your odds were just about right."

His anger apparently forgotten, Gates let loose a belly laugh. "I like a fellow who just lays a thing out. No hiding the damned pea, eh, Jim?"

Brady smiled indulgently. "Talking about not hiding the pea, John, I want my young friend here to be a player tonight."

This brought a sharp glance from Gates. "I don't do charity work, Brady. He can stand at the suckers' window with all the other rubes."

Brady, bless his heart, stuck to his guns. "That ain't the way I see it, John. I hold a few of your chits, and I'm calling one in right now."

Gates plunked down ten blue chips—nearly half a year's salary for me. "Twenty-three black!" he roared.

The croupier dutifully moved the stack to the designated spot. "Place your bets, gentlemen, place your bets," he chanted as a dozen hands shot out to position chips on the table.

"No more bets, gentlemen, no more bets," intoned the croupier as the ebony wheel inlaid with Madagascar ivory spun crazily. All eyes went to the tiny ball as it hopped here and there on the turning wheel before coming to rest.

"Twelve red! Twelve red!" called the croupier as he swept away Gates's chips once more.

Gates flashed scarlet but held his tongue. He reached grimly into a bulging pocket and hauled out another stack of chips. His luck would change; it always had in the past.

"Okay, Brady," he growled as he pondered his next bet. "I'll let him in. Just this once. And," he added with finality, "you got one chit less."

"Done," replied Brady, putting an arm on my shoulder and guiding me to a quiet corner of the casino.

"What was that all about, Jim?" I demanded when we were alone.

"Just a little wedding gift, Fenny, don't worry. Remember you told me today that you wanted to put together a big enough grubstake to make a killing on Chickamauga when he runs tomorrow?"

"Yes, I remember," I answered carefully.

"Well, I'm fixin' on giving you that chance."

"How?" I demanded. Something damned strange was afoot here, and I wanted to know what. By way of answering, Brady nodded his head in the direction of a massive brute of a man lounging near the bar. His neck was as thick as a tree stump, and his dinner jacket strained across his chest to the bursting point. Around him was a group of admirers, all smiling and clapping the big fellow on the back. One of them, I noted, was the odious Mr. Crawley.

"Do you happen to know who that strapping fellow might be?" asked Brady.

"Nope," I answered. "Can't say as I've ever made his acquaintance."

"Does the name Bob Fitzsimmons mean anything to you?"

"You mean 'Fighting Bob' Fitzsimmons? The heavyweight prizefighter from Australia?"

"The very same. What's more, Fenny, he's not here at the Spa to see the sights, if you get my drift."

"You mean there's going to be a prizefight? Here, in Saratoga?"

Brady nodded.

"But, but, prizefights are illegal in this state, aren't they?"

Brady exploded in laughter. "Of course they are! That's why people flock here to see 'em on the sly."

"You've got something up your sleeve tonight, don't you?"

"Could be," he replied vaguely.

"Come on, Jim," I demanded. "Level with me. What's all of this got to do with me?"

Brady eyed me appraisingly and then confided, "This could be a big evening for you, Fenny, if you do exactly as I say."

"I'm listening."

Looking about to ensure that no prying ears were too close by, Brady whispered, "There'll be a fight out behind the club in a short while. Bet everything you have on Fitzsimmons's opponent."

"And who might that be?"

"A slugger from Hell's Kitchen named Sunday O'Dwyer. They call him Sunday because he has a Sunday punch that's sent ten straight opponents to the canvas. He's a righty with a decent left jab. Fights mostly on barges in the East River. I've made a pretty penny off him over the past year or so."

I digested this intelligence for a moment and then said, "I'm no big boxing fan, Jim, but I know two things about Fitzsimmons. First, I know that he recently got KO'ed by Jeffries and lost his title."

"Yep," Brady said, beaming. "That's right. What's more, I think that loss probably took the steam out of Fitzsimmons for a long time to come. And what's the second thing you know?"

"I know that even on a bad day, Bob Fitzsimmons could knock your boy off any barge afloat."

Brady gave me an approving glance and then chuckled. "Now I see how you got your hands on that Filipino bandit, Fenny. You're no fool, are you?"

"Jim, stop flapping your jaws in the wind. I'm right, aren't I?"

Brady was unfazed by my brusque tone. "All right, I'll level with you, Fenny. Yes, you're right. O'Dwyer is no match for Fitzsimmons."

"Then why the dickens did you tell me to bet on O'Dwyer?"

Brady arranged his fleshy jowls into an enormous smile as he explained the obvious to me. "Because O'Dwyer's going to win, my young friend. That's why."

A fix! Of course! Jim had been hinting all day that the key to surviving in Saratoga was taking the chance out of games of chance. Obviously, I hadn't been listening—until now.

"Who else knows?" I whispered, glancing over my shoulder as I spoke.

"Gates, me, and now you. We'll bet against the other suckers who'll all go for Fitzsimmons. It'll be a perfect scam, Fenny. I don't mind saying that I'm plunging on this one."

"Who's taking the bets?"

"Any of Canfield's people. Write 'em a personal draft and mention my name. They'll honor it. Now get going, and I'll see you at ringside."

He gave me a chuck on the arm as I scurried off to find the nearest pit boss. I had about a thousand in the bank. Although I had emerged from the wilds of Mindanao with about eight thousand dollars, among my gaming losses, another thousand I'd spent on uniforms, two good mounts, and hunting trips to Canada, the thousand was all I had left. I'd bet it all, I figured. Since the odds were seven to one against O'Dwyer, I stood to win seven thousand dollars! I'd turn right around and put that amount on Brady's horse tomorrow. Jim had put those odds at thirty to one against Chickamauga. Why, that meant I'd be set for life. It was like a dream come true.

It was only as I was scribbling out my check that I noticed that Crawley had taken Fitzsimmons aside and was whispering forcefully into his ear. At that moment, though, my attention was diverted by the booming voice of Dick Canfield himself. He announced above the hubbub of the room, "Ladies and gentlemen, the main event is about to begin."

Apparently the fight had been a secret to nobody except me, for a lackey in a tuxedo threw open a bank of French doors and the crowd surged toward them. I followed into a garden behind the casino and along a narrow path lined with torches. The path led to a secluded meadow formed by an opening in a thick copse of Dutch elm trees.

Here rows of lanterns mounted on poles illuminated the field of combat. The ring was nothing more than a riotous circle of onlookers, and in that arena Fitzsimmons appeared, clad now in black tights and high-top leather shoes. His torso was bare, and the power in the man was readily evident. Heavy muscles rippled in his chest and arms as he shadowboxed in the center of the ring to warm his sinews for the combat to come.

Then the crowd roared, for Fitzsimmons's opponent had arrived. Sunday O'Dwyer was a lanky youth with a thick crop of disheveled red hair that gave him a wild and menacing look. His nose was smashed flat, a souvenir of some past barge fight, but the boy was fit and fully a foot taller than Fitzsimmons. Although Fitzsimmons seemed the stronger of the two, O'Dwyer had a clear reach advantage.

As was the practice, this was to be a bare knuckle contest, and I found my glance drawn to the hands of the opponents. Oh, O'Dwyer had the calloused knuckles of a prizefighter, all right, but Fighting Bob's paws were a sight to behold. They were the size of Virginia hams—the largest hands I had ever seen on a man. And they were reputed to be as hard as pig iron. Veritable weapons of war they were, and I shuddered at the sight of them. In a fair fight, I'd wager that Fitzsimmons would pulverize the kid, but then this was not to be a fair fight and so I relaxed and waited for the fun to start.

"Fitz! Fitz! Fitz!" the crowd chanted for the favorite.

Undaunted by this adulation, a seedy group from Brooklyn stood firmly behind their man. "Kill 'im, Sunday. Kill 'im!"

The referee, clad in white tie and tails and holding a glass of champagne, called the fighters and their seconds to the center of the ring. "There'll be three-minute rounds, gentlemen, unless there's a knockdown. On a knockdown the round ends, followed by a one-minute break. The fighter who fails to answer the bell"—here he pointed to a fellow on the edge of the crowd who held a cowbell and a hammer—"loses. No low blows, no holding, and no butting." There was nothing left to be said; this fight would end only when one of the gladiators was too battered to rise. "Are there any questions?"

There were none.

"Good," said the referee. He sipped his drink, then ordered, "Return to your corners. Seconds out, and good luck to each of you."

Grimly the fighters retired to their corners to await the bell. It came on the instant. Fitzsimmons stepped into the torchlight, his body gleaming as though he had been given a light sheen of oil. He raised his massive fists above his head to acknowledge the roar of the crowd.

O'Dwyer advanced more cautiously, his fists raised and his eyes fixed on Fitzsimmons. He closed on the ex-champ and immediately threw a looping right, his favorite punch.

"Ohhh!" gasped the crowd, but the blow sailed wide as Fitzsimmons danced away. He jabbed as he moved off, making O'Dwyer pay for his bold move.

Brady was at my side now, whispering intently. "Fitzsimmons looks like he's in no mood to let O'Dwyer get close. He'll keep him off with that jab for a decent interval. Then, of course, he'll let a convincing punch slip through. . . ."

And take the fall, just like Brady and Gates had planned. Everything was under control, I told myself, and my bet was perfectly safe. O'Dwyer chased after Fitzsimmons, but the older man kept him off with flashing jabs and surprisingly nimble footwork.

"Look at that fancy stepping," crowed an onlooker in the crowd. "Why, Jeffries didn't take a thing out of Fightin' Bob!"

Brady merely smiled serenely. Let the suckers enjoy the show while it lasts. They'll all be crying in their beer soon enough, and he would be the richer for it. It was just the way things were in Saratoga, you see.

Now O'Dwyer was flicking out his own jab and Fitzsimmons was covering up. It was clear that each man was trying to get the measure of the other in these opening minutes. O'Dwyer's jabs had zing to them and he held his right cocked, ready to unleash it at the smallest opening in Fitzsimmons's defenses. Fitzsimmons, however, covered up well, his ring savvy giving his younger opponent no opportunity to throw a haymaker. But O'Dwyer's vigor was beginning to tell, and slowly the sheer volume of jabs seemed to be driving Fitzsimmons back to his own corner. I flipped open my timepiece—only twenty seconds left.

"Not a bad first round for the kid," I murmured to Brady.

No sooner were the words out of my mouth than Fitzsimmons flicked out a jab and then unleashed a thunderous straight right. He caught O'Dwyer flush on the nose, sending a disgusting gob of red flying high into the air. O'Dwyer went down as though he had been shot, and the crowd went wild.

"That's the Bob we love!" they cheered as the bell clanged the round to a sudden end.

"What the hell?" muttered Brady, suddenly suspicious. "I hope that Bob's merely having a little fun before he takes his dive."

I wasn't so sure. Instinctively, I scanned the crowd for Crawley. What had he whispered to Fitzsimmons back inside the club? I spied him on the fringe of the crowd—right beside Rothstein. Rothstein had a roll of greenbacks in his hand and was in the act of placing a bet. Alarms instantly went off inside my head!

"Jim, didn't you say that Rothstein doesn't bet on fights?"

"Yeah, that's right. He sticks to the ponies, as far as I've ever seen. Why?"

"Because he's betting on this fight! Look!"

Brady followed my gaze. "Goddamn, Fenny. You're right!"

I felt the bile rise to my mouth now, and my knees were shaking. Things were coming apart, but just how I wasn't yet sure. "Jim, what's going on here?"

Brady's answer rooted me to the spot. "The fix ain't in no more, Fenny. Rothstein just double-crossed us. Fitzsimmons intends to win this thing."

"So, Rothstein has started in on that pushing you were telling me about."

"It seems so, my friend."

Clang! went the bell.

"Seconds out!" ordered the referee.

"C'mon Sunday," screamed the Brooklyn section. "Keep away from that big ox!"

No sooner had they cried out their warning than the big ox connected with a stunning left hook and then a smashing right. O'Dwyer dropped as though he'd been poleaxed.

Clang! went the bell.

"Jim," I rasped through a throat tight with fear as I watched O'Dwyer crawl to the stool in his corner. "Your boy Sunday's got no defense."

Brady sighed. "That's the way I see things too. Up until tonight, he's never needed one."

"What about our money?" I asked fearfully.

"Kiss it good-bye, Fenny. That's all you can do. Rothstein got to our man after we did. It was stupid of us to let it happen, but what's done is done. Oh, don't get me wrong; Fitzsimmons won't get off scot-free. He'll never get another money fight on the East Coast. Just leave that to me."

Punishing Fitzsimmons after the fight did me damned little good. It was a useless gesture as far as I was concerned, and I said so. "But that isn't fair, Jim! Can't we get back our stakes? I mean, we expected a nice, honest fix, right?"

Brady laughed hard at my croaking. "Why don't you just sidle up to Canfield, Fenny, and tell him your fix is out and Rothstein's is in, and, oh—by the way, you'd like your money back? I don't think you're going to get much sympathy. Why not just buck up and swallow the loss like a sport? After all, its only money."

"It's only money?" I nearly shrieked. "That's easy for you to say, Jim. Hell, you're made of the stuff! I'm not, though, and my life's savings happen to be at stake here. I'll be damned if I'll let a weasel-faced galoot like Rothstein rob me without a fight!"

"Fenny, don't do anything crazy," pleaded Brady. "That Rothstein is as dangerous as a snake!"

But Brady was talking to himself; I was already on my way to Fitzsimmons's corner. If O'Dwyer couldn't handle Fitzsimmons himself, well then, I'd lend him a hand. I bulled my way through the spectators to where the cornermen were toweling off the hulking Australian. Fighting Bob's eyes were fixed across the ring to where the bloodied O'Dwyer was being revived with smelling salts.

"Seconds out!" commanded the referee.

"Smash 'im, Bobby, smash 'im," Fitzsimmons's trainer urged as the bell rang. Moving forward like a mythical destroyer, Fitzsimmons did as he was told. Although O'Dwyer tried to cover up, Fitzsimmons delivered three short, chopping blows to O'Dwyer's ribs. When the kid lowered his arms to protect his aching rib cage, he gave Fitzsimmons the opening the Australian sought. A roundhouse right bounced off O'Dwyer's temple with a cracking sound, and O'Dwyer fell so hard he actually bounced off the ground.

Clang! went the bell.

"One minute," bawled the referee.

For a second there was no movement from O'Dwyer, and it looked as though the fight might be over. The kid's cornermen had his towel raised, ready to toss it in should their fighter fail to show some sign of life. Fitzsimmons was sauntering back to his corner with a smile on his mug when O'Dwyer stirred and then, incredibly, staggered to his feet. As O'Dwyer teetered back to his corner, I knew I had to act now, for O'Dwyer wouldn't last another round.

"You got 'im now, Bobby," bubbled Fitzsimmons's trainer. "He's ready to go. Work the body, Bobby, then go for the head. He's ready to go, I tell you."

"All right, mate," replied Fitzsimmons, the strange accent jarring my ears. "He's game enough, but the bloke's on his way out or me name ain't Fightin' Bob."

"Bawling Bobby's more like it," I jeered from right behind him through cupped hands. "I saw Jeffries lick you, you second-rate, hayseed Limey!" I lied. "He went through you without raising a sweat. Oh, you're good with youngsters, all right, but you can't face a real fighter!"

Fitzsimmons's head snapped around at this, and he fixed me with a glare of pure malice. I realized instantly that for all his toughness, Fitzsimmons had a particularly thin skin. "How'd you like a taste of this, mate?" he demanded, waving a bloody fist in my direction.

The threat was palpable, for none of the blood was Fitzsimmons's. I fought my instinctive impulse to flee from the presence of this human punching machine, and instead stood my ground. "Oh, that's tough talk from a loser," I retorted hotly. "Go tell it to Jeffries. I'm sure he'd shake in his boots."

"Shaddup, mister!" demanded a Fitzsimmons loyalist nearby. Another chimed in, "Yeah, beat it, you bum!"

Of course, I had no intention of doing either before pulling off my sudden plan, a scheme so low-down that it amazed even me. You see, all that was needed to end the fight was for either of the fighters not to answer the bell. No question about it, those were the rules. All I had to do was to make sure that the fighter failing to answer the bell was Fitzsimmons, not O'Dwyer. Since O'Dwyer clearly lacked the power to keep Fitzsimmons in his corner at the bell, I decided to do the job for him.

"I'll stand anywhere I want," I snarled in reply to the catcalls all around me. "I'll even stand in this buffoon's corner if it pleases me."

Clang! went the bell.

"Seconds out!"

"Who are you callin' a buffoon, you bloody bastard?" demanded Fitzsimmons, lunging for me.

Only his cornermen, thrusting themselves between their fighter and his quarry, saved me from being seized. "Forget 'im, Bob," they urged frantically. "You've got a job to do. Get in there and finish this fight before you pick another one."

"Oh, all right, damnit," swore Fitzsimmons, "but he's mine when this is over."

So saying, Fitzsimmons strode across the ring to where the dazed O'Dwyer was being propelled from his corner. O'Dwyer raised a feeble arm to ward off his foe, but Fitzsimmons swiped it away as though it was a twig. With a single jarring punch he snapped back O'Dwyer's head, bowed his legs, and dropped him unconscious into the arms of his anguished trainer. Then Fitzsimmons turned on his heels and headed straight for me.

Murder was in his eyes, and my guts churned with fear. He had not been kidding; he aimed to finish the evening's festivities by demolishing me. "A'right, now, let's you and me have a little talk," he snarled, his jaw jutting forward with anger. "How'd you like to step in this ring with me for a minute?"

Fitzsimmons's trainer, however, still had his eyes on O'Dwyer's corner. "Bobby, forget 'im for now. They're trying to bring the kid around. Let's see if he answers the bell."

It was good advice, but I refused to give the bruiser any peace. "Face it, you're washed up in this game against the real professionals. You're a joke, Fitzsimmons, a shabby, tired joke."

Fitzsimmons's rage knew no bounds. He had come to Saratoga for a quiet little payday, and I was turning it into a verbal hell on earth. Others in the crowd were beginning to snigger at Fitzsimmons's discomfiture now. He howled and roared at me as his cornermen wrapped their arms around his middle to keep him from plowing into the crowd after me. "'Ow'd you like to find out how much of a joke this is?" he shrieked, shaking a bloody fist at me.

"Look, mister, get the hell out of here while you still can," pleaded Fitzsimmons's trainer. "Beat it!"

"I'll go when I'm ready," I fired right back. "What's the matter with this big oaf anyway? Don't tell me he's afraid of me."

The crowd, which had earlier been put off by my churlishness, warmed to me now that I was showing some grit. Laughter erupted all around. "Don't worry, Bobby, we won't let him hurt you!" someone called jovially from the crowd.

Clang! went the bell. I glanced into O'Dwyer's corner. Sunday was on his feet but just barely. His cornermen were trying to slap some sense into him, but it looked hopeless. Suddenly, the brawler from Brooklyn sagged back on his stool. He couldn't go on, I realized. Something had to be done to stop Fitzsimmons. It was now or never.

"Tell us, Bobby," I shouted over the din of the crowd as Fitzsimmons readied himself to sally forth toward the hapless O'Dwyer for what promised to be the close of the match. "Is it true that your mother plied her trade in a British army brothel?"

A great gasp arose from the crowd. "Why, you filthy heathen!" roared Fitzsimmons, lurching toward me. "I'll have your head for that. You'll be spitting teeth for a week!"

He charged straight at me, knocking a Yaleman and two lawyers head over heels as he came on. Fitzsimmons leaped over the flattened bystanders, and it was only with the greatest of luck that I eluded his crushing grasp. In Fitzsimmons's wake, the Yaleman came up swinging.

"Get the hell off me!" demanded that dandy, his tails flying and his top hat crushed beneath his feet. In his rage, he decked a completely innocent fellow who had been standing beside him, whose companions in turn promptly pummeled the man of Eli senseless. The Yaleman, however, had friends, and now they rallied to his defense. In an instant complete pandemonium broke out. The brawling spread around the ring like wildfire, and one huge battle royal was joined by one and all.

"Fitzsimmons has failed to answer the bell!" cried the referee as torches and glasses sailed through the air above his head.

At this announcement, the ominous chant "Fix! Fix!" was on a hundred lips. The crowd's support for Fitzsimmons vanished in that instant. As the battle raged, maddened cries from Fitzsimmons supporters could be heard from all quarters: "You damned fool, get back in there!" Over it all came the agonized shrill of Dick Canfield himself: "I want no trouble here! Disperse, you rabble!"

"Bobby! Bobby, you fool!" screamed Fitzsimmons's trainer, but to no avail. "O'Dwyer's done for, can't you see that?"

Fitzsimmons, however, could see nothing but me and probably would have torn me limb from limb had not his own irate backers intervened. "You're throwing our money away, you Limey bastard!" they shrieked, shoving their way between him and me and trying to push their champion back into the ring.

"Don't tell me what to do, damn you!" bellowed Fitzsimmons. Maddened by their interference, Fitzsimmons dashed a few of his fans to the ground as though they were rag dolls. "Let me at him!"

Fitzsimmons's reward for these exertions was to become the quarry of an enraged mob. His former supporters began pelting him with empty glasses, binoculars, clumps of earth, and anything else they could get their hands on. "Booo!" they hissed. "Get him! Get him!"

This turnabout gave me the opportunity to push through the punching and kicking crowd to locate Brady and to be off. I found Jim flat on his back, unconscious. One eye was blackened and his elegant attire was in shreds.

"Let's go, Jim," I urged, slapping him awake and then pulling him to his feet with a tremendous effort. Pushing him through the crowd, I added happily, "I think I saved our money. All O'Dwyer had to do to win was stand up."

"Ohhhh, thas' good," Brady mumbled through a split lip.

As we fled, I heard the referee call over the din of battle. "This fight is over! Fitzsimmons has failed to answer the bell, and so has O'Dwyer! The match is a draw, gentlemen. A draw!"

Goddamn that meddling Rothstein, I raged as I retreated with nearly three hundred pounds of stunned sportsman in tow. I got Brady to his coach and soon the chaos of Canfield's was behind us. I went straight to the Anaconda, where I remanded Brady into the custody of a perplexed night manager. With Brady safely stowed, I headed for the saloon, where I steadied my nerves with two quick bourbons over ice. If Fitzsimmons had been only a tad more nimble, or if the crowd had not reacted at just the right moment, I doubt very much that I would be around to see the sun rise on the morrow. With that dreadful thought in my brain, it took a determined effort to calm myself down enough to attempt to get a little shut-eye. Paying off my tab, I went up to my lodgings. I lit the gas lamp as I entered—and then jumped back. I saw movement under the covers of my bed!

"Who's there?" I cried in alarm. Had I been followed from Canfield's? I wondered fearfully.

There was no answer at first, and I was half inclined to find the hotel detective and let him sort out this mystery for me. Just as I turned to go, however, the covers pulled back enough to reveal a mass of luxuriant auburn tresses.

"Fenny, aren't you glad to see me?"

"Alice!" I cried in relief. In my anxiety, I had completely forgotten about our tryst. "Of course I'm glad to see you, my love. It's just that I was, er, distracted by some business, that's all."

"Not the same dreadful things you were discussing with Uncle George, I hope."

"Er, no, my dear. These were some new dreadful things."

Alice giggled and lowered the covers. She hadn't a stitch of clothing on, and the sight of her banished all other thoughts from my mind. "We have to talk, Fenny. You seemed so upset when you left Sycamore. Come and tell me what's wrong."

Instantly, I was shucking off my clothes. "Your wish is my command, lovely lady. There's nothing I more ardently desire at this moment than some deep, soulful . . . conversation."

4

I was in a delightful dream. Alice and I were alone in golden fields in the middle of an earthly garden of Eden. Servants had set a sumptuous feast before us and then discreetly retired. As I ate, Alice rose and inquired whether she might perform the *magloonsy,* the love dance of the Filipino Moros, for my enjoyment.

"Yes, my love," I agreed huskily. "By all means do so."

Comely Alice slowly disrobed for me, stripping each garment from her lithe form so as to tease and provoke me to the fullest. Then, when she stood completely naked before me, she lifted her arms and began to sway her hips slowly, hypnotically. Somewhere a drum was beating, and Alice's swaying kept time with the rhythmic throbbing. The drums beat softly at first but soon became more insistent. Alice began to move more frenetically now, trying to keep in rhythm with the savagely pounding tempo, but the effect was being lost and I called out irritably: "Slow down, damnit. You're spoiling it."

"Fenny, wake up," came Alice's reply.

"No, I don't want to," I insisted, but now I became aware that someone was shaking me, and suddenly I aroused from my enchanting dream. Although my reveries were over, the pounding continued unabated.

"Fenny, who is it?" asked Alice fearfully.

Before I could fathom a guess, a voice cried out from the corridor. "Fenny! I've got to speak to you! Wake up, for God's sake!"

The pounding on the door was forceful enough to rattle the gas lamps on the wall, but still I might have slept on had not Alice Brenoble, my fiancée and the love of my life, sat bolt upright in the bed and shaken me urgently.

"Fenny, wake up! There's someone at the door!"

Slowly I sat up and blinked. Groggy from my long nighttime romp with Alice, I had a devil of a time rousing myself. When at last things came into focus, I saw hanging before me two absolutely perfect breasts. Instinctively, I reached for them. A whistling slap across my fingers brought me up short.

"Oh, no you don't. You get up and find out who's on the other side of that door."

From the door came more pounding, then a cry, "Fenny, for God's sake let me in! I've got to see you! The colt's sick, I say! He's in a bad way."

"Who's there?" I demanded blearily.

"It's me—Jim! I tell you the colt's dying. Do you hear me? He's dying!"

Now I was fully awake. The colt was dying? Why, that was Diamond Jim Brady out there in the hotel hallway hollering and carrying on. Was he drunk? No, that couldn't be. I'd never known Brady to drink; indeed, he was a teetotaler. It was one of his big shortcomings, but I tolerated him anyway. The important thing was that if he wasn't in the throes of a drunken stupor, then something awful must have happened to Chickamauga!

"Hold on, Jim," I called through a hoarse throat. "Just give me a minute, will you?"

"Fenny, what's wrong?" asked Alice tremulously, clutching the sheets about herself.

I shook my head. "I don't know, but it sure sounds like bad trouble. You had better fetch a robe, my love."

Obediently, Alice hopped from the bed and threw an elaborately brocaded peignoir around her lovely shoulders. I found a pair of trousers and hauled them on. When we were presentable I opened the door.

Brady burst into the room, sobbing and shaking, almost incoherent with shock. "My trainer just rang up the hotel from the stable, Fenny," he wailed. "Chickamauga's down on the straw, thrashing about. None of the stable hands has a clue as to what's the matter. I'm at my wit's end, I tell you. I swear to God I'm about to collapse from anxiety. That horse has never been sick a day in his life, and now on the eve of the biggest race of his career, the Saratoga Special, the poor thing's on death's doorstep."

"Have you called the vet?" I asked.

"My trainer, Anderson, sent a boy for him. Oh, my God, this is awful. What can we do, Fenny?"

I was already getting dressed. "We're going out there," I answered. "Alice, I don't know when I'll be back. I'll send word to you when I can."

"Oh, Fenny," she fretted, "promise me you'll be careful, won't you?"

"There, there, my sweet. It's just a matter of a sick horse, nothing more. Jim and I will see to the poor thing and then I'll be back at your side. What could be simpler than that, eh? Now, you slide back into bed and I'll return before you know it."

I kissed her distractedly, for in plain truth it was I who was in need of comforting. I had counted on that colt to win a bundle of cash for me tomorrow, and if what Jim Brady said was correct, all my hopes of a financial killing had been smashed to bits. In a few minutes I was dressed.

On a hunch, I decided to bring along my revolver. It was my .45-caliber Colt Single Action Army, the same pearl-handled beauty I'd brought to bear against the howling Moros on Mindanao. It would stop anything likely to be abroad this night in Saratoga. I made sure it had six rounds chambered and scooped up a pocketful of cartridges for good measure. Then Brady and I were out the door, leaving an alarmed and confused Alice to ponder the implications of this event upon our upcoming wedding.

We hurried down to the lobby, where Brady raised hell until a hotel carriage was rolled out and placed at our disposal. We were at the stable ten minutes later. An anxious group of trainers and grooms was clustered around Chickamauga's stall.

A slight fellow—probably an ex-jockey, I judged from his trim build—intercepted us as we entered the stable.

"I'm sorry, Mr. Brady. There was nothing more we could do."

"You mean, he's . . . he's . . ."

The little man nodded sadly. "He's passed on, sir."

Brady broke into great wails of grief that shook the timbers above us. Chickamauga had been more than a horse to him; it had been the child he never had. I left him to his sorrow and walked to the stall. The sight that greeted me wasn't a pretty one. The colt's body was still contorted in its death throes, its once beautiful eyes now wide and cold. The boards of the stall were bashed in, giving mute testimony to the agony the horse had endured in its last moments.

"My, God," I gasped involuntarily. "No animal should have had to suffer like this."

The jockey joined me. "I agree. We would have put the poor thing out of its misery if we suspected how bad off he was. But in truth the horse was fine all day. It was in the peak of fitness for tomorrow's race. Suddenly, about two hours ago, it started to get restless, and then it lay down. That's when we called Mr. Brady."

"Are you the trainer?"

He nodded. "Aye. Anderson's the name."

"Tell me, Anderson, has the veterinarian been here?"

"No. I sent a stable boy off for Doc Partridge right after I called Mr. Brady, and I ain't seen neither the boy nor the doc since."

It didn't matter now, of course. Chickamauga was dead and gone. "What do you think happened?" I asked.

Anderson shrugged. "I don't rightly know. It could have been something in the horse's feed. We checked the feed bag, but it seemed in order. Maybe Chickamauga got into some weeds that disagreed with him."

"Like locoweed?"

Anderson could only shrug his shoulders, so I stood there and thought the matter over a bit. Out in Arizona I had seen livestock browse on locoweed, which grew interspersed with other grasses. A horse would be perfectly normal in the morning, and by afternoon it would be clearly agitated. In extreme cases the beast would go berserk. There was nothing to do in such cases but to let the spell run its course. Rarely, however, did an affected animal die.

"You know," I said, thinking out loud, "when I was in the 7th Cavalry out west, we used to buy mounts from the Mexicans down in Sonora. You had to keep an eye on those vaqueros, because they'd always try to slip one over on you. They'd take a worm-eaten nag that was slow and lethargic and feed it locoweed a few hours before they trotted the beast out to show to the gringo buyers. It would be prancing and pawing like a right sprightly mustang, and sometimes the sale would go through."

"What's that got to do with all this, mister?" queried Anderson, perplexed.

"I think Chickamauga was drugged."

The other stablemen, who had gathered round, exchanged uncertain glances.

"You mean someone wanted Chickamauga to lose the Saratoga Special tomorrow?" asked Anderson.

"Perhaps. Or perhaps somebody wanted to pay Diamond Jim back for something that happened at Canfield's tonight."

"This is nonsense," insisted Anderson. "First, I never heard of anyone killing a horse like this. And even if you're right, mister, it would be impossible to prove that the colt was drugged."

"I'm not so sure," I countered. "Bring me a lantern." When one was hoisted over Chickamauga, I bent down to study the horse's carcass. "There's no locoweed in the East, Anderson. Besides, this seizure came on too quickly to be something the horse ate. I think someone slipped in here and injected the horse with some potion intended to make it sluggish for the race. I don't believe the death was intentional, though, because that would give away the whole scheme. No, I think that whoever did this simply didn't know the proper size dose to administer."

To Anderson's astonished ears, my suspicions sounded like wild speculation. "That's just you guessing, mister," he said. "There's no proof of anything you're saying."

Diamond Jim had recovered his poise enough to join us and was listening closely. "There may be no proof, but what Fenny's saying is making sense to me."

Just then the stable boy, the one Anderson had sent to find Doctor Partridge, burst in. "I couldn't find the vet, Mr. Anderson. His wife said that he had gone off to Mr. Canfield's for the night and hadn't returned home."

Brady and I exchanged glances. That meant that the veterinarian had lost a chance to make money on Fitzsimmons, which in turn meant that he might have a motive to sell some unscrupulous character a big dose of horse tranquilizers to get even with me through Brady.

"Hold that lantern up high," I ordered Anderson. "A horse syringe is damned big, and it leaves a bloody mark where it pierces a horse's hide. It usually takes a day or so to disappear, which means that if Chickamauga was drugged, we may find the needle mark."

The carcass was more or less on its side. I searched up its front leg carefully, across its flanks to its withers, and down its stiffening rear leg. I paid particular attention to the great raised blood vessels just under the surface of the horse's hide, which would serve as likely injection points. "Nothing here," I said, shaking my head. "Flip him over, boys."

I stood back and let Anderson and the others manhandle the carcass until the bottom side was now uppermost. Immediately I spotted it; low down near the fetlock of the rear leg was a small red dot, no bigger than a ladybug.

"There it is, Jim," I said.

Brady bent down to inspect the spot. "Damn! You're right, Fenny. No doubt about it."

The stablemen buzzed among themselves and shook their heads in disgust at the wanton destruction of such a promising beast.

Tears were in Brady's eyes again. "Who could have done such a thing? Who? My God, only complete savages could wish to harm such a lovely creature."

"I know who did it," I said.

"Then out with it, man," demanded the distraught Brady.

"Rothstein. He made a move tonight to set you down a peg or two, Jim, and it backfired in his face. Oh, I know I'm the cause of all of that, but the point is that Rothstein probably believes that I'm your man, the way Crawley is his. He decided to get back at you the only way that counts to him, which is by seeing you lose a bundle. So he drugged Chickamauga to slow him down. It was probably supposed to be a subtle thing, just enough tranquilizer to throw Chickamauga off his pace but not enough to raise any suspicion. You'd take a soaking and Rothstein would have his revenge."

"If that's so, how did this happen?" asked Brady, stretching his arms toward the stiffened corpse of his beloved Chickamauga.

"Simple. Rothstein must have sent Crawley to do the deed," I reasoned. "Crawley's no horseman. He probably pumped everything Doc Partridge sold to him into poor Chickamauga."

"Damn Rothstein, and double-damn Crawley," stormed Brady. "They can't get away with this."

"But what are you going to do, Mr. Brady?" asked Anderson. "I mean, everything that this fellow here has been saying is just a guess. You'd have to get Doc Partridge and Crawley to admit to what they did to have a case against 'em."

"He's right, Fenny," agreed Brady. "I don't see any way to settle the score."

"I do," I said with menace in my voice.

Brady looked at me with concern. "What have you got in mind, Fenny?"

I slipped out my Colt and spun the cylinder. Rothstein was a vile reptile, and his creature Crawley a monster. They would respect nothing short of brute force, and I happened to possess that particular commodity in abundance. Ruining the Fitzsimmons fight on me had been galling, but I suppose I could have let it pass. After all, gambling was an unscrupulous business, and one had to expect those sorts of things. Dashing my chances for windfall at the Saratoga Special, though, was going too damned far. Nobody dealt to me from the bottom of the deck twice in one day—nobody. What was more, I couldn't countenance the senseless killing of a beautiful horse; Chickamauga had not deserved to go the way he did. By God, Rothstein and Crawley would rue the day they ever hatched up this scheme.

"I aim to pay off those bastards in hot lead."

"Fenny, don't do anything crazy! This ain't the Wild West, you know."

"It is tonight," I replied, and then I was gone.

5

I took Brady's carriage before he could stop me and whipped the team into a gallop. I knew just where I was going and just what I would do when I got there. I pulled up to Canfield's and leaped from the carriage before the team came to a full stop. The place was mostly dark, but a few

lights burned on the upper floors. That's where I knew I'd find Rothstein—
at his all-night card game.

I tried the front door but found it was locked. One blow from the heel
of my boot sent it crashing open and then I was on the stairs, taking them
two at time. I threw open the mahogany doors to the upstairs game room,
my revolver in my hand. There, at a table on the far side of the room,
was Rothstein. With him were Crawley, Dick Canfield, and an old gent
with a black doctor's bag. That would be Doc Partridge, I concluded. Two
others rounded out the group of gentlemen gamblers in dinner jackets. Everyone
rose in alarm when they saw my six-gun.

"I say, my man," protested Canfield. "How dare you come bursting in
like that. This is a private game, I'll have you know."

"Stay out of this, Canfield," I ordered. "Me and Rothstein here have
got a little score to settle."

Rothstein sneered and spat out, "We ain't got no business, soldier boy.
And put that gun away; we both know you ain't crazy enough to use it in
front of all these witnesses."

He was wrong. I squeezed the trigger and the big Colt roared, the bullet zinging past Rothstein's cheek.

"Get outside, you bastard!" I ordered as Rothstein dabbed at his bleeding
face, a look of utter amazement in his eyes. Something else was there too.
Fear. He recognized too late now that he was dealing with as ruthless a
fellow as any he'd encountered in the teeming slums of New York City.

Crawley, unmanned by the specter of death, made his move first. "Let
me outta here!" he bellowed, bolting from the table and crashing headlong through a closed window. I fired a shot after him but missed. There
was the crash of shattering glass, the heavy thump of Crawley hitting the
roof outside, and then footsteps as he scurried away across the shingles.

At the instant of that shot, Rothstein was off in a second direction,
scampering through a side doorway. I ran after him, past the flabbergasted
Canfield. Rothstein was surprisingly fleet of foot. He was out the door
and down the driveway by the time I reached the ground floor. In the moonlight
I could see he had been joined by Crawley. There was no time to find
Brady's carriage. I set off afoot in hot pursuit.

My quarry lit out for the nearby village of Saratoga, where the narrow
streets might offer them some shelter. I was right on their heels as I saw
them try one shop door after another in their desperate attempt to give
me the slip. Realizing that all the doors were securely locked, Rothstein
and Crawley suddenly dashed down an alley.

I reached the mouth of the alley and paused. Carefully I peered around the corner and into the dark recesses beyond. In the dim light I could make out several large hogsheads, a pile of lumber, and a few ash bins. Nothing stirred, however.

I wasn't sure if Rothstein was armed. He probably relied on Crawley to pack the artillery. As for Crawley, he was primarily a hoodlum, not a sharpshooter. Up close I was sure he'd be dangerous, but as long as I kept low and didn't present too big a target, I figured that Crawley wouldn't be able to find his mark.

I slipped into the alley and huddled low, not wanting to be silhouetted by the relatively well lit street behind me. I held my breath, but still nothing stirred. Slowly I made my way to the first large barrel. It was easily big enough for a man to hide unseen on its far side. I'd have to assume that one of my targets was doing exactly that, and be prepared to ventilate him if he was. I took a deep breath and reached around the barrel, with my Colt leading the way. There was no one there.

I was just about to turn my head to focus on the next hogshead when I caught sight of Rothstein from the corner of my eye. He had hidden *inside* the first barrel and now towered above me with a nail-studded board in hand!

"Rest in hell, soldier boy!" he ejaculated as he swung the board downward.

He caught me a thumping blow across my head, driving me to my knees. Fortunately my hat saved me from serious damage, but for an instant I was stunned. Rather than finishing me off, though, Rothstein leaped from the barrel and fled out the mouth of the alley. On his heels came Crawley, trying to take advantage of Rothstein's blow to make good his own escape. Crawley was quick but not quick enough.

I raised the Colt and fired, spinning Crawley against a wall. "Oh, Jesus!" he howled, clutching at his shoulder with one hand. In the other I caught a glint of silver; he held an over-and-under derringer, a small-gauge street fighting weapon. "You son of a bitch!" he gasped at me through clenched teeth, then fired.

The derringer bullet slammed into the barrel at my side, missing me by no more than an inch. I returned his fire instantly, hitting Crawley in the thigh.

He screamed as the Colt slug smashed into bone. Dropping the derringer, he slid to the ground in agony, whimpering, "Oh God, oh God."

As I rose and closed on him, Crawley began pleading for his life. "Don't kill me, mister. For God's sake, don't kill me. It wasn't my idea. It was

Rothstein's idea. He said it was the best way to get back at Brady. You want Rothstein, not me."

"You're right, partner," I said. "I do want Rothstein. And mark my words, I'll get him. In the meantime, though, here's something for you to think about."

I took careful aim at Crawley's remaining good leg. The Colt roared again. "Eeeyiii!" shrieked Crawley, and then through a river of tears he cried piteously, "Are you crazy, for God's sake? Why'd you do that? Can't you see that I give up?"

"I don't care, you maggot," I said coldly. "As to why I did it, it's so that you can hobble around for the rest of your sordid little life as you ponder this night's work. What's more, I have a few more mementos to leave with you."

So saying, I hefted the board Rothstein had discarded in his flight. It was a two-by-four, and about five feet long. It would do the trick nicely, I decided. Standing over Crawley, I set to. I pounded him up and down, covering him in a welter of gore. He tried desperately to drag himself away as I beat out that grim tattoo, and as he did I followed merrily along, banging my club off his head every inch of the way. No, I wouldn't kill him, I had decided, but when I was done with him, he might wish I had.

I was enjoying my work so much that it wasn't until Crawley moaned, "Help me, help me, for God's sake," that I realized I had company.

I looked up to see two fellows in overcoats and bowlers at the mouth of the alley. Ominously, their hands were in their pockets. I tensed for action and tried to remember how many bullets I had left in the Colt. Just then, the nearer of the strangers spoke.

"Are you Captain Travers?" he asked.

"Who wants to know?" I replied carefully, dropping the board and backing away from Crawley, who collapsed sobbing where he lay.

Now I heard a police whistle and shouts in the distance. Either Rothstein or Canfield had raised the alarm. It was clearly time to be on my way. Then the stranger said something that amazed me. "I'm Agent McAllister. This"—here he gave a nod with his head toward his companion—"is Agent Patterson. We've come to fetch you."

"Fetch me? Fetch me where?" I demanded.

"We can't say at the moment, I'm afraid, but it's a matter of the greatest concern to the country."

Greatest concern to the country? What the hell was he going on about? I didn't have time to ask that question, for now we were joined by an impromptu posse of citizens headed by a constable with a shiny tin star on his coat.

"I'm Sheriff Weylan," announced the lawman. "I want to take that gentleman in to answer some questions." He was pointing straight at me.

I gulped. Rothstein evidently carried more weight in this town than I had imagined. He must have fled straight to the law and babbled out a complaint against me. I began protesting my innocence when the fellow who had identified himself as Agent McAllister spoke up.

"We're federal agents, sheriff." He and his partner produced badges and then printed credentials.

This slowed down Sheriff Weylan somewhat, for never before in his life had he encountered federal agents. But he rallied gamely. "Well, boys, I'm mighty proud to make your acquaintance," he said, "and I'd be pleased to pass the time of day with you, but I'm a mite pressed at the moment. I need to take that fellow over yonder into custody for assault and attempted murder."

"Attempted murder?" I cried, aghast. "Why, I was just handing out some just deserts, that's all."

Agent McAllister stayed me with an upraised hand. "We saw the whole thing. Captain Travers was attacked by this man and only defended himself. Both Agent Patterson and I are prepared to execute affidavits to that effect."

The sheriff considered this, then said, "Well, be that as it may, there's still a little matter of damage to Canfield's place. A broken window or two, and a few slugs in the walls."

Agent McAllister produced a wad of greenbacks and asked, "What's the amount of damage?"

"Hmmm. That's a mighty fancy place, so I reckon three hundred might do it," opined Sheriff Weylan.

Agent McAllister peeled off three one-hundred-dollar bills and handed them over to Sheriff Weylan. "I believe that settles Captain Travers's account."

Sheriff Weylan pocketed the money with a satisfied nod. "Well now, gentlemen, if you'll just step down the street to my office and give me those affidavits you promised," said the now genial sheriff, "I think this unfortunate matter can be concluded forthwith."

In no time the necessary papers had been drawn up, Crawley had been whisked off to see a doctor, and the two agents and I were at my room collecting my things. Alice hovered about as I packed, distraught from having heard the news about Crawley. "Fenny, my love, where are you going? What's to become of you?"

I looked at Agent McAllister, who said, "He'll be gone for a short while, ma'am. It's federal business and I'm afraid I can't say anything more."

Had someone told me two hours previously that I would be shanghaied to parts unknown by two federal agents, I would have kicked up a ruckus the likes of which Saratoga would never forget. Now, with a possible warrant hanging over my head but for the intervention of my newfound guardians, slipping out of town under escort was downright appealing. With my bags packed, I gave Alice a farewell kiss and headed for the door.

"Fenny, write to me as soon as you can," she implored, tears coursing down her lovely cheeks. "I'll wait for you, my love. I swear I will."

And then we were gone.

6

New York City
July 1903

At Saratoga Depot we boarded the *Cavanaugh Special* for its return trip to New York. The train was named in honor of John G. Cavanaugh, the Irish ruler of the New York bookies. Irish John was famed for the caravan of horseplayers he led to Saratoga each summer for the opening of the season. The special, consisting of six Pullman cars and two dining cars, was nearly empty. The food was quite good and the champagne even better, so despite the mysterious circumstances, all in all I rather enjoyed the trip down to New York City.

Once there I thought we would transfer for a train going on to Washington. Instead, upon our arrival at Grand Central Station, Agent McAllister announced to my surprise, "We're laying over in New York."

That made me wonder a bit, but it was his show and so I made no fuss when we checked into the St. James Hotel, on the corner of Broadway and East 26th Street. I did protest on the following morning, though, when Agent McAllister without explanation hailed a hansom cab, bundled Patterson and me into it, piled himself in behind, and then told the driver, "The federal pier at South Street."

"The federal pier? Where's that? And why are we going there?" I asked.

I received only silence in reply, despite my further demands for some answers. We arrived at a nondescript wharf not at all distinguishable from the commercial docks all along South Street, on the southern tip of Manhattan. There, lashed to the pier, was a two-masted schooner with a single funnel. Emblazoned on her bow in neat script was the name *Decatur*. Crewmen in naval uniforms labored on the schooner's deck, and from their hurried activity it was evident that they were about to weigh anchor. It was only when we had descended from the cab that Agent McAllister deigned to enlighten me further.

"We're going on a little boat ride, Captain Travers. It won't take long. The official who needs to meet with you is out on Long Island at the moment, on the North Shore. The *Decatur*'s been put at our disposal for the trip. So let's board, shall we?"

"Hold on, McAllister. I've been mighty patient with you boys up to this time, but it seems that I have a right to know who I'm setting off to meet."

McAllister and Patterson exchanged looks, then McAllister said, "Okay, Captain. We're taking you to President Roosevelt."

"Roosevelt? What the blazes does that galoot . . . er, what does the president want with me?"

Agent McAllister, however, would add nothing further. "I couldn't tell you if I wanted to. My orders were to fetch you. You'll just have to hold your question until you meet the president."

With great trepidation I boarded the *Decatur* and took a seat on a bench in the pilothouse. The schooner slowly backed away from the pier, swung about, and then gained speed. It nosed up the East River to Ward's Island, threaded through the Hell Gate, skirted Riker's Island, and then debouched into Long Island Sound, heading due east.

The morning was warm, and not a cloud was in the sky above us. Seagulls, as though hoping the *Decatur* might be a fishing trawler, wheeled and screeched around the funnel. I eyed the water skimming past the rails. It was amazingly clear, and I could see hundreds of mackerel and bluefish darting over the sandy bottom below. Far in the distance a school of porpoises leaped playfully from the waves. Then spying the *Decatur,* they hurried over to run alongside the bow like so many playful dogs. The skipper kept the North Shore just off the starboard bow and passed two headlands that jutted out into the sound. Just as we came abreast a third headland, he called out a sharp order. At once the bow came smartly around to starboard, and the schooner steamed into a snug little harbor.

"What's this place called?" I asked.

"Oyster Bay," answered the skipper, his eyes straight ahead as he guided his vessel shoreward.

"The president's summer home," added Agent Patterson, who was standing by my side.

The surface of the water in this haven was as smooth as glass, and the helmsman cut back his throttle until the boiler made only a low rumbling sound. Oyster Bay was evidently a summer playground, for it was dotted with a variety of ketches and dinghies and a few large yachts. It was a working port as well, for interspersed with the pleasure craft were a few worn fishing boats manned by hard-looking Yankees.

The *Decatur* headed for a small village nestled by the shore and came alongside a pier with only a slight jar. Instantly sailors leaped from the deck to the wharf and the hawsers were secured.

"Let's go, Captain Travers," ordered Agent McAllister. A one-horse trap was waiting at dockside, the reins held by a bumpkin whose obvious task it was to meet the *Decatur* when she docked. With a crack of the whip we were off, cantering through streets lined with fish stalls, marine equipment shops, and a few small cafés. Then we were out in the country. We followed a dirt track for two miles past pleasant fields heavy with crops and then turned into a macadam drive that led up a low hill. At the crest was a mansion, not of stone and mortar but of clapboard with brightly painted shutters, all set off with a gabled roof of cedar shingles. The dwelling rose three stories and was skirted on all sides by a spacious veranda. Over the veranda were spread striped awnings, giving the place the jolly look of a well-appointed resort.

"This is Sagamore Hill," announced Agent McAllister. "It's the Roosevelt family home and serves as the northern White House whenever the president wishes to get away from the public eye."

"Why does Roosevelt need privacy for a meeting with me?"

McAllister merely shrugged; if he had any guesses, he wasn't saying. We drew up to the front door and stepped down from the trap.

"We'll wait for you here," said Agent Patterson.

When I hesitated, Agent McAllister said, "Go ahead and pull the bell cord. You're expected."

I did as I was told and a butler opened the door. "Captain Travers?"

"That's right."

"Please come this way, sir." The butler led me down a long hallway to a pair of oaken doors. Above me, the ceiling rattled with the pounding of small footsteps and shrieks of laughter from what sounded like a pack of children. Roosevelt's brood was evidently in residence with him. The butler opened the doors and turned. "Please wait in here, sir. The president is in the gun room. I'll summon you when he is ready for your interview."

The gun room? I didn't like the sound of that at all. If the butler noted any disquiet on my visage, though, he didn't let on. He calmly motioned me into my holding pen and withdrew. I stepped into the chamber and saw immediately that it was already occupied. On a low divan sat two figures. One, a major of Engineers, eyed me sharply as I entered. The other rose to his feet in consternation.

"My God, if it isn't Travers!"

At first I couldn't trust myself to speak. When my tongue unfroze, all I could croak was, "Longbottom!"

Yes, it was Capt. Joshua Longbottom, the blight of my life who had dogged my steps from Peking to Manila. This was all very strange and unsettling, since nothing involving Longbottom had ever boded well for me in the past. I demanded warily, "What in Sam Hill are you doing here, Longbottom?"

"I was going to ask you the same thing, Travers," he replied with equal bewilderment. "All I know is that I was summoned from Plattsburgh Barracks late last night and brought here by Secret Service agents. The butler told me I was here to see the president, but for the life of me, I don't know why."

"My story is about the same," I rejoined, deciding to keep to myself the fact that I'd been interrupted in the middle of a murderous street fight.

My glance wandered to the major, who remained seated as he studied me. Following my eyes, Longbottom said, "This is Major Black, Corps of Engineers."

"Major," I said with a nod of my head.

"Captain," came the reply. It was formal, distant.

Engineers were like that, I knew. Only the very brightest West Point graduates were accepted by the corps, and consequently engineers viewed all other officers as stumbling dolts, fit to be entrusted only with the most menial of tasks. I waited for something more from Black that might explain his presence at this conclave, but he remained silent. Baffled, I turned to Longbottom.

"The major was called here from his annual leave, Travers," Longbottom explained. "He's as puzzled as you and I. My guess is that the president wants some service that only we three can offer."

Major Black didn't have the look of a fellow who was easily stumped, but I put that thought aside and said, "Well, let's think about this situation a moment. What do we have in common?"

Longbottom gave me a look that as much as said the question was preposterous. Nonetheless, he tapped his index finger along his jaw and ventured, "Well, we were both in Cuba."

"And China," I reminded him.

"And the Philippines," he added.

"And you, sir?" I asked Major Black. "Where have you been assigned recently?"

The major made it clear he wasn't much interested in playing our little game. He replied vaguely, "I've been on a mapping assignment, Captain. In Central America."

"Is that so?" I mused. "Well, the only common thread I can make out is that we've all been around a bit."

An idea suddenly occurred to Longbottom. "Say, that may be it, Travers."

"What may be it?"

"The major has expertise in mapmaking. You and I, on the other hand, have battle experience. We've been to Peking and all across the Philippine archipelago. Oh, yes, and don't forget Tientsin."

How could I forget Tientsin? That was where I saved the 9th Infantry's bacon, although Longbottom had gotten most of the credit. Still, Longbottom was right; there was a pattern in all of this. "Roosevelt wants officers for a dangerous mission overseas," I concluded worriedly.

"Yes, but where?" wondered Longbottom.

No sooner were the words out of his mouth than my head was swiveling toward Major Black. "Er, sir, just what part of Central America were you surveying?"

Major Black had no time to answer even had he been so inclined, for at that moment the butler reentered the room and announced, "Gentlemen, the president will see you now."

We followed him down the hall and up two flights of stairs to a high-ceilinged chamber whose walls were cluttered with bookshelves and the mounted heads of luckless big game. This evidently was the gun room. No sooner had the butler ushered us across the threshold than Roosevelt was upon us.

"Captain Travers!" he bellowed as he came on, his eyes aglitter behind his spectacles and a horse-toothed grin wreathing his face. "Dee-lighted, sir, dee-lighted!" He seized my right hand and pumped it as though he were a frantic fireman desperate to get a flow of water from a balky pump. With his left hand he gave me a thunderous clap on the shoulder, the sort that promised to leave a bruise on the morrow.

"I see you've magnificently weathered your sojourn among the savage Moros!" he fairly roared. "Will Taft out in Manila has kept me appraised of all your deeds on Mindanao, young man. If anything, they exceed the glory of your capture of Aguinaldo. By Godfrey, Travers, you have contributed more than any single man to the advantageous position we enjoy in the Philippines today."

That was spreading it on a bit thick, which signaled that Roosevelt was lining me up for something. That realization made me damned chary, and it was with narrowed eyes that I said, "You honor me, Mr. President."

Dropping my hand sharply, Roosevelt greeted Longbottom and Black, delivering knuckle crushing handclasps to each of them in turn. As he did so, I saw that Roosevelt was not alone. With him was Maj. Gen. Leonard Wood, whom I recognized from the days I had served with him in Cuba during the Santiago campaign. "Hello, sir," I greeted Wood.

"Glad to see you again, Captain Travers. I've followed your accomplishments with great interest. I echo the president's compliments."

Also present was a trim, mustachioed gent standing just to the side of Wood. This fellow studied me with alert eyes while I peered right back at him. He wore a pinstripe suit of rich weave set off by fawn-colored spats over glossy patent leather shoes. I gave a friendly bob of my head, since he looked the sort who was my social better, and said, "Pleased to meet you, sir."

"The pleasure is all mine, Captain Travers." The voice was well modulated, almost musical, like that of an accomplished actor—or perhaps a trial lawyer.

I had no time for further small talk, for Roosevelt held the floor, as it were. "Captain Longbottom, Major Black. Dee-lighted, gentlemen. Yes, I'm most pleased to see you all. I apologize for all the secrecy, but for the good of the nation it was better to summon you here with as little fanfare as possible. Now be seated, won't you?"

Good of the nation? What did the little rooster mean by that? I wondered. It was with no small amount of trepidation that I settled onto a sofa directly under the mounted head of a huge, snarling grizzly. Roosevelt stood before us, rubbing his hands with relish at the tale he was about to spin.

"Now, it's my understanding that excepting Major Black, none of you gentlemen has been to Central America. Is that right?"

Slowly, Longbottom and I nodded our heads. "That's correct, sir," said Longbottom. "We've only been to Cuba, China, and the Philippines."

"I've been to the Mexican border," I volunteered.

"I've already pointed out that fact to the president, Captain Travers," said General Wood. "I've also told him that you and Captain Longbottom are both fluent in Spanish."

That was true for me; I had picked up the lingo in Havana and I said so. As for Longbottom, I assumed he learned Spanish during his sojourn in Cuba or the Philippines.

"Good, good," bubbled Roosevelt, pulling up a chair and hunkering down before the three of us. "Gentlemen, you're all on your way to Panama."

"Panama?" Longbottom and I echoed as one. Black said nothing, the calm look on his face telling me he had expected this news.

"Yes, Panama," said Roosevelt, beaming.

"When?" I blurted.

In my anxiety, the question came out a bit sharply. Roosevelt took it for a note of eagerness and grinned anew. "That's what I remember about you, Travers," he said approvingly. "Always ready to charge into the fray, just like you did on Kettle Hill. I like that in a man, by gad. I think it's bully."

He took a deep breath and looked ready to launch a discourse on the general topic of gumption, when General Wood cleared his throat delicately and answered my question. "Immediately, Captain Travers. We need you to perform a rather important task regarding a possible Isthmian canal."

"A what?" I queried, only to draw a look of rebuke from Major Black.

Roosevelt, however, was more understanding. "You may not have been able to follow the canal debate while you were out on the vastness of the Pacific, Travers. I'll ask Secretary Root here to fill you in on the background of the mission I'm proposing for you gentlemen."

So that was the stranger—Secretary of War Elihu Root. I had heard of him, all right. He'd succeeded Secretary Alger, a rather easy act to follow, by all accounts. I knew a thing or two about Root from conversations with George Duncan over the years. For instance, I knew that he was a famed New York attorney before entering government service. And I knew that he was an astute businessman and a diehard Republican loyalist.

As instructed, Secretary Root addressed us. "Gentlemen, Congress has been debating a canal across Central America ever since the French canal effort collapsed in the 1880s."

"You mean the Ferdinand de Lesseps venture?" asked Longbottom.

"That's right," confirmed Root. "As you may know, the United States viewed de Lesseps's effort with alarm from the very beginning. To us, it signaled a period of European meddling in this hemisphere. Fortunately, the French effort was poorly planned and eventually went bankrupt."

"I had heard that disease and corruption played large roles in their failure," said Longbottom.

"You heard right," Root confirmed. "There was disease aplenty. Malaria and yellow fever decimated the workforce. As for corruption, well, the civil trials in France after the collapse of the French canal effort exposed a bottomless pit of malfeasance and chicanery. A stock company, called the Compagnie Universelle, had been formed to finance de Lesseps's effort. As things turned out, the directors had illegally dipped into the till of the company for personal expenses well before the first yard of dirt had been moved in Panama. In essence they bled the company dry. That, coupled with the disease lurking in Panama, sealed the fate of the French effort. It was a black mark for France but a reprieve for this country."

"A reprieve?" I asked, befuddled.

"Yes, Captain Travers," explained Root. "In the 1880s this country was in no shape to take on a project like the Isthmian canal. First, there were political considerations. Few Americans were ready to look beyond our shores back them. Also there were the twin demons of disease and terrain that had licked the French. Back then, they would have licked us too."

"But now, I take it, things have changed?"

"Yes, they have, Captain Travers. For one, Congress now favors a canal."

"There's still a big unknown there, Mr. Secretary," General Wood reminded him. "You know, the issue of the Walker Commission."

"What's the Walker Commission?" I asked.

Major Black rolled his eyes at my denseness, but Root was nothing if not patient. "Walker is a retired admiral, Captain," Root explained. "A very capable fellow, indeed. President Roosevelt appointed Admiral Walker to chair a commission to settle once and for all the vexing question of whether the Isthmian canal should be built across Panama or across Nicaragua."

"That fight's been raging in Congress for years," offered Longbottom.

"And a hot fight it's been," acknowledged Roosevelt. "The southern delegations in Congress want a Nicaraguan canal. It would be a shorter distance to their ports, you see, and they have gotten the notion into their skulls that the shorter route will spark a boom along the Gulf of Mexico and the lower reaches of the Mississippi."

"It stands to reason," I ventured.

Roosevelt frowned and shook his bull-like head, but not angrily, which suggested that he hadn't called me here because of my mental prowess. "It's not that simple, Captain Travers," he corrected me. "There are crucial advantages to the Panama route." Turning to Root, he ordered, "Tell him, Elihu."

Secretary Root obliged. "There's the Panama Railroad for one. It has spanned the Panama Isthmus since the 1850s and remains in perfectly serviceable condition. Its existence would contribute immeasurably to the success of a Panama canal. Also, the Panama route would take advantage of the excavations left by the French."

"To be fair, though," observed General Wood, "there are disadvantages to each route."

"Such as, sir?" inquired Longbottom.

"Your question leads back to the Walker Commission, of which Major Black here was a member," answered Root. "The commission studied both routes and concluded that each would be expensive and each had political complications. Ultimately, because of the lower overall cost, the Walker Commission recommended the Nicaragua route. In doing so, though, the commission discounted one of the more widely discussed shortcomings of the Nicaragua route, which was volcanoes."

"Volcanoes?" I squawked in alarm.

"Oh, there you go with that wild man Bunau-Varilla's tales," scoffed Roosevelt.

"Bunau who?" I echoed, now lost.

"Monsieur Philippe Bunau-Varilla," repeated Roosevelt gruffly. "A French pipsqueak who thinks he's the Almighty's gift to mankind."

"Er, perhaps I can shed some light on the president's observation," offered Root. "Mr. Bunau-Varilla is a French engineer. In fact, he used to be the chief engineer of the Compagnie Universelle. He's a devoted admirer of Ferdinand de Lesseps and was crushed when the French venture failed. More importantly for our immediate concerns, however, is Mr. Bunau-Varilla's financial links to the Compagnie Universelle. As I've told you, when that company failed, its directors were put on trial. It was a national disgrace for France and for de Lesseps. To retrieve some shred of dignity, the French government stepped into this embarrassing scene. Under its official auspices, a successor company was founded, called the New Panama Canal Company, which took title to all its parent company's property. It owns the dredging equipment, the steam engines, and most importantly, the right-of-way across Panama that was granted by the government of Colombia.

All the major financial backers of the Compagnie Universelle, of which Bunau-Varilla was one, were told in no uncertain terms that either they invested in the New Panama Canal Company or they too would be tried for fraud. The result, rather predictably, was that these large shareholders bought into the New Panama Canal Company."

This cleared up absolutely nothing for me. "But how does that relate in any way to what we're discussing?"

"Oh, quite directly," Root assured me. "Bunau-Varilla's interest in the New Panama Canal Company runs into the hundreds of thousands of dollars. The only truly marketable asset of the company, however, is the right acquired from the government of Colombia to dig a canal way across the isthmus. If the United States decides on the Nicaragua route, Mr. Bunau-Varilla will be ruined."

"Ah," I said, the light finally dawning.

"Exactly," said Root. "For that reason Mr. Bunau-Varilla has canvassed this country from coast to coast drumming up support for the Panama route."

"A damned nuisance," spat Roosevelt.

"But a useful nuisance," added General Wood.

"At times," Roosevelt conceded grudgingly.

Root continued. "Bunau-Varilla is a bit of a character, but one can only admire his ingenuity. He's showing Nicaraguan postage stamps to anyone who'll stop to give him the time of day."

"Postage stamps?" queried Longbottom. "Whatever for?"

Here Root actually chortled. "Because they're emblazoned with volcanoes. I guess the engraver who made them up needed a dramatic subject to stimulate his interest, and so the stamps portray volcanoes in various states of arousal. They're beautiful examples of the engraver's skill, but from a public relations point of view, they're a disaster for Nicaragua and for our southern representatives in Congress. You see, as Bunau-Varilla speaks to audiences across the country, he horrifies his listeners with visions of sinking hundreds of millions worth of precious capital into a Nicaragua canal, only to watch it all be blown to smithereens by some uncooperative volcano."

"The volcanoes are an issue, of course," allowed Roosevelt, removing his pince-nez and polishing the lenses with his handkerchief as he spoke, "but frankly they're not a major issue. There hasn't been a serious eruption in Nicaragua in more than eighty years, and there aren't any active volcanoes near the proposed canal route."

Tiring of this geography lesson, I asked straight out, "Then what is the problem?"

You might think this presumptuous of me, what with Roosevelt having risen to the status of a national icon in the view of most Americans. I had known him from our Cuban days, however, and familiarity does breed a certain amount of contempt. From what I'd seen of Roosevelt, everything he did centered about the greater glorification of Teddy and the progressive wing of the Republican Party. I was certain that this little gathering had been called to further Roosevelt's political aspirations, and if such was the case, I wanted all the pertinent facts.

"It's the political problem Secretary Root alluded to, and indirectly a military one," answered Roosevelt. "General Wood, why don't you enlighten the captains on that score?" He had not mentioned Black, causing me to surmise that the major was already privy to Roosevelt's machinations.

General Wood obeyed. "Nicaragua is ruled by a dictator, an unsavory gent by the name of General José Santos Zelaya. Zelaya's a bloodthirsty despot but a crafty one, and he's got a stranglehold on every element of Nicaraguan society. There's no meaningful opposition, and because of that, he feels secure when dealing with us. His terms are simply unacceptable. He wants millions just for entering into discussions about a canal in his country, and his position regarding ultimate sovereignty over any resulting canal is clear: Nicaragua will retain sovereignty, not the United States."

"Well, that seems understandable," I murmured, my naïveté showing for all to see.

"Understandable?" rumbled Roosevelt. "Why, it's no such thing. Zelaya's position is inadmissible, I say! Totally inadmissible. I will not commit this country to an effort so vast that it crushed a nation like France only to see some two-bit dictator flying his flag over the canal at the end of our labor. No, any canal we build will be American property. That point is beyond question."

Roosevelt folded his arms across his barrel chest and fixed me with his fiercest glare. If I had entertained any doubt on the matter, this outburst had settled it for good; Roosevelt had decided that the Panama route was the way to go.

Shifting uncomfortably under that piercing gaze, I said, "Well, I see you've given a great deal of thought to the matter."

"There's more than simple chauvinism at work here, Captain Travers," General Wood hastened to add. "Any canal across the isthmus will become one of the vital trade links of the world. In time of war, the United States must be able to defend that canal, and we cannot brook interference from a third-rate Central American power. We have negotiated this matter with Great Britain in the second Hay-Pauncefote Treaty"—John Hay was Roosevelt's secretary of state, I knew—"and that treaty secured British acquiescence to the right of the United States to fortify any future Isthmian canal."

Here Longbottom chimed in with a cogent observation. "Mr. President, if Nicaragua is off your list because of the sovereignty issue, then the Panama route suffers from the same infirmity. After all, the province of Panama is part of Colombia, itself a sovereign nation."

By God, Longbottom was right. I looked about for some indication that Longbottom's point was irrefutable, but instead Root cleared his throat delicately while Roosevelt studiously eyed the ceiling as though he had just noticed it for the first time. Their sudden shyness told me that Longbottom had come close to striking a raw nerve.

It was General Wood who answered Longbottom's challenge. "Ah, Captain Longbottom, you've raised an interesting point. I've told you about the shortcomings of the Nicaragua route, those being volcanoes, political obstacles, and pure greed. Well, the shortcomings of the Panama route also include political obstacles and pure greed. The State Department has been negotiating with Colombia for some time for the right to construct a canal across the isthmus, and the results of those talks are not promising."

Secretary Root picked up on this theme. "The problem with these negotiations is that we have been dealing with two different groups, gentlemen, each of them quite unsavory. On the one hand there are the French of the New Panama Canal Company. We offered to buy out their interest for forty million dollars, but they demanded almost triple that amount. That's where Monsieur Bunau-Varilla came in handy. He cajoled his countrymen into coming to their senses and seeing the reasonableness of our offer. The French finally accepted our figure, albeit reluctantly. That left only the government in Bogotá to be dealt with, but they have proven to be a major impediment. After much wrangling with a parade of emissaries from Colombia, in January of this year Secretary Hay was able to conclude a most generous settlement with Bogotá."

"A den of thieves, by gad!" thundered Roosevelt. He evidently had a dim view of the good faith of the Colombians.

"Yes, well," continued Root. "Secretary of State Hay offered the Colombian ambassador, one Dr. Tomas Herrán, a lump sum of ten million dollars plus an annuity of two hundred fifty thousand dollars per annum. That amount would replace the rent that Colombia currently receives from the New Panama Canal Company, which, by the way, represents almost all of Colombia's yearly income. So you can see how generous our terms to the Colombians were. After much wrangling, Dr. Herrán accepted our terms, and the resulting agreement is known as the Hay-Herrán Treaty."

Roosevelt punctuated Root's discourse with an irascible, "A damn giveaway to a bunch of jackals! Highway robbery, I say!"

Having evidently heard this particular fulmination in the past, Root didn't skip a beat as he continued, "The Senate ratified the Hay-Herrán Treaty in March. Despite the generosity of our terms, however, the Colombian government balked. Bogotá insisted that it, not the French investors, should get the lion's share of the forty million. That attitude stalled all progress, which is especially vexing since the concession of the New Panama Canal Company will expire next year. If the expiration date passes without an agreement, we will be facing a government in Bogotá with a much stronger hand to play than it currently possesses."

"That's not going to happen," vowed Roosevelt.

"Perhaps," demurred Root. "However, the current status of affairs is this. In view of the intransigence of the Colombians, Secretary of State Hay was forced to issue an ultimatum to them. Either ratify the Hay-Herrán agreement or place the traditionally friendly relations between Washington and Bogotá at risk."

"Has there been an answer from the Colombians?" queried Longbottom.

Secretary Root nodded gravely. "Yes. We received it just the other day. The Colombian senate rejected the treaty unanimously."

There was silence at this and a look on Roosevelt's face that bespoke frustration and determination. He clearly had no intention of letting this matter lie, and that, I knew, explained our presence here.

"Er, sir," I said, addressing myself to Secretary Root, "you've told us what we were prepared to give the Colombians under the Hay-Herrán Treaty. What exactly was it that we expected in return?"

"Nothing beyond reason," insisted Roosevelt, answering for his secretary in a tone that suggested he was cobbling together a stump speech for future use. "We asked only for the bare minimum concessions necessary to ensure the continued growth and prosperity of this great democracy."

"Meaning what?" I pressed.

"The treaty would have given the United States the right to build, maintain, and operate a canal zone ten kilometers wide across the breadth of the isthmus. The term of the agreement was to be one hundred years, renewable at the option of the United States. Perhaps most importantly, it also gave the United States the right to defend the canal."

"Ah, there's the rub," said Longbottom softly.

"It shouldn't have been if the Colombians were dealing in good faith," insisted Roosevelt strenuously. "After all, the treaty specifically stated that sovereignty over the zone remained with Colombia. In my book, that should have laid to rest any qualms those coyotes in Bogotá might have had about the deal."

I rather doubted that. Sovereignty was a joke if foreign troops were ensconced on one's native soil. I could just imagine Roosevelt's reaction to, say, a proposal from Kaiser Wilhelm to garrison German troops on Staten Island but promising to allow sovereignty over the island to remain with Washington. Why, after the smoke had cleared, it would have taken ten strong men with ropes and hooks to pull Roosevelt off the ceiling.

"So," I asked carefully, "where does all of this leave us?"

Root fielded the question. "A few weeks ago the Senate passed the Spooner Amendment. It says that unless the Hay-Herrán Treaty is ratified in a reasonable time, Congress will insist on going forward with the Nicaragua route."

"Then that's pretty much it, isn't it?" asked Longbottom, looking about the room uncertainly. His words were met by stony silence all around, and Root and General Wood exchanged furtive looks.

A very bad feeling was beginning to come over me now, and from the perplexed expression on Longbottom's face, I could see that he hadn't yet grasped the central point that our superiors were trying to make. I decided to enlighten him.

"Let's just suppose, gentlemen," I ventured slowly, "that Panama were to be somehow cut out of the Colombian herd. If that were to happen, we'd be able to deal with her directly without going through any middlemen, so to speak."

Root nodded sagely, as though the notion had never occurred to him before, yet upon hearing it from me just now, it struck him as a particularly sound idea. Roosevelt, less subtle than his secretary of war, was giving me his broadest grin, his lips stretched to within an inch of his flashing eyes.

"The important thing, though, Travers," he insisted, "is that those are your words, not mine. You never heard me say any such thing."

"Remember that, gentlemen," admonished General Wood sternly. Then he added, "The only comment I have in response to your observations, Captain Travers, is that we have become aware over the last several months that there may be, er, separatist sentiments among some elements of the population of Panama. Major Black, in fact, noted the existence of civic unrest in his classified reports to the War Department."

That crystallized Black's role in all of this. He was the man who had walked the ground and knew the politics of Panama. He was to be our guide.

Longbottom hadn't quite caught the significance of General Wood's comment, however, for he posited forthrightly, "Well, sir, you could say the same for the population of South Carolina." He ought to know, I thought silently, since he hailed from Charleston, a hotbed of Southern sore losers. "My point is that feelings mean nothing unless the populace is willing to translate them into action."

"Your point is well taken, Captain Longbottom," conceded Secretary Root. "If, however, the people of Panama *do* want to do something about their feelings, then their interests and ours are in alignment. In other words, while we won't start a revolution in Panama, we certainly won't do anything to prevent one."

"And if one occurs," I said, summing up what I'd been hearing, "Uncle Sam will be ready to treat with whatever government emerges for rights to build a canal across their new country."

"In a nutshell, that's it, son," confirmed General Wood.

"Then I see why we're here."

"You do?" asked Longbottom, still not grasping what our role was to be in all of this.

"Yes, I do. We're on our way to Panama, Joshua, to see whether the locals are ready to put their money where their mouths are."

Roosevelt's face creased anew with a smile of pure gratification at my unexpected astuteness, causing even the dignified General Wood to grin. Addressing Root, General Wood said, "Mr. Secretary, I told you these were exceptionally perceptive officers."

"It appears you were right, General," Root said nodding approvingly.

I, for one, didn't share their complacency. After all, I was being thrown into the cockpit, not they. For my money, it was time to get a lasso around what promised to be a runaway mustang of an assignment. Clearing my throat, I asked by way of clarification, "So that's it, sir? Just poll the locals and then report back?" I suspected, you see, that no definitive written orders would be forthcoming, and I wanted some guidance that would place limits on what could be a hopelessly open-ended mission. The answer I got was hardly encouraging.

"For now, Captain Travers," General Wood replied vaguely. "As for the future, well, things will just have to solidify a bit before we can hazard a guess about that."

Roosevelt stood; our interview was evidently at an end. "Gentlemen, you'll be provided with whatever you need for this journey. I see that the army has chosen the right men for the job. A bully team of warhorses, all right. I know that you men won't let your country down."

Just then the butler knocked and entered. "There's a telephone call for you, Mr. President. It's the secretary of state. He says it's urgent, sir."

"Thunderation," snapped Roosevelt. "I love Hay dearly, but, by George, he's like an old woman who needs hourly assurances that all is well. As sure as shooting, he's calling to see what I aim to do about those Colombians. Well, excuse me, gentlemen. This will take but a moment."

With Roosevelt away, General Wood and Secretary Root quickly outlined the overall scheme of the operation. Longbottom and I were to pose as land surveyors working for the Panama Railroad. Ostensibly, we were to lay out plans for improvements to several railroad trestles spanning the mountainous sections of the railway. In reality we were to contact a list of prominent citizens in the isthmus and attempt to gauge their feelings on the issue of an independent Panama. Black, who would travel separately, would be in Panama City to provide introductions. Also, similar arrangements had been made with the general superintendent of the Panama Railroad, one James Shaler. Superintendent Shaler was a Yankee, and thus his sympathies in this matter were beyond doubt. The necessary papers to perfect our cover were to be provided in a day or so, and then we were to travel by steamer from New York to Colón, Panama's Atlantic port. When General Wood was finished, he took questions from the floor.

"There are just two things, sir," I said.

"And what might they be, Travers?"

"First of all, I don't pretend to know much about Panama, but I expect that there aren't a whole lot of white men down there."

"That's true, Travers. The ruling class is Spaniards—white folks but dark enough. The poorer classes are a mix of Indian and Spanish—mestizos—and then there are black West Indians. The French hauled in the Blacks to dig their canal. But what are you getting at, son?"

"It's just this, sir. If we're supposed to get the lay of the land and to sniff out whether any revolution's brewing, the places we might need to visit are places where white men can't go without raising suspicion."

"Hmmm. You raise a valid concern, Travers," allowed General Wood.

"We hadn't thought of that," conceded Secretary Root, a bit chagrined since he was the sort to think of everything.

"Well, Travers, since you raised the problem, do you happen to have a way around it?" asked Wood.

I did. "Sir, there's a soldier I've campaigned with in the past who would fill the bill nicely. He's Sergeant Henry Jefferson of the 25th Infantry."

"A black regular, eh?"

"Exactly, sir," I confirmed.

"Henry Jefferson," mused General Wood. "It seems as if I've heard that name somewhere before."

"You may have, sir. Sergeant Jefferson was with me at Palanan, when Emilio Aguinaldo was taken. General MacArthur promoted him to sergeant at my recommendation."

"Well, Sergeant Jefferson would be a solution to the problem you posed," allowed Wood.

"Now hold on, sir," protested Longbottom. "I respectfully submit that we should not add any more members to this group. The greater our numbers the more likely we'll be detected by Colombian sympathizers."

Turning to me, General Wood asked, "What's your reply to that, Captain Travers?"

"I don't intend for Sergeant Jefferson to be part of our group, sir. You see, the last I heard he was at Fort Niobrara, Nebraska, with his regiment. I aim to have him travel to Panama alone. He can pose as a railroad worker when he gets there. I'll arrange to contact him surreptitiously; that way he won't be linked to Captain Longbottom and me directly. The important thing is that we'll have him available should we need an agent to move freely once we're in Panama."

"Well, if Jefferson's not visible," conceded Longbottom dubiously, "and as long as he understands that if he gets into hot water alone he'll have to get out of it alone, then maybe Captain Travers's plan might work."

"Done," decided General Wood. "I'll wire Fort Niobrara today. Sergeant Jefferson will proceed to Panama by steamer and once there he'll be under instructions to contact Superintendent Shaler. I'll have Shaler set him up with some nominal railroad job and have him stand by if you have need of his services."

"Thank you, sir."

"And what might be your second concern, Captain Travers?"

"Er, well," I stammered with an awkward grin, "there's a little matter I left hanging back in the quartermaster general's office. There was a little procurement irregularity, you see."

"Yes, I know all about it. Half the horses at Fort Bliss had to be killed, and the government has taken a loss of more than twenty thousand dollars. Fraud, malfeasance, God knows what else."

I stood there abashed as Longbottom looked on agog. "Fraud? Twenty thousand dollars?" he echoed, incredulous. He turned to General Wood for enlightenment but got none.

"That's all water under the bridge, Captain Travers. The president's needs are our paramount concern. If this mission hadn't come up, well, who knows where that squalid contracting affair might have ended." Here he shot me a piercing glance that suggested that a stay in some military prison might well have been my lot, but then he brushed away the whole affair with a final, "I disposed of the investigation. The loss has been written off the books. Now set your mind to the task at hand with my assurance that the matter is closed."

I was breathing a sigh of relief when Roosevelt returned, muttering that Hay was a complete prissy and, by gad, the man seemed about to swoon with the vapors because of Congress' uproar at the mulishness in Bogotá. Putting aside the interruption with a shrug, he wished us well and then sent us along our way with a flurry of backslapping and handshaking. Then, after a final warning from General Wood that none of what had transpired was ever to be divulged, we were out the door.

Once outside Major Black took his leave, promising that he would see us "down there." Agent McAllister then corralled Longbottom and me, and soon we were on our way back to New York to await further instructions.

7

New York City
July 1903

The St. James was in an area of New York with which I was well acquainted, being just two blocks north of my old favorite, the Fifth Avenue Hotel. Once Longbottom and I were settled in, McAllister and Patterson finalized all the necessary arrangements. Passports were produced for us as were letters of introduction from a fictitious Connecticut engineering firm to Superintendent Shaler. Oh, Shaler would know exactly who we were, all right; the letters were for the benefit of any nosy Colombians who might care to inspect our documents. Longbottom and I were given $1,500 each and told to contact the U.S. consulate in Panama City should we need more. There was no mention of any limit on that line of credit, a fact I stored away for possible future use. Finally, we were given tickets for a one-way trip on the steamer *Yucatán* from New York to Colón. I immediately recognized the ship's name. The *Yucatán,* you see, had carried the Rough Riders from Tampa to Cuba, and evidently the venerable ship was still chartered for special government business from time to time.

Both Longbottom and I pointed out to McAllister that we needed wardrobes consistent with our cover stories. We had a full issue of uniforms but damn few surveyor togs. McAllister, though, was ahead of us on this one too.

"There's an account set up in each of your names at Brooks Brothers down at Broadway and Twenty-second Street. Buy whatever you need." I knew the place well; indeed, I had bought my first full dress uniform there. "One note of caution, however," he added. "I want you to go one at a time, to attract as little attention as possible."

This sounded reasonable, and so it was agreed that Longbottom would go first and I when he returned. I amused myself playing solitaire for two hours until Longbottom's reappearance, then I threw down the cards and set out to the haberdashery. I was actually beginning to enjoy this lark. True, it had all come as a shock to dear Alice. How she was going to explain the groom's disappearance to the several hundred or so guests gathered today at the chapel at Saratoga was beyond me. I was confident, however, that she still loved me and was prepared to wait as long as it took to land her man. Free of any doubt on that score, I turned my thoughts to the beckoning adventure.

I knew this would be no China with massed armies of howling Boxers, and that fact comforted me exceedingly. In Panama there might be a few Colombian gendarmes but no real danger, or else Root or Wood would have pointed it out to us, right? The way I saw things, we'd go down there, probably spend a month or two lolling about in the sun, and return home all safe and sound by Thanksgiving—Christmas at the latest. It promised to be a pleasant excursion, topped off with a glowing letter placed in my file from Wood or Root, or maybe even Teddy himself. Now that I wasn't going to be cashiered for gross incompetence, I knew that a letter of that sort would come in damned handy when the time for promotion to major rolled around. Yes, Panama promised to be a tidy little opportunity for old Fenny, I congratulated myself.

At Brooks Brothers I was treated with the deference and courtesy I had come to expect in that establishment. I ordered an assortment of tropical-weight linen suits, a few cotton tunics, several pairs of durable denim trousers, and two pairs of sturdy boots. For a head covering I planned to use my wide-brimmed campaign hat; they were frequently worn by civilians out West, you see, and I was sure it would raise no suspicion in Panama.

A few alterations had to be made, and so the clerk said, "We'll have your order ready by noon tomorrow, sir. Where can we send it?"

I gave him my room number at the St. James. "Why, that's odd," the fellow mused. "Another gentleman was in here not an hour ago, ordered a wardrobe of tropical clothes, and told us to have them sent to the St. James too. The same room, in fact."

So much for McAllister's wish for discretion, I thought. "That's my brother," I lied. "We're off to New Mexico for the quail season, you see. It's an annual pilgrimage."

"As you wish, sir," replied the clerk, not accustomed to questioning any practice of his clients. I could have told him that Longbottom and I intended to dress up like explorers to search for Hottentots in Morningside Park, and he would have merely smiled and had our things sent around to the St. James at noon as promised.

I had gone only a few steps from the shop when a display in a store window caught my eye. The neat lettering on the window proclaimed the place to be Barlow's, Outfitter to the Active Gentleman. In the window was a collection of regalia of the sort that might be worn by a moose hunter in the north woods. There was a flannel shirt, a cap with earflaps, and a pair of the strangest-looking clodhoppers I had ever laid eyes upon. They were vulcanized duck-hunting boots with thick, cleated soles and laces clear up to the knees. Only an idiot would buy the damn fool things, for walking in them would be like stumping about with splints strapped to one's legs.

The thing that drew my attention, though, was a Krag rifle nestled among all these hunting togs. Affixed to the barrel of the Krag was a tubelike structure perhaps eighteen inches in length that was affixed to the upper portion of the rifle by means of various screws and clamps. I went inside the shop and was instantly attended by a bowing, smiling clerk.

"I say, isn't that one of those rifle telescopes I've heard about?" I inquired, pointing at the display.

"Yes, sir," replied the clerk. "It's made by the Cataract Tool and Optical Company especially for the Krag rifle. The sight magnifies objects to twelve times their actual size. You know, that Krag there is said to be the very one carried by Mr. Roosevelt when he stormed San Juan Hill."

Roosevelt had gone up Kettle Hill, of course, not San Juan Hill. Also, I had been with him through most of that battle and he hadn't once toted a rifle. No, he had spent the whole day waving his sword about like a conductor's baton, and he had let fly at the dons with nothing more lethal than a barrage of oaths. Despite the clerk's fanciful tale, though, I was much taken with the contraption.

"Is the sight for sale?"

"The sight? Hmmm, I really couldn't say, sir. It's just there for display purposes. If you'd like, though, I'll raise your request with the management."

"Do so," I ordered, handing the fellow ten greenbacks. "This is for your trouble. I'm having an order from Brooks Brothers delivered to my lodging tomorrow. If you can arrange it, have the sight and the bill sent along with those things."

As I gave him my address just in case things became muddled, he said, "Ah, you must be with the other gentleman who was in here earlier. He wanted me to send a few things over to Brooks Brothers for delivery to the same room."

I rolled my eyes; apparently every merchant in New York would soon know that Longbottom and I were holed up in the St. James and buying enough clothing and equipment to outfit an expedition to the Amazon. "You don't say," I muttered. "Oh, and give that sight a good coat of oil, would you? It may be in storage for a while."

I thanked him and sauntered up Broadway in the late afternoon, savoring this unexpected freedom on what was to have been my wedding day. I was in no hurry to get back to the room simply to spend an evening in Longbottom's company, I can assure you. Besides, the banks and stockbrokerages were emptying now, and the sidewalks were beginning to fill up with throngs of New Yorkers. Soon the restaurants would be packed with gay diners, and an hour or so after that the theaters along the Great White Way would be jammed. As I approached Madison Square and was just passing the white marble facade of the Hoffman House hotel, thoroughly engrossed by the spectacle of this vibrant city coming to life for the evening, I was startled to hear someone hail me by name.

"Well, if it isn't Lieutenant—no, forgive me, Captain Travers."

I stopped in my tracks and turned. There in the doorway of the Hoffman House was a dapper figure in a tasteful striped suit, yellow spats, bowler, and ebony walking cane. Why, it was none other than Richard Harding Davis in all his splendor.

"Why, I declare. Davis—Dickie Davis! By God, I haven't seen you since we marched into Havana back in '98. How are you, old man?"

We shook hands heartily. "I've heard quite a lot about you since, Fenny. Quite a lot," Davis assured me. "I knew you were going places from the first time I laid eyes on you down in Tampa, and by George, you've proven me right."

"Kind of you to say so, Dickie," I preened. "But tell me about yourself. I still see your bylines from time to time. I guess you're still chasing news stories for a living?"

"Oh, once a journalist, always a journalist, Fenny. It does tend to get in one's blood. But I've also expanded my interests some since we last met. I'm an editor now—I'm with *Harper's*."

"Why, congratulations, Dickie," I said with all sincerity. "Now I know who to contact when I'm ready to write my memoirs."

Davis chuckled good-naturedly. "Fenny, you're much too young to be thinking about memoirs. But when you do, I'm sure you'll have quite a few whopping yarns to relate."

That should have caused me to pause, but I was still under the assumption that my meeting with Davis was pure chance and so I merely laughed in reply.

"Fenny," Harding continued, "there are a few friends of mine you should meet while you're in town."

I cocked my head sideways, sensing that there was a message here that I just wasn't receiving. "How's that, Dickie? You know I can tolerate journalists in small doses, but groups of them give me the hives. You're about the only one of your breed I can stand for any time at all."

"I thank you for the compliment, Fenny, but I assure you the people I want you to meet are not reporters."

"Not reporters?" I was lost now. After all, I was a lowly soldier, and folks didn't normally line up just to have a chat with the likes of me.

Seeing my befuddlement, Davis explained. "Fenny, you're an exceptional military man, and your record proves my point. As for my friends, let's just say they come from many walks of life. They all have one common interest, however."

"Which is?"

"The emergence of this country as a power second to none."

This should have sent me scudding down the street with a vague promise to look up Davis the next time I blew into town. But I didn't go, for in truth Davis's line had fascinated me. If some substantial burghers thought I was an important cog in the national machine, well, who was I to disabuse them of the notion?

"When are you fixing to arrange this little palaver?" I inquired.

The answered floored me. "Right now. My friends are just inside. I'm certain you're very busy, Fenny, but this shouldn't take long."

Well, I'll be damned, I thought. Davis had been stalking me. He had positioned himself on my route back to the St. James and set up this cabal of cronies just in case he was successful in netting me. What did he have in mind? I had nothing of any value to anyone other than Alice, and so I felt little danger in Davis's proposal. Shrugging my shoulders and giving what I hoped was a winning grin, I said, "Why not, Dickie. I'd love to meet your pals."

He motioned me to follow him and led me through the glass doors and into the vast foyer of the Hoffman House. The interior was girded with huge carved columns that soared to a frescoed ceiling thirty feet above my head. Crowds of gents in top hats and women in fine gowns milled about, either on their way to dinner or out for an evening on the town. Davis motioned me through the stained glass doors that led to the Hoffman House's renowned saloon where Bouguereau's mural entitled *Nymphs and Satyrs* filled an entire wall. I was no stranger to this saloon, since Bouguereau's Rabelaisian work was a venerated landmark for all West Point cadets on leave in New York.

I followed Davis to a far corner of the saloon and through a door I had never before noticed. We entered a small, exquisitely decorated private dining room. Three gentlemen sat at the single table in the room. They rose as we entered and as they did, I stopped in my tracks. Why, one of them was Bet-a-Million Gates, from Saratoga!

"Fenny, I believe you know Mr. Gates," said Davis unnecessarily, for my prior acquaintance with the boisterous millionaire was written all over my face.

"Yes, indeed. I'm a bit surprised you do, however," I retorted, not quite fathoming this situation. I eyed the other two men. One was a tiny, bald-pated fellow with a great waxed Gallic mustache and the hungry eyes of a jackal that had missed a few feedings. Like a small scavenger, the tiny fellow was high-strung. Although he clasped his hands together before him, I could see his thin, pallid fingers twitching with nervous energy. Then he spoke, and I knew immediately two things: first, he was French; and second, this could only be the peripatetic Philippe Bunau-Varilla.

"*Mon capitaine,* I welcome you to our great enterprise," announced the Frenchman grandly, offering me his finely boned hand.

"A pleasure to meet you, Monsieur Bunau-Varilla," I replied as I shook a rather limp forepaw.

The fact that I knew the Frog's name caused the third gentleman to eye Davis meaningfully. This fellow next advanced with his hand extended, so I dropped Bunau-Varilla's and took his. I studied him as I did. He was of medium height, conservatively dressed in a dark, well-cut suit. I pegged him as being in early middle age, maybe forty. He sported a great mass of blondish silver hair that fell to just above his collar, rather in the fashion of a Shakespearean actor. This, together with our proximity to the theater district, led me to conclude tha this hombre might be a thespian of some sort. As things turned out, I wasn't too far off the mark.

"Fenny, this is Mr. Cromwell," introduced Davis. "*The* Mr. Cromwell."

"Not Oliver Cromwell," I said with a little smile. "I rather expected you'd be a bit older, sir."

The joke went right over Bunau-Varilla's bald head, but Gates let out a great guffaw and swore, "Jesus Christ, the boy's a wit, ain't he?" Subsiding, he sat down and began gorging himself from a platter of green hard-boiled egg yolks set before him.

Cromwell, however, was not at all amused. His blue eyes turned to ice and he said tightly, "I'm William Nelson Cromwell, Captain. I'm the senior partner of Sullivan and Cromwell, attorneys-at-law. I also just happen to be the general counsel of the New Panama Canal Company."

A lawyer. Damn, I should have known it immediately. Who else but a New York lawyer could look all-knowing yet inquisitive at the same moment? I swept off my hat and took a seat unbidden. Here was a true rogues' gallery, you see, so I immediately felt right at home. With a bemused shake of my head I said to Davis, "Dickie, you've got a French engineer, a New York lawyer, and the biggest gambler in America all in the same room. You're up to a bit of no-good or I'm not the much-acclaimed hero of Peking."

Davis grinned, not at all offended. "I wouldn't put it quite like that, Fenny. As I told you, these are gentlemen who care about the emergence of this country as a power second to none."

I had to bite my tongue to keep from laughing out loud. Gates cared only for his next killing, and the little Frenchman undoubtedly didn't give a tinker's damn about the greater glory of the United States.

Eyeing me purposefully, Davis asked, "Well, have you figured out why I brought you here?"

"Nope, but I'm sure you'll let me know. And in the meantime, I think I'd like a drink, if you don't mind."

Davis pulled a velvet cord near the wall and a waiter instantly appeared. "Manhattans all around," he ordered.The Manhattan cocktail was the drink of choice in the Hoffman House, seeing as it had been invented right on the premises by a bartender on a slow afternoon.

"Make mine a bourbon and branch water," I countermanded.

"Very good, sir," said the waiter, reappearing in an astonishingly short time with a tray of drinks, which he set on the table and then withdrew, closing the door behind him.

Davis raised his glass. "To the transoceanic canal," he toasted.

I raised my glass with the others, drank deeply, and then sat back. How Davis had learned about my involvement in this matter and what he wanted from me would all come out in due time, so I decided to relax and enjoy the show.

"Cigar?" queried Davis solicitously, tendering me a Hoffman House perfecto.

I preferred Cuban stogies, but the perfecto was free so I took it with an easy grace. I bit off the end and spat it into a nearby cuspidor, then struck a match on the underside of the table, lit my cigar, and took a puff. I exhaled a great cloud of blue smoke to the ceiling and readied myself to hear whatever proposition this checkered delegation might lay before me.

With the preliminaries out of the way, Davis nodded at Cromwell. The lawyer began to make his case. "Captain Travers, we know that you were out to see the president at Sagamore Hill. What's more, we know your mission—you're to travel to Panama to determine the viability of the independence movement in that country."

"I see you keep yourself well informed, sir," was my curt reply.

Cromwell allowed himself a crafty smile. "That I do, Captain. Especially on this issue."

Gates brusquely cut in, green bits of egg spewing from his maw as he did. "Cromwell, we don't have time for courtroom posing." This drew a withering glare from Cromwell, who disdainfully turned his shoulder to Gates and fell silent. "Travers," said Gates, picking up from the miffed barrister, "we're interested in you because you're a fella who gets results. Why, I saw what you did to Crawley. He was on public display in the sheriff's office after you were done with him. Crawley's a blooded street fighter who's feared from Chicago to Brooklyn. You went through him like Dewey took Manila, son. In my book that's a glowing recommendation for the job we've got in mind."

"Which is?"

Gates was equally blunt. "We want a canal built and we want it in Panama. Our reasons are none of your concern. The point is that you're being ordered to Panama to find out where the locals stand on independence. We know that pantywaist Hay has pleaded with Roosevelt not to snatch Panama from Colombia. I guess that would be too damn easy for his refined sensibilities.

Everything's got to be all nice and legal for him. By Christ, if the founding fathers of this great nation had been of Hay's mind, our frontier would still be the Blue Ridge Mountains. Well, that's neither here nor there. My point is this—if all you do down there in Panama is snoop around to see what the natives are up to, there'll never be any Panama canal."

"In which case there'll be a Nicaragua canal," I observed mildly.

The Frenchman bristled visibly at this. "Never!" he vowed, although it came out sounding, "Nay-vere."

"Phil's right," agreed Gates, his anglicization of the Frog's name causing Bunau-Varilla to sputter anew. "That dictator in Nicaragua, er . . . what's his damn name again?"

"General José Santos Zelaya," said Cromwell pedantically, his disdain for Gates for not thoroughly mastering the facts of the case dripping from each syllable.

Gates ignored Cromwell's venom. "Yeah, Zelaya. He wants millions just to sit down for a powwow, and everyone knows he won't allow the United States to have jurisdiction over a canal zone anyway. Damned highway robbery, I say."

"That's exactly what Roosevelt said," I interjected, "only he was speaking of the Colombians."

"That's because there are crooks on both sides of this deal," growled Gates. "The point is that this Zelaya character will string us along forever, raising the price at every turn. There'll never be a Nicaragua canal, and that means it's Panama or nothing."

"*Absolument,*" seconded Bunau-Varilla firmly.

None of this was news to me; Roosevelt and Root had told me essentially the same thing. "Well, you still haven't answered my question," I said. "What exactly do you want from me?"

"Action," snapped Cromwell.

I drained my bourbon in one gulp, placed the glass on the polished table, and said languidly, "Come now, Mr. Cromwell. That's a rather imprecise answer for a lawyer, isn't it? What specific kind of action have you got in mind?"

Here Davis took up the torch. "We want you to talk to the leading citizens in Panama, Fenny. Tell them who sent you and assure them that if they rebel against Colombia, they'll have a friend in Uncle Sam."

"But to what end, Dickie?"

"Damnit man, do we have to draw a picture for you?" fumed Gates. "If the Panamanians kick up a ruckus, we'll send down the navy and the marines and run the Colombians off like the lousy horse thieves they are.

It's as simple as that. Tell them that the United States is just itching to help 'em if they'll only give us the chance."

I took another puff on the perfecto and let out a great circle of smoke. "Well, I don't see how I can do that, gentlemen," I observed mildly.

Oh, this was essentially the mission I'd received from Roosevelt, albeit tacitly, but I didn't care to share that intelligence with this gathering of buzzards. Besides, with Gates in attendance, I sensed that there was money to be made here if I played my cards close to my chest. After all, wasn't Bet-a-Million one of the wealthiest men in the country?

"Why the hell not, Travers?" demanded Gates. "Damn it all, it's only the plain truth."

It was time to shake these fellows up, I decided, so I turned to Gates with just the hint of a sneer. "Says who, Mr. Gates? You may be a big wheel up in Saratoga, sir, but when I last checked, you didn't yet run the marines or the navy. What's more, just a short while ago I had a chat with the man who does. He didn't say anything about using the military against Colombia. No, not a peep on that topic, I'm afraid. What you're proposing is that I stir up a hornet's nest, and on no more authority than your say-so."

Now Cromwell eyed Davis with concern. "I thought you said Travers was with us," he muttered.

Davis, though, remained calm. "I said no such thing, Mr. Cromwell. What I said was that Captain Travers was a fellow with whom we could do business."

Davis had read me right. I didn't care to let on so fast, though, so I asked with a disarming smile, "Business, Dickie? Whatever do you mean?"

Davis rang for another bourbon and leaned forward to fix me with his most earnest gaze. "Fenny, you might have questions about our motives in all this—" he began.

"Not at all," I interrupted. "I understand them perfectly. Gates and Cromwell here are in it for money. Gates will profit, you see, because the canal will make it easier to ship steel from coast to coast. Cromwell, on the other hand, will collect fees in perpetuity and is probably billing each one of you for this meeting. You, Dickie, well, you're in it for the greater glory of Richard Harding Davis. The Frog probably can't decide between restoring the good name of France or recovering whatever's left of his battered stock holdings, or both."

Gates flashed red and seemed about to leap roaring to his feet. Instead, he threw back his head and declared with pure glee, "Hot damn! He really hit the nail on the head that time. Whooeee!"

No one else seemed amused, though—especially Bunau-Varilla, who threw me a look of indignation with his dark eyes. Davis, maneuvering between the Frenchman's silent outrage and Gates's guffaws, went on. "Let's suppose for the sake of argument that you've assessed our purposes correctly, Fenny. Even if you're right, a Panama canal will be nonetheless good for this country, for the world, and for everyone in this room." Then he leaned forward and said slowly, "It can even be good for you."

The waiter appeared and placed another bourbon before me. I took a sip before asking, "What's your offer, Dickie?"

Here Davis looked over to Gates. The disheveled plunger leaned forward toward me. Gates was the master salesman, and the time had come to close the deal. "Fenny—you don't mind me calling you that, do you?" he asked with an avuncular smile that failed to mask the glow of avarice in his eyes.

"That's my name—John."

"Well, Fenny, you undoubtedly know about the Panama Railroad, right?" I nodded.

"Good. You see, if there is a deal between the United States and the Panamanians, it's no secret that the railroad will be a necessary part of the bargain. That line will carry the men and materials that will make the canal a reality. That's the reason why shares in the railroad will shoot sky-high if the Panama route becomes a reality."

"That only stands to reason," I said noncommittally. "But what's that got to do with me?"

"Nothing," replied Gates before adding, almost as an afterthought, "unless you own some of those shares."

"Why, Mr. Gates, are you trying to bribe me?" I wasn't offended, you see, for I had been bought before. I simply wanted to clarify the proposition being laid before me.

Monsieur Bunau-Varilla was offended, however. "*Capitaine,* you impugn my sacred honor!" he exploded before Gates silenced him with an upraised hand.

"Phil, let's just sit back and let the attorney explain the situation to our young friend," suggested Gates.

Cromwell obliged. "Captain Travers, your characterization of our bona fide business offer as a bribe is rather artless," he commenced crisply. "An official can be bribed only if there is an arrangement whereby that official is caused to forsake his official duties in exchange for some pecuniary gain. Such is not the case in this instance. Your duties require you to facilitate civic unrest in Panama. We also desire that you facilitate civic unrest in Panama, and we wish to reward you for doing so. Our offer to you therefore does not fit the classic definition of a bribe and is hence perfectly legal. You should view it as, er, an incentive to the performance of your official duties."

Cromwell's bromides notwithstanding, I knew that Gates's proposal would be certain to raise eyebrows if it ever saw the light of day. For that kind of risk, the reward would have to be damned alluring. I did some quick figuring. The shares were probably priced at a reasonable value for a quiet rail line in a forgotten corner of the world. How would Wall Street value those shares if the Panama Railroad was to be the terminus for uncounted millions of Yankee dollars? The value would double—no, probably quadruple—within a week of a Panamanian secession from Colombia. As I made my calculations, I felt the palms of my hands begin to sweat.

"What size of incentive are we talking about here?" I asked a bit shakily.

Gates smiled hugely, for he sensed that the pigeon was almost in the snare. "Panama Railroad shares trade at about twenty dollars apiece. We'd like to make four thousand shares available to you."

Four thousand times twenty—why, that was $80,000! If that quadrupled, I'd be set for years to come, maybe for life! There was only one major flaw in Gates's proposition as far as I could see, and I let him know about it straightaway.

"Making four thousand shares available doesn't do me much good, Mr. Gates. It's not as though I just happen to have eighty thousand dollars lying around. If I did, I rather doubt that I'd still be in the army. So, you see, your offer is meaningless unless I have the wherewithal to purchase these stocks."

Gates nodded and reached deep into his coat pocket. He extracted a stack of brand new, banded bills and tossed them across the table to me. My eyes bulged as I realized I was staring at a wad of thousand-dollar greenbacks. "There's forty thousand there. Count it if you want."

I felt the breath go out of my body, and it was only with an effort I managed to wheeze, "That's half of it. Where's the rest?"

Gates looked at Cromwell and Bunau-Varilla. "The rest comes from the coffers of the New Panama Canal Company. Pony up, boys."

Cromwell's eyes hooded over at this, like those of a skinflint in a restaurant when the check arrives. Thus when Bunau-Varilla cleared his throat to speak, I could sense Cromwell relax ever so slightly, for he assumed that the Frenchman was about to ante up the $40,000 on behalf of his company.

"We accept your challenge, Monsieur Gates," announced Bunau-Varilla grandly. "The money will be delivered through my agents tomorrow to arrange the purchase of stock on behalf of Captain Travers. That amount, of course," he added with an aside to Cromwell, who, up to that point had allowed a satisfied grin to spread across his sly face, "will be deducted from any fee to be paid to the firm of Sullivan and Cromwell by the New Panama Canal Company."

"What? How dare you?" exploded Cromwell. "Your firm has signed an engagement, sir—a binding contract! My fee is directly related to the selling price your company receives from the sale of its assets to the United States government. There is nothing in our contract about any deductions of the sort you are contemplating. Nothing at all!"

Bunau-Varilla remained serene in the face of this outburst. He merely twirled his mustache as he eyed Cromwell with cool disdain. When Cromwell had subsided and resumed his seat, muttering direly about "breach" and "punitive damages, by God, punitive damages," Bunau-Varilla continued.

"What the lawyer Cromwell forgets is that he was engaged to consummate the sale of the New Panama Canal Company's assets. If that requires fomenting a revolution in Panama, well, *c'est la guerre,* no? What Mr. Gates has proposed, however, is that a major portion of the duties that my company understood were to be handled by lawyer Cromwell will now be handled by the brave *capitaine.* I see no reason to pay twice for the same services."

"He's got you there, Cromwell," cackled Gates, popping another green egg yolk into his mouth and swallowing it whole. "I say you either get on your horse and go south and get this show on the road yourself, or you agree to fork over part of your fee like Phil here says."

Cromwell didn't like this scheme one damned bit, and he said so for the next twenty minutes, but everyone's mind was made up on the issue, and in the end Cromwell reluctantly and ungraciously conceded the point.

"Good," said Davis when that order of business was finished. "If you want, Fenny, I can hold the certificates until you get back."

Right, I thought. Allow a free-spending reporter to roam loose in New York with negotiable stock certificates while I'm a thousand miles away. "That's awfully kind of you, Dickie," I responded with a smile. "However, I see no reason why you can't get the certificates to me at the St. James before noon tomorrow. The *Yucatán* doesn't leave until three in the afternoon, and that's more than enough time for me to drop them off at my bank." I had kept a modest account and a safety-deposit box at the Nassau Bank down on Nassau Street ever since my China days, you see.

"Well, that will be tight timing, Captain," said Cromwell dubiously.

"I'm sure it will. Of course, if I sail before I see the certificates, I will assume that you gentlemen have reconsidered this matter and no longer have any need of my services."

"Get it done, Cromwell," ordered Gates flatly.

"One last thing. If I need to communicate with any of you, how shall I do so?"

Gates answered. "Contact Cromwell at his offices. If that's not possible, wire me at my offices on Wall Street." He slid a business card across the table. "Identify yourself as the 'surveyor.'"

I slipped his card into my pocket. "If there's nothing else, gentlemen," I said, rising, "I must be off."

I took my leave with handshakes all around—Cromwell's being decidedly less than enthusiastic now that I was an expense to him—and made my way back to my suite at the St. James. I was elated; if the stock did nothing other than simply hold its value, I would realize a profit exceeding forty years' pay. And if it went up—and it certainly would if Uncle Sam bought out the New Panama Canal Company—well, the sky would be the limit. Oh, you might think me a mite greedy. After all, I was sure to be comfortable with the dowry Alice would bring to our postponed yet inevitable marriage. My view of matters, however, was that this little arrangement would give me a tidy nest egg of my own. How was a man to be expected to raise Cain unless he had his own bankroll, eh? And besides, wasn't independence what this great country was all about?

The best part, moreover, was that I already had a hefty profit in the bag. Oh, I could increase my windfall if things turned out the way my newfound sponsors desired, but if I failed, well, I walked away with a tidy bankroll nonetheless. I'd undoubtedly poke around Panama to see what kind of unrest I might stir up in order to maximize my profits, but the simple truth was that I could loll about in a hotel room in Panama City and I'd be $80,000 ahead upon my return to the States.

If that wasn't wonderful, I didn't know what was.

8

The certificates arrived the next day about noon. A posse of clerks from Brooks Brothers had arrived only minutes earlier and were crowding into the small suite. Among other things, they delivered my Cataract rifle sight in a beautifully embossed leather case, complete with a shoulder strap. They also delivered a pair of the duck boots, the ones I had seen in the window of Barlow's. Longbottom had fallen in love with the ridiculous things and decided he had to have them. Neither Agent Patterson nor McAllister, who had joined us in our room, had ever seen anything like them, and they crowded close as Longbottom modeled the outlandish things for them.

Distracted, the lot of them took scant notice of the entrance of a bell-hop bearing a sealed manila envelope. I accepted it and the fellow withdrew, a bit irritated, though, since I failed to tip him.

"Good news?" asked Longbottom as I opened the envelope and inspected its contents as best I could without withdrawing the papers. The certificates were in order from all appearances. There were four of them, each in a denomination of one thousand shares. That made four thousand, just as Gates had promised.

"Oh, tolerable," I replied, tucking the certificates into a valise.

Inside the hour our belongings were loaded into a dray that Agent Patterson had secured for the occasion. When everything was in order, Longbottom, our shepherds, and I all climbed into a waiting hansom and headed for the docks with the dray tagging along behind.

When I pleaded for a detour past the Nassau Bank, neither Patterson nor McAllister saw anything amiss with the request. Although Longbottom and I had each been provided with plenty of cash, and promised access to more should the need arise, there were always loose ends to be secured before a tour of duty overseas. Accordingly, our little caravan swung by my bank. I entered alone, called for my safety-deposit box, and stored away my valuable property. In minutes I was back in the hansom with no one the wiser.

That done, it was straight to the *Yucatán,* which was raising steam as we arrived. Our things were hustled aboard as Longbottom and I went up the gangplank, where the captain stood impatient to be off. We were his only passengers, you see, and he desired to take advantage of the favorable tide. We waved a cheerful good-bye to our escorts—for I, at least, was genuinely glad to be rid of them—and then the gangplank was raised, the ship's whistle gave out great hoots, and we warped out into the middle of New York Harbor. The *Yucatán* swung her bow southward toward Staten Island, then with a mighty shudder steamed out into the broad Atlantic.

With calm seas and idyllic July weather, our run down the East Coast was peaceful. Reaching the Florida Keys, we slipped into the Straits of Florida and from there traversed the Great Bahama Bank. Off the eastern tip of Cuba, we negotiated the Windward Passage between Cuba and Haiti and steamed on to the Caribbean Sea. I hadn't been in these waters since '98 when I'd sailed with Pecos Bill Shafter for the frolic in Cuba. The sights as the *Yucatán* rounded Cape Maisí off Cuba filled me with nostalgia and set me to wondering what the fiery Marguerite was up to these days. At the thought of my Cuban paramour, my ardor rose. She had been so passionate, so uninhibited, and so damned available. Had she not possessed a jealous streak as wide as Diamond Jim Brady's ample backside, which she had manifested by attempting to blast me with her derringer, I might have been tempted to settle down in Old Havana to lead a life of dissolute bliss. From thinking of Marguerite I started to cogitate about Fiona, the lovely siren who had most improbably become Mrs. Longbottom. I had trysted with sweet Fiona in Cuba and Luzon before she tied the knot, and had gamely made a few runs at her since. The thought of her delectable charms led me to indiscreetly ask Longbottom how the missus was these days. This drew a savage rebuke, which terminated the conversation and caused me to make a mental note to look up Fiona sometime to see whether there might not be trouble in paradise.

From Cuba, the *Yucatán* negotiated the Jamaica Channel, then set a southwesterly course across the gentle swells of the Caribbean straight for the Mosquito Coast, as the Caribbean shore from Honduras to Panama was known. My first glimpse of Panama came shortly after dawn, some ten days out of New York. I was on deck when the air, sea fresh up to this point in the journey, became gradually rank with the stench of rotting vegetation. In the current slipping past the bow an occasional log floated by, signaling that land was near. A heavy red sun had just struggled into the sky in the east, promising a day of blazing heat, when a voice rang out from the bridge above me, "Land ho!"

Then I saw it, a low line of green on the horizon slowly materializing through a bank of fog. As we steamed shoreward, coastal fishing boats appeared here and there as the haze dissipated in the growing light. Nearing the coast, I was able to make out an unbroken expanse of impenetrable mangrove swamps beyond which were the distant blue heights of the interior cordillera.

The *Yucatán* swung a little to starboard as the captain got his bearings, then we slowed to a steady three knots for the approach to the harbor of Colón. We arrived at an open roadstead and dropped anchor a quarter of a mile offshore.

"Yonder's Colón," said a deckhand near me as he worked the anchor chains, then added ominously, "the land of yellow fever."

I studied the town through my field glasses. From the charts I'd seen, I knew that the Isthmus of Panama was a narrow neck of land, no more than forty miles across at its widest point, that ran from Costa Rica in the west to mainland Colombia in the east. Colón, on the north shore of the isthmus, was situated on a big, flat promontory, called Punta Manzanillo, which jutted out into Limón Bay and was connected by the slenderest of natural land bridges to the rest of Panama. It was across this bridge that the Panama Railroad ran from the docks of Colón across the isthmus to Panama City on the south shore.

As I inspected Colón, I saw nothing but a collection of ramshackle huts slapped together with unpainted boards. Few people were stirring at this hour, giving the place the appearance of a tropical ghost town. The only substantial buildings that Colón did boast were clustered hard by the shore, where I could see five wharves protruding into the turgid waters of the roadstead. From north to south they were Piers 1 and 2, belonging to the Panama Railroad Company; then an unnumbered pier used by the Royal Mail Steamship Company; next Pier 4, which was a general purpose wharf; and finally the pier for the Pacific Mail Steamship Company. At the head of Pier 2 loomed a large stone freight house, and directly across the street from the freight house was the train station.

Because we were too excited to wait as the harbor pilot laboriously maneuvered the *Yucatán* to its berth, the captain ordered the ship's boat lowered, and Longbottom and I were rowed ashore, our things to follow. "No firearms, Travers," insisted Longbottom firmly as we went over the side. "We don't want to attract attention to ourselves."

"I couldn't agree more, Joshua," I assured him, secure in the knowledge that my .45-caliber Colt single action army revolver was tucked discreetly into my belt beneath my khaki tunic, and there it would stay, by God. I had no intention of going onto this forbidding shore without it. I also brought along my telescopic sight, dangling from my shoulder by the strap of its case. In a pinch, I figured, I could use it as a spyglass.

Our boat steered for Pier 2. Waiting there was a tall, elderly gentleman in a white flannel suit and a straw Panama hat. As we disembarked he called heartily, "Welcome to Colón, gentlemen. I trust you had a pleasant journey."

"Pleasant indeed," Longbottom assured him. "Might you be Superintendent Shaler?"

"At your service," said Shaler. "And you're . . . ?"

"Captain Longbottom." Motioning toward me, he added, "And this is Captain Travers."

We shook hands all around, then Shaler told us how pleased he was to see us and that there was much work to be done about "the problem," which was apparently his term for the fragile political balance on the isthmus. The first order of business, though, insisted Shaler, was to get us installed in the Washington House, the best hostelry in these parts, according to him. Shaler escorted us to a waiting coach with the legend "Panama Railroad" emblazoned on its side.

As we walked he proposed genially, "Boys, how about a quick breakfast? After that, I'll arrange rail passage for you over to Panama City. There are some people there who are anxious to make your acquaintance."

"That would be ideal," agreed Longbottom.

The coach took us through muddy streets to the Washington House, which turned out to be a simple yet clean establishment. An excellent breakfast of thick steaks and scrambled eggs was laid before us, and we set to. Shaler, pleading a delicate constitution from years in the tropics, ordered a glass of fruit juice for himself. When it came, I was amazed to see ice cubes floating in it.

Catching my glance, Shaler smiled. "We live a spartan existence in these parts, Captain Travers, but we're not completely without amenities. Colón boasts a perfectly serviceable ice plant, you see." Then, as we chomped away contentedly, Shaler proceeded to give us the lay of the land. "Let me tell you a little bit about the history of this place," he began. "It'll help you to understand just what a powder keg you'll be playing with. Panama has little past and damned little future." Here he paused and gave a chuckle. "The place isn't even really named Panama. What we call Panama is in reality the State of Colón in the sovereign nation of Colombia. Years ago, moreover, when the conquistadors landed here, they knew this land by yet a third name, Golden Castille. That was because they thought there were gold mines in the vicinity."

I stopped in midchew. "Well, were there?"

"Yes, in a way, Captain Travers. You see, it was the custom of the headmen of the Cuna—"

"The who?" interrupted Longbottom.

"The Cunas. They're the main Indian tribe along the Caribbean coast, although the Indians refer to themselves as the Tule. Savage fellows they are, and you'd be well advised to steer clear of them. You might see some Cunas, or more accurately, some of their arrows, if you wander too far into the cordillera or east of here along the offshore islands, the San Blas Islands, as they're known. In answer to your question, Captain Travers, it seems that the Cuna have always loved gold, and in years gone by they traded far and wide to get it for their chiefs. When a chief died, you see, he was sent off to the happy hunting ground covered from head to foot in gold plate. Unfortunately for the Cunas, the conquistadors found out about this burial practice. All those gold-plated cadavers just a'moldering in the ground sent the dons into a frenzy. In no time they were pulling up long-dead Cuna chiefs like potatoes at harvest time. Yep, plucked them right out of the ground and stripped them of their finery. The bullion was shipped back to Madrid in such quantities that Panama became known to the Spanish as Golden Castille. It was a mighty profitable business for a while."

"For a while?" asked Longbottom.

"The lode played out, Captain," explained Shaler. "The Cunas, as I said, traded for their gold, both up into Mexico and down into South America. When the last grave had been robbed, well, that was it. The festivities were over."

So was my interest in this story; I went back to eating. Longbottom, though, was intrigued. "What happened when the gold ran out?"

"Well, Panama had other attractions to the dons, the foremost being that it was the narrowest point between the Pacific and the Caribbean. It was a natural place to cross the continent, so the Spanish garrisoned Portobelo on the Caribbean and Panama City on the Pacific side. The treasure convoys from Manila and Acapulco landed each year in Panama City, where the goods were loaded onto mule trains and hauled across the central cordillera to Portobelo. In fact, the paving stones of the old Spanish gold trail are still visible up in the hills, or so the campesinos say. Once the treasure reached Portobelo, it was loaded into galleons and shipped off to Havana and Santo Domingo and eventually found its way back to Spain. Panama became the very center of the Spanish Main and enjoyed its time in the sun for many years."

Everything Shaler was saying rang true, for years ago on faraway Luzon, Señor Segovia, the Spanish turncoat, had told me all about the fabled galleon trade.

"The Spanish Main eventually declined," observed Longbottom. "What happened to Panama then?"

"Why, Panama declined too," came the answer. "This place lapsed into the dark ages and stayed there. It's a backwater even today. Other than the Colombian employees of the Panama Railroad, the few big cattle herders on the Pacific coast, and the campesinos clustered in squalid barrios along the railroad line, there's nobody on the isthmus—nobody, that is, except savage Indians and the soldiers sent here to put them down."

"Well, if the place is such a wasteland, why's your railroad spanning it from coast to coast?" I wondered aloud.

"That's a good question, Captain Travers. The truth of the matter is, however, that the existence of the railroad has little to do with any events in Panama."

"Eh? How's that?"

Shaler sipped his juice and then explained, "It was the California gold rush of 1849 that gave rise to the Panama Railroad. The forty-niners tried to cross the isthmus on foot, and lots of 'em didn't make it. Some investors back in the East, though, saw that California was the future of the United States and that a rail line across the isthmus was necessary to keep the trade links open between the east and west coasts. In short order, the railroad was laid out and open for business, and it's been running in the black ever since."

"Were you here when Ferdinand de Lesseps attempted his canal?" probed Longbottom.

Shaler nodded gravely. "Indeed I was. Back then I was the deputy superintendent, and I saw the whole tragedy unfold. The French came in with fire in their eyes, convinced that de Lesseps would build this canal just like he had his earlier one in Suez. Yes, their beginning was magnificent, but their end was godawful."

"What's your view of what happened to them, Superintendent?" asked Longbottom.

Shaler sighed. "It's hard to put a finger on any single thing. Let's just say that a lot of little things went wrong at the same time. And a few big things. One of the biggest was that the capital raised didn't all go for machinery and labor."

"That's what we were told," said Longbottom. "There was corruption at every level. We've also heard all about the yellow fever and malaria."

"Well, they're still here," said Shaler grimly. "The French died in droves, as did the Blacks they imported from the Antilles. Nobody really knows how many perished, but my best guess is that it was more than twenty thousand."

I let out a whistle. "Twenty thousand? My God, that number dwarfs our losses in the war against Spain!"

"It was a first-class disaster," affirmed Shaler. "The bodies are buried outside of Colón on a rise called Monkey Hill. At least the French are. The Blacks were thrown into ravines and streams wherever they fell. In the end, the whole effort just collapsed in on itself as each man tried to save himself from a pestilence nobody understood."

"What's to keep it from happening to us?" asked Longbottom uneasily.

Shaler had a ready answer. "Our experience in Cuba," he replied confidently. "Doctor Walter Reed—an army doctor, by the way—thinks he's got the problem licked."

I'd heard of Reed and his yellow fever experiments. The details, however, were a bit fuzzy to me, so I asked, "How?"

"By fighting the cause of the problem rather than the symptoms. The French had hospitals in Panama, you know. Damned fine ones, too. The trouble was that the French never made the connection between the fever and the skeeters. Instead they tried to treat the fever symptoms, and, of course, they were unsuccessful. Doctor Reed has a different approach. He wipes out the skeeters and thereby prevents the disease in the first place."

"How can you wipe out mosquitoes in a place like Panama?" I asked dubiously. "I mean, the jungle starts at the edge of town and just keeps going."

"Nobody said it'll be easy," conceded Shaler, "but it's my understanding that what will be done is to coat all the freestanding water near any human habitation with petroleum. That's where the skeeters lay their eggs, you see. If they can't breed, then their natural cycle can be broken. I know it's all yet to be proved, but for my money it sounds damned promising."

I finished my meal and called for more coffee. The brew in these parts was delicious—a thick black java laden with generous dollops of sugar. "Well, Superintendent," I said, shifting the subject away from pestilence, "since you're an old hand hereabouts, do you have words of wisdom for two young, er, surveyors?"

Shaler smiled at the allusion to our ostensible mission; clearly, he knew our true purpose. "Well, the most important thing is not to call attention to yourselves. Oh, by the way, Captain Travers, I'd get rid of that campaign hat if I were you. It sticks out like a sore thumb. Get yourself a Panama hat like mine." As I flushed at my stupidity, Shaler sailed right along. "Bogotá, you see, views Panama as almost an occupied territory, and that's why the provincial government views the presence of strangers with suspicion. The war here never really ended, you know."

"War?" I asked with alarm. "What war?"

"It was called the War of a Thousand Days, and it raged from about 1899 to mid-1902, although for my money it has yet to end. The war pitted the liberals—folks who wanted a measure of local autonomy—against the conservatives—adherents of the reactionary junta in Bogotá. The conservatives viewed any loosening of the central government's reins as tantamount to a loss of sovereignty over the isthmus."

Politics of any stripe bored me, so I posed the only question important to a military man. "Who won?"

"Arguably, nobody. In purely military terms, though, the conservatives ultimately prevailed on the battlefield. Comandante Reyes, the military commander of Colón, was a major contributor to that victory, making a name for himself by eradicating the insurgents with fire and sword. The death toll was staggering, and the effect on the local economy—well, let's just say that the place was backward to begin with, but now except for the areas immediately adjacent to Colón and Panama City, it's completely moribund."

I eyed Longbottom with concern. Nobody at Sagamore Hill had mentioned that Panama was essentially a war zone.

"Well, sir," said Longbottom, clearing his throat, "that's all very interesting. Our main concern, of course, is how all of this recent unpleasantness might relate to our mission. Specifically, are there any Panamanians still living who are willing to stand up for freedom from Colombia?"

Shaler carefully looked about to ensure that we were out of earshot of the waiters and our fellow diners. In a hushed tone he said, "That there are, Captain Longbottom. But I warn you, they're extremely shy. Some of them are clandestine liberals who remain under cover to save their necks from a hangman's noose. Others are nominal conservatives, well-educated gentlemen who chafe under Bogotá's despotic rule. They dare not challenge

Bogotá directly, but if an independence movement should gather steam and look as though it might prevail, well, I would expect the better circles to rally to the cause."

"Great," snorted Longbottom. "We come looking for men of principle and find sunshine patriots."

Shaler smiled with the understanding gleaned from more than six and a half decades on this earth. "Son, I can appreciate how you might disapprove of people who are a bit reluctant to show their true colors. The fact is, however, being completely forthright in this land is just a tad suicidal. Let me just comfort you with the knowledge that one of these sunshine patriots, as you call them, just happens to be Bogotá's provincial governor, Señor José de Obaldia. He has separatist sympathies, but he's very fearful of being discovered. If he's handled right and"—here Shaler pronounced each word slowly for emphasis—"made to feel secure, if you follow me, he will be a valuable partner."

Longbottom digested this in concerned silence, but I took the broader view. If the fervor of the locals had been drained by the recent war, perhaps a little jawboning from two American officers might change that. I could be wrong, of course, but I had eighty thousand reasons for wanting to give the thing a go.

"When do we get to meet these secret allies?" I asked. "That's what we came here for, and the sooner the better, I say."

Shaler was pleased by my directness. "That's what I miss—good old Yankee spunk. You don't find that attitude too often here, but you've got it in spades, Travers." He finished his juice and then leaned forward and whispered, "Today, in Panama City, all the people you need to see will be gathered to listen to what you have to say."

"That's splendid, Superintendent. We can get our message across in one fell swoop and then be on our way back to the States. What could be simpler, eh?"

"Let's hope so, Captain," Shaler said and seemed about to add more. It was then, however, that the shots rang out.

9

"What the hell was that?" I yipped, leaping to my feet.

Shaler was up too. "Damned if I know, Travers. Let's have a look-see."

The three of us hurried out into the street. The angry sound of a mob came to us from around the corner where Front Street met Bolívar Street. As we hurried in that direction, the sight that met our eyes stopped us in our tracks. A furious crowd of Blacks had gathered in the narrow thoroughfare. Facing them was a squad of tense Colombian soldiers commanded by a burly sergeant. The sergeant was trying to lead a black prisoner through the jostling multitude. A puff of smoke wafted away in the heavy air above the sergeant's head; what we had heard was the warning shot he had just fired with his pistol in a vain effort to cow the threatening mob.

The prisoner was bound but far from subdued. He was a muscular fellow, not especially tall but with a thick, powerful torso and huge neck that dwarfed the Colombian soldiers ringing him. "Help, lads!" cried the prisoner in English. "For the love of God, rush the bastards!"

His plea struck my ears as, "Hep, lads! For de lub o' Gawd, rush de bastards!"

I tried to place the accent. It was almost British, perhaps from British Guiana or maybe the British Antilles. His cry galvanized the Blacks pressing in on the soldiers on all sides, and it was only the Colombians' leveled bayonets that kept the would-be rescuers at bay.

"By jiminy, it's Kingston Jack!" exclaimed Shaler.

"Who's he?" demanded Longbottom, at my side.

"Only the most notorious bandit in these parts. He's one of the Antillean Blacks brought here by the French to work on the canal. When the French left, the Blacks were cast off to fend for themselves. Most are destitute, trapped in a Latin world that shuns them. Some went to work for the railroad, but others—like Kingston Jack—took to the hills to become bandits. Make no mistake, he's a folk hero to these poor beggars." Here he nodded at the dirty, ragged Negroes around us. "He gives 'em handouts from time to time but mostly hope and a little pride."

"He looks damned short on pride at the moment," I observed.

"Old Jack's in a fix, all right," conceded Shaler. "He must have gotten a little too bold for his own good and wandered into town in broad daylight. Either these Colombians spotted him, or one of their spies fingered him. Whatever the story, his goose is cooked now."

And Kingston Jack knew it; he bellowed for succor at the top of his lungs and struggled so hard against his bonds that suddenly one of the Colombians slammed the stock of a rifle hard against his head.

"My God, they be killing me," he moaned as he sank to his knees.

An angry growl came forth from the mob at this assault, and several of the more daring bucks pressed forward. This caused the burly sergeant to level his revolver and cock back the hammer. The Blacks sullenly backed off but not far, and there they stayed. It was a Mexican standoff; the Antilleans stood defiantly screaming at the soldiers for the release of their countryman, and against their fury the small squad could make no progress. This impasse lasted no more than a minute, however, before the tramping sound of many boots striking the damp earth filled the street.

Reinforcements. A platoon of Colombians hurried onto the scene and pushed their way through the mob to the beleaguered squad. At the head of the relief column, splendid in a sparkling white uniform and red kepi adorned with gold braid, strode a glowering officer with a drawn saber. From the French-patterned uniform and the gilt-edged brim of the rakish kepi, I could see that this hombre was a field grade officer. Dark eyes shone forth from his swarthy face, eyes that promised murder at any moment.

"That's the infamous Comandante Reyes," muttered Shaler as the crowd, uncertain in the face of this sudden show of force, drew back. "He's sworn to have Kingston Jack's hide, so things should get hot now."

Comandante Reyes formed the reinforcements into a square around the prisoner and then barked out a flurry of sharp orders in Spanish. "Sergeant Gómez," he said to the noncommissioned officer, "fetch a rope. Shoot any man who tries to interfere with you."

Sergeant Gómez pushed through the crowd to a dry goods store and returned with a coiled length of rope. Reyes uncoiled it, tossed one end over a streetlamp, and tied off the other end around a hitching post. The sergeant then stood up on a small barrel and hurriedly fashioned a crude but perfectly serviceable noose.

"They aim to string him up, right here and now," observed Shaler, quite unnecessarily.

"What? Without a trial?" protested Longbottom.

"None is needed," replied Shaler. "Comandante Reyes is the law in Colón. He has the authority to execute bandits on the spot, and whatever due process a Colombian might be afforded—and that is damned little, I can tell you— wouldn't apply to Kingston Jack. He's an Antillean, a noncitizen. He has no rights."

Appalled, Longbottom insisted, "But surely there must be some appeal of a capital sentence."

Shaler shook his head grimly, for there was no recourse from the hard law of Comandante Reyes. Now, however, the crowd, which had fallen back at Reyes's initial show of force, buzzed anew as the *comandante*'s purpose became clear. Here a muttered "No!" was heard, and there a "Don't let 'em do it, lads!"

"Disperse!" commanded Reyes as Sergeant Gómez, who had finished forming the noose, dragged the prisoner to the barrel, prodded him up with the business end of a revolver, and slipped the rope around his massive ebony neck. Clearly, Kingston Jack had only seconds left on this earth.

"No, no!" he protested. "For the sake of God, no!"

The prisoner's remonstrances only brought a cruel smile to Comandante Reyes's lips. "Sergeant Gómez, do your duty," he ordered harshly.

It was then I heard a voice rise clear and steady above the angry murmur of the crowd: "There ain't gonna be no lynching."

That was an American accent—a Black one. Moreover, it was one I recognized instantly. I searched the crowd; yes, right under the bayonets of the Colombians, I saw him. It was Henry Jefferson!

"There ain't gonna be no damned lynching," Henry repeated.

Comandante Reyes, who may not have understood Henry's words but certainly understood his tone, ordered stonily, "Strangle the beast, Sergeant."

Gómez nodded and was about to kick the barrel out from beneath Kingston Jack's trembling legs when Henry let fly with a rock the size of a baseball. It sailed through the air and caught Sergeant Gómez flush in the face. Gómez clasped his head convulsively and then fell unconscious to the ground, a stream of crimson flowing from the gash that ran from the bridge of his nose to his hairline.

"Free Jack!" roared someone else in the crowd, and with that battle cry the Blacks surged forward. A Mauser roared, and then another. Here an Antillean was skewered on a bayonet, shrieking his life away, while a few feet away a comrade cried out in agony as a high-velocity bullet ripped through muscle and bone. In an instant five Blacks were down, but they had the superior numbers and, more importantly, were spurred on by Henry's defiance. Their blood was up. A Mauser was snatched from a startled Colombian, and then another, and in an instant the gunplay became general, with the Antilleans giving as good as they got.

"Get down!" cried Shaler as hot lead whizzed everywhere. He turned to find me already crouching. Longbottom, stupefied by the deadly fight exploding around us, had to be pulled to the ground.

"Get them! Get them!" thundered Henry as he flailed his way into the square of soldiers and hurled himself upon Reyes. Behind him the Antilleans followed. In the close combat that followed, Blacks were at an advantage, for many of them had secreted machetes under their shirts, which they now used to deadly advantage.

"Henry," I called over the din, "get out of there while you still can!"

"Henry?" shrilled Longbottom. "Not Sergeant Jefferson from Fort Niobrara?"

"The same," I admitted reluctantly as a strapping Antillean staggered by, his hands clamped to a ragged red gash on his neck where he'd been bayoneted by a Colombian.

"You mean that fellow who started this donnybrook is the sergeant you personally requested, and in fact vouched for?" demanded Longbottom, incredulous. "Why, I'll . . . I'll, I'll have him court-martialed! Yes, court-martialed and run out of the service."

And probably keelhauled and drawn and quartered if he'd been allowed to go on, but at that instant the mob parted enough for me to spy Henry again. He was locked in combat with Reyes, flat on his back struggling for his life!

"Boys, we've got to make tracks," insisted Shaler. "It won't do to have either of you two identified with this affair."

Longbottom was more than eager to be gone, for several ricochets had landed uncomfortably close to him. "He's right, Travers, we have to go."

Longbottom was preaching to the choir, for as much as I liked and admired Henry, I had no stomach for this lethal brawl. Silently wishing Henry well but thinking I'd never see him alive again, I rose to follow. Suddenly, the desperate Colombians sallied into the crowd with their bayonets leveled. A knot of them headed straight for me, and in a flash I was faced off against a wild-eyed private who advanced behind a flurry of savage jabs, doing his damnedest to bury his bayonet deep in my guts.

Longbottom turned as he ran and called crossly, "Travers, you heard me! I order you to come this instant!"

"God Almighty, can't you see that this madman is trying to kill me? Help me, blast you!"

Rescue was immediately out of the question, however, for now a second Colombian was on Longbottom, thrusting lustily with his bayonet. Terrified, Longbottom swatted at the fellow with his hat, as though his assailant could be shooed away like a pesky fly.

I saw no more of Longbottom's plight, for my attacker suddenly lashed out with a sweeping butt stroke that caught me a stunning blow to the side of my head. I hit the ground, dazed. Planting his foot on my chest, the Colombian lunged downward with the point of his bayonet. His cold steel would have skewered me had not the bayonet first rammed into the hard wood of the maple-handled Colt tucked into my belt.

That did it for me. In a flash my Colt was in my hand and aimed right for the startled soldier's face. I pulled the trigger and the Colt roared, lifting the Colombian a foot off the ground and depositing him in a lifeless heap. Rising shakily, I could see both that he was dead and that my shot had drawn the attention of his fellows. Retreat was now impossible; the only way out of this brawl was to put the Colombians to flight. Once I identified my salvation with offensive action, I sprinted toward Henry.

"Travers, come back here and help me!" shrieked Longbottom, his arms locked around his antagonist so that the latter could not bring his weapon to bear.

He was talking to himself, though, for by then I was plowing forward past struggling men, dodging a bayonet thrust here and a machete swipe there. "Henry!" I called. "Hold on, I'm coming!"

Henry heard me, although his eyes were locked on Comandante Reyes. With a desperate effort he suddenly threw off Reyes and then slammed the Colombian with a roundhouse right. Reyes went down, but Henry didn't finish him off. Instead, he whirled and lurched toward Kingston Jack, who still perched precariously on the barrel as the battle royal raged around him.

"Look out, Henry!" I cried, but Henry was blind to the danger. A soldier, seeing his commander felled, reversed his Mauser and hefted it as a club. With a looping swing, he smashed Henry to the ground. Flat on his back once more, Henry watched helplessly as his attacker raised the rifle stock high for what promised to be a death blow.

"No!" I cried, firing from the hip as I did. The Colombian screamed and jerked convulsively as the heavy .45 slug pierced his chest and ripped a fist-sized chunk from his back on its way out of his body. Then I was over Henry, hauling him to his feet with one hand, keeping the Colt ready with the other. Henry was grunting out his gratitude when I felt a burning, stabbing pain in my left shoulder.

"Damnation!" I groaned in anguish, dropping Henry and my Colt to clutch at my shoulder. Whirling, I saw a saber blade pulling away and instantly realized what had happened. As I had been distracted by Henry, Comandante Reyes had regained his feet. Watching me slay his man and seeing his opportunity for revenge, he had delivered what he hoped would be a fatal saber stroke. He had come damned close; the blade had sliced through the brim of my hat, missing my skull by a fraction of an inch, and then bit into my shoulder. Luckily, the broad leather band of the case for the telescopic sight across my shoulder had absorbed the full impact of Reyes's stroke. Although my blood was flowing copiously, I dully realized that I still had the full use of my injured arm.

Desperately, I twisted out of the way of another blow, only to become entangled in the sprawled body of the soldier I'd slain. Off balance, I fell at the feet of Comandante Reyes. "Henry, help!" I babbled in terror.

Reyes drew back his saber for a third slash as I flopped about like a fish desperate to avoid a gutting knife. "Die, *yanqui*," he sneered, and I was certain I was about to do just that.

His blow never came, however, for suddenly, incredibly, Henry was on his feet, fighting with the fury of a tiger. He threw himself on Reyes once more, insanely raining blows on the startled *Comandante*. A straight right staggered Reyes, buckling his knees, and then a wicked left hook cracked into his ribs. With Henry well inside the effective cutting arc of Reyes's weapon, the saber tip wavered and then lowered as Reyes lifted his free hand to ward off Henry's relentless blows. For a second it looked as though Henry would overpower his foe barehanded when suddenly Comandante Reyes's booted foot shot out and slammed between Henry's legs.

The kick to the crotch rocked Henry, stopping his attack instantly, but Reyes—his face now a bloody mask from the furious pummeling Henry had delivered—was too winded to press his advantage. Henry's surge had given me the respite I needed, though, for I sprang to my feet once more, my recovered Colt in my good hand.

"This fight's over, partner," I vowed, leveling the big muzzle in Comandante Reyes's face. "*Adiós, amigo.*"

Reyes looked down my looming barrel and caught the cold resolution in my voice. For the first time I saw fear in his eyes. Longbottom, locked just feet away in his deadly waltz with his foe, saw this drama unfolding before his astounded eyes. Even as he fought for his own life, he realized the catastrophic consequences that my impending action would have for our mission.

"Don't, Travers!" he protested. "For God's sake, there'll be an international incident!"

Reyes heard Longbottom's call and guessed his concern. "That's right, *yanqui,* have a care," he taunted. "Don't forget whose country you are in." His eyes dared me to fire, knowing that in the end I'd back down.

He was wrong. International incident be damned, I thought—this bastard was on his way to hell! I pulled the trigger and the Colt bucked. Unfortunately, I was weak from the blood I'd lost, and my aim was erratic. At this range Reyes should have been dead, but instead my shot only clipped his ear and spun him in a half circle. Without an instant's pause, he was scampering away through the melee, screeching, "Retreat! Retreat!"

His men followed, including the one belaboring Longbottom, and I fired once more to hurry them along their way. In seconds it was over. Ten bodies lay sprawled in the dust—four soldiers and six Antilleans. Kingston Jack, however, was quite alive, hurling imprecations at the retreating Colombians as his followers with their machetes hacked him down from his makeshift gallows.

"That's it! Run, you dago filth! Run before I get my hands untied and do real damage to you!" When he was freed, however, he showed no inclination to press the fight. Instead he sought out Henry and, seizing his hand, said thankfully, "You saved my life, man. Do me the great favor of telling me your name."

"Henry. Henry Jefferson."

Kingston Jack shook his head, not being able to place the name or the strange accent. "What island are you from, Henry? Aruba maybe?"

Henry blinked at this. "Island? Why, I'm from Elm Grove."

"Elm Grove? Is that in Bermuda?"

"Naw, it's smack-dab in the middle of Illinois. I'm an American."

"Well, I'll be," said Kingston Jack, laughing with delight. "I've seen some Americans, like Mr. Shaler and those other railroad gentlemen. But I've never seen one as black as you, my friend. Have you been brought here to work on the railroad?"

Henry's eyes darted to me and I gave a barely perceptible nod. "Er, yes, that's right. I'm here to work for Mr. Shaler."

Shaler was nonplussed now, never having heard of Henry before this instant, but he wisely held his tongue.

"Well then, Henry, you go right ahead and work," said Kingston Jack. "Ordinarily, I'd take a dim view of a new man coming into Panama when so many of my neighbors need work"—here he indicated his fellow Blacks— "but under the circumstances, you feel free to make yourself right at home. And if you ever need help, you just spread the word on the streets of Colón. I have ears everywhere. I'll hear."

With that he shook Henry's hand once more and padded off down the narrow street. When he was gone, Longbottom rounded on Henry. "That was a damn fool thing to do, Sergeant," he snarled. "Thanks to you, we're within inches of having our mission compromised during our first hour ashore. I can't believe you were so indiscreet."

Maybe Longbottom was right, but then again Henry's instincts had been uncannily accurate so many times in the past that I wasn't inclined to question them now. Besides, I liked Henry, whereas I could barely stomach Longbottom. That was probably the reason why I interrupted bluntly, "Let's get something straight here, Longbottom. First, nobody put you in charge of this little fandango, so stop acting like you are. The days when I was the lowly plebe and you were the lordly upperclassman at West Point are long over." Longbottom had been three years senior to me at West Point, but that disparity in grade had been erased by my unnaturally rapid advancement following the Boxer Rebellion, a fact that galled Longbottom no end. "In case you haven't noticed, my date of promotion to the rank of captain precedes yours."

He had forgotten, for he sputtered in outrage that he was still senior by virtue of his superior length of service as an officer, and that I was being impertinent, by God.

I cut him off brusquely, for this was a lame argument and he knew it. All that mattered was our respective dates of rank, and I had him trumped in that respect. "And second, I go back quite a way with Henry. He was with me on Mindanao, don't forget. In fact, if it wasn't for him, your dear wife might still be a love slave to the sultan of Jolo. *I* asked for Henry to be here, so if he answers to anyone, he answers to me."

"You simply make my point for me, Travers," retorted Longbottom. "You selected this man and he's already evidenced a willingness to do as he pleases whenever the notion seizes him. It's obvious he doesn't have the discipline necessary for a delicate assignment like this. It's equally evident that you are a questionable judge of character. I want him packed off back to the States before he gets into any more trouble."

"He stays," I said flatly. "I need someone I can trust in a tight spot, and that someone is Henry."

Unspoken, of course, was the fact that Longbottom by definition wasn't that person, and he seethed at the implied insult. "All right, Travers, have it your way. But if this dolt foils our efforts, you can rest assured that both he and you will figure prominently in my report back to Secretary Root."

"Gentlemen, please," interrupted Shaler worriedly. "All this wrangling must wait. Comandante Reyes may be back at any time. No doubt he's rousing the rest of the garrison at this very moment."

That silenced us both in a hurry. "What do you suggest we do, Superintendent?" I asked.

"I say you get while the getting is good. Reyes might imprison you all."

Longbottom bridled at this. "Washington wouldn't allow such a thing."

Shaler looked unimpressed. "Washington's far away, Captain Longbottom, and Reyes holds the reins of power in Colón. He commands a company of troops here, and like I said, that makes his word law."

Clutching my bleeding shoulder and feeling damned vulnerable, I said, "I say that we vamoose, and quick."

"I've made a special train ready for a trip to the Pacific coast," said Shaler. "I suggest we board immediately. If there are no landslides or damaged rails on the way, we'll be there by afternoon."

"What about Reyes?" Longbottom objected. "Won't he watch the depots for us?"

"Yes, he'll watch, but if we hurry, we'll be aboard before he can rally his forces. Once you're on board, moreover, he'll be stymied."

"Why's that, sir?" asked Henry.

I knew the answer. "Because free passage on the railroad is guaranteed by treaty with the United States. Any interference by Comandante Reyes would guarantee American retaliation, perhaps even outright intervention."

"Exactly, Captain Travers," confirmed Shaler. "The relationship between Washington and Bogotá is like a dance between two scorpions at the bottom of a pit. Neither wants to be the first to use its stinger, because then all hell would break loose."

There still seemed to be a flaw in our escape plan, though, and I raised it. "Won't the Colombians simply wait for us to disembark in Panama City and hustle us off to the calaboose there?"

Shaler shook his head. "No. Reyes's writ runs only to the edge of Colón.

The king of the roost in Panama City is a little squirt by the name of Colonel Esteban Huertas, commander of the Colombia Battalion."

"So what?" I pressed. "Won't Reyes just send a wire there and ask for our arrest?"

"He might, but he'll be wasting his time," answered Shaler. "You see, Huertas and Reyes are rivals, each jostling for control on the isthmus. They guard their jurisdictions like personal fiefdoms, and they're so jealous that cooperation between them is impossible. No, Huertas won't come for you merely at the request of Reyes. Now, enough talk. Let's get going."

10

Shaler got us to the depot unharmed and slipped us aboard the waiting special. Before we pulled out, he saw to my wound. Using makeshift bandages, really nothing more than strips torn from the curtains of the station waiting room, and a bottle of tincture of iodine he kept in his desk in the station office, Shaler trussed me up quite satisfactorily. Henry inspected Shaler's work and assured me I would be just fine. Shaler even managed to provide me with a replacement shirt fetched from my bags, which had been landed in the meantime.

As we made ready to depart, we drew glares from several Colombian guards. They made threatening gestures at us, but having received no orders from Reyes as yet, they did nothing to halt our progress. They were especially cowed by the fact that Shaler, a man of immense prestige in these parts, was sitting right beside us as we pulled away from the station.

Once out of Colón, the train began its slow ascent to the continental divide—the cordillera. We had gone only about two miles when I asked Shaler to slow the train.

"Why?" challenged Longbottom.

"I want Henry to hop off. He'll slip back into town when things quiet down." I had decided, you see, that Henry would be most useful as a pair of eyes and ears to cover our rear when we were on the other side of the isthmus. "He's to check with the telegraph office from time to time to see if there are any messages from me, but otherwise I want him to lie low until we return."

Shaler did as I asked, and Henry dismounted. Before he went, though, I handed him the telescopic sight and told him to safeguard it for me. With a wave of his hand he was gone, and then the locomotive raised steam and we were under way once more.

For half an hour we climbed steadily through thick jungle, broken only by occasional clearings where sad barrios with names like Gatun, Tiger Hill, and Lion Hill clung precariously to the mountainsides. The track seemed to hug the course of the mighty Chagres River, an enormous torrent that plunged from the central highlands headlong into the Caribbean Sea. As we climbed the heights, the tropical foliage gradually yielded to stands of conifers. These trees signaled our arrival at the high passes, and then we began our descent past Emperador and Culebra, and down even farther to Paraiso, Pedro Miguel, and Miraflores. As we went, we came into open grasslands whose sweeping vistas were more reminiscent of an African savanna than the jungle we'd just left.

"The prevailing winds from the Pacific cause all of this," explained Shaler. "Cool, dry air. It makes this side of the mountains healthier. That's why the ruling elite live in Panama City, not Colón."

The train now picked up speed, and by late afternoon we were chugging into Panama City or, more accurately, the suburb of La Trinchera, which lay a mile beyond the walls of Panama City proper. Shaler had been right about the limits of Reyes's power. The murderous *comandante* had apparently not even tried to raise a hue and cry in advance of our arrival.

A railroad official, was on hand to greet Shaler and to provide the three of us with saddled horses. We mounted and followed a broad avenue called the Carrera del Istmo to Panama Vieja, the walled part of Panama City that was built after the pirate Henry Morgan destroyed the original site back in 1671. We pass through the walls at the Revellin quarter of the city and turned onto the Carrera de la Constitución, which led to the Carrera de Bolívar.

These thoroughfares, although grandiosely named, were little more than filthy alleyways. Panama City struck me as a crumbling relic of a bygone age that made Manila look like a modern metropolis. The plaster was cracked on the facades of the tall, narrow houses lining the cramped streets, and a thin veneer of mold seemed to cover everything. Wrought iron balconies festooned the decrepit house fronts, looming out over the narrow streets below in the Spanish fashion. The shadows cast by the balconies heightened the heavy sense of gloom that blanketed the city. On every corner, small, thin men with dark faces and eyes that revealed nothing watched us warily as we made our way to the Parque Catedral and halted before an uncharacteristically spruce residence off the Calle de Miranda.

The marblework on this abode was free of grit and mold, and the elaborate iron balconies that graced the wide windows above me gleamed with fresh paint. Shaler dismounted and strode up the wide steps. Longbottom and I followed as Shaler pulled at a bell cord. A liveried footman opened the door.

"Senator Arango is expecting you, Señor Shaler," he said.

We were all bowed across the threshold and down a carpeted foyer into a drawing room crowded with gentlemen who were obviously awaiting our arrival. Major Black, whom I had last seen at Sagamore Hill, was among them. Like Longbottom and me, Black wore mufti. He gave a slight nod of recognition as we entered.

A vigorous-looking fellow, sporting a magnificent white Vandyke beard, advanced upon us at once. I took this to be Senator Arango, and I was right. "Superintendent Shaler," Arango hailed, "I have gathered the friends of liberty as you requested. Are these our esteemed visitors from the north?"

"Yes, indeed, Senator. May I present to you Captains Travers and Longbottom." As we shook Arango's proffered hand, Shaler informed us, "Gentlemen, Senator Arango represents Panama in Bogotá, and he's also an attorney of the Panama Railroad. He's a man of great stature on the isthmus, and because of that he's referred to with great respect as El Maestro."

"Señor Shaler," said Senator Arango with a smile, "you greatly honor me." Arango seemed tickled to death by the compliment.

"Pleased to meet you, Senator," I assured him, much heartened by the political standing of this collaborator. Why, if representatives of the government of Panama, in addition to the governor, were in on our little scheme, maybe the coup had some chance of success after all.

"The pleasure is all mine, señors," Arango said genially. "But the most important person for you to meet here tonight is not me. No, it is Doctor Manuel Amador Guerrero." He gestured toward an octogenarian in glasses sporting an unkempt walrus mustache. Even as Arango spoke, the fossil was stumping toward us with a surprisingly spritely step for one his age.

"Honored guests," gushed Dr. Amador as he seized each of our hands in turn, "we are at your service."

The moment was awkward, you see, for I got the sense that Amador was expecting some sort of announcement from us. If so, he was bound to be disappointed, for Longbottom was silent and all I could muster was, "Well, er, that's just dandy, sir."

Amador gave Shaler a quizzical look, and the superintendent broke the strained silence that followed by remarking, "Doctor Amador's a good friend of us Americans. Like Senator Arango, he too is an employee of the Panama Railroad. He's our chief physician."

As more introductions were made, it rapidly became clear that everyone in the room either worked for Shaler's railroad or was a relative of someone who did. Also, I learned that in addition to Black and Shaler there was another Yankee present.

"Gentlemen, this is Herbert Prescott, my deputy superintendent," said Shaler. "He's truly my right-hand man."

Prescott seemed a well-knit, stalwart sort of fellow, the type to make a railroad run no matter how adverse the circumstances.

"Glad to meet you, Mr. Prescott," I said.

"Glad to meet you, Captain," Prescott assured me in return.

When all the introductions had been made, Amador said, "Gentlemen, time is short. Let's get down to business, shall we?" He led us to a large table with chairs lining all sides. Spread upon the tabletop was a map of the isthmus showing both coasts and the railroad.

"Sit, please," he said, and we did as he bid. Dr. Amador sat to Longbottom's right and Senator Arango sat directly across from me. Arrayed on the other side of Arango were Shaler and Prescott. The others, the cream of Isthmian society, perhaps twenty in all, sat or stood about as space permitted. Among them were Carlos Arosemena and the two Arias brothers, all three scions of great Colombian families. Present also was Fredrico Boyd, whose family controlled the press on the isthmus. When the company was settled, Senator Arango began.

"We are the committee dedicated to the independence of Panama from Colombia. When the government in Bogotá rejected the Hay-Herrán Treaty, it became clear to us that there was no other alternative but independence. If things are left in their present state, there will be no progress in the negotiations with the United States on a Panama canal until the concession of the New Panama Canal Company expires in 1904. After that, Bogotá will attempt to renegotiate the Hay-Herrán Treaty on terms so unfavorable that the United States will be forced to build its canal through Nicaragua. If that happens, the isthmus and its people will be robbed of the bright legacy that by rights should be theirs." Longbottom and I nodded solemnly in unison, but so far Arango had told us nothing new. "Our plans are advanced enough now, however," continued Arango, "for us to see the outlines of our future Isthmian government. It will be a democracy, of course, along the outlines of your own great republic." Shaler beamed widely at this and gave us an approving wink. "We have decided by consensus, moreover, that the interim president to be installed upon the declaration of independence will be our esteemed colleague, Dr. Amador."

Muted applause broke forth, and Dr. Amador bowed his grizzled head. Arango's announcement, though, brought Shaler up short, and down the table a look of concern was in Major Black's eyes. I surmised that both he and Shaler rather expected that the leadership role would go to El Maestro, who seemed to be the bull of the woods hereabouts. Amador, to the contrary, struck me as being more suited to bouncing fat grandchildren on his knee than to leading a nascent secessionist movement.

"Well," managed Shaler with forced enthusiasm, "please accept my congratulations, Dr. Amador."

"*Gracias,*" he replied, which brought on another round of polite applause. Despite the honor accorded him, old Amador did not look particularly thrilled with his nomination.

Longbottom, evidently concerned by this nomination, decided it was time to interject some sense of reality back into this cabal.

"Er, do any of you," here he looked from Senator Arango to Dr. Amador and back, uncertain as to whom to address his question, "have a plan to deal with the Colombian army units in Colón and Panama City?"

Predictably, it was Senator Arango who answered. "*Sí,*" he said. Referring to the map, he explained, "The military commander of Panama City, Colonel Esteban Huertas, commands one battalion. Also, in the harbor is a Colombian gunboat, the *Padilla,* commanded by General Ruben Varon."

Shaler had told us about Huertas and his battalion. Arango's revelation about the *Padilla* was news, however. Ominous news.

"A general in charge of a gunboat?" muttered Longbottom. "That's odd, isn't it?"

"Things are a little different down here, Captain," Shaler whispered back.

Senator Arango continued. "Colonel Huertas is quartered in the Caserne de Chiriqui"—Chiriqui Barracks—"by the seawall looking out on the Pacific. That means he controls this town. Fortunately, Colonel Huertas is a man who understands business. It is my judgment that he would rather be a general in the army of an independent Panama than a forgotten colonel in the army of Colombia."

It was Shaler who now asked the key question. "Just what is Huertas's allegiance going to cost?"

From the pained expression on Dr. Amador's face, I could tell that the notion of someone's fealty being on the auction block was distasteful to him. It seemed perfectly natural to me, though, and it didn't seem to offend Senator Arango either, for he answered matter-of-factly, "I'm not certain yet. Many thousands of Yankee dollars, I'm sure."

Major Black seemed to squirm at the way Arango emphasized the word *Yankee*. The good senator evidently expected Washington to provide the bankroll required for the coup he was hatching.

"Colonel Huertas's battalion is not the only force to be reckoned with," observed Longbottom. "There's also Comandante Reyes's troops in Colón."

Senator Arango nodded. "What you say is true, my friend. We feel, however, that we can handle Reyes. The chief of police in Colón is on our side, as are the majority of the citizens. Most importantly, Mr. Shaler and his railroad are on our side. That means that we control the main transportation link between the coasts." Here his well-manicured finger followed on the map the trace of the railroad as it snaked from Colón, along the mighty Chagres River, and through the steep gorges of the central cordillera, then debouched onto the gentle plains of the Pacific coast. "Controlling the railroad means that the garrisons in Colón and Panama City are isolated, allowing us to deal with them separately."

"What about reinforcements coming from Colombia itself?" I pressed. "How would you handle them?"

Now Senator Arango's smile faltered a bit, and from the uneasy looks exchanged around the room, I realized I'd found the plotters' Achilles' heel.

"Well," suggested Senator Arango unconvincingly, "if we strike quickly, the coup can be a reality before the junta in Bogotá can react."

Now Dr. Amador spoke up, showing me clearly why he was less than enthusiastic about his prospective elevation to the presidency of a Panamanian republic. "The American captain is right. If reinforcements come, our cause is finished. We cannot hope to defy the full might of Bogotá."

The silence that greeted this sobering pronouncement was deafening. "Well, I don't understand, then," said Longbottom at length. "Are you going to revolt or aren't you? I mean, we came down here with the understanding that you gentlemen had more or less made up your minds about the matter."

Dr. Amador eyed Major Black and then Longbottom. "The answer to that question, Captain Longbottom, lies in what specific commitments to our movement you have brought with you."

Ah, I thought. That explained the awkward silence upon our arrival. These gents were waiting for us to pledge the wholehearted support of the United States to their cause.

"Commitments?" asked Longbottom, perplexed, looking to Major Black as he spoke. "I haven't been charged by my superiors to relay any commitments to you."

An angry buzz erupted around the room. "Impossible!" exclaimed Senator Arango. "We were told by Cromwell that the both of you met with President Roosevelt before you left New York."

"Cromwell? Who the dickens is he?" asked Longbottom, confused.

"A human ferret whose nose is in everybody's business," I answered, clearing up nothing for Longbottom. Turning to Arango, I demanded, "How the blazes do you know Cromwell?"

Shaler answered for Arango. "Cromwell's the general counsel for the Panama Railroad, Captain Travers. He also happens to be a major stockholder and sits on our board of directors. So, you see, Mr. Cromwell keeps in close touch with Senator Arango and me by telegraph from New York."

I saw now that Cromwell had his fingers in many more pies than I had suspected. As the lawyer for the New Panama Canal Company and the Panama Railroad, he had all of the action on the isthmus sewed up tightly. No wonder he had seemed so insufferably arrogant back in the Hoffman House; no matter the outcome of this tawdry affair, Cromwell was likely to show a profit.

"Since you mentioned Cromwell's name, Senator, why don't you tell us exactly what he told you?" I said.

"He wired to inform us that you two were representatives of the United States, and that your very presence here was proof that if the Colombians sent reinforcements to the isthmus to quell our revolt, your country would intervene with military force."

Major Black looked damn grim at this but continued to hold his tongue. He clearly had no intention of divulging the much less ambitious instructions we had received from Root and Roosevelt. I wasn't about to spill the beans either, but at least Arango's recitation of his communication from Cromwell illuminated one point for me. Specifically, it explained why such a large group of the city's leading citizens had been bold enough to meet with us in Senator Arango's house. They figured that the days of Bogotá's sovereignty over the isthmus were numbered, and that with Uncle Sam's protection the chances were slim that any of them would swing from a rope for committing treason.

"Well, I'm afraid that you have been misinformed," insisted Longbottom. Sudden gasps and ashen faces greeted this unwelcome news. Heedless of the bombshell he had dropped, Longbottom plowed forward. "We have no commitment to make. Our president never offered American forces to ensure the success of your movement. He wishes you all the best, but this must be your effort."

Turning to me for support in the face of the stunned silence that greeted this pronouncement, Longbottom demanded, "Isn't that so, Travers?"

Instinctively, I looked to Black for guidance. The army had made him a major for some reason, and as his junior I had a right to expect direction from him at a moment as ticklish as this. What I received was a small sign; he brought his finger to his lips, as though cautioning me not to fully endorse Longbottom's blunt statement.

I had but an instant to interpret this gesture, and in that moment I decided it was best to hedge. I quickly thought back to what Roosevelt had said when I surmised that what he wanted in Panama was a nice tidy little revolution. His response had been, "The important point, Travers, is that those are your words, not mine. You never heard me say any such thing." That meant but one thing to me: Roosevelt desired a revolution in Panama, but he didn't want the blame for the thing roosting on his doorstep.

Taking Roosevelt's unspoken intent as my guide, I cleared my suddenly dry throat and said, "I agree with Captain Longbottom that President Roosevelt's sentiments are very much with you and your compatriots, Senator Arango. I hesitate to suggest, however, that you are completely on your own. What is clear is that the opening moves must be made by Panamanians. After that, well, who can say where events might lead the United States?"

That was as far as I could fairly stretch what had been hinted at back in Sagamore Hill, and Black seemed to heave a slight sigh of relief. The Panamanians, although pulling back a bit from their sudden panic, were far from sanguine. In fact, Dr. Amador shook his head with discouragement. "Even if we succeed in overcoming the garrisons already in Panama, we cannot fend off an attack from the sea, and without the intervention of the United States, one will surely be attempted. No, *amigos,* I say this is the end of our dream."

Senator Arango, who appeared to be the head dreamer, was not ready to give up quite so easily. "Wait," he implored his fellows. "Our Yankee friends have spoken plainly with us, and for that we must thank them. I, however, do not choose to view this as the end of all we have worked for. The American president must be told that we are ready to fight but that we can win only with his help. We must make him understand that if he will stand by us, we won't fail."

Dr. Amador, to whom age had brought a well-founded distrust of puffery, was not easily swayed by Senator Arango's flowery oratory. "We have sent such messages in the past, my friend, but they have gotten us nowhere. Señor Cromwell assures us that he has laid our entreaties at the doorstep of both Secretary of State Hay and President Roosevelt."

That could well be so, I thought. Cromwell did strike me as the persistent sort.

"Then we must take new measures," insisted Senator Arango.

"New measures?" asked Dr. Amador. "Please be reasonable, Senator. What more can we do?"

"We can send you to see President Roosevelt," proposed Senator Arango dramatically.

An excited hubbub greeted this as I eyed Longbottom sideways. If Roosevelt wouldn't admit in the privacy of his own den that he favored a revolution in Panama, he sure as shooting wasn't going to publicly embrace one of the prime instigators of such a revolt. In my humble opinion, Roosevelt would as soon shear his head, cover himself with ashes, and don sackcloth as grant Dr. Amador an audience.

The conspirators in the room, however, liked the notion just fine, and even old Shaler was enthusiastic. "That's a dandy idea, Senator. No doubt Mr. Cromwell will approve. I'll send him a cipher in the morning and then I'll make the arrangements. The sooner Dr. Amador is in the United States, the better for us all."

Dr. Amador remained unconvinced, but his fellows would brook no argument. By acclamation it was decided that he was to go north, and that was the end of the matter. Senator Arango ended the conclave by throwing open a double door leading to a salon where a mahogany sideboard held chilled magnums of champagne.

"Señors, please do me the honor of toasting to *el Istmo Libre*—free Panama." Glasses were filled by servants, and El Maestro lifted his.

"*¡Viva el Istmo Libre!*" chorused the conspirators. I greedily quaffed my drink and motioned a lackey for a refill when I noticed we'd been joined by a bevy of señoritas, the distaff side of this conspiracy, if I guessed right. One, a stout matron with a grim face and too much rouge, took her post by Senator Arango's side. "Gentlemen," he said, addressing us Yankees, "allow me to introduce Doña Maria Estaban Arango."

Longbottom gave a courtly bow and I followed suit, but my attention was not on Señora Arango. Instead, I was captivated by the pair of ladies who had just joined Dr. Amador. The older of these two was perhaps forty—

his daughter, I surmised. She was a woman of striking good looks, with a fine carriage and a high, proud face. Here, I knew, was a woman with a will of her own. Her companion was no more than twenty, I guessed, and as lovely a gal as ever I had set eyes upon. Her skin was fair and was exquisitely set off by dancing fiery black eyes and luxuriant raven tresses that flowed down her slim white neck. I found myself drooling involuntarily, and only an elbow surreptitiously driven into my side by Longbottom broke my trance.

"For God's sake, don't be so damned obvious, Travers," he hissed.

I closed my mouth with an effort as Dr. Amador introduced his lovely companions. He turned first to the eldest. "Captain Travers, Captain Longbottom, this is my wife, Señora Maria Amador."

His wife? Why, he was a least twice again her age. The old codger evidently had more fire in his furnace than I would have guessed. "Charmed, ma'am," I fairly leered, taking her hand in mine and bestowing a soft kiss upon it.

The señora was not taken aback by my forwardness. I had judged her right, you see. She was damned independent and not afraid to show it. "Welcome to our country, Captain," she said with a warm smile.

Longbottom gave Señora Amador a stiff bow and murmured, "My pleasure, ma'am."

"And this, gentlemen," continued Dr. Amador, "is Señora Serafina Gómez Viscaya, my wife's second cousin. She is staying in my household for the time being."

Staying with him for the time being? What the blazes did that mean? She would not have been introduced as señora unless she was married, yet where was her husband? All of this flashed through my mind as I dropped Señora Amador's hand in an instant and seized the lovely one of Serafina with an alacrity that caused Amador to blink.

"Señora," I breathed, "we are privileged to assist your brave countrymen in their quest for freedom."

Serafina smiled demurely and gave me a tender yet penetrating gaze. What was it that I read in those wide, clear eyes? It was evident that she was curious about this tall, blond *norte americano,* and I hoped that curiosity went well beyond her desire to see independence for the isthmus.

"*Gracias,* Captain," she said with a silken voice that melted my heart and stirred my loins.

Unable to be silent but not having much of substance to say, I babbled, "It is my great honor to offer whatever meager assistance I can to your country, señora." My ardor for the independence movement, you see, had increased dramatically over the past few moments.

"Captain Travers is merely expressing a personal opinion," interjected Longbottom quickly, noting with disapproval that I had not yet released Serafina's hand. "My country is not in a position to act as guarantor of the success of your revolution."

"So we understand, Captain Longbottom," said Dr. Amador. "You have made that point perfectly clear."

His wife gave him a quizzical look, so Dr. Amador quickly apprised her of Longbottom's disappointing intelligence that the United States was officially on the sidelines, hence the need for his trip to the United States. Señora Amador appeared momentarily crestfallen but recovered her composure quickly.

With calm dignity she addressed herself to Longbottom and me. "Panama's destiny is in the hands of her people. Although we naturally would welcome the assistance of any friends of liberty, the road down which we are going is one that we ultimately must walk alone."

Said like a committed patriot, I thought—or a smooth political wife. Whichever was the case I couldn't tell, nor did I much care, although I had to admit that the lines were delivered masterfully—so masterfully, in fact, that they brought a grudging smile to Longbottom's face.

"Exactly, ma'am, exactly. And my country wishes you all the best on your way down that road."

Dr. Amador did not share his wife's sangfroid. "Wishes, wishes," he chided Longbottom irritably. "We could do with more arms and money and fewer wishes from your country, Captain."

Well, they weren't coming, at least not right now, and Longbottom knew that, so he shut up for lack of a convincing rejoinder. His silence allowed me an opening to chat with Serafina. "Are you from Panama City, señora?" I pried, using all the charm I could muster.

She shook her lovely head, setting the delicate gold earrings that pierced her earlobes to twinkling in the gaslight. "No. I am from Bogotá, but I have been in Panama for many years now."

A perfect white smile accompanied this response, and I grinned wolfishly in return. Devilish plans were already flitting through my head, but I decided it would be wise to pinpoint the present location of her better half before I went too much farther. "And Señor Viscaya. Is he, er, attending the festivities tonight?"

Serafina cast her eyes down and was suddenly silent. Dr. Amador coughed awkwardly. I sensed I had blundered into trouble, but for the life of me I couldn't figure exactly how. Señora Amador rescued me from my predicament. "Captain, you could not know. Please do not be embarrassed. Serafina is a widow. Her husband, Oscar, was killed in the war."

By God, I exulted, she's unattached! What a blessing! I struggled with the look of glee that threatened to sweep across my face and instead marshaled a suitably grave countenance. "My dear señora," I oozed, "I had no idea. Please accept my deepest apology. You must think me a complete fool."

Serafina's eyes met mine once more. "No, I do not think you a fool, Captain. I think you are a brave man who will rid Panama of the tyranny of Bogotá."

That comment kept me from wondering on whose side her late spouse had fought. Clearly he had been with the liberals, a bad choice for him but a wonderful opportunity for me. To assure Serafina that I was squarely in her corner, I hastened to say, "Then the señora will be pleased that I helped strike a small blow against the soldiers from Bogotá this very day."

Dr. Amador and his lady exchanged concerned glances. "And how did this come about?" Dr. Amador asked, anxiety in his voice. "Give me the details at once."

Superintendent Shaler had made the rounds of the small room and rejoined us just in time to hear the question. He answered it in my stead. "The garrison in Colón tried to arrest Kingston Jack. Captain Travers here intervened on behalf of a, er, friend, and exchanged blows with Comandante Reyes."

Serafina drew in her breath with an audible gasp. "Reyes the butcher!" she hissed.

"You know him?" I asked with surprise.

Dr. Amador nodded. "Sí, she knows him. You see, Captain Travers, it was Comandante Reyes who killed Serafina's husband."

"And worse," added Señora Amador.

"Worse?" I asked, confused. Killing Serafina's spouse would pretty much seem to be the bottom of the barrel, I would think.

"Sí, worse," Señora Amador assured me hotly. "Comandante Reyes desires to have Serafina as his mistress in Colón. He is a filthy pig!"

"Well, I'll be," exclaimed Longbottom, and even I had to shake my head in amazement. The customs in these parts did take a little getting used to.

"That is why I must stay here," added Serafina. "Panama City is beyond the jurisdiction of Comandante Reyes."

"I see," I murmured. "As long as you're on this side of the isthmus, you're safe."

"*Sí,* as long as Colonel Huertas remains in command of the Panama City garrison. But if he should return to Bogotá, or if he reaches an arrangement with Reyes, then . . ."

She didn't finish the sentence, nor did she have to. If Reyes ever got his hands on her, she would be in his thrall. I had seen the savage ferocity in Reyes's eyes, and there was no doubt in my mind what would lay in store for the lovely Serafina should she ever fall under the *Comandante*'s dominion.

It was Longbottom who broke the awkward silence that followed. "Er, is that very likely? I mean, could Comandante Reyes reach some sort of accord with Colonel Huertas?"

Dr. Amador was uncertain about that and he admitted it right out. "Well, Colonel Huertas is an officer of Bogotá, and he was sent to the isthmus to keep law and order in the wake of the civil war. All I can say with certainty is that for our revolution to succeed, we must either rally Huertas to our side or neutralize him."

Amador was talking pure treason now, but to my amazement Señora Amador joined right in. "There is no way to neutralize the hundreds of men under Colonel Huertas's command. They must either be for us or they will surely be against us."

Having been a soldier for a few years, I knew how most regulars thought. They couldn't give a tinker's damn about great political movements; what mattered to them was their comrades around them and their next payday. Wondering if the Amadors were cognizant of this central fact, I posed a question from the floor. "Er, do you have a strategy for wooing Huertas's battalion to your side?"

"No, we don't," admitted Dr. Amador. "We have been hesitant to approach Colonel Huertas too openly with our plans lest he clap us all in irons. Time, however, is short, and we know we must act soon. There is a complication in all of this, however."

"Complication?" I asked, my smile fixed to my face. What I had heard thus far was as convoluted as six lovers in a single bed. What, I wondered, could this further complication possibly be?

"It seems, Captain Travers, that the Panama City garrison is becoming restive. The soldiers haven't been paid in three months, and they are in an ugly mood."

"Haven't been paid in three months?" I fairly hooted. "Why, man, there's your opening to Huertas!"

Dr. Amador was confused. "Eh? I'm not sure I follow you, Captain."

It was as plain as the nose on his face, but I politely led the old fellow into the light. "You simply offer to pay off Huertas's men, and perhaps add a savory annuity for Colonel Huertas to seal the bargain."

"But how?" asked Señora Amador. "The soldiers are owed thousands of pesos. We do not have that kind of money."

"Of course you do," I countered, undaunted. "You are all men of substance, are you not? Certainly the city's bankers defer to you and to Senator Arango. Have them advance you the money—in Yankee gold dollars, not worthless paper pesos. You pay off the Panama City garrison, the soldiers come over to your side, Panama becomes free, and the new government can underwrite bonds to pay off the bank loans."

"Hmmm," pondered Shaler. "It might work." I rather thought that Shaler might approve of my hastily contrived scheme, since it didn't call for the use of railroad money.

The Amadors were less enthusiastic, though, and from the look they exchanged I guessed that parting a Panamanian banker from a dollar was about as easy as squeezing blood from a rock. Yet old Amador was determined to be gracious. "Captain Travers, you have suggested a most intriguing possibility. If for no other reason, I count tonight as a success. I think it must have been destiny that sent you to us in our hour of need."

Destiny, hell, I thought. It had been that thieving Rothstein who had started me rolling south, but I took the compliment graciously. "My fondest wish is to advance the future good relationship between your country and mine."

This was a bit thick even for Longbottom, and he wasn't at all comfortable at the meaningful glances I continued to lavish upon Serafina. "Well, Dr. Amador, you have honored us by inviting us to this stirring occasion," he interrupted. "Time, however, is short for us and there are many things to accomplish. I think Captain Travers and I should be taking our leave."

I for one was not ready to go, since there was still plenty of champagne and my little solution to the Huertas problem appeared to have kindled a perceptible glint of admiration in Serafina's lustrous eyes. Unfortunately, however, Superintendent Shaler agreed with Longbottom, so there were farewells all around and more toasts to *el Istmo Libre,* and then I was on my way out the door.

It was only at the last second that lovely Serafina contrived to bar my way with a sweet smile. "You are very clever, Captain," she said with a voice that seemed to tinkle like small bells.

"I was inspired by your company, señora," I said with a gallant smile. There was no lie there, since her very presence brought my faculties to full screaming alert.

"Perhaps," she suggested coyly, "before you leave Panama City, Dr. Amador might invite you to his residence for, er, further discussions on the political situation. Would that interest you, Captain?"

I read the invitation clearly. A summary interview with the old boy and then off to some secluded niche for a tumble with this lovely, and evidently quite lusty, young widow. I couldn't have proposed a more splendid arrangement myself. "I shall hold myself at the good doctor's disposal," I promised.

I had barely enough time to plant a final kiss on Serafina's outstretched hand before Longbottom took me by the elbow and propelled me out the door in Shaler's wake.

11

Panama City, Panama

Outside, we took our reins from a groom who stood at respectful attention as we mounted. It was a still, humid night and the moon was hidden behind a heavy bank of clouds. In the distance thunder rumbled, and occasional flickers of lightning lit the otherwise black sky. With Shaler leading the way, we proceeded down the Carrera de Santander to the Hotel de la Compagnie du Canal.

As we rode, Shaler spoke. "Boys, that affair was handled about as well as I could have expected. Captain Longbottom, you may have been a bit harsh in deflating some expectations, but it was probably just as well that our friends understand the limits of our capabilities. The main point, though, is that prior to tonight it was all they could do to steel themselves up for a clandestine meeting. Now they've agreed to send Dr. Amador to Washington. This is wonderful, gentlemen. Simply wonderful."

"I suppose, then, that our mission here is concluded," Longbottom ventured hopefully. "I mean, we were sent to test the political winds down here and report back. We've done that, and what's more, spurred old Amador to pay a visit to Washington. I'd say we've done everything we were sent to do, and more, eh?"

Shaler agreed, so the two of them began to make plans for our return trip, something I might have looked forward to until my meeting with Serafina. We'd stay on in Panama City for the night, they decided, and slip into Colón late tomorrow. Shaler would go on ahead to arrange ship passage for us. After we were safely aboard, he would scour the city and send Henry along on his way, too.

About the time the general outline of our departure had been worked out, we found ourselves at an unpretentious establishment that stood on the corner of the Carrera de Caldas. It was a three-story building with tightly shuttered windows. A lone gas lamp illuminated a sign that announced it to be the Hôtel de la Compagnie du Canal. No sounds emanated from within. The silence gave the place more the air of a fortress than that of a hostelry. The whole town, in fact, had seemed to settle into a deep melancholy with the coming of the night. On the streets I had seen only small groups of men who hurried by with nary a sideways look at us gringos. Their furtive behavior, and the dour gloom of the Hôtel de la Compagnie du Canal, reminded me that I was in a land where civil war could flare anew at any time.

We dismounted and went inside, where a sullen desk clerk lounged in a rattan rocker. Shaler quickly took him in hand, ordering the fellow to put us in his best room and to send the chit over to the railroad's bursar for payment. Then Shaler took his leave, promising to send a messenger in the morning when all the arrangements had been settled. When he was gone, I instructed the clerk to send up two bottles of his best wine—after all, Shaler was paying—then Longbottom and I went up to our lodgings. We'd just settled in when there was a knock at the door.

I opened it, expecting a bellhop with my libations. Instead I found myself staring into the mug of Major Black.

"Let me in," he insisted, rushing past me.

"Major Black!" exclaimed Longbottom. "Is something wrong? Is Superintendent Shaler all right?"

"He's fine, Captain Longbottom," replied Black as I shut the door. "It's the two of you who may be in danger."

"Danger? What do you mean, sir?"

Before Black could explain, there was another knock at the door. This time it was the bellhop, or, more accurately, a shambling pensioner sporting an Indian poncho and a toothless grin, who handed over two dusty bottles of cheap red wine. I ordered him to pull the corks from both, which he did using a stiletto he produced from up a loose sleeve, and then withdrew with as much of a bow as his arthritic spine would allow.

"Either of you gents care for a swallow?" I asked genially.

Major Black sternly shook his head. Longbottom chided me, "In view of the major's news, I rather think it's important to keep our wits about us, Travers."

"Suit yourselves." I smiled and took a deep pull straight from the bottle. The stuff was surprisingly good and had a hell of a lot more kick than El Maestro's champagne. "Ahh," I sighed, smacking my lips. "Now, Major, what's all this about danger?"

Black first peered through the shuttered window to ensure that the street was empty, then he put his ear to the door. Satisfied we were alone, he explained, "Your mission, gentlemen, is slightly different from mine. I was assigned to the Walker Commission because of my engineering skills. I was tasked with evaluating the feasibility of the Nicaragua route as opposed to the Panama one. As such, I was quite visible in the process, and I've been to Congress to testify regarding the commission's findings."

"Meaning what, sir?" asked Longbottom, not following Black at all.

"Meaning that I'm too closely linked to our government to operate with the same latitude as you. That's why I refrained from speaking tonight before our Panamanian friends. I must be seen as being scrupulously neutral in this matter."

"Latitude?" murmured Longbottom, still totally lost.

I was getting Black's message now, although it was a damned oblique one. I decided to lay the major's unwelcome tidings straight out for Longbottom. "Let me translate, Longbottom. You and I are junior officers. Junior officers have notoriously bad judgment, and sometimes they take into their heads notions that have no official sanction whatsoever."

"Damnit, Travers, quit speaking in riddles. What's your point?"

I obliged him. "If the Colombians see through our guise as surveyors, Washington will suffer us to be thrown to the dogs to appease Bogotá."

"That's nonsense, Travers," retorted Longbottom. "We're American officers."

"True, but without any official portfolios. If we prove to be an embarrassment, the War Department will insist we overstepped our bounds and put our noses where they had no business being."

Longbottom looked confounded as he suddenly grasped the exposed position we occupied. After all, he had assumed all along that we were here with the full support of the administration. "But, but, we're here at the express direction of the president," he protested.

"Longbottom, open your eyes," I scoffed. "You and I could swear on a stack of Bibles that we were ordered to rouse the local rebels, but if Roosevelt denied it, that would be the end of the matter. How many members of the general public or the press knew we were at Sagamore Hill? Why, even our friend Major Black here would back up Roosevelt if he insisted that such a meeting never occurred. Wouldn't you, Major?"

Major Black gave me a hard look that only confirmed my suspicions. "I don't deal in speculation, Captain Travers, and I don't discuss any meetings I may have had with high government officials. I suggest you don't either."

At this point I was disinclined to take Black's suggestion about anything. "The danger you were speaking of—what exactly did you mean?" I demanded.

"The gentlemen who run Bogotá are hardly naive," he replied. "They understand that matters between our two countries have come to a critical pass. They also understand that an important segment of the ruling circles on the isthmus are dissatisfied with Colombian rule. On top of all that, they are undoubtedly aware that we three are in the country."

"Comandante Reyes," I said flatly.

"And others," rejoined Major Black. "Bogotá may be incapable of exercising good government, gentlemen, but its espionage system on the isthmus is quite functional. The Colombians seem to know the gist of what occurs between Washington and the local independence movement. Fortunately, the precise membership of the independence movement has remained secure, at least so far."

I exchanged an uneasy look with Longbottom, who gazed at Black with trepidation. "If Bogotá learns of tonight's meeting, what will happen?" he asked.

"I expect that the ruling junta will react."

"In what manner?" I snapped. I was getting damned tired of prying critical information from Black.

"That I don't know," admitted Major Black, but he added darkly, "although I expect that the eventual reaction will be lethal."

Longbottom was pale now in the light of the hissing gas lamp. "Is that why you're here? Are the Colombians rounding up the plotters tonight?"

Black shook his head. "Things don't happen that quickly in these parts, Captain Longbottom. Bogotá has just finished one bloody war in Panama and certainly doesn't relish the prospect of a new one. They'll want to nip any revolt in the bud, in a way that ensures that they excise the threat in one quick stroke. I expect that the Colombians will move carefully at first, trying to ensure that they uncover all the traitors. In fact, they may wait for the plotters to declare openly for secession. Meanwhile, I suspect that the Colombians will begin shifting reinforcements to the isthmus, so that when the plotters are unmasked publicly, Bogotá can bring overwhelming force to bear and eradicate the entire movement in one fell swoop."

Feeling the need for something to steady my suddenly shaky nerves, I quaffed down a great draft of wine, then demanded of Black, "Reinforcements? From where?"

He eyed me distastefully before answering. "From Barranquilla or Cartagena. There's a regiment at each of those locations and another two in Bogotá. Bogotá, though, is landlocked, and those regiments would take weeks if not months to get into play. There are no sizable Pacific garrisons other than Huertas's battalion, meaning that the reaction, when it comes, will be from the Caribbean side of the isthmus. Such a coup de main would eliminate all local support for the Hay-Herran Treaty and give Washington but three choices."

"Which would be?" I prompted him.

"It could either deal with the Colombians on their terms. Or it could abandon Panama in favor of Nicaragua. Finally, of course . . ." Here he let his words hang in the air, as if unwilling to speak the unspeakable.

Longbottom's curiosity would brook no delay. "Finally what?" he demanded.

"Invade Panama with no pretense of succoring a budding democratic movement. Just show the mailed fist to the world and seize this pesthole, legalities be damned."

"Is that possible?" gasped Longbottom, shocked. "Wouldn't Congress forbid it?"

"Anything's possible once the stakes get high enough, Captain," came Black's cold reply. Then, as though the thought had just occurred to him, he added, "You know, there might be a course of action available to the Colombians short of a wholesale slaughter of the plotters. It's an option that could also minimize the risk of an American invasion of the isthmus."

"And that is?" asked Longbottom, dread evident in his voice.

When Major Black answered, there was not the slightest hint of emotion in his voice. "Bogotá could arrange to have the two of you assassinated as an object lesson to Senator Arango and the others. After all, if the junta were to show that it wouldn't shrink from killing American 'surveyors,' just think what it might do to bona fide traitors."

Longbottom seemed about to swoon. As for me, I had had about enough of Black's dramatics. Oh, don't get me wrong; I was as scared as Longbottom, if not more so. What angered me, though, was Black choosing to keep all this to himself until after we had foolishly exposed ourselves to danger. Perhaps it was the cheap wine on top of a bellyful of champagne, but for whatever reason I blurted hotly, "Now see here, Major. All of this should have been told to us back at Sagamore Hill. I'm disappointed that you kept us in the dark the way you did. I want some straight talk from you, and I want it now. Let's have your best estimate about what the Colombians will do as the result of tonight's palaver with Arango and Amador."

"They'll move more troops to the isthmus, like I said—under a reliable commander. The very fact that the meeting was allowed to occur must raise questions about Colonel Huertas's loyalties."

Longbottom was aghast. "You mean the military commander of Panama City knew about the meeting?"

"Undoubtedly. He may not have a detailed roster of the attendees, but he certainly knew something was afoot. Huertas could have thrown a cordon around the city and forbidden any gatherings tonight. By staying his hand, however, he demonstrated that he is very much on the fence. I think Huertas's vacillation is known in Bogotá, moreover, and for that reason I think the real reins of power are no longer in his hands."

I was confused. "If Huertas is not Bogotá's man on the isthmus, then who is?"

"That's a damned good question, Captain Travers. Huertas outranks every other officer on the isthmus, and up until about six months ago I would have said that he was unquestionably Bogotá's trusted agent. With the coming of the Hay-Herran Treaty, however, and the increasing dissension among the locals going unchecked by any military countermeasures, I believe that Bogotá stopped putting its trust in Huertas. It stands to reason, though, that the Colombian espionage net in Panama is under the centralized control of one supreme agent. I hear rumors of someone called the Raven. Unfortunately, there's quite a field of likely suspects for that role. That worries me, gentlemen, because those unseen eyes are even now trying to uncover the identities of Arango's faction and to relay that critical information to Bogotá. If powerful formations of loyal troops land in Panama soon, and they happen to be handed the names of all of Arango's supporters, they will be in a unique position to effect the swift annihilation of the independence movement."

At the mention of the Raven, I thought of Reyes's dark, malevolent eyes. "Comandante Reyes," I muttered.

"I agree," replied Major Black. "He's young, particularly vicious, and solidly on the side of Bogotá. Besides, he's made numerous enemies among the locals because of his depredations during the war. I have a hunch that he'd be only too happy to fill the void left by Huertas's fall from favor. That's why, Captain Travers, I was especially distressed to hear of your run-in with him earlier today."

"Well, he started it," I hastened to point out, only to be quieted by Black's upraised hand.

"Captain, please. I hardly care who started it. After all, this is not a schoolyard brawl we're discussing. The point is that you and Captain Longbottom are both marked men, and your usefulness has been compromised. I know that you intend to slip out of the country tomorrow night"—he'd been talking to Shaler, I could see—"and I concur in that course of action. My purpose in coming here tonight has been accomplished. I've warned you to be extremely alert until you're at sea. Don't allow anyone into your room after I leave, and for God's sake avoid becoming separated until Superintendent Shaler is able to spirit you back to Colón and aboard a steamer."

"What about you, sir? Aren't you coming along?" asked Longbottom.

"No. The very visibility that compelled me to keep my distance from you two at Senator Arango's house serves me as a shield. I'm too closely identified with Washington to risk harming. A blow at me would inevitably bring swift intervention, probably with the support of Congress. Accordingly, I'll tarry behind a bit. When you get back to New York, tell General Wood that I intend to survey the harbor defenses and see what I can glean about the armaments on the *Padilla*. After that I might slip over to Colón for a bit and perhaps leave for home in a few weeks. I wish you Godspeed, and heed well my words. Watch your backs until you're away from these shores."

His message delivered, Black hastened to take his leave. He opened the door and peered out cautiously to ensure that the corridor was empty. Then he slipped from the room and was gone.

Longbottom and I spent an uneasy night, one of us awake at all times to watch the street. Black's dire warning had set our nerves on end, and we expected treachery at any moment. Thus, when at dawn there came a knock on our door, we were both instantly alert. My Colt was out and trained on the door as Longbottom slowly opened it, ready to leap out of the way should I commence to blaze away.

Expecting the worst, we were surprised to see a young man of about twenty years of age. "Yes, what is it?" inquired Longbottom, opening the door wider as I hastily hid the revolver behind my back.

The young fellow pointed to his mouth and shook his head.

"What's the matter, can't you speak?"

Another shake of the head was the only answer to Longbottom's query. Then our visitor handed Longbottom a scrap of paper. On it was written my name.

"Eh? Are you looking for Captain Travers?"

He received a nod this time.

"Well, that's him over there," he said, jerking his thumb toward me.

The fellow marched in and handed me a folded note. I exchanged a puzzled glance with Longbottom and then flicked open the note. Why, it was from Serafina! I read it quickly.

Captain Travers,

   Please put yourself in the care of Pedro, the bearer of this note. I must speak to you. It is urgent.

                                          Serafina

Longbottom had slipped behind me and was reading the note over my shoulder. "Her request is out of the question, Travers. We have to lay low and then skedaddle when we get the word from Shaler, just like we planned."

I was reaching for my hat as he spoke, visions of Serafina's lovely face swimming before my eyes. Longbottom read my thoughts instantly. "For God's sake, man," he upbraided me, "you're engaged to be married. Besides, weren't you listening to a thing that Major Black told us?"

"I'm not married yet," I shot back. "As for Black, he seems a mite too inclined to share secrets with us after we're in the thick of things. Serafina's note tells me she has news for us, Longbottom, and we happen to be in a spot where we need all the information we can get. I'm going with this hombre, and that's all there is to it."

Longbottom didn't like that one damn bit and commenced to threaten and blow, trying to keep me put. He was in the act of promising to report me for dereliction of duty, in fact, when I slammed the door in his face. I followed Pedro down to the street where I found, to my great surprise, my horse saddled and ready. That told me that Pedro had been damned confident that I would follow him.

He mounted a burro and cantered off ahead of me. We rode through the narrow streets as the city came to life around us. Women were afoot with water jars on their heads, and vendors were setting out mangoes and bananas for sale on the tiny kiosks that lined the way. We passed through a portal in the city walls, turned west, and set off on a highway that paralleled the coast. Soon we were past the edge of town and into a region of orchards and meadows. We traveled on for about ten miles, then Pedro turned off the road onto a narrow drive that led up a grassy hill to a spacious hacienda. Herds of black cattle ranged the grasslands past the hacienda, their numbers beyond counting. Among them I could see riders, probably cowhands who served the lord of the manor. We rode up to a wide portico where Pedro reined in.

"Is Señora Gómez Viscaya in there?" I asked.

He nodded, then he cantered off, his burro braying to a jenny in a nearby paddock. I dismounted and then strode up to the heavy wooden door. I gave it a few good knocks and stood back. It opened, and before me stood a round little Indian woman with glistening black hair.

"I'm here to see your mistress," I announced.

"Sí, señor," she replied with a curtsy, opening the door wide.

There, striding down along the corridor and headed straight for me, was sweet Serafina! The maid, seeing that her services were no longer needed, quietly withdrew.

"I knew you would come, Captain Travers."

"Fenny, please," I insisted.

"Very well," she readily agreed. I noticed she was dressed much differently than the night before. She sported a short jacket and, of all things, breeches. On her head was a wide-brimmed hat with a flat crown in the

Spanish style. Serafina appeared dressed for a gallop, and my surmise proved to be completely accurate.

"I am about to ride down to the surf to gather some cows with calves who congregate there in the evenings. The weeds along the dunes are not good for them; they must be driven to the higher pastures to feed. Will you join me?"

"A ride?" I asked, flustered. "I mean, where are we? Who owns this place?"

"This is the hacienda of my late husband. I come here sometimes . . . to be alone. The Amadors have treated me as a daughter, but, still, the past year has been very hard for me."

"You must have loved your husband very much," I chanced, hoping that such was not the case. I carefully watched her eyes as she answered.

"*Sí,*" she said sadly. "I do miss Oscar."

Damn, I thought, she means it. That would make my advances a bit more ticklish than I would have hoped. Nonetheless, I had overcome greater odds in making past romantic conquests, and Serafina was certainly a prize worth exerting the utmost effort to possess. The first thing I needed in that regard, of course, was a bit of privacy.

That's why I said with a broad grin, "I think a ride with you on this lovely morning is a splendid idea."

Stepping from the house and into the bright sunshine, Serafina called for her mount. A ranch hand dutifully appeared, leading a dainty mixed-blood Arabian mare with a white blaze on its nose. The mare pranced about nervously as a silver-inlaid saddle was thrown across its back and the cinch tightened. I wondered if the mare didn't have a bit too much spirit for the demure Serafina. My doubts, however, were laid to rest when she took the reins and vaulted into the saddle.

The mare, instantly recognizing its master, settled right down. "Let us fly together, Fenny!" she called.

I was still swinging up into my saddle when she pounded out across the fields, leaped over a low rail fence, and then was off in a straight-out gallop. I dug my heels into my nag's flanks, drove straight for the fence, and cleared it awkwardly, my mount's rear hooves knocking the top rail from its moorings as I did. My horse landed heavily, wobbled, and seemed about to go down but then recovered and set out after the Arabian.

Serafina clearly wanted a race, but after a few furlongs it was evident that there would be no contest. She flew over the grassland before me, widening the distance between us with every stride. Finally, when she was a full half mile ahead of me, she reined in and waited for me to draw even.

"Is your horse lame, Fenny?" she giggled mischievously.

"I'm afraid I have no excuse, Serafina. Your mare is exceedingly fleet, and her rider quite skilled."

She threw back her head and seemed to revel in the compliment. No Latin man, I guessed, would readily admit the superior skills of a mere woman, and Serafina drank in the compliment with gusto. We were on a bluff above a sandy beach now, and Serafina suddenly turned in the saddle and pointed off toward the surf. "There—can you see them?"

I nodded. A small knot of cows and calves, sheltered in the lee of the bluff, grazed on the hardy grass that clung to the base of the incline.

"Come, let us corral them together," she cried and then dug her spurs into the Arabian. The little mare bounded down the bluff, its agile feet seeming to barely touch the earth. Serafina had her lariat off her saddle horn now and was spinning the loop in the air over her head as she rode.

She was a perfect horsewoman, I saw, and she handled her rope with a skill that approached that of the grizzled wranglers I had seen during my stay in the Arizona wilderness. Before my horse had gained the beach, Serafina was among the startled cattle, cutting between bawling calves and their panicked mothers. The herd began to bolt, heading up the bluff for the most part, in the direction Serafina wanted. One pair, however, a calf and its mother, ran off along the beach. It was these two that caught Serafina's attention. She was after them in a flash.

"Be careful!" I cautioned as she leaned forward in her saddle, and then the lariat snaked out and expertly caught the cow around her back leg. Serafina's mare, evidently an expertly trained quarter horse, immediately halted, then began backing away from the cow to tighten the rope. The panicked cow ran until the slack was exhausted, then stopped and tugged madly at the restraining rope. Timing the moment perfectly, Serafina jerked on the rope just as the cow seemed the most off balance, sending it sprawling helplessly on the sand. In a twinkling she was off the Arabian and at the cow's side, trussing its feet so that the befuddled bovine was completely immobilized.

"Well done! Where did you learn to rope like that?"

"Panama is a wild place, Fenny. If you don't learn to look out for yourself, you will be lost."

I took this to be a reference to her husband's fate. To break the sudden awkward silence that followed, I leaped from my horse and pulled the lariat

from the disgruntled cow's leg. She struggled to her feet and went low-
ing after her fellows as they climbed to the high pastures. Her calf scurried along behind her, bawling fearfully all the way.

Serafina tethered her mount to a driftwood log. "At times I come here
to swim in the ocean," she said quietly.

"Oh, you're a swimmer too? Why, there seems to be no end to your
accomplishments. You know, Serafina, I rather admire women who aren't
afraid to take a bit of exercise."

She seemed to eye me questioningly, and then, deciding something for
herself, inquired boldly, "Would you mind if I swam now?"

"Mind? Why, no, not at all. Er, perhaps I could join you?"

Incredibly, for a widow in a Catholic country, she seemed amenable to
the idea. In no time we were both stripped to the buff. Her face clouded
over, though, as I revealed my Colt. Catching her glance, I hastened to assure
her, "It's for snakes, my dear. Please, don't trouble your mind about it."

Then I stripped off my tunic and bandages, and she saw the red gash
from Reyes's sword stroke. "A bite from one of those snakes I was telling you about," I said with a smile. "It's nothing, really, or at least nothing that will, er, slow me down, if you get my meaning."

She did, for soon we were gamboling through the waves like a pair of
young otters in the middle of a mating ritual. She stayed out of my reach,
though, diving from time to time to give me an inspiring view of her shapely
legs and firm buttocks. Try as I might, I couldn't seem to lay a hand on
her—until that is, a heavy roller came in from the deep water and pushed
Serafina into my grasp. As the force of the water propelled us both up
onto the beach, she showed no inclination to free herself.

I held her close, feeling the soft swell of her breasts. Serafina had
the body of a goddess, and the look she was giving me at the moment
told me that she had too long denied herself the pleasures of the flesh.
As the water receded, we lay entwined on the edge of the beach, her
face just inches from mine. I gave her a tender, oh so tentative kiss.
Women are funny about sparking, you know. A gal who had not the slightest
compunction about baring all before a fellow might become suddenly
shy at a stolen kiss, while another lady might kiss you all night, yet
shriek to the high heavens if you so much as raised her hem. One could
never tell about matters of the heart, and therefore I aimed to go slow
with Serafina.

Guessing that a little talk was in order before I advanced any farther,
I murmured, "Tell me something, Serafina. Your message said that it was

urgent for you to see me. Now, what was so all-fired important that I ride this considerable distance?"

The dark glow in her eyes told me the answer before she spoke. "I took one look at you last night, Fenny, and I knew that I must be with you one time before you left my country forever. Forgive me if I led you here under false pretenses."

The smile I gave Serafina at this confession told her that somehow I'd manage to get over the deception. "In truth, my dear, if I had left Panama without seeing you again, I would have felt a pang of regret for the rest of my days." It seemed like the perfect rejoinder, and I was so buoyed by the tears of emotion that seemed to well up in the dear girl's lustrous eyes that I impulsively followed my words with a second kiss on her upraised cheek. Expecting some resistance on her part, if only for the sake of form, I was amazed when my second buss drew a deep, tongue-devouring kiss in return.

Praise the Lord, I crowed silently! Serafina was randier than a dance hall girl between cattle drives. As we lay in the wet sand, her legs locked around me so tightly that I could not have disengaged had the thought even occurred to me, it was clear that Serafina needed more than kissing. She was in desperate need of something she had not had since the demise of the late, lamented Oscar. It was just her good fortune that old Fenny stumbled into her neck of the woods when he did.

Rising to the occasion, I did my duty. With exquisite care, I mounted sweet Serafina, exhibiting all the virtuosity acquired in more than a decade of attentive study of the art of love. I drummed her soft buttocks off the sand for a full hour, whispering sweet nothings in her ear all the while. Serafina went wild, caterwauling and kicking, raking my back and biting my shoulder. Then, with a sudden shudder, we were done, and I rolled over her to regain my breath. As I recovered, I was sure of two things. First, I had upheld the honor of the United States Army, and second, I was certain that Serafina would miss me when I left Panama.

Rather expecting dear Serafina to need some time to recover from the throes of her passion, what with her as a widow being out of practice and all, I was a mite surprised when she rose suddenly and cocked an ear to the wind.

"Get dressed, Fenny," she ordered. "Riders are coming this way."

I heard nothing and said so, but Serafina was already climbing into her silky underthings. "Oh, all right," I muttered, disappointed now since I had rather hoped that I might have another go at her. As I was buttoning my shirt, I looked up at the bluff to see that Serafina had indeed been right.

Two horsemen crested the bluff and pounded down to the beach. One was the ranch hand whom Serafina had sent to fetch her mount.

"Señora," he called as he came on. "El Diablo! We have found him! Come quickly!"

El Diablo—the devil? What the blazes was the fellow babbling about? I turned to ask Serafina exactly that, but she was already sprinting for her mount. "Quick, Fenny!" she cried. "We must be off!"

She flew into the saddle with a speed that belied the amorous exertions she had just undergone, and without a backward look spurred off. I mounted and hurried after her, calling all the while for her and her vaqueros to slow down, damnit. To no avail, however, for on they galloped, ever upward, past the vast herds I had seen earlier.

Ahead I could see Serafina and her men as they vaulted fences and plunged through thickets where briars pulled at boots and bridles and threatened to rip the unwary rider from the saddle. Then I heard the baying of a hound, then another, and Serafina disappeared into a thick copse of *cuipo* trees. Her outriders followed her into the thicket.

As I neared, I could see that just inside the grove was a small group of men, vaqueros all. They were gathered around the mangled carcass of a steer. Dogs were everywhere, barking wildly. More of them were deeper in the undergrowth, out of sight of the men. Their barks were shrill, as though they had something treed. As it turned out, they did.

"El Diablo! El Diablo!" the men were shouting excitedly to one another as I galloped up. Serafina was afoot now and called out for a carbine.

A carbine? What in Sam Hill was she up to? I wondered. She quickly cleared up my confusion.

"Fenny, there is a jaguar in there. One that has preyed on these herds for years. The dogs have it treed, and now it is for me to kill it."

"You?" I cried. "What about them?"

There had to be twenty sturdy men standing about, all of them rough-looking hombres who were armed to the teeth. In fact, these gents were so uniformly frayed and weatherbeaten that a good mauling by the jaguar could only improve their appearance. Why in heaven's name take a chance on having a hair on lovely Serafina's head mussed when such oafs were lounging about?

Reading my look, she explained, "I must do this, Fenny. My men all know it. Oscar vowed he would kill El Diablo, but he died before he had the chance. He has no sons, and so it falls to me to fulfill his vow. Do not try to stop me."

Then she rushed off into the tangle of vines and bushes toward where the pack was yelping itself hoarse. Apparently there was a code about such things, for not one of the cowboys made a move to follow. Serafina would either uphold the honor of her late husband or join him in a hideous death.

"Damn that stubborn woman," I fumed and drew my Colt. Before anyone could make a move to halt me, I was on Serafina's trail, shoving my way past creepers that coiled about my ankles and tripped me with each step I took. I could only guide on the call of the dogs, for I could not see past the solid wall of vegetation that loomed before me. Cursing and sweating, and wishing I had a Luzon bolo to clear a path, I made my way forward.

Suddenly I burst into a clearing to behold a primeval scene of bestial savagery. In the center of the glade was a tree, a powerfully muscled jaguar crouched warily on one of its lower branches. Beneath swarmed the enraged pack of dogs, two of its members lying eviscerated and lifeless on the ground. El Diablo evidently had managed to do quite a bit of damage before he ascended to his perch.

The thing that struck me was the awful stench that wafted to my nostrils from the big cat. There was a deep musky odor to the beast, all mixed in with the nauseating reek of rotted meat. The latter seemed to emanate from the beast's grooved claws, probably because it had not had time to thoroughly cleanse itself since its last kill. Those awful claws were fully extended as I neared Serafina, and I realized instinctively that were I to receive so much as a scratch I would die a miserable death from infection and fever.

If Serafina was shocked by the gory scene, she gave no evidence of it. Instead, she slowly squared up to the big cat, which watched her with baleful yellow eyes. El Diablo's glare flicked to Serafina's rifle and then to the revolver in my hand. I may be crazy for crediting an animal with thinking, but for my money it appeared that the jaguar realized that the game had changed, and that the odds were suddenly stacked against it. Whatever the reason, it suddenly rose and let out a great hiss.

At the ghastly sound, Serafina froze in place, then slowly raised the stock of the carbine to her slender shoulder. The great cat tensed, and I could see its powerful haunches bulge.

"It's going to leap!" I cried, and as the words left my mouth the cat was in the air. I fired my Colt, too high, I thought, and then a second shot rang out.

I blinked as the jaguar hit the ground with a great thud. It didn't move. The hounds held back an instant, for they had seen what this fiend had done to their mates. Then, with full-throated snarls, they fell on their prey.

Pushing through them, I kicked the carcass. There was no movement. The jaguar was dead, with a bullet through its great heart. I turned to Serafina.

"You—you did it! Wherever did you learn to handle a gun like that?"

"At my father's knee in Colombia," she answered. "This is a harsh land, just like the old frontier in your nation, Fenny."

I needed no further proof of that statement, so I told Serafina she was a veritable Annie Oakley, and then spent some minutes explaining that comment to her. In the end she rather liked the simile, and she beamed brightly as her men piled into the clearing and trussed the body of the great cat to a sturdy sapling that had been quickly cut and trimmed for that purpose.

With three men on each end of the pole, El Diablo was hefted from the scene of his last stand and into the grasslands, where the cadaver was strapped to a skittish mule for the trek back to the hacienda.

"Come, Fenny, let us return together." We rode off, leaving her ranch hands to follow along at their own pace. As we went, I could no longer contain my curiosity about this remarkable woman.

"Serafina," I asked, sweeping my hand about me to indicate the vast lands all around us. "Are these yours? I mean, upon your husband's death did his estate pass to you?"

She shook her head. "No. Oscar did not own these lands. His family did. They are from Cartagena. Oscar was sent here to manage the property for them, and all he earned from his labors went to them. I am allowed to stay here from time to time, as a guest, nothing more."

"Then what's to become of you?" The question was damned artless, but it was out of my mouth before I thought to stop it.

"Whatever becomes of a widow in my society?" she said with a bleak smile. "I exist at the sufferance of others. Perhaps," she added wistfully, "I will find another husband. If not, well . . ."

She didn't finish the thought. She didn't have to. I knew instinctively that unless she remarried she would remain attached to her husband's distant family, a charity case for the rest of her life. As she had said, this was indeed a harsh land.

"There has been much disappointment for me, Fenny. Last night when I heard your friend, Lowthing—"

"Longbottom," I corrected her.

"Sí, Longbottom. When Longbottom told Dr. Amador that your great country was not prepared to make any commitments to Panama, well it just seemed too much to bear. We had heard that emissaries from Washington were on their way, and we expected so much more. Today, when I saw you again," here she turned and was looking directly at me, forcing me to meet her gaze, "I thought that perhaps he said those things because there were too many ears present to say otherwise. That's why I must ask you now, is it true? Can poor Panama expect no help from her American friends?"

Giving Serafina bad news was the last thing I wanted to do, but I could see no point in stringing the poor girl along. The sooner she got the truth through her skull, the sooner I could steer the conversation around to more appealing subjects.

"Longbottom did not lie. He spoke the truth."

Serafina fell silent, and we rode along without another word until we arrived at the hacienda. There the plump Indian woman laid out a festive lunch in an ornately appointed dining room. The food and the ambience seemed to revive Serafina's spirits markedly. I took my meal with her at my side, laughing and exchanging meaningful looks all the while.

When we were finished and the table had been cleared, she gave me an appraising look with her eyebrows arched high. "Tell me, Fenny, has your morning completely tired you?"

I caught her meaning at once. "Oh, I think you'll find that my recuperative powers are astonishing, my dear."

"That I will judge for myself," she announced. Rising, she gave me her hand.

"Lead on," I whispered in her ear, and she did—straight to her boudoir.

12

It was twilight before I gained the outskirts of Panama City. As the sun set, I savored once more the afternoon of sweet bliss that I had shared with Serafina. The hot passion she had kept in check for so long had spilled over, engulfing me in a torrent of exquisite delights. I was groggy and tired but as happy as any man will ever get in this life—so happy, in fact, that I was humming a jaunty tune when I neared the hotel. Under the gas lamp before the hotel stood two figures. One was Longbottom, and with him was Shaler.

Longbottom, stamping with impatience, saw me as I neared. "Travers, you nincompoop! Where the devil have you been? Superintendent Shaler here has been scouring the city all day for you."

"I went for a ride in the country, Joshua," I replied good-naturedly, for even the sight of Longbottom could not sour my buoyant mood. "The people out there are wonderfully hospitable, you know. You ought to get about a little yourself. It would do you worlds of good."

I was feeling so supremely satisfied, that as I dismounted and tied my horse to the hitching post, I barely noticed two shadowy figures slip from an alley beside the hotel. Shaler, however, saw them at once as they moved slowly forward to confront us.

"Bushwhackers, Travers!" he warned.

Instinctively, I whirled about. As I did, I saw that from the opposite direction two more shadows were approaching.

"We're surrounded!" I yelped, reaching for my Colt.

"Who are they?" cried Longbottom, fear in his voice.

Shaler had time only to growl, "Don't know, son. Could be common thieves, or could be assassins."

Assassins? Immediately I recalled Black's dire warning. In that instant Shaler slipped his hand into his coat pocket. When he withdrew it, he was clutching a silver derringer. It was a two-shooter, I saw, as I began calculating the odds that we were facing. My Colt had but two shots left, since I hadn't been able to secure any fresh cartridges after the confrontation with Reyes yesterday. That meant that we'd have to make every shot count.

Our attackers padded silently forward like wolves closing upon helpless prey. I saw no evidence of guns. They'll use knives, I thought, but then I heard the unmistakable rasp of a saber clearing its scabbard. "Swords! They aim to hack us apart!"

Shaler, though, was unfazed. He merely observed matter-of-factly, "Blades don't make noise. These boys don't want to attract too much attention."

"Get ready!" I warned, crouching as I spoke. Shaler stood firm, holding his fire for a point-blank shot, while Longbottom, unarmed, sheltered behind us.

Then, with nary a word, our assailants charged from all sides at once. The figure nearest to me closed for a killing slash, and I leveled my Colt. It roared and the swordsman dropped to the cobblestones. Behind him, his cohort dodged to the right, dropped low, and leaped in for a disemboweling stab. I caught him in midflight with a shot through his forehead. He dropped in a heap at my feet just as I heard Shaler's derringer discharge twice in quick succession from behind me. Whirling, I expected to see two attackers sprawled in the street.

Incredibly, I was wrong; they were both alive. One had Shaler by the throat while Longbottom struggled wildly with the other. By God, Shaler had missed twice at a distance of less than ten yards! Cursing his ineptness, I seized the saber from the corpse at my feet.

"Travers! Help, for God's sake!" pleaded Longbottom.

I sized up the situation; Longbottom was slowly losing his battle, but old Shaler was being totally overwhelmed. An assailant shook him by the throat like a terrier might worry a rat. I went to Shaler's aid first, letting Longbottom twist in the wind a bit longer. I pried the hand from Shaler's throat and with an effort hurled back his attacker. Rather than fleeing, this fellow coolly sneered in Spanish, "I was told not to kill the old man, but you are dead, gringo."

Before I could grasp the import of what he'd said, the fellow struck furiously. A flash of steel was all I saw as he thrust forward. I parried the blow desperately and then lunged in a quick counterattack, feeling the pain from my already wounded shoulder as I did so. The throbbing slowed me, for my assailant danced easily away from my point.

"I see you are no bladesman," he taunted.

He was right, for although I'd slaughtered a passel of Moros out in the Philippines with nothing but cold steel in my hand, shooting irons were my true forte. I was painfully aware of that fact, and of the fact that my opponent was evidently a master duelist. This contest, I realized forlornly, could not last too long.

"Finish him!" implored Longbottom just before he was slammed to the street by his attacker. He clung grimly to his assailant's sword arm, but it was only a matter of time before he weakened. Shaler was out of the struggle, sinking to the cobblestones as he labored to force air through his constricted windpipe.

Then my attacker was on me again with a flurry of ringing blows, each one from a different direction. I barely blocked these, retreating clumsily as I did. I felt the rough stones beneath my boots and realized with mounting panic that if I lost my footing I was a goner. Sensing my fear, the swordsman bore straight in with a huge lunge. I jerked convulsively to the side, just as his blade promised to skewer me, and with the reflexes of the truly desperate I lashed out with my booted foot.

I caught him on the outside of his knee with sufficient force to buckle both his legs for an instant. That instant was all I needed; I plunged my blade into his side, low enough not to catch on a rib. He gasped and staggered back two paces. Then with a huge geyser of blood cascading from his torn flank, the vicious brute slowly sank to the ground, convulsed a time or two, and then lay still. Seeing his last companion die, Longbottom's assailant ceased his onslaught and sprinted down the street to disappear into the gloom.

Shaken by the suddenness and savagery of the attack, I helped Shaler to his feet. When he could speak, I asked, "Who the hell were they?"

By way of an answer, he took the saber from my hand and held it up to the light. It was of French design, the sort of épée an officer might carry. "Those fellows were military men. They must have been stalking Captain Longbottom all along but stayed their hand until they could set upon the two of you together."

Longbottom, still gasping with exertion and terror, managed to wheeze, "Was this the work of Colonel Huertas? Did he order our assassination?"

"I don't think so," opined Shaler. "You've done nothing to offend him, at least not overtly. No, I think these boys were put on your trail by Comandante Reyes."

This was disheartening news, since we had to pass back through Reyes's bailiwick in order to take ship for home. Moreover, this night's work had been a close call. We might not be quite so lucky the next time. "We've got to get out of here," I said.

Shaler nodded. "It goes without saying that your lives are in real danger. You need to leave Panama, and pronto. I was telling Captain Longbottom that the *Yucatan* is still in Colón Harbor. I've arranged for a special train to carry you over to the Caribbean side tonight, and for guides to meet you when you arrive. My primary concern now is to get the two of you on board the *Yucatan* and under steam before Reyes realizes that his attempt on your lives has failed."

I'd heard enough. "You're absolutely right, Superintendent. We should be on our way without delay."

We hurriedly mounted and galloped through the dark streets to the railroad station. The special was just raising steam when we arrived. It consisted of a locomotive, a coal tender, and a single passenger car. We leaped from our mounts and hurried for the train. We had but twenty feet to go when suddenly a group of figures stepped out from the shadows of the station.

"Not again," I moaned.

Shaler peered into the night and then said, "Good evening, Colonel Huertas."

The leader stepped into the light cast by a lantern in one of the station windows. He was a small, dapper man, clad in a white uniform cut in the French fashion. Perched on his head was a red kepi at a jaunty angle, and a long scarlet cloak was thrown carelessly about his shoulders. The cloak gave the fellow more of the aspect of a carefree boulevardier out for a night on the town than that of a military man on duty. In the light I could see that he was young, no more than thirty years of age. His features were passingly handsome but in a feral sort of way. His dark eyes were all business, and I watched them for signs of trouble. I saw none, though. Even more reassuring was the fact that the saber swinging by his side remained sheathed.

"Ah, Señor Shaler, what a pleasant surprise. I was just out for a stroll with some of my officers. I had heard that there might be bandits afoot tonight, and ordered heightened vigilance everywhere. I trust that you have encountered no unpleasantness?"

"None that we couldn't handle, Colonel," replied Shaler gamely.

"Good, good." Huertas stopped before us and studied Longbottom and me. He pulled a slender cigarillo from a case in his tunic pocket and put it to his lips. At once a tall captain stepped forward with a match and lit it. Huertas inhaled and then loosed a stream of smoke into the heavy night air. "These gentlemen, Señor Shaler, must be the, er, surveyors who landed in Colón the other day. Did you know that I received a message from Comandante Reyes about them?"

"Oh? Nothing bad, I hope."

Huertas didn't reply to Shaler directly. Instead, he said over his shoulder, "Look at these hombres, Captain Salazar. Don't they have the look of fighting men about them? I suspect that their true talents are wasted working for Señor Shaler's railroad."

What was Huertas saying? I wondered. Did he know that Longbottom and I were American officers? If so, what did he intend to do about it?

Nothing, as things turned out. He stepped aside and said genially, "Forgive my manners, gentlemen. Here you are obviously in a hurry to catch your train and I occupy you with trivialities. You must pardon me."

"Think nothing of it, Colonel," said Shaler carefully, stepping quickly past Huertas with Longbottom and me right on his heels.

We climbed aboard as the engineer and fireman watched curiously, and when Shaler gave the signal they engaged the throttle and pulled out without the customary hooting of whistles. Once inside the car, Longbottom and I relaxed a bit. After all, the United States guaranteed the right of way for the railroad. Colonel Huertas and even Comandante Reyes would not be foolish enough to provoke a confrontation with the colossus of the North over two insignificant junior officers.

"What was all that about?" I asked Shaler as we cleared the outskirts of town.

"I don't know, Captain Travers. Something's afoot, though, and I'm willing to bet it's nothing that bodes well for us."

The track ahead was evidently clear, for we climbed easily into the cordillera, negotiated the more difficult stretches of track in the highlands, and began the descent to the Caribbean. We had just crossed over a trestle bridge about a mile outside the station at Tabernilla when I felt the locomotive's steam brakes engage, shaking the train with a great groan of metal on metal. Slowly, we rolled to a halt. Longbottom and I leaped to our feet to peer out into the darkness.

I hurried to the platform at the front of the car, then leaned out and cried to the engineer, "What's the matter?"

"Debris on the track," came the shouted reply. "Come up here and lend a hand. We need to clear it before we can go on."

Debris? Damn, that had all the earmarks of some ploy by Reyes to waylay us. But the engineer was right; there could be no further progress until the obstacle was cleared.

Fearfully, Longbottom and I dismounted and joined the fireman in front of the locomotive. A huge mahogany tree had been felled and dragged across the track. If we had hit it at full steam, we would have been derailed.

"Look at the size of that monster," marveled Longbottom. "It must have taken a gang of men to put it there."

That was exactly what worried me, and I looked around nervously. Flighty and at the end of my tether, I just about jumped out of my boots when a voice called softly from the encroaching underbrush, "Fenny!"

"Who the hell . . . ?" I exclaimed. Longbottom was poised to flee to the protection of the train when a group of men stepped from the shadows. By the light of the locomotive's lamp, I could see they were Blacks.

"Bandits!" gasped the fireman.

Maybe, I thought, but one of them knew my name. "Who is it?" I demanded with what I hoped was a note of authority.

"Fenny, it's Henry." He stepped into the lantern light and I could see him clearly now. With him were three other Blacks, all armed. At their head was Kingston Jack.

"Henry, what the blazes is going on here?"

"We had to warn you, Fenny," explained Henry. "Reyes sent gunmen to the station at Tabernilla. They know about the special train and are going to waylay you."

"Damn!" I swore to Longbottom. "We never should have let that last killer slip away. He must have sent a wire to Reyes."

"He sure enough did," confirmed Henry. "One of Superintendent Shaler's telegraph operators took the message on the Colón end. He delivered it to Reyes, but not before he told Mr. Prescott about it. Mr. Prescott found me and I put the word on the street that I needed help. In no time Kingston Jack here appeared. He rounded up some men and we came out on a handcar about an hour ahead of the Colombians. We cut down this tree to stop you, and it looks like things worked out just fine."

Kingston Jack spoke up. "Reyes has vowed to kill both of you, and Henry too. He is a very dangerous man."

That was the understatement of the day. "Well, what do we do now? We just got run out of Panama City, and now we can't go back to Colón."

"You must do what I do from time to time, Captain," replied Kingston Jack.

"Which is?"

The answer was swift. "Take to the cordillera."

Longbottom eyed me uneasily. "You mean wander off into this jungle?"

Kingston Jack smiled jovially, as though he were suggesting nothing more strenuous than a stroll through a city park. "That's right, man. But do not worry, for I will go with you. You will be safe enough, and after a while when the Colombians let down their guard, we can slip back into Colón and smuggle you aboard a steamer for home."

"What do you think, Travers?" asked Longbottom uneasily. He clearly didn't relish the notion of traipsing off into the wilderness with Kingston Jack any more than I did.

"I don't like it, but I don't see that we have any choice in the matter."

Henry agreed. "That's the way I see it too, Fenny."

"Then lead on," I told Kingston Jack.

I hastily arranged it with Shaler that we would make contact with either him or Prescott once the danger had passed. They would stand ready to hustle us out of the country as soon as we reemerged from hiding. We all put our backs into clearing the track so the locomotive could go along its way. Once it disappeared into the night, we bedded down for a few hours of sleep in the brush by the track. Kingston Jack roused us at dawn, and after a meal of dry corn provided by the Antilleans, we struck out for the highlands.

Kingston Jack set a leisurely pace, explaining that there were several secret campsites in the vicinity, any one of which could be made habitable with a minimum of effort. He stated his intention to set us up in an area where game abounded, leave us a rifle or two, and come fetch us when

all the uproar died down. It seemed like a feasible plan, and I was actually looking forward to a few days of uninterrupted hunting when we crested
a rise and paused to rest. One of Kingston Jack's men was scanning the
trail behind us when he saw movement.

"Colombians!" he called, and all eyes followed his pointing finger. One
ridge over I caught a flash of the sun off metal. Focusing on that spot, I
saw a group of about twenty men passing through a clearing on the hillcrest.
Although the men were obscured in foliage that rose to chest height, I could
see that about half of them were in uniform, and the others were in mufti.
These latter had the look of veteran woodsmen, and I instantly recognized
them for what they were—trackers. All of them had backpacks and, more
ominously, they all bore rifles.

Henry squinted hard. "Look, Fenny," he said.

I nodded. "It's Reyes." It was his gleaming saber that had caught my
eye. Beside him was a man with a bandaged head. It was Sergeant Gómez,
whom Henry had felled with a stone during the melee back in Colón.

Kingston Jack took in the situation at a glance. "They must have taken
the train from Tabernilla to where we camped last night. From there they
followed our trail. They look well armed, and I'm willing to bet they have
plenty of food in those packs. We must run deeper into the hills than
I expected."

This worried me no small amount. What about the plan to sustain our-
selves by hunting? We couldn't hunt and run like the dickens at the same
time. We had no traveling rations other than the cracked corn of the Antilleans.
In a few days we'd be reduced to skin and bones. What's more, only Kingston
Jack and his two men had rifles. The latter carried old Remingtons, whereas
Kingston Jack sported a Krag he must have purloined from some visiting
U.S. Marine in Colón. I carried only my empty Colt; Henry and Longbottom
were unarmed.

"Let's go," ordered Kingston Jack, pushing deeper into the bush.

Thoroughly alarmed but unable to think of any alternate course that might
shake our pursuers, I followed. In this region the cordillera ran east to west,
with spurs branching north and south toward the Caribbean and Pacific
coasts, respectively. Kingston Jack stayed on the crests, running the ridges
like a *cimaroon* of old. He followed a faint trace, one probably known
only to the runaway slaves fleeing their Spanish overlords. The trail wound
through stands of mahogany trees, conifers, and an occasional large, stately
cuipo tree, whose branches soared to the very top of the triple-canopy jungle.
Everywhere the jungle was perfumed with the heavy scent of the white-

flowered frangipani tree, which looked rather like a magnolia in full bloom. In the valleys below us, swift-flowing mountain streams laced their way through an unbroken wilderness of kapok, *tagua,* ficus, and cashew trees.

Despite the haste of our passage, the abundant wildlife of the Panamanian backcountry revealed itself. Herds of squealing peccaries bolted from our path as we pushed through the brush, an occasional specimen turning to grunt truculently at us before hurrying away. In the trees above, white-faced monkeys and flocks of quetzals, birds with plumages of vibrant greens and reds, hooted and squawked their disapproval at our intrusion into their domain. Through the heavy brush we caught sight of anteaters and tapirs, and once we heard the stuttering cough of an angry jaguar. The sound reminded me of the awesome power of El Diablo, and I prayed that the big cat had tastier prey to stalk. Through the occasional break in the dense canopy of leaves I saw huge harpy eagles, gliding silently through the tropical air in search of monkeys to eat.

We pushed on all that day until dusk fell and the way was totally obscured in darkness. I figured we had gone perhaps fifteen miles through exceedingly rough terrain. We had not caught sight of our pursuers since the morning, but we had no reason to think we had shaken them. Kingston Jack sent one of his men back down the trail to act as a rear guard while the remainder of us foraged about for some provender. We looked for berries or the ubiquitous Panamanian breadfruit, but finding none we curled up to sleep on empty stomachs. I drifted off with a single thought in my mind: how long could we endure this uneven contest?

The answer came with the dawn. A booming shot split the morning calm, sending a thousand fruit bats squeaking into the air from the branches above our heads. In a flash we were awake, the Blacks hastily chambering rounds in their rifles. Then I heard the beat of feet on the soft earth and our rear guard appeared at a dead run.

"The Colombians are coming! They must have started on the trail before dawn!"

"How far behind you?" demanded Kingston Jack.

"No farther than I can shoot this rifle," the man replied.

That was a quarter of a mile, a half at the most. We had to be off. Kingston Jack bawled out his order of march—his two men to the rear, we Americans in the middle, and he in the vanguard. Then we were off.

The foliage if anything became thicker as we went, but it did not dampen the shouts from our pursuers. "Run, *yanqui* pigs!" they called. "We will follow you to your deaths!"

I had no doubt they intended to do just that, and the thought spurred me into a dogtrot. I took the lead now with Kingston Jack and Henry keeping up quite readily, but after three miles of this Longbottom began to flag.

"We need to slow down," he huffed, sinking to the ground.

Behind us came the sound of shots being exchanged between the rear guard and the Colombians. "Longbottom, either keep up or you'll spend the rest of your career in some Bogotá calaboose."

"Damn it all, Travers," Longbottom protested, "I'm doing my best, but my feet are blistering in these damned boots." He pointed to his duck-hunting oddities.

If Longbottom expected me to make some sort of suicidal last stand at this spot simply because he had torn up his feet in his ridiculous footgear, he was sadly mistaken. "There are a few principles of war they don't teach at West Point, Longbottom. A key one, for instance, is the rule that during retreats the devil takes the hindmost. Make sure you give my regards to our friends back there when they catch up with you. *Adiós.*"

With that I turned and started away. Longbottom pleaded behind me, "Travers, wait. You can't just desert me, for God's sake!"

I was intending to do exactly that when, to my utter amazement, Kingston Jack took pity on Longbottom. He put a hand on my shoulder to stay me and said, "Captain Travers, I have a plan. There is an old Spanish trail that once crossed the isthmus from Old Panama City to Portobelo. We're not too far from it."

Here he pointed through the foliage to a long ridge visible some five miles to the north. That far ridge ran parallel to the one we were on. I recalled that Shaler had talked of an old Spanish gold trail that crossed these hills.

"What's your point, Kingston Jack?"

"If we can get to that road before the Colombians, we can find mules. Campesinos still live along that old road in small villages. They do not like the Bogotá soldiers because they are tax collectors and thieves. Besides, the campesinos know me and will help us."

"Listen to him, Travers," beseeched Longbottom. "The only way I'll get out of this fix is to ride out."

I shook my head. "It won't work. The Colombians will just follow us down this ridge into the flatlands as we make our way over to that far ridge. If we're dragging you along, they'll overtake us for sure."

"No, they won't," insisted Kingston Jack. "You slip down the ridge here and I'll hide your trail. Make straight for the Portobelo road. Meanwhile, my men and I will lead the Colombians down this same path for a few more miles. When we're certain you have enough of a head start, we'll leave the trail for the lowlands too." With a twinkle in his eye, he added, "Only we'll go down the other side of the ridge. That will make the Colombians think we've decided to go south instead of north. After a few miles of that, I'll lead my men around the Colombians and back up this same ridge, then we'll cross over to the north side and join you on the far ridge."

"How will you find us in that trackless wilderness?" I protested. "Once we split up, we'll never see you again."

"Do not be concerned, Captain. I know these hills. If I say I will find you, I will do so."

"It might work, Fenny," allowed Henry.

I wasn't sure. After all, if Kingston Jack was so damned omnipotent, why had he needed our intervention to save him from a good old-fashioned lynching? I looked from him to the now-forlorn Longbottom and back. "Oh, all right," I conceded reluctantly. "It's worth a try, but don't fail to rejoin us because I'm out of ammunition. Without your rifles, we're defenseless."

Henry and I hauled Longbottom to his feet, and between the two of us we were able to support him tolerably well as we started our descent down the steep slope. Above us Kingston Jack used a small bough to smooth over the earth where we had trodden, then he carefully arranged dead leaves to cover any depressions we made in the soft soil. Once satisfied that our tracks were undetectable, he disappeared.

We gained the valley floor and struck out for the distant ridge across a boggy swamp. Our way was barred by a swift stream with steep banks and a muddy bottom. We proceeded with care, for these wetlands looked like the perfect abode for the dreaded fer-de-lance and bushmaster. As we waded into the stream, our passage was contested by a large, spotted ocelot on the far bank. The feline spat in our direction, then sullenly withdrew. When it was gone, we pressed forward, breasting the flow with difficulty. Thoroughly soaked and exhausted from keeping Longbottom's head above water, we gained the far bank. After a few minutes of precious rest, we staggered to our feet and headed north once more.

We reached the foot of the far ridge after an hour of painfully slogging through swamp grass with blades as sharp as honed bayonets. After an arduous climb up a slope slick with moss and mud, we mounted the crest.

Almost at the end of our endurance, we were overjoyed to find that just as Kingston Jack had promised, a respectable path ran along the crest of the ridge. Here and there were flagstones, strewn about randomly by the ravages of time. Clearly they had not been hauled to this place by Indians or apathetic campesinos. No, I was looking at the ruins of what could only be a work of the long-departed dons, a *camino real* of the Spanish Main. That meant we were indeed on the road to Portobelo, and since Kingston Jack had been accurate in that regard, perhaps he might also have been right about the possibility of securing mules along the way. Only that thought enabled us to summon the strength to hobble off to the northeast.

We had gone but a mile when Henry heard something. "Shh!" he cautioned us.

"What is it?" I demanded fretfully.

Henry waved away my question, instead standing quietly with his ear cocked in the direction we had been walking. "There it is again. I hear children laughing. They're somewhere up ahead."

Children? Why, that meant a village, just like Kingston Jack had promised. That in turn meant burros or maybe even a mule or two! By God, we were saved!

Galvanized by the prospect of salvation, we rushed forward until we rounded a bend. There we stopped in our tracks, our mouths hanging open slackly at what we saw. The "village" consisted of two dilapidated straw hovels, populated by a litter of naked mestizo children. A woman who looked like she was sixty, but in truth might have been but thirty, stood in the door of one of the hovels. She wore naught but a grimy skirt wrapped about her skinny loins. Her bare, pendulous breasts hung halfway to her waist. She gripped a clay pipe between her toothless gums, and at our appearance she put her hands on her hips and blew a great cloud of smoke as the children fluttered to her for protection.

I eyed this dismal encampment with dismay. The biggest animal in sight was a black goat, which baaed loudly and then scampered out of sight. "We're done for," I announced grimly.

Longbottom sank to the ground as despair overwhelmed him. It fell to Henry to advance and palaver with the hag for some grub. He showed her a few copper coins and she quickly got the idea. She hastily whipped up a wooden bowl full of maize porridge for each of us, then spooned out the food as fast as we ate it. When I flashed a piece of silver, she magically produced bananas and breadfruit as well.

We ate like pigs at the trough for as long as the food held out, then sat back in blissful surfeit. I must have dozed off, for the sudden chatter of children's voices close at hand roused me from a deep slumber. I sat up groggily just as Kingston Jack and his two men strode into sight.

"Ah, Captain Travers," he hailed me with a broad, white smile. "I see you have found food."

"Yep, but no pack animals. I reckon we'll have to walk out of here."

"That is no problem now. The soldiers are far from here. You are quite safe."

I produced more coins and the woman set out fare for our deliverers. Kingston Jack ate enough for two men, and when he'd had his fill he produced a fine cigar from the pocket of his shirt, lit it on an ember from the woman's hearth, and sat back contentedly. "We will rest here for the night and tomorrow head for Portobelo. Maybe there we can find a boat and slip back up the coast to Colón to get you on a ship for home."

That sounded fine to me. A good night's sleep, another meal in the morning, and then off to find safety. I was contemplating that happy thought when one of the naked urchins bolted into camp, terror evident in his eyes.

"¡Soldatos!" he shrilled, pointing in the direction from whence we had come.

"Soldiers?" I yelped. "But how could that be? You shook 'em, didn't you?"

"Yes, of course I did! I have no idea how they could have followed us so quickly—"

A low baying in the distance cut him off.

"Bloodhounds!" exclaimed Henry. "They must have had them all along but kept them muzzled until now! We never saw them earlier because the underbrush was so high."

"Damn!" swore Kingston Jack. "We must flee. Now!"

He didn't have to convince me. I was up and moving, stepping over the prostrate form of Longbottom in the process. Henry dragged the still-somnolent Longbottom to his feet and roused him enough to hurry him along in my wake. Kingston Jack's two men lingered behind, nervously fingering their Remingtons.

"Give us some time," Kingston Jack called to them over his shoulder as he darted along after us. Obediently, they scattered into the brush, determined to slow the pursuit.

My sleep had refreshed me, and I made good speed down the uneven path. As I hurried along, I noticed that the surrounding foliage was thinning a bit. Then a dull roaring sound came to my ears from somewhere up ahead.

"Kingston Jack! What's that noise?"

"The river!" he shouted in reply. "Keep going! You'll see!"

See I did, for the path suddenly terminated on the edge of a yawning chasm. Between us and the far side swung a pitifully narrow footbridge of woven hemp. Below us boiled an enormous river, easily ten times the size of the troublesome stream we had crossed earlier.

I hesitated before the bridge. "Go on!" ordered Kingston Jack. "The bridge is safe. My men will hold off the enemy."

As if to punctuate his words, wild gunfire broke out behind us. Bullets were whistling through the air now, and there was clearly no time to lose.

"I'll go first!" I blurted, and bolted for the swaying span. The bridge was no more than two parallel ropes for handrails and a stout hemp hawser beneath one's feet. Spindly cords connected the handrails to the hawser. The slightest misstep would send me hurtling into the boiling white water below. Only the direst of circumstances could have driven me out onto such a frail contraption—such as the present circumstances, for instance. Holding my breath, I seized the handrails and edged forward.

The firing grew louder now, and I felt the bridge swing alarmingly as first Henry and then Longbottom crept out behind me. "Hurry! Hurry!" Kingston Jack urged as he anxiously looked over his shoulder.

The sound of shooting was quickly getting nearer. From the corner of my eye I saw Kingston Jack's two men scamper into view. Both were wounded, and one had lost his rifle. Then a fusillade erupted from the foliage, dropping both of them in the dust and sending Kingston Jack fleeing onto the flimsy bridge at full tilt.

"Run for it!" he screamed at the top of his lungs. "They're on us!"

He was right. As I redoubled my efforts to reach the far side of the chasm, Comandante Reyes, at the head of his men and the yelping bloodhounds, emerged into view. He saw the four of us floundering away on the rope bridge, the river below, and instantly realized that we had no chance of reaching the far side alive. I heard him bark out his orders, and then the woodsmen stood aside, pulling the hounds off with them. The soldiers stepped to the fore and shouldered their Mausers. At a command from Comandante Reyes, they began pouring a deadly fire in our direction. I felt a stinging blow to my thigh that knocked me face forward, ripping the handrails from my grasp. For a sickening instant I balanced above the raging river with no support whatsoever, and then, just as I started to slide from the hawser, I managed to hook an arm through one of the connecting strands to halt my fall.

"Help! Henry, save me, for the love of God!"

Henry had his own hands full, however, for as I dangled I craned my neck around far enough to see that all of my companions were similarly clinging to the hawser, twisting wildly as they attempted to dodge the hot fire from the Colombians. Our forward progress thus arrested, escape was impossible. We were pinned in place and certain to be picked off one by one!

It was at this moment that Comandante Reyes revealed his truly nefarious nature. "Cease fire!" he cried. Turning to Sergeant Gómez, he snapped, "Finish these *yanqui* pigs and the black bandits."

Gómez grinned wickedly and waved a hand toward the bridge. At this, the trackers, heretofore only amused spectators, produced hatchets and sprang forward. They began to hack feverishly at the bridge's hemp moorings. For a second I could only blink uncomprehendingly, until their diabolic purpose became evident.

I screamed in panic. "They're going to cut the bridge loose!" Shooting, apparently, was too gentle an end for us to suit Comandante Reyes. Instead, he intended to send us on a dizzying swing against the far side of the chasm. If the force of our bodies striking solid rock at high speed didn't kill us outright, then the fall into the river far below certainly would. We were helpless prey. I realized forlornly that this uneven contest would be over as soon as the last fiber of hemp was chopped through.

Kingston Jack, however, had managed to hold onto his Krag; it was slung around his neck as he hung from the hawser. I saw it, and hope surged through me once more. "Shoot, for God's sake!" I screamed.

He nodded in reply. Wrapping a leg around the hawser for support, he unslung the Krag and drew a careful bead on Sergeant Gómez as he supervised our destruction. Kingston Jack squeezed the trigger, and Gómez jerked convulsively, then fell in a twitching heap. He was alive, but from the way he clasped his beefy arm, it was clear that the shot had at least slowed him down.

For this act of bravado, Kingston Jack was immediately subjected to the concentrated fire of the enraged Colombians. A torrent of lead plucked at his clothes and tore great chunks of hemp from the bridge all around him. He was doomed, I knew. No sooner had the thought entered my mind than Kingston Jack let out a great scream and dropped from the bridge, turning slowly head over heels as he fell. He struck the water and then disappeared beneath the raging torrent.

Now the trackers sprang back to their task, the bridge shuddering with every blow. The strained cords groaned and popped until first one of the handrails fell away from its anchorage and then the other. Now only the hawser connected the two banks of the chasm, and the trackers turned their full attention to it. Their blades flew with a maniacal determination, and strand after strand of hemp popped loose under their ceaseless blows. As fewer and fewer cords remained to bear the weight of the bridge, the structure seemed to emit low groans of protest and commence a terminal sag. In no time, only a single strand remained.

Comandante Reyes stood on the edge of the chasm, laughing uproariously as perdition loomed before us. *"¡Adiós, yanquis!"* he called in farewell.

"This is it, Fenny!" cried Henry.

I had time only to howl out, "You son of a bitch, Reyes!" before an ax blade flashed in the sun and we all pitched into the vortex below.

13

I hit the water with a thunderous crash that seemed to pop both my eardrums. The shock of the impact was so awful that at first I feared I had struck some rocks. It wasn't until I plunged far below the surface that I realized I still had the use of my limbs. Immediately I started kicking madly for the light above, frantic to regain the air. I breached like a harpooned whale and drew in a great breath, only to be promptly submerged once more by the ferocious current. Struggling for breath and terror stricken by the river's awesome power, I managed to resurface and cast desperately about for something to support me. A log dashed straight for me and would have staved in my head had I not dodged it in the nick of time. As it shot past me, I grabbed one of its stunted branches, and like a vaquero leaping into the saddle of a wild mustang, I hauled myself up on the log and held on for dear life.

The white water tried to sweep me from my perch, but I hung on grimly as the log careened downstream between vast boulders and around underwater snags. None of these obstacles was able to throw me from my saddle, though. I was just on the verge of getting my panic under control when I noticed something odd. The thunderous roar of the river seemed if anything to be growing louder.

Louder? I wondered. That seemed damned queer, unless . . . Then the awful realization hit me. I abandoned my log in a flash, striking out wildly for the nearest shore. The roar I had heard was a waterfall, by God, and I was nearly upon it! I battled futilely against the current as it swept me to the very edge of an immense cascade. I watched in horror as the big log teetered at the brink and then plunged out of sight.

"Oh, God! Oh, God!" I screamed into the foam. "This can't be the end! It can't beeeee . . . "

And then I was hurtled into space.

After an awful drop that seemed to last for minutes, I dimly realized that I was still somehow alive and that I was again far underwater. With the last ounce of my remaining strength, I kicked out feebly. Fortunately, the force of the current seemed to have abated, and even in my diminished state I was able to surface. Weak and sore all over, I paddled to the shore.

"Hello, Captain!"

Why, it was Kingston Jack! "You're alive!" I cried, amazed.

Indeed he was, standing on the bank as saucy as you please but cradling a bloody hand through which a steel-jacketed Mauser bullet had passed.

"Aye, I'm alive. I've got a broken bone or two in this hand, but I'll be fine."

"And you saved your rifle!" I exulted, for with his good hand he grasped the sturdy Krag. Around his waist was an ammunition belt with extra cartridges.

"I thought that river would tear my arm from its socket, but I intended to die rather than let go of this beauty," he said proudly.

"Any sign of Henry?" I asked anxiously.

Kingston Jack shook his head sadly. "No, nor Captain Longbottom."

No loss there, but Henry was a genuine friend. I would miss him badly. I was just thinking how badly when a high-pitched scream interrupted my reveries. I glanced up just in time to see the better part of a tree launch itself over the lip of the falls with two human figures enmeshed in its branches.

"It's them!" sang out Kingston Jack as the tree hit the water below with a sickening splash. I dove in after Henry, while Kingston Jack lit out after Longbottom as best his injured hand would let him. Henry was unconscious when I got to him and didn't stir until I pulled him ashore.

Longbottom was wide awake, though, and babbling nonstop. "We got caught in that tree and it got hung up at the edge of the falls for what seemed an eternity. My God, it was awful."

For a few minutes it looked as though Henry might have been seriously injured, but then he groaned and painfully sat up. "I guess we made it," he said faintly.

"I'm afraid that still remains to be seen," I replied tersely. I coaxed him to his feet as quickly as I could, for I had no idea when our pursuers might appear once more. In ten minutes Henry was able to walk, and Longbottom had managed to get a grip on his frayed nerves. I used that time to bandage Kingston Jack's hand with strips of cloth torn from my shirt. My thigh wound fortunately proved to be nothing but a nick, but between it and my still-tender shoulder, I was looking quite the worse for wear.

Taking stock of our precarious situation, I said, "The way I see things, we have a party of hostiles between us and the Portobelo trail. That means the only way to the coast is down this river."

Kingston Jack nodded his agreement. "If we're going to get out, Captain, it'll have to be by water."

"Then the river it is. By the way, Kingston Jack, where exactly on the coast does this river emerge?" Once I knew that, you see, I could calculate the time it would take us to haul ourselves back to Colón.

The Antillean smiled brightly and said, "Ah, but I have no idea."

"Then why are you smiling, damnit?" I demanded crossly.

"Because this will be an adventure, Captain Travers, and we will be in it together."

I looked to Henry, and he just shrugged. Maybe the bullet wound or the drop over the falls, or both, had addled Kingston Jack. Or maybe he was just addled all the time. Whatever the reason, he seemed in high good humor about being stranded in a howling wilderness on the banks of an uncharted river.

"That's just dandy," was all I could muster. Turning to Henry, I said, "We'll have to lash together a raft."

Henry looked around. "I've made a raft or two in my time, Fenny. We don't have any tools, but we can take some of these dead logs that have gathered below the falls and tie them together with vines. It won't be much to look at, but we should be able to launch a right serviceable craft."

"Then let's do it."

Kingston Jack and even Longbottom pitched in, and within the hour we had a big, flat raft tethered to the banks. We had even managed to fashion some poles from the bamboo trees that proliferated along the riverbank. They would greatly ease the task of guiding our craft to the sea.

Henry gave the vessel a final inspection, tightened a knot here and ordered another log lashed there, and when he was satisfied that this was as good as we were likely to do with the materials at hand, we all went aboard and cast off.

The river broadened and slowed beyond the falls, but the current was sufficiently brisk to ensure rapid progress. The muddy waters coursed first through mist-shrouded highland groves populated by screaming bands of long-tailed marmosets, and then on to gentle bottomlands where herds of placid tapirs wallowed languidly on the mudbanks and an occasional alligator watched our passage with unblinking eyes. At night we tethered the raft to an overhanging tree and used Kingston Jack's rifle to down an unlucky tapir or two. The eating was fine and the pace was rapid enough. All would have been ideal had not the true terror of the tropics raised its ugly head.

Disease. First it was Longbottom. His fatigue from the march never truly left him. Slowly his exhaustion gave way to lassitude accompanied by a worsening fever and sudden chills. In three days' time we all recognized his symptoms for what they were. Longbottom had malaria, and without help he would eventually lose consciousness and perhaps die. If he recovered he might never be the same as before—not, of course, that Longbottom at his best had ever been much of a prize.

As for me, I had suffered scrapes going over the falls, and those scrapes, plus the gash in my thigh, had become infected over the passage of days. Ugly red welts covered my arms and torso, and now pain was beginning to throb through my body at each push on my barge pole. By our fourth day on the river, Longbottom was delirious and I was showing signs of joining him.

Henry and Kingston Jack recognized our danger and redoubled their efforts to reach the sea, although the stolid Antillean was himself but a one-handed man. At the end of the fourth day, we decided to forgo docking for the evening and instead pushed forward through the night so as to hasten our arrival at the Atlantic.

Dawn of the fifth day found us mercifully at the river's mouth. Ahead was a low, swampy delta, and beyond that was a line of breakers marking where the muddy river met the azure hues of the sea. The raft could not breast the swells of the open ocean, so Kingston Jack made for the bank. There we would consider our predicament and decide our next move. He and Henry grounded the raft upon a shell-strewn strand and helped Longbottom and me ashore.

Just inland from our landing point lay a deserted Spanish fort of some kind, perhaps a blockhouse guarding the approaches to the river. It looked as though it had been deserted for centuries. Creepers and vines snaked up its limestone facade, and startled bats fluttered from the darkened confines of its guano-whitened turrets.

The deserted fort seemed just the place to lie up until we had settled upon a course of action. Henry and Kingston Jack hastily constructed a litter for Longbottom, and with me following along as best I could, we entered the silent bastion. In the interior courtyard, furtive iguanas scurried along stone flagstones, and two startled deer took flight and escaped through a gap in the walls. Whatever troops had once walked these battlements were long gone, probably carried away by pestilence or wounds. I suspected that damned few of them had ever again laid eyes on sunny Spanish shores.

Henry and Kingston Jack settled Longbottom on the worn flagstones and eyed me expectantly. "Well, Captain," asked Kingston Jack, "do we go on with him or leave him here?"

I looked down on the fast-fading Longbottom. I had no love for the dolt, and he had proven himself time and again to be an insufferably pompous ass. Leaving him to his fate in this tumbled-down ruin was mighty tempting, yet I knew I would lose face in front of Henry by cravenly abandoning a fellow officer to the cruel elements. So, as much as it would have gratified me to toss Longbottom aside like so much excess baggage, I hesitated. "How far is Portobelo?"

"Maybe thirty miles down the coast," estimated Kingston Jack.

In our condition I knew that was a three-day walk. Longbottom would never make it.

"And how far to Colón?"

Kingston Jack shrugged, for in truth he was lost. "Maybe forty or fifty miles in the other direction."

Those distances were certainly grounds for abandoning Longbottom. Why, we would wear ourselves out trying to haul his carcass back to civilization. I was just about to say exactly that when Henry spoke up.

"If Captain Longbottom can't go on, Fenny, I can stay put with him. You and Kingston Jack can go on up the coast and return with help."

I nodded as though I were seriously considering this. Henry had evidently overlooked the fact that the authorities most likely to be in a position to render us any assistance on this coast were actively seeking our hides at this very moment. No, Longbottom would have to fend for himself. Oh, I'd doctor up the report of his demise to the War Department, of course. I'd make it seem as though I'd rendered him every possible assistance but that ultimately Longbottom had just slipped off when we weren't looking. I'd speculate that Longbottom had probably decided not to burden us any longer. Who can figure out how a man thinks when his brain is racked with fever, eh? The details were all a bit fuzzy, but I was certain that I'd concoct a tale that would leave me completely blameless. What's more, if I inflated my own role to sufficiently heroic proportions, I just might induce poor Longbottom's widow-to-be, the lovely Fiona, to pay me a visit to express her gratitude. Yes, a few private sessions with the well-endowed Fiona might make this miserable trek worth the trouble.

"Henry, your brave offer notwithstanding, I'm afraid we can't afford to allow you to stay behind. We'll just have to fix Longbottom up here as best we can . . . ," I began, but I never finished the sentence.

As he watched me fall silent, a look of concern came over Henry's face. "Fenny, are you all right?"

It was only when I didn't answer that his eyes followed my gaze. Then he too fell mute. On the ramparts above us stood twenty-five savages, some with bows drawn taut and the rest with blowpipes leveled.

"Don't move or we are all dead," warned Kingston Jack in a low voice. "Those are Cunas."

14

"Cunas?" I gasped.

Shaler had warned us to steer clear of these hombres, and now I saw why. They were as rough looking a set of customers as I had ever laid eyes upon, and that included the battle-mad bodyguards of the sultan of Jolo. The Cunas were short, like Apaches, for none of the silent warriors above us stood more than five and a half feet in height. Yet their heavily muscled torsos and the lurid tattoos on their arms and chests created an aura of chained power ready to be unleashed at any instant. Their attire consisted of no more than palm-frond penis sheathes tucked into leather thongs tied about their lithe waists, a getup that left their testicles freely exposed. Their savage regalia was set off with bands of beautifully wrought copper fastened about bulging biceps and upper calves, and small golden nose plates that dangled from their septums.

Several of the Cunas sported feathered headdresses of quetzal feathers, with the odd hawk, owl, and raven plume thrown in for good measure. I took these fellows to be the chiefs, and as things turned out, I was right. It was the Cuna with the grandest headdress of all who finally spoke.

"Spanish man. This is Cuna land," he snarled in pidgin Spanish. "Spanish man die."

That was it; we were goners. Tensing for the sting of the arrows these beasts would probably loose at us at any moment, I slowly edged sideways to shelter behind Henry. If I could just survive the first volley, I might be able to sprint back to the raft and shove off before these hellions could take me. I was measuring the distance to the fort's front gate when Kingston Jack called out to the Indians. To my utter surprise, he seemed to know them!

"El Tigre," he called, "these are my friends. Amigos, *sí?* They are not Spaniards."

Not knowing just what Kingston Jack's relationship with this crowd was, I was uncertain whether being identified as a friend of his was good or bad. El Tigre—the Tiger—seemed wholly unmoved by the Antillean's entreaty and merely repeated accusingly, "Spanish man."

"No Spanish man," insisted Kingston Jack urgently for he knew we had but seconds to live. "We *cimaroon. Cimaroon!*" He pointed excitedly at his black skin and then to that of Henry. Cimaroons, I knew, were African slaves who had fled into the hills to escape from their Spanish masters. I gathered that the slaves who had escaped into Cuna lands over the past few centuries had done the natives no irreparable harm, or else Kingston Jack would not be making such a point of his dusky complexion.

Kingston Jack seemed to be making some headway, or at least he was until Tiger fixed his angry gaze upon Longbottom and me. "They Spanish!" he declared. "Enemy. Cuna kill them!"

"No Spanish!" objected Kingston Jack strenuously. "Tiger, these are American fellows. North man." Here Kingston Jack gestured vaguely in the direction of Mexico, as if making an understandable argument to the Indians, but I could tell from the chief's smoldering eyes that the Antillean was not getting his point across very well at all. Longbottom and I were white, and in these parts that evidently was a major character flaw.

Tiring of Kingston Jack's palavering, Tiger nodded his head, and a nearby archer drew a bead on my heart. The bow bent as the string was drawn to its fullest extent, and I tensed for the cruel bite of the arrowhead when suddenly Henry stepped forward, completely shielding my body with his.

"They gonna have to go through me to get to you, Fenny," he vowed stolidly.

"Bless you," I gasped, not mentioning that I had been just about to throw myself behind him at that very instant.

The bowman hesitated, apparently reluctant to slay a *cimaroon*. He looked to his feathered leader, who in turn crossed his arms as he considered this novel proposition. An escaped Black willingly shielding a Spaniard? Never before had he seen such a thing.

Kingston Jack seized on the confusion of the moment to resume his explanation at the top of his lungs. "Tiger, he no Spanish man! He *amigo!*" Then in an inspired gesture he pulled off my hat and displayed my golden locks. "See! His hair is golden. *¿Sí? ¡D'oro!*"

The Cunas began murmuring among themselves at this, and I sensed turmoil go through their ranks. I was certain there were blond Spaniards. Hell, I'd seen dozens of 'em in Cuba. The important thing, though, was that apparently these ruffians had never before laid eyes on a blond human being, and the sight seemed to disturb them considerably.

Completely unknown to us at the moment was the fact that Kingston Jack had fortuitously blundered across one of the latent superstitions of the Cunas—their profound reverence of albinos. Not knowing this, all we saw was some hurried grunting between Tiger and his fellows, then inscrutable gesticulations in my direction, all followed by more frantic conversation. The Cunas didn't know what to make of me, you see. Clearly I was a strange beast, and most probably a dangerous one, yet exotic enough to require a trip to the reigning shaman to determine my fate.

"You go Cuna land," decided Tiger. "All you go. Go now!"

And go we did. With a bloodcurdling shriek the Cunas leaped from their perches and set upon Longbottom and me. We were bound securely head and foot, trussed to the poles from our own raft, and then carried to the bank of the river like two pigs on their way to a communal roasting. Three large canoes, which the Cuna referred to as *cayucos,* were concealed beneath fresh-cut boughs on the riverbank. The *cayucos* were fashioned from hollowed-out cedar trunks that had been equipped with outriggers. They seemed sturdy enough and quite capable of navigating the shallow coastal waters. Henry and Kingston Jack remained unbound but closely watched as they were escorted along in our wake. Longbottom and I were unceremoniously dumped in the bottom of Tiger's *cayuco,* the biggest of the three. Henry and Kingston Jack were ordered to get in and take their seats, and we were off, our chanting captors paddling furiously for points unknown.

The three *cayucos* emerged from the mouth of the river and headed into the wide Caribbean. The Cunas paddled due east, keeping the coast in view to our right. They paddled steadily all that day and well into the night, beaching their craft only for a few hours of hurried shut-eye. They were awake before dawn, paddling ever eastward. After the sun sank on the second day, we passed lights on the coast. This, I surmised, was Portobelo.

The Cunas slipped unmolested past Portobelo in the dark, and then rounded a vast headland which I knew from my studies of the maps provided by McAllister could only be Punta Manzanillo. Beyond Punta Manzanillo lay the Darien wilderness, a primeval forest into which few white men had ever ventured and from which even fewer had returned. Recalling as best I could what Shaler had said about these heathens, I surmised that they were making for the chain of low-lying barrier islands that hugged the Darien coast from beyond Punta Manzanillo all the way to the distant Gulf of Darien. This was the Comarca de San Blas, the stronghold of the proud and haughty Cunas, a race that had successfully rebuffed every attempted Spanish incursion. Once we were safely spirited into the Cuna domain, I thought forlornly, our already slim chances for escape would dwindle to nonexistent.

When the sun rose on the third day of our journey into captivity, I began to feel the effects of the increasing infection in my body. My brain was racked with fever, and I lay in the bottom of the canoe drenched in sweat as Longbottom lay nearby shaking with chills. Oh, we were a pair, all right, yet throughout our passage our captors barely cast a glance our way. I could hardly blame them for ignoring me, I suppose, since they couldn't be expected to know the difference between a white man at the peak of health and one at death's doorstep. But Longbottom's malaria was so bad now that he moaned and tossed endlessly. His violent shivering in the midday heat was a dead giveaway about his deplorable condition. The Cunas, though, offered no aid or comfort; all they did was paddle inexorably onward.

If it hadn't been for my utter misery, I might have marveled at the breathtaking beauty that was unfolding all around me. The weather was majestic, as it often is in Panama right before the November rainy season. Only a few soft clouds on the far horizon marred the vista as the *cayucos* coursed across aquamarine shallows. Below us were coral reefs of immense proportions over which glided schools of brilliantly hued tropical fish, eels, and the occasional sea tortoise. Farther out beyond the reefs lurked the big Atlantic tarpon, while in the air above soared pelicans and gulls, the boldest of which swooped down to inspect the *cayucos* for a possible meal.

It was late afternoon when I noticed a dot on the horizon. At first I paid it no mind, since I had been slipping in and out of hallucinations since noon. When the dot didn't disappear of its own accord, however, I awkwardly sat up and took notice. It was a real island, all right, and as we neared it I saw more islands beyond it in the distance. The Cunas, chattering excitedly now, paddled directly for the looming island.

The *cayucos* landed on the sandy beach in the shade of palms that reached almost to the water's edge. The warriors leaped ashore with shrieks of triumph to announce the capture of their prisoners. The women and children waiting on the beach, however, took one look at the white and black faces of the *wakers*—the strangers—and ran screaming for the shelter of their palm-thatched huts. All except one woman, that is. This gal held her ground and studied me closely as I was dragged ashore, and if my eyes were not deceiving me, there was no trace of revulsion in her gaze.

I had no time to exchange pleasantries with my admirer, for immediately a crowd of excited warriors gathered around. Brown fingers yanked at my hair and prodded my white skin, and then Longbottom and I were hauled from the beach and carried into the surprisingly congested village. Living on small islands as they did, the Cuna had to use every square foot of available living space, you see. Most of the island was given over to cassava fields and palm groves, and the acreage available for habitations was necessarily restricted. The village was laid out on a circular plan about a sandy interior plaza. On the perimeter of the plaza perched a fringe of rounded, palm-thatched huts, each one built only inches from its neighbor, and the whole ring was broken only by the single gateway through which we had passed.

In the center of the plaza stood a large structure on stilts, which, judging from the numerous warriors it disgorged upon our approach, I guessed to be the bachelor house of the village. Near the bachelor house was a smaller hut and before it several sturdy poles were embedded in the sand. Each pole was twice the height of a man and as thick around as a hogshead. Demonic figures carved into the poles gave them a sinister look, and I noted worriedly that the sand at the foot of each pole was blackened with the ashes of past fires.

The boisterous warriors circled us ominously. Some began blowing on conch shells, while others made a hideous racket with reed flutes and small, flat drums. To this din was added their otherworldly refrains until the noise reached an infernal crescendo. Just as I thought the clamor might unhinge my fevered brain and drive me into howling insanity, the cacophony suddenly stopped. In the utter silence that followed, a figure stepped from the small hut. I blinked twice and then shook my head. Clearly, my fever had overborne my senses, for standing before me was one of the weirdest sights ever beheld by mortal eyes.

It was a wizened old codger, one so old and wrinkled that I was certain he had managed to put a full century behind him. He was decked out in the obligatory headdress of quetzal feathers and sported the largest gold nose plate of the entire lot, an enormous sheet of metal half the size of a tin canteen. He was tattooed from head to foot with garish designs, which no doubt represented the unseen demon deities that these folks worshiped. Bowed by the weight of his years, the old fellow supported himself on a polished staff of black palm as he shambled forward across the dusty plaza. The head of the cane, I noted with distress, was carved in the shape of a batlike gargoyle.

The ancient one wore a necklace thick with what I first took to be small white seashells. It wasn't until he drew closer that I saw they were teeth—human teeth, hundreds of 'em, each drilled clear through and strung like so many pearls. Oh, he was horrible to behold, and had I the power to do so, I would have run screaming from his presence. The thing that riveted me to the spot, however, other than my bonds, that is, was the fact that the old man was as white as snow—he was an albino! Long hair, the color and consistency of bleached cotton, hung in limp strands down his shrunken shoulders. His wrinkled skin was so translucent that the purplish veins were clearly visible beneath the surface. His eyes were weak and rheumy, and pink like those of a pet rabbit. Yet they held power, for they flashed in my direction and I involuntarily recoiled in horror.

Tiger drew himself up erect and began gibbering at the old fellow in the Tule tongue, with Kingston Jack translating as best he could. "Tiger hails Great Turtle, the *nele,* the all-powerful medicine man, the one who knows the lore of the Tule people."

With the preliminaries out of the way, Tiger launched into the circumstances of our capture. I didn't need Kingston Jack to interpret Tiger's meaning for me when the war chief yanked several strands of hair from my scalp and handed them to the *nele.*

Great Turtle studied my locks for a moment or two, and squinted up at my blue eyes. Then, in a soft, barely audible voice, one cracking with age and decay, the *nele* spoke. Kingston Jack interpreted. "You got big trouble, Captain. Great Turtle says you are not a moon child, an albino like him. He says he has seen people like you on these shores before, from big ships that could not cross the reef. He says you have no special magic, and . . ." Here Kingston Jack gulped and fell silent.

"And what?" I demanded, alarmed enough by the *nele*'s utterances to have temporarily thrown off the effects of my fever.

"He says you and Captain Longbottom must die like all Spaniards who have ever found their way to these islands."

"And you? What about you?"

"I can go, as can Henry. We are *cimaroons,* as I have told you. We are not a threat to these people. I'm . . . I'm sorry, my friend."

Sorry? I raged. Not half as sorry as I was, by God. Was this what it had all come down to? Had I traveled around the world and courted death on a dozen battlefields only to die like a dog on this flea-bitten speck of an island? And at the direction of a pink-eyed octogenarian albino the size of a twelve-year-old? By Christ, the indignity of it all was galling beyond endurance! I wanted to scream and cry, to run looking for mercy. I struggled to speak, to find the words to make these heathens see that what they were proposing was nothing less than cold-blooded murder. When I found my tongue, though, the only word I could utter was, "When?"

"Tomorrow. When the sun is high. Tiger has been told to kill both of you himself."

15

Comarca de San Blas, Panama
August 1903

It was a night I shall long remember. Longbottom and I were fastened with rawhide cords to the thick poles in the middle of the plaza. The warriors kindled a great blaze and then commenced to dance in long, undulating lines around us. As they danced, they bellowed out songs of wars long past, and of their profound pleasure about the coming extinction of the two *wakers* on the morrow.

It was damned hard on my nerves to have these leaping, tattooed savages swirling around me all night. Oh, they shrieked and cavorted wildly, all the while quaffing gourds filled with *chicha,* their native beer made from fermented plantains and cane juice. As the heady brew worked its magic on the Cunas, an occasional brute broke from the mass to threaten me with an upraised war club.

As the level of violence increased by the minute, I wondered whether I would survive to see the dawn. What made it all the worse was that Longbottom, hanging slackly in his bonds in the throes of a fever-induced stupor, could share none of my terror. I never thought I'd envy a man in a coma, but I did that terrible night, especially when one tipsy hellion loosed an arrow into the pole directly above my head. His shaft struck so close to my head that it nearly parted my hair, and the Cunas roared with delight.

Another reveler charged forward with a lance at the ready, plunging the tip into the pole so close to my flank that he actually drew blood. I howled and cried and cursed a blue streak at my assailant. My antics, though, seemed only to drive my tormentors to new heights of devilish merriment, and soon I was dodging a rain of hurled clubs and assorted brickbats. I was battered by this fusillade, torn and bruised so much that I thought the trauma alone would be the end of me. Longbottom suffered his share of punishment at my side, but unconsciously, for he smiled dreamily as a stone-headed ax opened a nasty gash from the crown of his skull all the way down to his ear. He looked positively contented as blood spurted from his jagged wound, drenching him in streams of scarlet.

Mercifully, our captors eventually tired of these diversions. One by one, and then by groups, they succumbed to the rigors of their exertions, retiring to the *casa grande,* as they termed the bachelor house, to sleep off their intoxication and to await my demise. Finally I was alone, sobbing at the starry sky above as I hung from the thongs that held me like a sheep awaiting slaughter.

I must have drifted off at last, for the sun was high when I was nudged awake by the sharp jab of a javelin in my ribs. I awoke to see Tiger, his face painted a garish vermillion, staring hard at me. He grunted a few commands and I was unbound. I had no time to rub life back into my constricted limbs, however, for I was immediately prodded away by a corporal's guard of five sullen Cunas. Through the village gate we went and down toward the beach as the entire village trailed behind to watch the show. Longbottom was carried along as well, slung like a sack of oats over the shoulder of a particularly robust Cuna.

At the beach we were greeted by the repulsive sight of Great Turtle stripped stark naked. He was smeared with vermillion from head to toe, and in his hand gleamed an ancient Spanish cutlass. I knew with one glance that this was to be the instrument of our death. Henry and Kingston Jack were there too, dismay written all over their faces.

"Kingston Jack," I cried in one last attempt to avoid the inevitable as I was hauled before Great Turtle. "For God's sake, do something! These people are crazy!"

Kingston Jack shook his head sadly. "There is nothing I can do, Captain Travers."

Henry, tears in his eyes, confirmed this. "We tried, Fenny, we tried. We told the Great Turtle that our government would give him much gold if the white captains were released unharmed. He laughed at us. He said their laws were more important than our gold, and that their laws must always be obeyed."

The orderly administration of Cuna justice was damned little solace to me at the moment, and I said so in a screaming tirade to everyone within earshot, but all for naught. As I ranted against my fate, I was spread-eagled on the sand and immobilized with lianas, vine ropes, tied to palm stakes.

"What the hell are they going to do to me?" I sobbed, nearly out of my mind with fear now as the climactic moment was fast approaching.

Henry looked away and could not answer, but Kingston Jack, feeling that it would be an act of kindness to tell me what was about to unfold, said quietly, "Captain Travers, they are going to cut out your heart while you are still alive."

The piercing shriek that reverberated in his ears told Kingston Jack that I had not taken this information in quite the manner he had intended. When I managed to stop gibbering hysterically, I cried out in horror, "Cut out my heart? For God's sake, stop them! In the name of sweet Jesus, you must stop them!"

But Kingston Jack could only cast his eyes downward and step back. He was powerless to intervene in this matter, and he knew it. Now Tiger came forward stonily, chanting a keening song that I took to be a lament of some sort. As he sang, he looked to Great Turtle, who promptly handed him the wicked Spanish cutlass. Tiger raised the blade to the sun, calling, no doubt, for the aid of some guardian spirits to strengthen his hand as he dispatched the *wakers* to the land of the dead.

When his prayer was over, Tiger straddled me. His face was a mask of pure hatred, and I knew that he would not be stayed until his bloody task was done. Grasping the handle of the cutlass with two hands, he raised the blade high above his head. There he stopped, poised to plunge the killing blade downward and into my exposed chest. I heard Tiger inhale deeply, stiffening his sinews for the fatal strike. I closed my eyes and waited for the blinding pain that would signal my departure from this world.

It never came. Instead an excited shouting rang out, and then an angry roar from a hundred warrior throats.

I opened my eyes. "What the hell is going on?" I cried.

"It's the Colombians, Captain!" shouted Kingston Jack. "They're here!"

He pointed out to sea, and I craned my neck around as best I could to follow his finger. Beyond the white line that defined the island's sheltering reef some four hundred yards off the beach, I saw the shape of a steam-driven trawler. It was perhaps a half mile away, heading toward land and bearing down on a lone *cayuco*. The canoe was making for shore as fast as its paddles could propel it. I took in the scene with a glance and immediately recognized two things: first, the canoe was filled with Cuna children; second, they would never reach the safety of the reef before the trawler was upon them.

"They're slavers!" exclaimed Kingston Jack.

"Slavers?" I echoed uncomprehendingly. "What the devil do you mean, man? Talk straight, damnit. This is no time for riddles."

"It's like I said, Captain," explained Kingston Jack. "They're slavers. Comandante Reyes sends slaving raids out from Colón to capture young Indians along the Darien coast. The captives are hauled off to work on the banana plantations of Bocas del Toro, way up north by Costa Rica. The Colombians sell the children to the plantation owners, you see. That is one of the ways Reyes enriches himself."

The Cunas evidently realized what was afoot, for dozens of them took to their *cayucos,* paddling furiously to head off the Colombians before they could overtake the canoe filled with children. I could see, however, that these would-be rescuers had no hope of stopping the Colombians. Tiger was the most vocal of all as he hurled imprecations in broken Spanish at the fast-approaching trawler.

"His boy is in that canoe," explained Kingston Jack. The tears of frustration streaming down Tiger's painted cheeks were the first hint I'd seen that a flicker of humanity burned within his warrior breast.

It was Henry who first saw the opportunity that this dramatic change of circumstance offered to us. "Fenny," he urged, "you can stop the Colombians. You can pick them off from the beach."

At first I could scarcely believe my ears. When I spoke, it was with tones of incredulity. "You want me to help these savages? Henry, I don't know if you've been paying close attention to what's been happening to me. Tiger here was just moments from plucking my still-beating heart from my chest. I rather think he intended to gulp it down for his breakfast as I expired miserably before his eyes. You'll excuse me if I don't seem anxious to save his son from slavery, won't you? For my money, the Colombians can have the son, the father, and the whole damned tribe to boot."

"No, Fenny," insisted Henry, "don't you see? You're a crack shot with a Krag. If you save his son, Tiger might save you! It's the only chance you have, but you've got to be quick about it. Those children have only minutes left."

Now I saw his logic. By thunder, he was right! It was the only way. My eyes flew wide with sudden hope. "Tell them to cut me loose, Kingston Jack," I ordered. "Henry, get me Kingston Jack's Krag, and make sure it's loaded."

Henry ran off to the village where our belongings had been stored. Meanwhile Kingston Jack began remonstrating with Tiger in Spanish and Tule, explaining Henry's inspired plan and repeatedly pointing from me to the fast-approaching Colombians. At first Tiger balked, as did Great Turtle, but as the Colombians neared the doomed canoe, Tiger weakened. His paternal instinct overbore his hatred for *wakers*. He swung about and added his voice to Kingston Jack's before Great Turtle. The *nele* fell silent before their united appeal, and then after a deliberation that lasted only a few seconds but felt like an hour to me, Great Turtle made his decision. He gave the signal with a motion of his hand that I should be freed.

Machete blades flashed and my bonds were cut. Kingston Jack helped me to my feet, and by the time I was able to stand unassisted, Henry had returned with the Krag and the ammunition belt.

"It's loaded," he said.

I took the Krag and worked the bolt to chamber a round, then looked up to take stock of the desperate situation before me. The Colombians were about a thousand meters from where I stood, directly off the beach. The fleeing *cayuco* was only a hundred meters farther in, and the gap was closing fast. The trawler could come in as far as the reef, which meant it had another six hundred meters of maneuvering room before its draft would cause it to go aground. The fleet of canoes that had been launched once the danger had been perceived was only two hundred meters from shore, about halfway to the sheltering reef.

The Colombians plainly planned to close upon the fleeing canoe, seize the children, and beat a hasty retreat long before the warriors could effectively interfere. Already a dozen uniformed soldiers were gathered along the bow rail of the trawler, near where the name *Chagres* was emblazoned in black paint. They would do the actual snatching, I surmised, while above them in the pilothouse a knot of officers supervised the operation.

Even at this distance I could make out the swarthy figure at the center of this group. It was Comandante Reyes himself! He no doubt had doubled back to Colón after he tumbled us into that mountain torrent and then set out down the coast in the *Chagres*. He probably aimed to mix a little commerce with a patrol to see whether there was any word of the fugitives along the coast. Oh, he was thorough, all right, not assuming that we were dead until he saw our cadavers with his own eyes.

"Can you make this shot?" asked Henry dubiously.

"I don't know," I replied, "but I'm damned sure going to give it a try."

I shouldered the Krag and drew a bead. The thing to do, I knew, would be to aim at the soldiers gathered along the rail. They formed the biggest target, you see, and if I could wing one of them, the trawler might turn about to get out of range. That would give the children in the canoe time to gain the shelter of the reef, beyond which the trawler could not pass.

I would be firing from extreme range with a rifle I had never handled before. Each Krag had its own quirks, and my first shot was bound to go wide in one direction or another. If I could see it splash into the water, though, I could quickly adjust and send my next shot true to its target. I raised the Krag and took a deep breath to steady my quivering arms. Then I squeezed the trigger and fired. The Krag recoiled in my hands as I kept an eye peeled for the splash of the bullet.

"Did you see it hit?" I asked Henry.

He shook his head. "Nope. The waves out there are too choppy, Fenny. There's little sprays of white everywhere."

"Damn, you're right," I agreed in exasperation. A steady wind was moving across the water, swirling the surface into little puffs of spray every few feet. "If I don't see the splash, I can't adjust my aim."

To continue firing under these conditions would be simply firing blind. I was licked and I knew it. I lowered the Krag as Tiger's dark eyes burned into me. I had the sinking feeling that explaining this pass to him would be about as easy as imparting the wonders of a Texas barbecue to a devout Hindu.

"It's no use, Tiger—" I started to say in Spanish when suddenly Henry remembered something.

"Fenny, the sight!" he cried out.

"The what?" I asked.

"You know, the one you brought from New York."

"Damn, you're right! Where is it?"

"In the *casa grande*," he said, and he was off like a flash.

I turned to watch the plight of the children. The Colombians, oblivious to the fact that they had even been under fire, had closed the gap to fifty yards. The children were still two hundred yards from the safety of the reef. As for the rescuers, their *cayucos* were just clearing the white water washing over the reef, but it was evident to all that the game was about up, absent some outside intervention. It was then that Henry returned once more.

The leather case was covered with a soft layer of green mold. I brushed away the nauseous stuff as best I could and tore open the case. I reached in and nearly plunged my fingers into a mass of bright red spiders huddled within. When I had shaken the last of the interlopers from their nest, I slid the Cataract telescopic sight from its berth. Fortunately, the sight itself was in working order.

"Not too much the worse for wear," I said with relief. The coat of oil I had requested the clerk at Barlow's to apply had served its purpose well.

I fished about in the case for the screwdriver, found it, and then set hurriedly to work. First, I positioned the sight over the left side of the rifle and screwed the forward bracket to the Krag's wooden grip near the point where my left hand normally rested when sighting. I then affixed the aft bracket to the Krag's receiver plating at a point just forward of the trigger housing. Satisfied that the fit was snug, I raised the sight to my eye and peered out on the drama unfolding before me.

The sight was set at twelve magnification, and the faces of the terrified children in the canoe literally jumped out at me. I shifted my aim to the pursuing trawler. I could clearly see the coarse, pitiless expressions of the soldiers as they hooted and jeered at their prey. I sighted on a likely fellow—a corporal, to judge by the chevron on his sleeve—and fired.

The bullet kicked up a plume of white spray near the trawler's waterline, at a spot about fifteen feet to the left of my aiming point. Judging from the way they recoiled in alarm at the sight of the splash, I knew that the Colombians finally realized they were under fire. I would not have much time before they fired back.

The Cataract's mechanism for compensating for windage and drift was simplicity itself. The forward bracket incorporated a ball and socket mechanism that allowed the front end of the sight to be moved vertically or horizontally, or both, as required. Normally, of course, I would have adjusted the sight, fired again, watched where the bullet struck, readjusted the sight accordingly, and so forth until I had zeroed the weapon accurately. Under the present circumstances, I didn't have the time required for such precision. I would have but one chance to fiddle with the sight, and I would have to do it right the first time. The fate of the fleeing children would depend on pure luck and a little Kentucky windage.

I hurriedly made what I thought was the proper adjustment to compensate for the drift I'd seen, then threw the Krag to my shoulder and sighted on the corporal again. I exhaled slowly and squeezed the trigger.

Chips of weathered paint exploded from the side of the cabin behind the corporal's head. The whole crowd of soldiers around him dove for cover and began returning fire toward the shore. Bullets rained all around me, dropping one Cuna not ten feet away and sending the others scurrying for cover. I ran for the nearest palm tree and threw myself behind it, with Henry tagging along to serve as my ammunition bearer.

"They're firing blind," I said to Henry. "They just want to keep our heads down so they can snatch the children."

Henry nodded. "Yep. Only now *we're* not firing blind. Let 'em have it, Fenny."

And let 'em have it I did. With Henry feeding me cartridges, I opened a withering fire on the bewildered Colombians. They had been raiding this coast for years with impunity and had never before encountered this type of resistance from the Cunas. It was an ominous development, and although they fought back angrily I could tell from the startled looks on their faces that this was a new game for them.

I slammed bullet after bullet into the group of soldiers huddled at the trawler's rail, dropping two into the clear waters and wounding three others. Each time the trawler rolled in the gentle ocean swells, I could see blood streaming down its side from the deck to the waterline. My fire was touching them up considerably, and the thought gave me grim satisfaction. It also had another effect: shark fins appeared from nowhere and clustered around the trawler, drawn by the blood upon the water.

Yet still the trawler bore down on the canoe until it was only ten yards away from its quarry. Despite my efforts, the children were doomed. The nearest rescue *cayuco* was a hundred yards distant, and in its bow a warrior had notched an arrow. I realized that the distance was too great for Cuna arrows to be effective; indeed, when the Cuna loosed his shaft it sailed wide of the mark. The children had but one slim hope; if the trawler could be forced off its course somehow, they might gain the precious seconds needed to reach safety. As I chambered a round, my eyes roamed to the pilothouse where Comandante Reyes and his staff stood, just to the side of the helmsman.

"It's time to start paying back our friend Reyes, don't you think, Henry?" Henry got the point immediately. "I sure do, Fenny."

I sighted on the cabin, only to see Reyes peering at me through a set of binoculars. There was no doubt that he recognized me, for the rage on his face was unmistakable. He still had the glasses to his face when I fired.

My shot caught a mustachioed dandy at Reyes's side clean through the chest. The fellow made a graceful little leap into the air and then went down hard. A look of sudden fear crossed Reyes's face; he dropped his glasses and yammered at his men on the deck below to cut me down. Before they could obey, I fired again, blowing a compass from a bulkhead directly behind Reyes, who promptly ducked out of sight.

Now only the helmsman remained in sight within the pilothouse. Through the Cataract sight I could see that his face was chalk white with terror, yet he stoutly remained at his post, holding the wheel steady. Already soldiers were leaning over the rail, their hands only inches now from the cowering children who could not abandon their canoe because of the hungry sharks that thrashed everywhere.

"Fenny! Fire, for God's sake!" demanded Henry, repelled by the thought of anyone being seized as a slave.

I drew a bead on the helmsman, but the yawing of the vessel caused him to dance in and out of the sight's field of vision. Then, just as the *Chagres* rose on a new swell, I aimed again. At the moment when the trawler ascended to the apex of its vertical motion, there was a fleeting instant of immobility before it began its inevitable descent into a trough. At that precise moment I fired.

"Bull's-eye!" I cried as a bright geyser of blood erupted from the helmsman's forehead. Slowly he toppled to the deck, and the wheel spun crazily as he released it from his dying grasp. Immediately the *Chagres* heeled to port, away from the terrified children, the abruptness of the turn hurling one soldier over the rail and into the maw of a waiting shark.

As Henry whooped with glee, I continued to fire into the pilothouse at about the level where I figured Reyes and his officers might be lying on the deck. I hoped to ensure that nobody regained control of the wheel for a few precious moments. Round after round slammed home, tearing loose great chunks of planking and making it impossible for anyone to take the place of the fallen helmsman.

Those moments were all the children needed; they pulled hard, gained the outer edge of the protective reef, and then were engulfed by the sheltering flotilla of *cayucos*. As I watched, the *Chagres* cut a near semicircle through the sea beyond the reef, then straightened her course and headed at high speed for the horizon. Reyes had been thwarted once again.

16

The elated Cunas mobbed me, clapping me on the back and lifting me to their shoulders for a spontaneous promenade around the beach. Tiger was at their fore, giving loud thanks in Tule for the deliverance of his son, and adding for my benefit, "Spanish man, he great warrior. His arrow fly true. Kill the enemy, *sí*?"

"*¡Sí!*" I replied with a ready smile, quite willing to let bygones be bygones between us since my survival depended on being in his good graces. The happy procession bumped about in a rambling, jubilant fashion, but then it stopped cold when Great Turtle stepped in its path.

The potent *nele* had taken shelter during the gunplay. His black magic, while just the thing for cowing ignorant villagers into awed compliance with his dictates, didn't seem quite up to the job of stopping hot lead. If Great Turtle seemed at all abashed by his less-than-puissant showing in the face of the Colombian onslaught, he certainly didn't show it. Instead, he had the same malevolent countenance as when he had announced my doom. I shuddered as I looked into those weak, liquid eyes, for I could read nothing good in them. It was as though Great Turtle was looking through me at specters in the air that were visible only to him. Had he decided to order that my death sentence be carried out? Had all my fancy shooting been in vain? I couldn't fathom what destiny lay in store for me as Great Turtle lifted his face to the sun and raised both hands, palms upward in a supplicating manner. As he did, the assembled Cunas looked on with reverential silence. The only sound was the gentle wash of the surf on the sand and the stirring of the palm fronds in the breeze. Then, in a labored, brittle voice that sounded like chalk scratched across a slate, Great Turtle mewled out an eerie ditty. The words evidently were ones of great power, for around me I could hear awed gasps escaping involuntarily from warrior lips. As the *nele* wheezed on, a wide smile spread across Kingston Jack's face. Whatever Great Turtle was saying, it was evidently good news.

"Great Turtle has changed his mind," announced the stalwart Antillean. "He believes you are a moon child after all. He has decided you are one of the golden people who wandered away at the creation of the earth, and now he's prepared to welcome you back into the tribe."

"A golden one, eh?" Well, well. If that's the way the old huckster chose to see things, who was I to object? Turning to Tiger, I said in Spanish, "Tell Great Turtle and all my brothers that I'm simply delighted to be home."

Joyous shouts greeted Tiger's translation. Now that the *nele's* benediction had been obtained, the celebration resumed with heightened fervor. The children were hauled ashore at last and introduced to their deliverer. Tiger's boy was a chipper lad whose Tule name escaped me but which Kingston Jack translated as The One Who Watches. I quickly dubbed the boy Watcher and told him I was damned pleased to have pulled his fat from the fire. Then the whole congregation retired to the *casa grande*. Here I was led to understand that hurried preparations were being made for a completely unanticipated initiation ceremony. First, Tiger held out a gourd of *chicha*. I took a pull, found the taste to be bitter yet passable, and then threw back my head and downed the contents. Tiger's eyes opened wide at this, and I surmised that the locals didn't quaff entire gourds in a single gulp. Next, I was stripped naked and provided with a penis sheath and thong for my waist. I donned this outlandish garb in good humor, wondering all the while what dear Alice might say if she were to see her loving fiancé parading about in Cuna haute couture.

Tiger then commenced to pluck out my mustache, a hair at a time. I had a devil of a time staying my tongue as I endured this slow torture. When I was as bare as a baby's bottom, a Cuna appeared with small pots of paint. This fellow daubed me liberally with the stuff, and wasn't satisfied until I was completely coated with every hue of the rainbow. When he was done turning me into a living mural, Tiger took me aside and explained what was to follow.

Tiger, it turned out, was the *sahila,* the tribal chief of this band of Cunas. He made it clear that he planned to adopt me. Henceforth I was to be a warrior in the Jaguar Clan. "You be big jaguar," Tiger assured me with pure glee.

"I'd like that, Tiger," I assured him fervently. "I'd like that just fine." Indeed, had he said he wanted to initiate me into the clan of the three-toed sloths and have me hang naked from a tree all day, that's the very thing I would have done, just as long as my heart was allowed to stay right where it was.

Taking my quick smile for enthusiasm, Tiger launched into a lecture on Cuna theology. It was hard to follow his guttural patois, but as he spoke

I got the general gist of the Cuna version of the Creation. "The Great Father in heaven created the Cuna. They are the golden people favored over all other races. They live on their islands and await the day that the Spanish will be overcome and the Cuna will once again roam the isthmus from the great mountains in the south all the way to the volcano lands in the north." I nodded, understanding that this area encompassed roughly the area between Venezuela and Nicaragua. The Cunas evidently thought big, I could see. "While we wait," Tiger continued, "it is the duty of the Tule to maintain their purity and to resist the demons that move through the air all around us. Our *nele,* Great Turtle, protects us from these demons. He teaches us the chants to ward off sickness, and he alone is able to detect witches among us. As a Tule, you must never hurt another Tule, and that means never casting the evil eye or making hexes."

On he went in this vein, listing a plethora of strictures. It seemed about everything that was appealing to me was forbidden to the Cunas, especially helping oneself to the charms of the opposite sex. Woman-chasing was completely out of bounds among the chaste Cunas. Both male and female among them, you see, tended to save themselves for marriage. It sounded like a perfectly boring custom, but I saw the wisdom of it when Tiger went on to explain that adultery was punishable with death. Being in Tiger's clan was going to be like living in a monastery without walls.

When he finished outlining the tribal taboos, Tiger looked me earnestly in the eye and lapsed back into rapid-fire Tule. "I knew you were a moon child when you saved my son," translated Kingston Jack. "A true Tule always comes to the aid of other Tules, no matter what physical form they may take. Sometimes I think I see a jaguar in the jungle, but that jaguar lets me know that it is really the spirit of a departed clansman. It is because we are used to seeing Tule ghosts in the guise of animals that we were able to recognize you as one of the golden people."

"Well, *gracias*—I guess," was all I could muster in response to this faint praise. After some more chanting and mumbling of incantations, Tiger stood there eyeing me expectantly. I suspected that this part of the ceremony required some sort of speech from me. I cleared my throat and declared fervently in my most grandiloquent Spanish, "The greatest dream of my life is to be a Tule once more. Always I have known that it was my destiny to travel to this island, Tiger, and rejoin the good old Jaguar Clan. Let it be known now that Moon Child has returned home and is anxious to serve his noble father, the *sahila.*"

Oh, I could dollop out the fluff with the best of them when the need arose, and I could tell by the delighted expression on Tiger's mug that I had hit the nail right on the head. Tiger called out to one and all that the moon child was properly grateful for the great honor to be bestowed on him, and that the adoption would make the Great Father very happy indeed.

A huge chorus of acclamation greeted this pronouncement, and more toasts were offered to my eloquence. After I'd downed the better part of a gallon of *chicha* with Tiger and his cronies, I staggered out to the plaza where several hundred Cuna warriors were drawn up in a tight phalanx behind Great Turtle. There, amid the din from the flutes and drums, the ceremony reached its peak.

In flowing Tule, Tiger delivered a long discourse on my worthiness to be inducted into the clan. Kingston Jack at my side translated, and through him I learned that to this point my adoption was no more than a proposal, a motion from the floor, if you will. The motion would not carry until each warrior present seconded it. The Cunas apparently ran a damned exclusive club, with each member carrying a veto around in his hip pocket. When Tiger was done with his pitch, he polled the electorate. This was accomplished by voice vote from the floor, a long and tedious process. It wasn't until the assembled throng let out a great bloodcurdling yell that sent startled birds winging from trees a hundred yards away that I knew the motion had carried.

At this, Great Turtle stepped forward, mouthed some mumbo jumbo, rattled some chicken bones over his head, and did a little jig for good measure. Then he produced a pot filled with a noxious-smelling paste that looked like a mixture of clay and animal blood. He anointed my brow with the awful, oily stuff, and before the mess could fully congeal, my newfound kinsmen paraded past one at a time to clasp my arm and deliver resounding thwacks to my shoulder, all of which I bore with exceedingly good grace considering the fact that not two hours before, the whole pack of them had been of a mind to publicly eviscerate me and toss my entrails into the sea. When the last of them had passed, it was over. I was now officially Moon Child, the junior member of the Jaguar Clan.

At that moment Henry appeared and quickly brought me back to reality. "Fenny, what about Captain Longbottom?"

"What about him?" I asked casually as I looked about for more *chicha* to swill.

"Is he still gonna be executed?"

"I suppose so," I replied. "You needn't worry, though. It should be quite painless. Longbottom doesn't seem to be able to feel a thing in his present condition."

"You can't let it happen, Fenny. You're a Cuna now, and they'll listen to you. You can't let Captain Longbottom die while you have it in your power to save him."

On and on he went, insisting that as an officer I was duty bound to rescue Longbottom, and that I would never forgive myself if I didn't. I could see that I was going to get no peace until this issue was resolved, so at length I stayed Henry with an upraised hand.

"Okay, okay. I'll see what can be done."

"When?" Henry pressed.

"Later," I stalled. "After all, this is my party, and I'm not quite done celebrating."

"Fenny, your new daddy, Tiger, is down at the beach right now. He's fixing to split Captain Longbottom wide open like a hog at slaughter."

"Oh, damn it all," I muttered and allowed myself to be led to the water's edge. Longbottom, still trussed, lay where he had been dropped hours before. The tide had come in since then, and he was in grave danger of drowning. As the salt spray washed between his slack jaws, he was oblivious to the small committee of Cunas gathered about him. Tiger was there, as Henry had warned, and he was hefting the Spanish cutlass that had scared the dickens out of me when first I saw it.

"Tiger," I cried as we neared. "That man is my, er, servant. He is my property, you savvy? Turn him loose and give him back to me."

"He is your property?"

"That's right. I, er, won him in a card game up north. A wager, you understand? A contest, *sí*?"

Tiger considered this. He had no idea what a card game might be, and in Cuna culture it was not possible for one human to own another. He did understand the concept of property, however, and if this *waker* belonged to Moon Child, it would be contrary to Tule law to take that property without just compensation. Fortunately, at the moment he had nothing on hand to trade.

"If this is Moon Child's property, then Moon Child may keep it."

That was it; the *sahila* had spoken. The other Cunas cut Longbottom loose just as a wave washed over him. He might have drifted off to Africa had not Henry caught hold of one of his feet and dragged him to higher ground.

Kingston Jack, who had followed along, suggested that I ask Tiger for fever medicine for Captain Longbottom. "The Cunas can cure the marsh sickness," he assured me.

I did exactly that, telling Tiger that my property was in danger of losing all its value. He readily assisted me, sending off for the *nele*. Great

Turtle, pleased to be the center of attention, took over the case at once. He produced bits of ground bark from a pouch he carried at his waist and called for freshly boiled water. It was produced in a metal kettle, and the bark was dropped into the steaming liquid.

"Quinine bark," whispered Kingston Jack into my ear.

That, I knew from my time in Cuba, was just the stuff to cure Longbottom. When a weak bark tea had been brewed, it was poured down Longbottom's gullet. Not content with this feat, Great Turtle went on to address himself to my fever and the suppurating scrapes all over my body. He insisted that I swallow some of the tea, and then he packed green mold into my wounds. I wasn't at all keen on this palliative, but Kingston Jack assured me that the Indians were masters at herbal cures and that to object would only offend them. When Great Turtle was done with me, he cleaned out Kingston Jack's wounded hand, set the bone, and packed his gunshot wound with green mold as well. Then, satisfied with his work, the old rascal padded off with the smug air of a famed surgeon whose craft was beyond question by other mortals.

17

Great Turtle's confidence was well placed, as things turned out. In two days Longbottom was on his feet, and both Kingston Jack and I were feeling like new. As I recovered, I adjusted quite nicely to my new circumstances. I quickly learned, for instance, that Cuna warriors were expected to do real work. They fished in the sea or hunted on the lowlands of the Darien coast. They were also the ones who cultivated the fields. The women, on the other hand, remained largely in the environs of the village, venturing into the fields only to check the condition of the crops and to bring water to the men. An exception in this regard was the care of the coconut groves. It was the women who harvested the coconuts, which served as both a staple food and a form of currency for trading with other Cuna clans. Also, when the occasional campesino trader anchored off the island with a boatload of pots and knives, it was the women who did the bartering. Except for the awesome power accorded to the *nele,* and the wartime authority of Tiger, in fact, the government of the clan seemed to rest in the hands of the ladies.

Despite their social prominence, though, I rarely got to see the damsels. Cuna ladies were a notoriously shy lot, and they scurried off whenever I or the three other *wakers* happened by. In those brief encounters, moreover, I saw practically nothing, for the prudish Cuna were always garbed in ankle-length skirts and voluminous, gaily painted blouses, which they called *molas*. Over their heads were shawls, which offered only a peek at the distaff charms they concealed. Life among the Cuna, I could see, promised to be a celibate time for old Fenny.

Or so I thought until fate took a strange twist. Just a two weeks after my unanticipated adoption, I was stirring at the crack of dawn and had just stepped from the bachelor house when I was confronted by Henry. With him was Kingston Jack. From the set look on their faces, I could tell that Henry was about to raise the same tired subject with me. Specifically, he wanted to know when we were leaving for civilization.

"Fenny," Henry called as soon as he saw me, "have you spoken to Tiger?"

"About what?" I asked, feigning ignorance.

"About leaving this place," answered Kingston Jack for him.

"Hmmm, let's see. It seems I did raise that very subject with him just the other day. We were over on the mainland hunting tapirs and . . . oh, by the way, that reminds me. Have you heard about the golden frogs?"

Henry shook his head. "No, I haven't."

"Well, they're the key to success if you're a hunter hereabouts, my friend. Tiger told me all about them. The golden frogs are all over the trees and bushes on the mainland, you see."

"I know, Captain," interrupted Kingston Jack irritably. "They're poison. A bird or an animal that eats one will drop stone dead in seconds."

"Exactly," I continued unflappably, "and that, my friend, is the point. Tiger showed me how the Cuna scrape off the substance the frogs ooze through their skin. They smear the stuff on their arrowhead, and the result is a poison arrow that will drop a tapir faster than a buffalo gun. We all know how delicious tapir tastes, now don't we? Yes, a thick tapir steak and a few yams on the side, all washed down with a few pints of *chicha,* will make a man a fine meal. Say, have you boys had any lately?"

"No, damnit," snapped Henry. "We haven't had tapir, or pig, or anything bigger than a snake in days. The Cunas won't help us hunt and they won't feed us. Your damned frogs are of no use to us either, Fenny, because we don't have any arrows. The Cunas won't even let us pick coconuts from their groves, although there are so many of the blasted things around that they're left to rot in the sun. We're living hand to mouth, and I'm telling you we can't go on too much longer."

I knew all this, of course, and in truth both Henry and Kingston Jack had lost so much weight that they looked a sight. The problem was that the Cunas were a bit chary of *cimaroons*. On the one hand they recognized them as an ancestral ally with whom they had made common cause from time to time in the past. On the other hand, however, they hardly relished the thought of a horde of unemployed railroad workers making their way south from Colón to share the abundant delights of this earthly paradise. Their solution was exquisitely indirect; they took great care to offer expressions of friendship to Henry and Kingston Jack at every turn, and then froze them completely out of Cuna society. Whenever my friends appeared in the village plaza, communal kettles filled to the brim with turtle stew would be whisked away. Baskets of cassavas and breadfruit would similarly disappear. It was only when Henry had protested to Tiger that he was slowly dying of starvation that he had been provided with a leaky dugout barely fit to reach the mainland, visible some three miles distant. The canoe would certainly never make the long journey to Colón.

As for me, well, I was living a life that only millionaires enjoyed back home. I avoided all work in the fields by pleading lingering weakness from my fever. That meant that when I wasn't hunting on the mainland, I spent most of my days off fishing among the nearby reefs. The catch was good, and it was not unusual for me to return before midday in a *cayuco* piled high with fish and sea turtles. After a leisurely repast, usually washed down with a few gourds of *chicha,* I'd turn in for a well-deserved nap. Then, after an afternoon snack, it was time for supper, which was usually followed by some leisurely spearfishing in the early evening hours. It was one big campout, you see, and I was having a roaring good time. Unlike Henry and Kingston Jack, therefore, I had no desire to see my idyll end anytime soon.

"You need to see Tiger about all this, Henry, not me," I explained patiently for the hundredth time. "He's the one who can make a place for you two at the village meals, and he can provide you with a better boat if he wants. Yes, and nets to fish, and maybe even a bow and arrows."

"He'll never give us weapons," snorted Kingston Jack. "He even snatched away my rifle after you used it to save Watcher. Why, Henry had a devil of a time holding on to your rifle sight."

All this was true, and the plain fact was that Tiger wanted to drive off his guests. They had already overstayed their welcome, and the whole village was on edge over their presence. Yet the insular Cunas were reluctant to make a serviceable *cayuco* available to Henry and Kingston Jack, fearing that a comfortable trip back to civilization might encourage visits by other *cimaroons.* So it was a bit of a Mexican standoff; the Cunas wanted to be rid of their visitors but wouldn't help them leave, whereas Henry and Kingston Jack, anxious to be off, were fearful of expiring along the way for lack of supplies.

"Get us back the rifle," pleaded Henry. "If we had that, we might be able to walk back to Colón along the coast. Tell Tiger that he has no use for it here. The Cunas don't use rifles, and in fact they despise them."

"I'm afraid Tiger won't listen to reason on that score, Henry. He saw what the Krag did to those Colombians, and he won't let the thing out of his sight. He keeps it in his hut right next to his hammock, and there I'm afraid it will stay."

"Then get us enough food to tide us over until we can reach Colón. Five days' worth, that's all I ask. Some corn and rice, and maybe a little dried fish. Tiger will certainly see that such a request is reasonable."

"Perhaps," I replied, fully aware that Tiger had already decreed that not a morsel was to be given to the *cimaroons,* on penalty of death. I couldn't say this to Henry, of course, for there was no telling what he might do if he realized that his exile on the Comarca de San Blas was likely to be permanent. "I'll make it a point to bring it up with him first thing this morning. I promise."

"You got to, Fenny," said Henry. "We're desperate, and we're depending on you."

"Henry, you must realize that I've done all I can to help you. Every time I sense an opportunity, I raise your plight with Tiger." My words were true enough. I didn't have the heart, though, to add that on every occasion Tiger had turned a deaf ear to my pleas.

"I understand, Fenny," he said. "Kingston Jack here, though—well, he's not so sure that we'll ever leave this coast alive."

"Kingston Jack," I chided, "how could you even think such a thing? Where's that carefree attitude of yours? After all, weren't you the fellow who said that all of this was just a big adventure, and all that mattered was that we were in it together?"

"Aye, I said that, Captain. But that was before three of us had our feed bags snatched away."

Henry, not liking the way the veins on Kingston Jack's neck were bulging, intervened. "I told him, Fenny, that I know you and that we've been through thick and thin together. I'm certain you won't let us down."

"You're absolutely right, Henry."

"You might tell Tiger, Captain Travers," observed Kingston Jack, "that he has an interest in letting us go."

"Oh, how's that?"

"Never before have the Cunas defended themselves with rifles. That is because the Spanish never traded weapons to them. When Reyes returns to Colón, he will raise a force large enough to return to these islands and track down Tiger and his band and kill them to the last woman and child. That is the Spanish way in these matters. If Tiger releases us, though, we may be able to stop Reyes before he takes his revenge."

"Maybe, but I've talked to Tiger already about exactly that subject. He says the Cuna are not afraid. Let the Spanish come."

"He's never seen what massed Mausers and cannons can do," said Henry. "Reyes will cut through this place like a hurricane."

"I'll tell him, Henry," I promised, "but I can't say that it will do any good."

Having made his point, Henry put his hand on my shoulder and said, "I just know you'd never let me down, Fenny. I'll hold on and be patient. I'm sure you'll find a way to help us."

I laid a hand on his shoulder in return. "I couldn't have put it any better myself, old friend. Patience must be your watchword. The Cunas are mighty damned touchy about strangers. One has to approach 'em in just the right way. I'll belabor Tiger with your concerns until he sees things your way. I'll wear down the poor sot, eh?"

Henry gave a forlorn smile. "Thanks, Fenny."

Just then Watcher rounded the corner of the bachelor house. He was coming to me from the *casa del fuego*—the fire house—the village cook house where all the viands were prepared. Watcher was hefting a wooden platter heaped high with steaming, fresh-broiled fish and baked plantains. As soon as he saw the hungry faces of Henry and Kingston Jack, though, he did a parade ground about-face and disappeared from view.

I laughed nervously. "The boy spoils me shamelessly, you see. He's really become a little bother ever since I saved him. He knows I couldn't possibly eat such a portion, but he brings it nonetheless. I'll have a word with him about wasting food when there are others in need."

Henry nodded, his jaws slack at the sight of food almost within his reach. "Talk to Tiger, Fenny," he implored as he took his leave. "Do it before I do something we'll all regret."

"You have my word on it. Before you go, let me give you a little something to tide you over." I slipped into the *casa grande* and emerged with a small basket of mangoes and yams. Making sure that no prying eyes were watching, I handed my cache over to my famished friends, who accepted my gift with many thanks.

When they were gone, I whistled for Watcher to return. The boy laid the platter on the sand before me, and I squatted on my haunches to wolf down my breakfast as I had every morning since my adoption. Unlike poor Henry and Kingston Jack, the Cunas treated Moon Child like royalty. Food was offered wherever I went, for I was welcome at every hearth. Only old Great Turtle remained aloof. I got the impression that the wily shaman hadn't yet decided whether I was a portent of good fortune or doom, and until he did he intended to keep his distance.

As I gorged myself, Watcher explained that today something special was in order. Deepwater tarpon had been spotted the evening before. Great masses of the delicious fish were schooling in the blue water some two miles off the reef. Under Tiger's leadership, every man in the village would sally forth to catch them. It sounded like good sport to me, so when I was finished eating I meandered down to the line of *cayucos* on the shore where already men were gathering excitedly. Nets were checked and loaded, and long spears with fishbone tips were loaded into the canoes. As the junior member of the firm, seeing to these details should have fallen on my shoulders. That was the Cuna way, I had come to learn. One started off doing the menial chores, and if these were done to the satisfaction of the senior warriors, then promotions could be expected. I was told more than once that I might even aspire to the coveted position of lead rower in Tiger's war canoe. No promises could be made, of course, but good things would certainly come in time if I applied myself diligently.

My adoptive brothers were due for a bit of a disappointment, though, for diligence was entirely foreign to my nature. Despite their best efforts to get me interested in the hundreds of chores that went into maintaining the clan's readiness to hunt and fish, I seemed impervious to their pointed hints. That was why as preparations for the great tarpon expedition unfolded all around me, I walked right by a group of men scraping barnacles off a canoe and never offered to help. It was the same reason why as, I sauntered past a warrior mending a net, I couldn't seem to see the fellow despite the meaningful glance he cast my way.

This blindness on my part seemed to puzzle the Cuna a bit, but since the bloom was not yet quite off the rose they were inclined to tolerate Moon Child's little *waker* idiosyncracies, at least for the present. He would come around, they assured themselves; just give him time and he would remember the Tule ways.

Suddenly Tiger appeared and with a great shout ordered the expedition to shove off. Oh, it was a spectacular day to frolic about on the sea. The water was perfectly smooth, and in the blue sky only the softest and gentlest of clouds appeared. As the sun climbed high, a lone gull spotted the tiny flotilla, glided overhead to have a look, and lingered. In no time there was a noisy collection of seabirds wheeling and crying above us. Between their piercing calls and the lusty chants of the Cunas, the noise was perfectly deafening. As for me, well, sure, I looked forward to hauling in a few tarpon. I was especially cheered, though, by the fact that Tiger had thoughtfully brought along enough *chicha* to stun an ox. I couldn't wait to drop anchor and indulge in nonstop libations until I couldn't tell one end of a paddle from the other.

The tarpon were just where we expected them, and by the time the sun was directly overhead, the *cayucos* were filling with wriggling fish. Although the tarpon were mainly juveniles, the sheer volume of the catch surpassed even the most optimistic expectations, and Tiger decided to send his canoe to shore with the catch that had been taken to that point. He hailed a nearby canoe, and when it pulled alongside he nimbly leaped aboard. With his flag transferred, as it were, he ordered the other Cunas to pile their tarpon into his canoe. This done, he instructed Watcher and me to ferry the fish to the village while he and the others remained behind to fill the rest of the canoes.

Watcher and I did as we were told, and when we beached our craft all the young boys eagerly pitched in to unload the catch. Soon tarpon guts were everywhere, and boned fish by the hundreds were spread on palm frames to dry in the sun. All of this was too much like real work to suit my taste, so I left Watcher and his little companions and set off to do some exploring.

On a whim, I strolled out into the cassava fields. There I saw Longbottom, tethered to a post and grubbing about in the dirt like a helot in bondage. Over him stood an old Cuna hag, a switch in her hand. Her job was to make sure the *waker* put in a full day's work. Longbottom's lot had been a rather harsh one, for once I made my claim of property on him, the Cunas treated him as such. He had no more status than would a burro—that is, had the Cunas possessed such critters. Since all Cunas worked hard, moreover, it was only natural that they expected Longbottom, a *waker* of the commonest sort, to work hard as well. I suggested he be sent out to the fields, and Tiger had seen to it. What was more, although Longbottom was Moon Child's property, as long as he was in their midst, the whole village had a vested interest in wringing the fullest measure of labor from him before he expired from overuse. That explained the presence of the old woman; she was Longbottom's personal slave driver.

Longbottom saw me coming and cried out, "Travers, for God's sake bring me some water. This old bitch is working me to death."

I shook my head sternly. "Water will only slow you down in the heat, Joshua. Didn't they teach you anything at West Point?"

"Don't talk nonsense, damn you," he protested. "My mouth is as dry as a salt mine, and I'll expire unless I have water at once."

By way of an answer, the old crone cracked her switch across Longbottom's naked back. He shrieked in anguish and made as if to throttle her, but the spritely old gal hopped just beyond the range of Longbottom's tether with surprising agility. Then she turned and fetched him another blow for his troubles, only this time across his snout. Although neither of us could understand the Tule lingo, it was clear that she wanted him back to work, and right now, thank you.

Longbottom let out another howl of pain, but his Cuna keeper was unmoved. Careful to stand just beyond his reach, she proceeded to worry Longbottom with a flurry of stinging whacks until he was sobbing with pain and frustration.

I merely cocked my head and chuckled at his predicament. Longbottom, after all, had been my superior at West Point when I was a lowly plebe. After having endured hazing at his hands for a solid year, turning the tables in this manner was a rare treat to be relished.

"I'd say you had just better forget this foolish notion about having some water and get straight back to work, Joshua," I advised him cheerily. "Your lady friend here seems to mean business, I'm afraid. Unless I'm far off the mark, she'll brook no further delays."

"Oh, damn her and all the rest of these blasted savages," railed Longbottom. "Travers, what about the president? What about the secretary of war? They expect certain information from us—information we can't provide while you're lolling about the beach in paradise. Where's your sense of duty, man?"

I pointed at my temple and whispered. "Don't think that I've forgotten about it, Joshua. I'm memorizing every square inch of this island. When the time comes, why, I'll be a veritable font of information."

"It's not details about this fly-blown manure heap that are needed, you imbecile! It's the goings-on in Colón and Panama City that are vital. We need to be gone from—"

That was as far as he got, for his keeper had recovered her strength
and came on more savagely than before, whipping Longbottom into a lather.
Leaving the two of them to work out their differences, I waved a languid
farewell and passed on to the edge of the cassava field and peered into
the palm groves beyond. Here was an area of the island where I had yet
to set foot. There had been no strict limits placed on me, you see, but the
menfolk simply didn't wander into the palm groves. Why that might be,
I had no idea, but the implication was that this was the domain of the ladies
and the children, and proper gentlemen respected that claim of right.

I, of course, was no gentleman, especially not a Cuna one. What was more,
it had been nearly a month since my tryst with the lovely Serafina, and I
had for some time now been suffering from familiar urges. With Tiger and
the other men safely at sea, I rather fancied that the time had come to scratch
that itch.

Casting a look about, I saw that the harridan and Longbottom were still
locked in their imbroglio. The few other women in the fields had their eyes
glued to the drama. When I was certain that no one was watching, I slipped
into the forbidden precincts. Once in the shadows of the trees, I stepped
lightly. I heard naught but the humming of the insects and the calls of
weaver birds nesting high in the branches above. Here and there were piles
of coconuts, evidence of the industry of the village ladies. To my right as
I walked I could hear laughter; evidently a distaff work party was busy in
that direction. I steered clear of the noise, desirous of completing my covert
exploration before my absence from the village was noted.

I had a rough idea of the lay of the island and knew that it was no more
than two miles across. Figuring that the grove was about a half mile at its
widest point, I pressed on. Soon I heard the gentle rush of the waves upon
the sand, and then the vegetation thinned. Ahead of me was a white strand,
and at the water's edge was a figure. I crouched behind a thick palm and
scrutinized the scene. It was a young woman, clad in the obligatory wrap-
around skirt and gaily painted *mola*. She had something in a straw pannier,
and when I studied it I saw it was a catch of lobsters that she evidently was
in the process of cleaning. In the midst of her labors she had laid aside her
shawl, and her long, glossy tresses hung freely down her back.

Watching that feminine form bent to her tasks roused my passions. I
was hungry, by God, but not for tarpon. It was female companionship I
craved, and here was some right before my eyes. Suddenly the girl turned
and walked from the surf. I recognized her at once; she was the gal on
the beach when first I had been brought to the island. She was the one

who had not run off with the others. Encouraged by my good fortune at finding her alone like this, I stepped from the shadows.

The woman looked up and gasped. As she stood transfixed, I studied her closely. Cunas as a race have long heads and great Roman noses, you see, and this lady was no exception. What was more, she, like all her sisters in the clan, sported a black line drawn from a point between her eyebrows to the tip of her nose. This mark was evidently calculated to accentuate the proud proboscis, and I was a witness that it did exactly that. All of this, coupled with her gold nose ring, would take a bit of adjusting to. Given my randy state, though, I was ready to do some adjusting.

"I am Moon Child," I announced. I spoke in the Tule tongue, for I was rapidly getting the knack of the local lingo, and I wanted to place her at ease as quickly as possible.

She recovered from her surprise with amazing quickness. "I am Harvest Wife," she replied. Her answer was in Spanish, not Tule. It was a curious thing I was starting to notice about the clan, you see. They affected disdain for all things Spanish, and were stridently vocal in their praise of Cuna ways and culture. For all their posturing, it seemed that nearly all of them spoke Spanish passably well.

"I saw you on the beach when I arrived, Harvest Wife."

She smiled. "So, you remember me, Moon Child."

"How could I forget such loveliness?" I replied in my best Spanish. I was shading the truth a bit, for in reality Harvest Wife was rather on the plain side. She had a slight crook to her long nose, and one eye seemed just a bit off center. I couldn't make out too much of her shape beneath her voluminous *mola* and skirt, but if I were to guess, I would say she was on the sturdy and substantial side. My face betrayed not a hint of these thoughts. Instead I followed my flattery with my most dazzling smile. The sudden blush on her cheeks told me that Cuna damsels were as vulnerable to honeyed words as any other females. Harvest Wife would be putty in my hands.

"*Gracias,*" she murmured, but then she seemed to remember that she was standing scarfless before a strange male. To a Cuna, this was the equivalent of parading about Madison Square Garden in the buff. It just wasn't done, you see, and Harvest Wife instinctively moved as though to correct the situation. She swept her scarf over her head, but then she hesitated. A look passed over her copper features, a calculating one if I was not mistaken, and then she set aside her scarf once more.

Fenny, you're about to strike pay dirt, I congratulated myself. Pointing to her catch of lobsters, I asked sweetly, "May I help you?"

She shook her silky locks determinedly. "No, this is woman's work. Men may not do women's work. It is not the Cuna way."

That was damned refreshing to hear, and I readily conceded the point. "As you say, Harvest Wife." Aware of the ferocity of Cuna males, I needed a bit more information about my intended quarry before I went too much farther with her. I needed to know, you see, whether making advances on Harvest Wife was likely to result in retribution from a jealous warrior. "Er, tell me, Harvest Wife, did your man catch those lobsters?"

She flashed me a searching glance. I read curiosity in those dark eyes, and something more. Unless I was badly mistaken, I saw passion.

"No. I have no man. Mine was killed in battle. Far away."

She pointed across the channel separating us from the Darien interior. I surmised that she had been widowed as the result of some savage brawl between the Cuna and the upland tribes that bordered their dominions. All this explained her frank appraisal of me when I first came ashore; Harvest Wife was looking about for a replacement husband.

She was not about to find one in me, of course. Yet I was thrilled that she was a widow, for that told me that the coast was clear. Careful to keep the same huge grin on my face, I hunkered down at her side. Harvest Wife did not move away but instead went unconcernedly about her task, dunking the lobsters one after the other into the surf until they were free of sand and seaweed and then setting them back down in her basket.

As she worked, a scent of hibiscus flowers reached my nostrils. She seemed to have rubbed herself in them, and the aroma was wonderful. I found my passion growing, and Harvest Wife seemed to be aware of it. She paused in her work to inquire matter-of-factly, "Does Moon Child have a woman?"

"No, of course not. I arrived in your village only three weeks ago."

"No, I mean before you came here. When you were with the *wakers*. Did you have a woman in that world?"

There weren't enough hours in the day to recount for Harvest Wife the assorted dalliances of my life. As for informing her of my postponed nuptials with Alice, I dismissed the notion as soon as it popped into my head. You see, I knew enough of the straightlaced Cunas to surmise that for them a promise to be wed was inviolate. In their eyes, Alice and I were probably already married. No, a simple Cuna gal could never grasp the inherent subtleties of a *waker* engagement. All of this went through my mind in a flash—so quickly, in fact, that all Harvest Wife saw on my countenance was a look of utter sincerity as I assured her softly, "No, Moon Child has no woman."

This seemed to please her immensely, or at least she unleashed a string of chatter about her lobsters and how fine they were, and then went on about her family. She prattled away for the better part of an hour while I nodded attentively and wondered how to initiate the first move in Cuna sparking. Should I slip an arm about her shoulder, or should I just lean over and kiss her? Having long since stopped listening to her, I was weighing these two options when from behind me I heard a twig snap. Startled, I turned. There, in the palms, being true to his given name, was Watcher.

"Watcher, you little imp," I scolded him. "Have you been there all this while?"

He didn't answer but only stood stock-still, paler and more shaken than when the Colombians had nearly hauled him away into slavery. Irritated at the intrusion, I demanded, "Come on over here and quit skulking about like that. Hasn't anyone ever taught you that it isn't polite to snoop about when a fellow is trying to cuddle a girl? Come on over here, I say."

Watcher, however, did no such thing. Instead, he gave me one last look of pure revulsion and ran off through the trees, hallooing all the while.

What the dickens was the matter with the brat? I wondered. Why, he acted as though he had looked upon some act of monstrous evil, judging from the way he lit out from me. "What is wrong with that young fool?" I asked, turning to Harvest Wife.

I got no answer from her, for now she was up and running. "No, don't tell the *nele*!" she was screaming. "Don't do it!"

"Harvest Wife! Stop, damn you! What the blazes is going on here?"

There was nothing to do but sprint off after the two of them. It was a footrace, all right, for stocky though the Cunas were, they could run like antelope. As I dashed past rows of swaying palms, I could hear Watcher ahead of me blubbering as he ran. His words sent chills down my spine.

"Great Turtle! Great Turtle, you must come. Moon Child has broken the marriage law!"

18

By the time I broke out of the tree line bordering the cassava field, I knew the game was up. From every corner of the field women were eyeing me angrily, and from the village more were streaming out to see what the matter could be. Hobbling along behind them was the bent figure of the dreaded *nele*.

"Now, just wait a minute, folks," I implored as an angry crowd gathered about. "It's not what you think. I was merely talking with the lady. I don't know what Watcher thinks he saw, but it was nothing, I tell you, just a little chat."

Harvest Wife too was protesting her innocence, with about as much success as I was having. The village women rounded on her, gibbering in Tule so quickly that I could not follow all that was being said. I could make out, though, repeated references to the law of the clan and that Tiger would be summoned to judge the transgressors. Harvest Wife, I, and Watcher were then all marched to the plaza to await the *sahila*'s appearance.

But what was Tiger to judge? I wondered fearfully. What in Sam Hill had I done wrong? Why, I hadn't so much as stolen a kiss, and these savages were acting as though I'd violated the virginity of every Cuna maid in the village. Great Turtle only added to the tension by commencing a frenzied caterwauling that sounded like the buzzing of an angry wasp. All the while he glared at me with those horrid pink eyes. It was clear that he had second thoughts about ever having allowed my adoption.

My confusion lasted until Tiger returned with the other men. He heard out the *nele* as I waited on the plaza, surrounded by a knot of muttering women. Seeming to make up his mind about something, he marched through the women and squared up before me.

"Moon Child, you have not remembered the Tule laws as quickly as I hoped. The widow, Harvest Wife, cannot be approached by a man without following the code of the clan. You failed to consult me or the *nele*. You went into the grove of the women, and thereby upset the spirits of that sacred place. Great Turtle says that it will be weeks before he can appease those spirits so that the coconuts will continue to grow in abundance as before."

"Tiger, you must believe me," I pleaded. "I meant nothing by any of this. I just took a stroll, that's all. As for Harvest Wife, well, where I come from it's not a crime to say hello to a lady." Then I addressed an appeal to the *nele,* for I had been on the Comarca de San Blas long enough to know that these superstitious heathens wouldn't pass wind without the *nele*'s permission. "Great Turtle, I'm sorry. I did not mean to offend the spirits of the palms, and I will do anything I can to appease them."

All of this talk of spirits and broken laws was claptrap; the only thing that mattered was how all this unpleasantness would affect me. In that regard, Tiger didn't keep me guessing for too long. He looked to the bleached shaman, who in turn stopped his infernal chanting and eyed me damned sternly. It was clear that I was beginning to wear on the *nele*'s nerves. I had been nothing but trouble from the day I had arrived, and but for my wondrous rescue of Watcher and the other children, I guessed that Great Turtle was inclined to invoke the death penalty here and now, my very recent adoption into the clan notwithstanding. As it was, though, he suddenly began hopping about and emitting little whinnies and snorts, then stopped and stood glaring at Harvest Wife and me. He took a leather pouch from around his neck and opened it wide. The Cunas stepped back at this, for within lay the charms that were the source of all the shaman's power.

Great Turtle produced assorted bones of small birds and tossed them on the ground before me. He followed these with a few odd-colored pebbles and then what seemed to be tufts of human hair. He squatted down and arranged these fetishes into a pattern that seemed to have some significance for him. Satisfied, he stood and whined out a final incantation, then turned and shuffled off. The magic show, I concluded, was over.

When the *nele* was gone, Tiger spoke. "Great Turtle has decided that the spirits would be too greatly offended if Moon Child was to be punished for this transgression." Oh, ho, I thought. So the old mountebank was still unsure whether my magic was stronger than his. Thank heaven for his uncertainty, for it meant he still feared me. If he ever got over his shyness toward me, I suspected that my days among the Cuna would be numbered. "Instead," continued Tiger, "Great Turtle believes that Moon Child needs more time to remember the Cuna laws. Also, Moon Child will remember faster if he has a wife to help him recall them."

"Wife?" I asked, uncertain whether I had heard Tiger correctly.

"*Sí.* Harvest Wife needs a warrior. You have shown that you need a wife. Great Turtle has decreed that the two of you shall be joined. It is the will of the spirits."

"But, but what about Harvest Wife?" I stammered, not at all certain that I liked where things were going. "I mean, has anyone asked her if she agrees with all this?"

Tiger's face was hard and his eyes were narrow when he replied, "One of our strictest laws is that an unveiled woman may be looked upon only by her husband or her father. The penalty for violating that law is death. Only if the two of you join can you escape with your lives."

That put things in a perspective that even I could understand. "When's the nuptials?" I asked brightly.

I had done a bit of quick calculating, you see. First, it was obvious that the wedding would have to go on whatever my feelings on the matter. Marriage, though, might not be such a bad thing. After all, it certainly ended my problem of spending too many lonely nights swinging in a hammock in the *casa grande.* Now I would have Harvest Wife instead of Watcher to wait on me hand and foot, and I could pretty much go about my sylvan life as before. No, I saw no drawbacks to the arrangement now that Tiger had made the alternative clear to me.

As to her views on the matter, Harvest Wife made them clear by immediately bolting into the crowd and returning with a squatty little fellow with a horribly pockmarked face. "Moon Child, this is my father, Fish Hawk," she announced proudly. "Tule custom says that once we marry, you become his son."

Harvest Wife's runt of a pater had the look of a fellow who had survived the smallpox by no more than a cat's whisker. Given that, and his numerous other scars, no doubt from battle wounds, it was a sheer wonder that he was alive at all. Yet he seemed animated enough when he laid eyes on me, and in keeping with the spirit of the moment I grasped him by the shoulder and gushed, "Father, I crave the honor of being your son."

The bandy-legged little villain gave a lopsided grin at this, while all the while the assembled villagers, who not a moment before were quite ready to roast me slowly over a fire if that had been the wish of the *nele,* crowded about and congratulated both of us. Things might have gone on like this longer had not Tiger stepped in to get the festivities rolling.

He grunted out the banns to the hushed Cunas, gave some explicit directions to Fish Hawk, and then clapped his hands loudly. Immediately wild activity broke out everywhere. Fires were lit and soon long lines of women formed, each lady sporting a bright *mola* and a heavy necklace of Spanish coins strung together on a hemp cord. Thus adorned in their finery, the ladies of the Jaguar Clan commenced the wedding dance.

As they swayed about the plaza, singing men, called *ikarwisits,* moved among them. The *ikarwisits* warbled out ballads of creation and fertility while drums banged and flutes played. After an interval, the long lines of women dancers were joined by lines of painted warriors.

Now the volume of song soared, and the lines neared each other, surging back and forth as though they were giant serpents re-creating a mythic coupling from some mist-shrouded Cuna legend. The lines teased each other in this fashion for what seemed forever, and then, finally, they joined. Great yelps broke out as the orderly lines dissolved into masses of celebrating Cunas. This, apparently, was a signal for bacchanalian revels to commence, for gourds of *chicha* appeared everywhere. For hours the warriors drank and carried on until the sun set far in the west. As the flames of the many fires glowed brightly in the gloom, all eyes turned to Harvest Wife and me.

On some unspoken cue, a woman appeared before me and took me by the hand. She led me to a reed mat and bade me sit. A hush fell over the Cunas at this, and the only sound was a slow tune from a single flute. Harvest Wife rose, tossed some herbs into a fire, and then approached and danced before me. She wiggled her hips a bit and cast suggestive looks my way. Overall, though, it was a demure little exhibition, nothing like that wild waltz of love danced by the Moros in far off Mindanao. Nonetheless, Harvest Wife's dance made her point clear; she was ready to bed me and wanted the whole village to know that fact.

With her ritualistic capering complete, Harvest Wife offered me a small gourd of *chicha*. I accepted it and quaffed the fiery brew in one gulp. When I did, Harvest Wife seated herself at my side on the mat. An old woman approached—the same crone, in fact, who had belabored Longbottom out in the cassava field. She bore a platter of breadfruit. Harvest Wife took a serving of this, broke off a small piece, and handed it to me. I knew my part immediately, for this could only be the equivalent of the wedding cake. Alice had made certain to drill this part of the ritual into my brain, and so I executed my role flawlessly.

I broke the morsel in two, ate one, and then offered the remaining piece to Harvest Wife. She opened her mouth to accept it, and the night was split by the raucous acclamation of a thousand Cunas.

"Harvest Wife chooses Moon Child! Let the gods smile on them!" Tiger announced. "Now, Moon Child, is the time to retire to the abode of Harvest Wife. Go with her and do as she says."

Harvest Wife was already rising, pulling me along in her wake. Into her smoky, cramped hut we went, and straight into her hammock. If she was ready to consummate this shotgun wedding with most of her neighbors listening in at the hut's entrance, well, I was game. I merrily rolled over upon my blushing bride and commenced to haul up her cumbersome skirt.

"Come to me, you wild little filly," I murmured into her ear.

To my surprise, though, my advances were rewarded with a prompt cuff across the side of my head.

"Oww!" I cried. "What the devil did you do that for? We're married now, aren't we?"

"Not married," insisted Harvest Wife.

"Not married?" I retorted hotly. "Now see here, you silly woman. That old bugger Great Turtle gave us his blessings, didn't he? And then I just fed you, didn't I? That's it, now, isn't it? Now, why don't you be a proper little lady and just lie back. Old Fenny will take things from there, okay?"

No sooner had I said this, though, than a dozen screaming warriors, all from Tiger's lineage, burst into the hut. Petrified, I began bawling and begging for mercy, thinking that somehow the *nele* had changed his mind on this matter and decided to send me to perdition after all. Prying my fingers from the cords that secured the hammock to the hut's central posts, the warriors hauled me from the hut kicking and screaming.

"Let me go, damn you. We had a deal! A deal, I say!"

Expecting a deathblow at any instant, I was amazed when just feet from the hut they set me down and turned me about. Pointing me at the entrance, they shoved me back in that direction once again.

Tiger was among them now. "Go back," he insisted. "Moon Child must go to his woman."

Mystified by these shenanigans, I did as he bid. For her part, Harvest Wife lay in the hammock as though nothing amiss had transpired at all. She smiled coyly at me and patted the hammock at her side. Warily, I crept into the wedding bed once more.

"What was that all about?" I asked shakily.

"Cuna law," was the vague reply.

"Are they gone for good?" I asked, casting a questioning glance at the entrance.

Harvest Wife said nothing but instead grasped my hand. I had a great deal more in mind than simply holding her hand through the night, and so I rolled over on her and proceeded once more to get down to business.

"Not married!" she growled, then followed this up with a straight right to my eye.

"Ooof!" I grunted, the unexpected punch snapping my head back. Grasping her wrist, I demanded angrily, "Damnit woman, are you loco? This marriage isn't going to last too long if you wallop me every time I get near you!"

These words had just erupted from my throat when once more a knot of warriors boiled into the hut. "Damn you pests!" I swore at them. "Don't you have the brains to see that this is not the time to be playing your infernal games? Shove off, I say!"

My protestations were to no avail, however, for once more I was dragged from the hut, and then, inexplicably, freed as soon as I passed the portal. Once more Tiger was there, and once more he ordered me to return to my ill-tempered spouse. Grousing each step of the way, I did as I was told, but my patience with Cuna ways was beginning to come to an end.

Again I climbed into the hammock, but this time I kept my hands to myself, and well above my waist to ward off any sudden attack from my loving bride. None came, and after a quiet interlude the warriors appeared once more, dragged me out into the plaza, and again released me. Dully aware now that this was part of a ritual about which I had not been made privy, I demanded in exasperated tones of Tiger, "How much longer does this farce go on? I mean, a man can stand being the rope in a tug-of-war for only so long."

"It is over," Tiger assured me. "Go to your woman now. If she allows you to lie at her side, you are joined."

I returned to the hammock, eased in ever so carefully, and lay perfectly still. Harvest Wife didn't stir for the longest time, and when she finally did, I gave a start of fright.

"There's no need to get nasty about it!" I cried. "I'll just be on my way, never you fear."

Harvest Wife, though, had her arms open wide. "Come, Moon Child. Be my man now. Share my hearth."

Hmmm, I thought. This could be a trap. Maybe she wanted me in her embrace to strangle me. She had no visible weapons, but if she could manage to get my head wedged between the hammock's cords, they would do the job rather handily.

Seeing my hesitation, Harvest Wife reached for one of my hands and placed it upon her breast. I felt a soft fullness there, and an undeniably erect nipple. Maybe, just maybe, she was willing to settle down and act the part of the adoring wife. Gingerly, I rolled over and climbed aboard. Tensely ready for any offensive reaction from below, I set about coupling as best I could under the circumstances.

Harvest Wife, whether because my edgy performance exceeded the capabilities of her late husband on his best day, or because she was so lonely that any love play would suit her, seemed to warm to me as things progressed. Satisfied that I was safe for the moment, I settled down to ride my new mate into the wee hours of the night. A strange ride it was though, not at all unlike the tentative mating of black widow spiders. She lay there with her eyes closed, grunting heavily and taking her pleasures with not a care in the world. I hovered above, doling out that pleasure in controlled packets, careful to keep my eyes open at all times, and wondering fretfully when the fatal sting might come.

19

The following morning I emerged from my humble abode, tired and stiff from a night of fitful sleep, to find most of the males of the village gathered about my threshold to greet me. A great laughing and stomping of feet broke out, and I took this to be the good-natured jibing of the sort that generally accompanies wedding nights.

Then Harvest Wife emerged, coyly seeking my side as her friends and relations quizzed her about her first full night with Moon Child. Harvest Wife, so modest and reserved last night in my arms, made it graphically, almost shockingly, clear to all present that she was satisfied with her new mate's performance. She rubbed herself in a most indiscreet way and made as if to seize me by my penis sheath. I scampered from her grasp, to the vast amusement of all, and Harvest Wife mercifully concluded the audience.

My stock went up immeasurably with Tiger and the other men at this report, and I was feted to a breakfast of smoked fish in the *casa grande,* where I was asked to discuss the merits of my bride, which, knavishly, I did. The earthy details about Harvest Wife's well-muscled thighs and not inconsiderable breasts were soaked up by my rapt listeners. Like most puritans, the Cunas it seemed had a covert fascination with all things sexual. Indulging their curiosity, I even described the curious little yips emitted by Harvest Wife as she reached her moment of release. I imitated them as best I could, letting out a noise that struck the ear like the sound an enraged mouse might make. This convulsed my fellow clansmen, setting them to rolling about in the dirt and holding their sides with helpless laughter.

Later in the morning when I strolled about the village, I came to the conclusion that Harvest Wife too had been telling tales out of school. The village women smiled as I passed them, with more than one of them studying my private parts with undisguised curiosity. It all got a bit embarrassing, and I started hankering for my britches, which I had been without since my landfall among the Cunas.

After a bit, I decided it was time to return to Harvest Wife and let her know her man was hungry. As a married man, I would no longer eat at the *casa grande* but instead was expected to take my meals at my own hearth. I found my bride on a mat before the hut, weaving cotton on a crude loom.

Screwing up my face into what I hoped might pass for an adoring smile, I asked, "Is it time for breakfast yet, my love?"

Harvest Wife did not look up. "When you have finished your labors." Her tone was flinty and unyielding.

"Labors? Whatever are you talking about?" I demanded, angered no small amount by her impertinence. "I have nothing to do, except maybe go fishing later with Tiger."

"You go and work for Fish Hawk."

"Your father?" I snorted. "That mangled piece of leather can do his own damned drudgery, by God. I'll not be made into his lackey by you or anyone else."

Harvest Wife was uncowed. "You go work," she commanded.

"Don't you presume to tell me—"

I never finished my sentence, for just then Fish Hawk arrived and with him several burly sons.

"Moon Child, you come. I am your father now, and you are my son. Come now."

"Come where?" I demanded, only to be seized roughly by the wrist and hustled along to where a great log lay propped up between two stumps.

"This will be my new *cayuco*," announced Fish Hawk, tossing me a dull adze as he spoke. "Start the work," he ordered. "I will be back when the sun sets."

Incredulous, I threw aside the adze. "You expect me to stay here and hollow out this log all day? You're out of your mind, friend. Loco, *comprende?*"

Fish Hawk was not amused. "It is Cuna law, Moon Child. The son obeys the father." He squared up and slapped me hard across the face.

I went to slap him right back but was stopped by a sharp kick to my shin and a hard punch to my ribs. I staggered back, breathless. It was instantly clear that I'd need a weapon of some sort to settle matters with this hombre, for I could not overpower him barehanded.

Fish Hawk read my mind, for he growled, "Moon Child, do not make me seek the counsel of the *nele*. You broke our law yesterday. If you do so again, I think the *nele* may become very angry."

Damn! He had me buffaloed, and from the look on his mug, I could tell he knew it. Fish Hawk picked up the adze once again and shoved it at me. "Do not cease your labor until I come for you."

Then he was gone and I was left to spend the rest of the day under the broiling sun chipping away at the tough cedar log with a tool dulled from generations of use. My arms ached and I was hungry, and worst of all there was nothing to drink. I saw Longbottom in the distance out in the fields toting water to the irrigation ditches. He stopped and ladled himself out a long drink, and for the first time since we arrived among the Cuna I actually envied him.

Fish Hawk did not return until the sun was well behind the Darien mountains. He inspected my work, pronounced it shoddy, and berated me for my wastrel ways. I remonstrated with him that his damned adze was about as useful for this sort of work as a teaspoon, but this outburst merely triggered a barrage of cuffs and kicks. Fish Hawk hounded me all the way back to Harvest Wife's hut, scolded me in front of her, and then stomped off.

"You are lazy," she hissed when her father was gone. "You disgrace me before him."

"Listen," I rounded on her, "I've had about enough of your father. I don't want to hear about him for the rest of the night. Now you fetch me some broiled fish and yams, and get them pronto. Oh, and whip up some roasted pork too. I'm starved, do you hear?"

"You will have two yams, nothing more," she pronounced. "Until you learn to obey, you will not have meat."

"Now see here, woman. I'm your husband, and you'll damn well do as I say."

Starving and exhausted, I had lost my fear of her fists. By God, I was prepared to settle the chain-of-command issue with her once and for all. If a good old-fashioned shellacking was what Harvest Wife needed, well then I was just the boy to deliver it. With balled fists I advanced upon her and demanded tersely, "Get my meal, woman, and get it now."

I never really saw the big iron kettle coming at all. Harvest Wife, in one fluid movement, scooped the thing from where it sat before the fire, hefted it high in the air like a Scottish hammer thrower, and brought it crashing down on my skull. All I knew was that one moment it seemed as though I had mastered the situation, and the next I was stumbling from the hut in blinding pain, screaming in terror as I blinked stars from my eyes.

"Help! Stop her!" I cried as I staggered into the plaza with blood streaming down my crown. The Cunas, however, hung back, as Harvest Wife followed me into the open and commenced to belabor me with the kettle as though it were a mace. With awesome ferocity and surprising strength, she pounded me across the head and shoulders until I was rolling senseless in the dust. When she was satisfied that I was thoroughly bludgeoned, she finished with a few quick kicks to my midsection, then huffed back into the hut.

I lay motionless for what seemed an eternity with a strange buzzing in my head. When I awoke it was morning, and Fish Hawk was standing over me, impatient for me to be off to work.

Properly chastened now, I went. The next week was a pure hell of backbreaking labor. I finished Fish Hawk's canoe and then dug irrigation ditches in the cassava fields until my arms felt as though they would fall off. Once I was done there, my father-in-law decided he needed a new roof on his vermin-infested hut.

I was up on his roof, standing knee-deep in palm thatching, when who should happen past but Henry and Kingston Jack. Peering around to make sure none of my new kin were watching, I hopped down.

Kingston Jack let out a low whistle. "Jesus, Captain, you're black and blue from head to foot."

"We heard you tied the knot, Fenny," added Henry. "I guess honeymoons end early among these folks."

"Henry, you don't know the half of it. Ever since I got hitched, my life's been one long thrashing. These people are plain crazy, and mean as spit to boot."

"All this is only normal for a new husband, Captain," explained Kingston Jack. "It's the Cuna way. This tribe is really run by the women. They own all the property, and they make all the major decisions. The men are the warriors, all right, but other than that, they have little status compared to women. No man may sell or trade anything of value unless his wife gives her permission. She, on the other hand, can trade and sell as she pleases. Because of this, the women dominate the men. If a man wants a rooster for a cockfight, he must ask his wife. If he wants a coin to gamble, he must ask his wife. Being a Cuna husband is no easy task."

"Now you tell me," I groaned. "Why didn't you deign to enlighten me on these facts before I got hitched?"

"Now, Captain Travers, be fair. You never asked me."

He was right and I knew it. I had been living such a pleasant existence that I failed to open my eyes to the harsher realities of Cuna life. I had blundered into a snare and now I was caught fast. The fact that it was all my own fault, though, didn't mean that I couldn't go on complaining bitterly.

"My wife is bad enough, but her father is completely overbearing. He acts as though he owns me."

"In a way he does," commented Kingston Jack. "Once a Cuna male marries, he owes his father-in-law service. That means that a man with many daughters is lucky, since as he marries them off he can rely on the labors of many young men. Marriage is the way that older Cuna men escape the bondage of their own married lives."

"But I thought that Tiger said the Cuna didn't own other people."

"They don't own each other like slaves, Captain. These bonds are ones of tradition and heritage. To be a Cuna is to be bound to the clan and to your wife's family."

An existence of eternal toil was hardly appealing. Suddenly, Henry's desire to escape the Comarca de San Blas was very alluring to me. All I wanted now was the answer to one question, and I put it to both of them straight out: "How can we vamoose from here?"

Kingston Jack shook his head. "We've been through all this. We would need Tiger's permission to leave."

"Or the *nele*'s," added Henry.

"Oh, that old rascal would love to send me on my way," I said with a rueful laugh. "The only problem is, though, the destination he has in mind for me is hell, not Colón."

"Work on Tiger then, Captain Travers," urged Kingston Jack. "After all, you did save his son, and by all rights he still owes you. Convince him to help before his memories fade."

I spotted Fish Hawk ambling along in the distance. "Off now with the both of you. Keep your eyes on me, though. I'll think of something. What that might be, I don't exactly know at the moment. I've decided to leave here, though, and by God, I will."

Henry and Kingston Jack made off, and I climbed back onto the roof. Fish Hawk, well rested from a day of loafing and *chicha* swilling, lit into me for not finishing my task in the allotted time. He pulled me down from my perch and pummeled me to the ground before sending me home with a swift kick to my backside. Warning me to be back at dawn, he stumbled into his abode to sleep off his debauch.

When I returned home, I found my two yams, stone cold and barely cooked, on a platter before the door. Harvest Wife was within, spinning as usual. If she wasn't at her wheel, she was counting her horde of coins. Truly, she was the most overtly acquisitive woman I had ever met, and I had seen some truly greedy damsels in my time.

I morosely ate as much of my yams as I could, gagged on the rest, and then tossed the whole mess into the dust. It was then, as I sat hugging my knees and damning the fates that cast me up on this alien shore, that the scent of roasting chicken came to my nostrils. My head jerked about as if by its own accord and pointed directly at a hut just three doors down. With saliva running down my slack jaws, I was on my feet and moving before I was conscious of doing so.

As I walked, I was forming and rejecting plans. Perhaps I could just slip in and seize the fowl and pound away before I was spotted. Although theft was anathema to the Cuna, and a burglar taken in the act could expect to be stoned to death, I was building my resolve for a bit of smash and grab. By God, I was being slowly starved to death, and if I didn't get some proper food under my belt soon, I wouldn't have the strength to flee back to civilization.

I stopped at the portal through which the aroma was emanating and gave one final sniff. My course fixed in my mind, I entered. When my eyes adjusted to the darkness within, I saw that the place was not empty. At the hearth stood a Cuna woman, and she wore no shawl. What's more, she evidenced not the slightest surprise that I had passed her threshold unbidden.

"So, you came, Moon Child," she giggled. "I am pleased."

"Who, who are you?" I asked, looking hungrily past her at the spitted chicken slowly cooking over the fire. I could hear the fat of the bird popping and hissing as it dripped into the flames, and it was all I could do to keep from throwing myself upon the fowl and gulping it down my maw in huge, steaming chunks.

"I am Morning Star. I have watched you, Moon Child, ever since you married my cousin, Harvest Wife."

Ah, I recognized her now. She had indeed made it a point to flutter about whenever I was at the hut of my beloved spouse. I hadn't had much time to take notice of Morning Star before, though, since whenever I was under my own roof I spent most of my time ducking cudgels.

"Are you hungry, Moon Child?" she asked coquettishly.

"Did Sherman burn Atlanta?" I shot right back in English, but seeing her blank stare went on in Spanish, "Er, yes, Morning Star, I'm very hungry. I'm starved. You savvy? I need food."

She got the point, all right. "It is as I thought," she said with a smile. Taking me by the hand, she led me to her fire and gestured for me to sit. Once I was settled, she produced a wooden bowl and ladled out great spoonfuls of turtle stew from a kettle set in the flames. I ate without utensils of any sort, slurping the broth noisily and then greedily digging out the pieces of tender turtle meat with my fingers. When I was done, my companion slipped the chicken from its spit, set it on a wooden platter, and whacked it into quarters with a butcher knife.

I practically pulled the platter from her hands. As Morning Star watched with evident satisfaction, the bird disappeared before her eyes. Smacking my lips when the last bone had been licked clean, I belched loudly and rose to go.

"This has been simply fabulous, Morning Star. You must have me by more often. Say, do you happen to be open for breakfast? I could slip by here on my way to the salt mines."

Before I could go, though, Morning Star was between me and the door. She pulled a cloth curtain across the entrance and pressed herself against my chest.

"Do not go, Moon Child. There is much I still want to share with you."

What in tarnation was this gal ranting about? I wondered. I might have pushed past her and been on my way had not I felt a feminine hand very definitely closing about my all-too-exposed privates. By thunder, the lady was in a mood for a quick after-dinner fling!

"Now see here, my dear, what you're suggesting is extremely dangerous. Why, I damned near lost my life for just looking at a woman without her veil."

"Yes, it is dangerous, Moon Child," she agreed, "but it is possible. Women take lovers even among the Cuna, but we must hurry. Do not hesitate, or the moment will pass."

Then she demonstrated her resolve in a breathtaking manner. Morning Star doffed her clothes to stand naked before me, naked, that is, except for her *winis*—the bands of brightly colored beads strung about her wrists and ankles. There was no question about it; my hostess was a first-class beauty blessed with high, firm breasts and deliciously curved loins. She was petite and well proportioned. Why, compared to her, Harvest Wife was a misshapen troll. As I surveyed these feminine charms so provocatively displayed before me, my penis sheath shifted in silent salute.

Morning Star's sharp eyes did not miss the movement. "Moon Child likes, *sí?*"

"*Sí,*" I panted through a suddenly constricted throat, "but let's be quick about it, shall we?"

Besides being a damned good cook, Morning Star possessed another laudable attribute; she wasn't the least bit shy. Taking my hand, she led me to her hammock and climbed in. I piled in right behind her, and the little lady went straight to work with a vengeance. Now, I've known the favors of skilled courtesans from Tientsin to Toledo, but for my money this little Cuna miss stood right near the top of the list in terms of raw talent. Oh, she was a mite clumsy, but that was only from the lack of practice. Within minutes, though, it was clear that if I could ever get Morning Star away to a proper bordello, she could be shaped up into a top earner within a month.

She was so good, in fact, that my fear of detection soon yielded to my mounting urgency. I slipped into my companion as soon as she had brought me to full arousal, and then the horses were away from the post. Off we went on a ride of pure bliss, me groaning in delight as Morning Star huffed noisily at the feel of my deft thrusts. Soon she was rocking along in some dimension completely divorced from reality, for she commenced a curious sideways motion with her buttocks that set the hammock into wide, looping swings. As the amplitude of the swings increased, our coupling took on more the aspect of a circus ride than a tryst. Gasping and grunting, we swung left, then right, picking up speed and height as we went.

"More, more!" Morning Star demanded, and I complied as best I could, thrusting so hard that the hammock threatened to revolve in full circles about its moorings to the hut's central posts.

Now her legs were wrapped about me, and her nails were raking my back as she arched forward for what she craved. I couldn't have escaped her grasp had I wanted to. But why would I? In her embrace I had found an earthly paradise. No, it was a feeling even more exquisite than that, as though I had been bodily transported to a realm of pure delight, with no earthly cares whatsoever. Yes, that was it; I was in the Muslim seventh heaven, the very peak of sensual fulfillment.

Then I was in hell, for suddenly the curtain was torn aside and the room filled with both light and the enraged screams of Harvest Wife! "Moon Child, I will kill you!" she shrieked.

Immediately my eyes flew open and, despite Morning Star's awesome grip on me, I flew from her arms. I left the hammock just as it reached the peak of its arc, firing off on a trajectory straight for the ceiling and tumbling Morning Star to the dirt floor as I went. I slammed into a bamboo rafter, let out a great howl of pain, and then plummeted straight down to land in the open hearth with a huge puff of ash and sparks.

"Great jumping Christ, I'm afire!" I bellowed, leaping immediately to my feet and twirling about like a dervish. I slapped wildly at my feet and then sprinted for the exit. As I cleared the entranceway, from the corner of my eye I saw Harvest Wife grab a flat *cayuco* paddle and deliver Morning Star a resounding whack across her comely buttocks. I sprinted away from the love den, followed by my paramour and then my wife, all three of us hallooing and thundering as we went. Immediately I was collared by Fish Hawk, who had happened by his daughter's place for some free victuals. Then village women laid hands on the naked Morning Star. Her story was plain enough for all to see; she was buck naked, her behind was a bright pink, and her enraged cousin was hot on her trail. It was a case of adultery, pure and simple.

The *nele* was summoned at once, as was Tiger. All the villagers were on hand now, and among them were Henry and Kingston Jack, drawn to the scene by the hue and cry raised by Harvest Wife. It was clear there would be no easy way out of this mess. The stormy visage of the ancient shaman only heightened my sense of dread. He ordered a fire lit on the plaza, and a cauldron of water was set to boil. When it was bubbling he opened his magic pouch and began tossing herbs, seeds, mushrooms, and bits of bark into the pot, stirring all the while with a stick. When the potion was to his liking, he ordered it pulled from the flames. As soon as it cooled, he yammered out an order, and the Cunas rose as one and filed by the cauldron. Each of them took a sip from a ladle held by Tiger. Even Longbottom, who had been hauled from the miserable hovel where he generally spent his evenings, was given a dollop of the foul brew. When all except the two *cimaroons* had partaken, Tiger held the ladle out to Harvest Wife, Morning Star, and me. Each of us drank, but I certainly didn't relish the stuff. No, it tasted like the runoff from a tannery, and I nearly gagged as I forced my portion down my gullet.

With his stage set, Great Turtle held his spindly arms high. As he did, the flames of the fire seemed to rise higher, although no breeze fanned them. Then the ancient one spoke.

"Since the coming of Moon Child, there have been both wonders and evils among our people. Children have been saved, true, but also laws have been broken. Adultery has raised its ugly head among us, the golden people of the pure hearts."

How could this be? I wondered. Great Turtle was speaking Tule, yet I was understanding him as plain as day. It didn't make sense, you see, for my grasp of Tule was still rudimentary. Something had changed, but for the life of me, I couldn't fathom what that might be.

The *nele* continued. "Golden people, hear me. I have seen what has caused this trouble in our midst." He paused here, gazing out on his awed people with those awful pink eyes. When he spoke again, his words fell on my numbed brain like the ringing blows of a sledgehammer: "There are witches among us!"

Witches? Why, I knew enough about the Cuna to know that witches were their worst nightmare. A witch could conjure up a storm at sea to sweep away a *cayuco* without a trace. A witch could cause the coconut palms to wither and women to grow barren. Witches were menaces that had to be rooted out as soon as they were detected.

"Where are the witches, oh Seer?" cried Tiger, fear in his voice.

Great Turtle did not answer directly. Instead, he said, "I shall summon the totem of the Jaguar Clan. Our guiding spirit will point out the evil ones among us."

As racked with fear as I was, I was still coherent enough to realize that the shrunken little huckster was talking pure balderdash. Spirits didn't just waltz into Indian encampments, you see. He had some sort of mummery up his sleeve, I was sure, and if his scheme threatened to put me at risk, I'd expose him for the faker he was. That thought put a little steel into my backbone, and I was nearly on the verge of recovering my nerve when the most amazing thing happened. From somewhere deep in the sacred palm grove came an earsplitting yowl. I had heard that awful sound before; it had come from El Diablo, the huge jaguar killed by Serafina!

"It can't be," I murmured to myself, but before my disbelieving eyes, the impossible happened.

As the frightened mass of Cunas gave way before it, a huge jaguar strode into the village. It came on silently, swinging its massive head from side to side as it did, as though searching for something—or someone. There could be no doubt that the cat was real. It had the same spots as El Diablo, and the same bold, piercing yellow eyes. But how could this be? Jaguars just didn't appear at the behest of withered old albinos. This defied every principle of science I had ever known, which meant that I was either insane or else Great Turtle was a magician of the highest order. Perhaps I had been wrong about him all along, and now my very soul would be forfeit because of my stubborn foolishness.

"Oh jaguar spirit," intoned the *nele*, "guide us in this troubled moment. Tell us if there are witches in our midst. Point them out, so that they may not do harm to the golden people. Aid us in our need, we beseech you."

As he prayed, Great Turtle's pink eyes seemed to glow luminously red in the gloom. I blinked disbelievingly; a man's eyes couldn't glow like twin fireflies. Such things just weren't possible, yet seeing was believing. The *nele*'s rosy orbs were suddenly the least of my troubles, though, for now the jaguar swung its great head about and locked right onto me. Silently, it padded across the plaza, heading straight for old Fenny.

God in heaven, I prayed, deliver me from this devil! Oh, I promised to put my wastrel ways behind me and to set my feet firmly on the straight and narrow. Please Lord, I begged, just let this hellish cat pass me by. Pray as I might, though, nothing of any note happened in response to my celestial entreaties. Instead, I stayed rooted right where I was, and the jaguar came on until its whiskered muzzle was but a foot away from me. Then, with awful deliberation, the beast lifted a great forepaw—and pointed at Harvest Wife!

My churlish wife, so brazen just minutes before, collapsed in a dead faint; her eyes rolled up into her head until nothing showed but the whites.

"She is a witch!" declared Great Turtle.

"Kill the witch!" roared the Cunas, and they made as if to rush upon the fallen Harvest Wife.

"Yes, yes!" I cried, vastly relieved that the jaguar had not singled out yours truly. "She's the one, all right! Get her!"

"Hold!" commanded Great Turtle, and the crowd fell back.

I cried out in protest, "Why stop them, Great Turtle? You have your witch, don't you? Leave the golden people to deal with her and turn me loose. Turn me loose, I say."

Oh, you may damn me for a poltroon for turning over my own wife to the tender mercies of a Cuna mob, but look at things from my perspective. After one week of marriage to her, I was not at all inclined to intervene if Harvest Wife's friends and neighbors wished to tear her limb from limb. Moreover, if pure orneriness was the measure of being a witch, she was a charter member of the broom-riding club.

The *nele,* though, did not deign to respond to my remonstrances. Instead he looked to the eerily silent jaguar, which in turn looked at me. Its yellow eyes seemed illuminated with an inner light when it gazed upon me, and then its great jaws opened and I saw awful rows of white fangs. God, was it going to bite off my head? I wondered fearfully. Instead the great jaws closed and the beast raised its front paw—and pointed straight at me!

"He too is a witch!" proclaimed Great Turtle.

A great "Ooohhh!" erupted from the crowd, for never in Tule lore had witches been male. Yet Moon Child had been a *waker* before he had been adopted into the golden people, and perhaps among the *wakers,* witches could be male. Whatever the case, if the *nele* was certain that Moon Child was a witch, then none present would question his judgment. The witches would burn before the sun rose in the east.

"No! No!" I cried. "There must be some mistake! I couldn't cast a spell if my life depended on it! You've got to believe me!"

They didn't; as one the Cunas advanced on me. I stood there, quaking miserably, certain that this was the end of the trail. Nothing could save me now. I was destined to die screaming my life away as I was consumed in a sacrificial inferno surrounded by gibbering heathens. Yet as I faced my end, my brain insisted that I had missed some important detail about the jaguar. The great cat was so palpably real and so dangerously close, yet something seemed wrong.

Then it hit me! There was no smell. Hadn't El Diablo been enveloped in an awful musk combined with the stench of rotted meat? Hadn't his roars shaken the leaves of the tree in which he lay? This jaguar was odorless even though its maw was only inches from my face. Also, it had not roared once since it entered the village. The only jaguarlike sound I had heard had come before the cat appeared.

What all this told me was that the jaguar was not real. It was an apparition, somehow conjured up by Great Turtle. If the apparition was a sham, though, how could Great Turtle have made the same vision appear to hundreds of people at the same instant? My eyes went to the cauldron. Yes, of course! Great Turtle had dropped herbs into the brew, hadn't he? He must have whipped up some sort of elixir that caused people to have visions. Why else would he have insisted that everyone except the *cimaroons* drink before he summoned the jaguar?

Everything my eyes had beheld, I reasoned, was an illusion. There was no two-hundred-pound cat standing inches from me. Telling my mind to ignore the plain intelligence I was receiving from my eyes was one of the hardest things I have ever had to do. Yet trembling though I was, and on the verge of losing control of my bowels should my desperate surmise prove erroneous, I decided to call the *nele*'s bluff.

"My kinsmen!" I cried out. "Great Turtle has not summoned the jaguar spirit as he promised. There is nothing before me but thin air!"

A gasp went up at my blasphemy, and the lips of the jaguar pulled back into a wild snarl as though the thing was about to leap for my throat. Yet still no sound came from the beast. With a trembling heart, I balled my fist and raised it high. Then, with a gulp, I lashed out at the beast before me.

My hand went right through it!

Around me, the Cunas were babbling wildly, for they had seen my hand pass through the jaguar as though it were not there.

"Great Turtle," called Tiger. "What is this? Why can Moon Child pass his hand through the jaguar?"

"He is a witch, I say!" rasped the *nele*. "He has powers that others do not possess! The jaguar is there, but the witch's powers are great."

Now, though, I felt my courage flooding back as I realized the truth. Great Turtle had mesmerized us en masse and put only a projection of the cat before us. As for rendering the arcane Tule tongue comprehensible, maybe Great Turtle was really speaking Spanish but my dazed mind thought he was speaking Tule, or maybe the drug truly had powers beyond belief. Whatever the truth of the matter, it was clear that we were all victims of a narcotic effect of some sort, a black art that the cunning shaman had undoubtedly wielded to great effect in the past.

"That's a lie, Great Turtle," I challenged him, "and you know it. There is no cat here. Look, I will show you."

With that I kicked out at the vision and then danced a hasty jig all through it. It grew dim as I did so, as though my reason was asserting itself once more and the effect of Great Turtle's herbs began to wane. Now others saw the jaguar grow dimmer in their sight, and muttering against the *nele* began.

"Kill the witch before his powers overcome mine!" commanded Great Turtle. "I cannot hold him at bay much longer."

He looked to Tiger to carry out his command, and I could see the doubt on the chief's face. He was uncertain about what he was seeing, but if Great Turtle was right and I was a witch, then my power had to be contained while there was still time. Yet on the other hand, I had plucked Watcher from slavery, and that did not seem to be the sort of thing a malevolent witch would do.

Reading the hesitation on his face, I knew that I had to dispel the last vestiges of Great Turtle's authority, and quickly. I had a sudden inspiration, and I acted upon it. "Quick, Henry, get me the telescopic sight from the Krag!"

"The sight? Whatever for?"

"Just do it!" I screamed.

Henry reached into the haversack at his side. "Here it is, but for my money, what you need is the Krag, not the sight."

I seized the device and held it high. "Great Turtle, hear me. You saw me drive off the Spanish when I put this object on the fire stick. This is my looking glass, and it holds great power."

"What kind of power, *waker?*" demanded Great Turtle, already demoting me back into the ranks of the unclean.

"It has the power to capture souls. Hear me now, oh shaper of illusions. I can seize your soul, and surely I will unless you do as I say."

"You have no such power," scoffed the *nele*. "Only the greatest of wizards can seize the soul of men. You are an ordinary witch, a seducer of women and a maimer of pigs."

"You are wrong," I said, smiling. "My power is much greater than you suspect." I called to the *sahila*, "Tiger, come look through my magic looking glass. See that I already have begun to enslave the soul of Great Turtle."

Appearing deeply troubled, Tiger stepped forward. "Gaze upon your shaman," I directed, "and see whether my words are true or not."

I handed the sight to him, but reversed, and indicated that he should peer into the front aperture of the device. "Careful now, Tiger, this thing is big medicine. Handle it gently or it might release the spirits within and turn the whole clan into toadstools."

As he did so, I could see Henry beginning to nod his understanding. By looking through the front aperture, whatever image Tiger saw would be reduced, not magnified, and reduced by a factor of twelve. That meant that when he looked upon Great Turtle, it appeared that the *nele* was shrunken to the size of a chipmunk.

"Aiieee!" gasped Tiger, turning pale as he beheld Great Turtle. "Moon Child's medicine is strong! I see your soul, great wizard, and it is but the size of a small plantain!" He held his thumb and forefinger about two inches apart to emphasize his point.

Now Great Turtle was alarmed. The report was unquestionably accurate, for Tiger was a man of unimpeachable integrity. If he said the *nele*'s soul was in danger, then, by the gods, it was.

"Release my soul, *waker*," demanded Great Turtle, "or I will—"

"You'll what?" I taunted him. "Send a make-believe jaguar to growl at me? Or perhaps cause a troop of nonexistent monkeys to silently perch in the trees above me and make faces until I go away?"

Faced with mortal danger to himself, the old fraud capituiated. "What is it you want, *waker?*"

I knew my price and I laid it before him like a patron ordering at Delmonico's. "A seagoing *cayuco* with sturdy outriggers and a sail. Enough victuals for a week. Oh, and I'll have the Krag too, and all the ammunition."

"They are all yours. Now go."

"Hold on, partner," I retorted. "I'm not done yet."

The *nele*'s eyes, which had stopped glowing once I was able to see through his chicanery, narrowed now. "So, you want gold too. You are just like all the others. Well, there is no gold, *waker,* other than what we use to adorn our bodies."

I knew that, of course, for Shaler had told me so. Further, I rather doubted that the Cuna would live in crowded pigsties if they could afford better. No, I was certain there was no lucre to be had in these parts. "It's not gold I seek, Great Turtle. What I want are my companions, the *cimaroons,* and my servant."

He nodded. "They are free to go with you."

"And I want you to protect Harvest Wife and Morning Star from all harm when I leave."

"But one is a witch and the other an adulteress," protested Tiger. "What you ask, Moon Child, is impossible."

But it was Great Turtle's soul, not Tiger's, that was in my magic looking glass, and the wily shaman was painfully aware of that fact. He yielded.

"The adulteress is pardoned. She was under your spell when she committed her crime. Obviously she was hexed and could not know her mind. As for the other, Harvest Wife . . ." Here he paused, for his magic had boxed him in. How could he explain to the assembled tribe that the woman pointed out by the jaguar spirit itself was in fact not a witch?

I watched his ancient visage as he made his calculations, for I was convinced that it was he who had caused the apparition to point out Harvest Wife. When Great Turtle spoke, it was with all the impromptu bravado of a Tammany politician breaking a campaign pledge a month after the election. "The jaguar spirit pointed true, but at the aura cast from Moon Child. That aura enveloped Harvest Wife, who sat by his side. I see this now, and because of this I am able to say that Harvest Wife was falsely accused. No harm shall come to her."

Nobody seemed inclined to query the shaman on why, if what he had just said was true, the jaguar spirit had not also fingered Tiger and Morning Star, who were equally close to me. The Cunas were warriors, though, not lawyers, so this inconsistency went unchallenged. Tiger gave the necessary orders, and at once a *cayuco* was placed at our disposal. Provisions were stowed aboard, as was a sail and paddles. When all was in readiness, we prepared to shove off into the night.

Tiger stood in the sea up to his hips. He pushed the canoe out past the surf, and right before releasing us into the current he said to me in Spanish, "Whatever you may be, Moon Child, I will remember that I am in debt to you for the life of my son."

I paused, for I genuinely liked Tiger. Oh, he was a bloodthirsty killer, all right, and he would have split my skull had the *nele* but given the word. Yet, all in all, Tiger had done right by me, and I could count on the fingers of one hand the number of people about whom I could say the same. For that reason, I paused and replied, "Tiger, Kingston Jack said something to me that I think you should know. He said that Comandante Reyes would raise a force large enough to return to your island and kill your people to the last woman and child. Beware of his return."

Tiger nodded. "I have thought much about him, Moon Child. When the moment comes, I will be ready."

Then he gave me a crushing hug that drove the air from my chest, and when he released me I fell breathless into the canoe. Henry and Kingston Jack pulled for the deep water beyond the reef, then turned the prow to the northwest. Kingston Jack unfurled the sail, which caught a promising breeze, and then we were off.

20

Colón, Panama
14 September 1903

It was dawn when we paddled quietly into Colón Harbor. We pulled the *cayuco* ashore not far from Pier 1 and secreted it beneath a pile of flotsam washed in by the tide. Then we made our way to the railroad office, where I borrowed a pair of trousers and a shirt until my baggage could be made available. When Deputy Superintendent Prescott arrived for work a few hours later, I regaled him with the details of our harrowing adventure. Once I finished he rang up the telephone line to Panama City with the news of our reappearance. Shaler came on the line and Prescott handed me the receiver.

"Travers, I'm glad to hear your voice. Your disappearance put the fear of God into Amador and the others. They've been in virtual hiding, fearful that Comandante Reyes would come for them next."

"Well, you need to help them get over their bashfulness and get this show on the road." I was blunt with Shaler, for with my sojourn among the Cuna behind me, it was time to wrap up what had been started in Panama City and then sail for home. "We've got to get Amador up north to see the necessary officials in Washington."

"I agree," replied Shaler. "And you've got to go with him to ensure he doesn't get cold feet along the way."

"Then bundle him over to Colón on one of your trains," I said.

"I'll do so at once," Shaler assured me. "Meanwhile have Prescott see about booking passage on the next steamer for the United States." Then he rang off.

Prescott was waiting at the station three hours later when Amador arrived, alone and with no luggage. Shaler had decided that it would attract too much attention to have the elderly physician travel laden with baggage. If any curious eyes happened to be watching, his trip to Colón would seem to be no more than a short jaunt, perhaps to see about some routine railroad business, followed by a quick return trip home.

I waited out of sight in the ticket office, since Reyes's men were on patrol in the streets.

"Captain Travers!" cried Amador as soon as Prescott escorted him inside to meet me. "It's true, then. You are alive. I feared that you had perished when I was told that you had fled into the Darien. And your companion, Captain Longbottom? I trust he too is safe?"

"Safe enough," I replied. "He's suffering from a touch of the fever, I'm afraid."

"That's putting it mildly," interjected Prescott. "Captain Longbottom is, unfortunately, raving. He's been insisting that he saw a giant jaguar spirit, and that Captain Travers tried to enslave him while they were both among the Cuna."

"Oh, the poor fellow," commiserated Amador.

"Yes, he is a mite touched in the head. As you can imagine, I am concerned about him." Meaning, of course, that I was concerned lest someone lend him an uncritical ear and begin asking me some rather pointed questions about my conduct during our journey through the wilderness.

Fortunately for me, Henry and Kingston Jack had slipped away before Long-bottom could enlist them as witnesses, but even if he had, neither of them had been under the *nele*'s spell. They had seen no jaguar spirit. "Mr. Prescott thought it was best to place him in the French hospital here in Colón."

"Ah, excellent," said Amador, nodding. "There are some top-notch phrenologists on the staff there, Captain Travers. I've been told that they have experience with cases like this."

"Well, I hope they can do something with poor Longbottom," I said absently as I helped myself to a cigar from the humidor on Prescott's desk and lit it.

"I believe they will, Travers," said Prescott. "The French used to send their worst cases here from a place called Devil's Island off the coast of French Guiana. Ever heard of it?"

"Can't say that I have," I replied, exhaling a great cloud of blue smoke.

"Devil's Island is a pesthole that has unhinged more than one poor soul," Prescott continued. "The French discovered, though, that when a patient has severe fixations such as Captain Longbottom's, a cure can be effected by rather straightforward means."

"Oh? And just what might they be?"

"The French specialists chain the unfortunate wretch to a wall and smack him with ax handles each time he insists that he's had a vision. I've been assured that after a dozen or so such treatments, the cure rate approaches one hundred percent."

"Ah, good, old-fashioned, no-nonsense medicine," I said approvingly. "If you're out to administer a cure, I say, don't dither about. No, get right to the heart of the matter. Why, I've half a mind to drop by the hospital and give Longbottom a few whacks myself."

"Eh, how's that?" queried Prescott sharply.

"Oh, don't mistake my intent, sir," I hastened to assure him. "I merely wish like the dickens to do something for poor Joshua. The French cure seems severe, but I would not hesitate to lay it on, if I but had the chance. All in the name of science, you understand."

"Ah, I see," replied Prescott, mollified. "Well, I hardly think that will be necessary. I've spoken to the doctors and they tell me they have things well in hand. In fact, they tell me the prospects for Captain Longbottom appear very good. They hope to have him sound in mind and body in two weeks, a month at the most."

"My prayers are with him," said Amador gravely. "He was such a fine young man."

An opinion I certainly didn't share, for I knew Longbottom a mite better than did Amador. At the moment, though, I had more pressing matters on my mind. "Our immediate concern, Dr. Amador, is getting you out of the country. Are you ready to travel?"

"I have no more than the clothes on my back, but they will have to do."

I nodded and said to Prescott, "Let's go. We'll get Dr. Amador a wardrobe when we land in New York."

Prescott hustled us out the back of the ticket office, through some narrow alleys, and then, after peering carefully up and down Front Street, across the avenue into the stone freight house at the foot of Pier 2. There a gang of railroad workers awaited us in a dory. We bid Prescott a hasty farewell, and the men rowed Amador and me out into the roadstead where the *Yucatán* rode at anchor. No sooner were we aboard than the ship raised steam, drew up her anchor, and headed for New York. Henry, as prearranged between the two of us, remained behind in the company of Kingston Jack. If I needed to contact him, I would send a message through Prescott.

We enjoyed good weather the whole way and landed safely in New York eleven days later. It wasn't until minutes before we went ashore that Amador shared with me the extent of the assistance he had come north to seek. Senator Arango and he had decided on a figure of $6 million—enough for several gunboats and sufficient rifles to equip a small army.

As we disembarked, we found we had a welcoming committee. Shaler, it seems, had wired the news of our departure directly to Cromwell. The oily barrister greeted us in loud tones as "Paul" and "Uncle Bob," then warned us in a whispered aside to say nothing of substance in public. He shepherded us into his private coach and whisked us off to his plush offices at 49 Wall Street. There, in his richly appointed suite, Cromwell got down to business.

"Dr. Amador, please tell me who, besides myself and Captain Travers, knows that you are in New York."

"Why, only my fellow patriots, of course, and Superintendent Shaler and his men."

I eyed Cromwell as he pondered this piece of information. What was going on within that grasping mind, I wondered.

"Good," Cromwell announced. "You did well to keep your movements guarded. I know your purpose, of course, and I want you to leave all arrangements in my hands. I'll send a wire to Washington immediately. I have friends there in the highest circles. Through them I believe I can secure the sort of commitment from the American government that you need for your revolution to succeed."

"Not just commitments, señor," Dr. Amador corrected him. "We need money too."

Cromwell nodded. "And money. Make no mistake, sir, I'll see to it that you have every asset necessary for this enterprise to prosper." I saw no reason to doubt Cromwell's sincerity on this point, for unless the revolution succeeded, his fee would not be forthcoming. When Amador nodded his satisfaction, Cromwell continued, "Now, Doctor, I suppose that you're exhausted after your journey. I've taken the liberty of arranging accommodations for you at the Fifth Avenue Hotel. One of my associates will take you to your lodgings straightaway. I urge you to remain out of sight until I contact you again. Remember, Colombia has a vested interest in your mission failing. Please exercise the utmost discretion in all your activities until you hear from me."

Amador looked at me quizzically; he had not come all the way to the United States only to be quarantined in a hotel room by Cromwell. No, he had expected to pass straight to Washington at once and present his case in person to the American administration. Never had he imagined that his message would be conveyed through intermediaries. Why, he could have stayed in Panama if that was to be the case.

Amador looked to me for some guidance, but I merely shrugged. He was in Cromwell's bailiwick now, and if the lawyer was inclined to take the old boy off my hands, so be it. All that mattered was that Amador return to Panama filled to the brim with the spirit of revolution. If Cromwell could accomplish that while keeping Amador under lock and key the whole while, well that suited me just fine.

Seeing that he would get no help from me, Amador turned to Cromwell. "When will I see officials of your government?" he demanded. "I have traveled a long way, Señor Cromwell. I want specific guarantees, not vague promises."

"I can't say until I make some telephone calls, Dr. Amador. I'll contact you first thing in the morning and tell you what I've learned."

Amador considered this. He really had no choice but to place himself in Cromwell's hands, at least for the moment. After all, who did he know in the American government? Absolutely nobody. Cromwell, on the other hand, was the railroad's lawyer and had been currying political favor in Washington and Paris for years. Bowing to the inevitable, Amador sighed. "I will do as you say, señor."

"You shan't be sorry," promised Cromwell as he rang a bell on his desk. A young lackey appeared instantly, and Cromwell ordered the fellow to take Amador to his accommodations and to stop at a haberdashery on the way so that the doctor could augment his one suit of clothes.

Once we were alone, Cromwell turned his steely blue gaze on me. "And you, Captain Travers?" he asked crisply. "What are your plans?"

My agenda included a quick trip to the Hoffman House saloon for a few hours of carousing, after which I would most probably prowl through the Tenderloin in search of a likely piece of baggage for a romp under the covers. I didn't think Cromwell needed to know any of this, though, so I answered mildly, "Oh, I imagine I'll stay in town for the night and then be off to Washington in the morning, Mr. Cromwell. I rather think the War Department would expect me to stop by for a chat regarding my travels."

Cromwell eyed me sharply, almost coldly, although he kept a careful smile in place all the while. "Yes, I agree, and I expect there will be some well-deserved recognition for your accomplishments. After all, convincing Dr. Amador and his compatriots to send an emissary to the United States was no small feat. I rather think his presence in our country will go a long way to rousing the necessary support both in Congress and in the administration for a revolution in Panama."

"Assurances of support are fine, Mr. Cromwell, provided that Amador gets everything on his shopping list. If that happens, then the revolution is a sure bet."

"I agree completely, Captain," said Cromwell with that same strange smile.

"I'm glad to hear you say so, sir, since my, er, investment in your railroad depends on the success in our little venture."

It was only then that the barrister's smile slipped. "Ah, yes," mused Cromwell, half to himself. "You do hold some of our stock, don't you?" Then, leaning back in his leather chair, as though readying himself to share the most wonderful tale, he added, "You know, Captain Travers, I'd almost forgotten about your financial ties in all of this. Why then, I'll bet you'll be interested to hear the latest news about the railroad's stock."

I felt my guts tighten as I listened to these honeyed words. Cromwell had a mind like a steel trap, and there was virtually no possibility that he'd forgotten about my stock, especially since his firm's fee was underwriting a large part of the purchase price. My hackles were up now. What news was he going on about? Unless I was badly mistaken, there was mischief in the air.

"Just what are you trying to say, Cromwell?" I demanded hotly.

"Oh, nothing really. It's just a routine matter but one that affects the value of the stock a tad."

He was making no sense at all, but I could tell from his tone that he was enjoying himself immensely at my expense. "Out with it, damn you. What are you talking about?"

Now the smile dropped completely, and I was looking into the rapacious stare of a master manipulator. "Why, the plan that I'll present to the board of directors tomorrow. It will propose the issuance of a new class of stock at a discount rate to all holders of preferred stock. Something along the order of a thousand shares of the new stock for each share of preferred presently held. And the price? Oh, I don't know, let's say a dollar for those thousand new shares. Holders of common stock, unfortunately, will not be invited to participate. If I recall correctly, Captain Travers, your stock is all common, is it not?"

I was stunned. I'm no financial genius, to be sure, but I knew exactly what Cromwell was up to. He was watering down the stock, pure and simple. If the directors bought his plan, there would be thousands of new shares issued against the same company equity that presently existed. In other words, he would dilute the value of my stock with the stroke of a pen. Thus his outlay for the cost of my stock would plummet. He could meet the obligation he had made to Gates and Bunau-Varilla for a pittance. All I would end up holding would be worthless paper.

"You wouldn't dare!" I roared.

"You don't think so, eh? Well, we'll just see about that, Captain," retorted Cromwell, not at all cowed by my outburst. He swiveled about on his chair and tapped a pile of papers stacked high on a credenza behind him. "These are the necessary papers, in fact. I'll have them filed first thing in the morning."

I fought a sudden impulse to throw both him and his cursed papers through the window and onto his beloved Wall Street. It was only with the greatest of difficulty that I restrained myself. "We had a deal, Cromwell; you can't back out now," I snarled.

Cromwell's brows arched high in sudden pleasure, as though I had just invited him to play a game with which he was well acquainted. "I see you wish to be legalistic, Captain," he said with an approving smile. "Good. Yes, very good indeed. In my experience, most military men who are faced with an obstacle immediately resort to violence. They try to batter down barriers instead of employing their wits. I congratulate you, Captain, on your unexpected complexity."

Now he leaned forward, his chin in his hands and his face screwed up as if concentrating mightily. "It remains to be seen, though, how you will fare, but let's give it a go, shall we? Now, first off, it's axiomatic in the law that a contract will be enforced according to its terms. We must know, then, exactly what our agreement was. Perhaps, Captain Travers, you can produce our agreement. Yes, lay it right here on my desk so that I can inspect its terms to see whether your position has any merit."

"Why, I can't do that, and you damn well know it, Cromwell. Our agreement was oral; it was all done on a handshake."

Here Cromwell grinned like the cat that had swallowed the canary. "Ah, but exactly. You make my case for me, Captain. You see, there is no written evidence of any agreement between you and me. In the absence of a written contract, you must first prove that an agreement ever existed. Assuming you're able to carry that substantial burden, proving what the precise terms were will be another battle. Let's suppose though, for the sake of argument, that you are eventually able to prove the existence of a stock transfer agreement between you and me. Why, it should be clear to even a simple soldier that the provisions of an oral agreement are whatever the parties might recall them to be. I, for example, might recall that you were guaranteed to receive 4,000 shares of railroad stock. I might also recall that you in fact received that stock. That, however, is all I would be likely to recall."

"Quit toying with me, Cromwell. If you have a point, then just lay it out in the open."

"I'll be glad to, Captain Travers. The point I'm making is simply this. Even if all of these facts were to be established, I'm certain that neither I nor any other parties to this agreement that you insist exists would ever admit to guaranteeing that your stock would retain its original value. No, I'm quite certain that such a provision would never be included in any agreement to which I was a party."

"Damn it all, Cromwell, of course it was, and more I say. That stock was supposed to go through the ceiling, and you know it. Why do you think I would have come with you in the first place unless I expected a tidy little reward for my troubles?"

"That remains to be proven, Captain Travers. I trust you have some compelling evidence to support your assertions."

I had damned little, of course, other than my word against his and the four thousand shares sitting in my safety-deposit box. How they got there, though, would be anybody's guess should Cromwell choose to dispute the fact that we had a deal. In a quandary now that I realized the vulnerability of my position, I blurted, "Does Gates know what you're up to? Or Bunau-Varilla?"

"Not yet, but they will," Cromwell assured me with seemingly complete insouciance.

The mention of their names had not caused Cromwell to flinch. That told me that Cromwell felt that his shabby treatment of me would not be overruled, a thought that frightened me. In my fear I struck back as hard as I could. "Your blasted scheme won't work, Cromwell. I lived up to my part of the bargain, by God, and evidence or no, I'll see to it that you do the same!"

If Cromwell was perturbed by my rantings, he didn't let on. Instead, as he reached for the little bell once again, he observed languidly, "No, you won't, Captain Travers, and the reason is that you have precious little leverage to make me do anything you might desire." Here he gave a dry, mirthless laugh. "You must excuse me, Captain, but I find the irony of your predicament doubly delightful in view of the fact that you are the author of your ruin."

I was tired of his riddles and I told him so straight out. "Quit your games, Cromwell. I find them boring and, frankly, beneath me."

I hit just the right tone that time, for Cromwell retorted bluntly, "Very well, Captain Travers. The unvarnished truth is that you did your job down in Panama a tad too well for your own good. Amador, you see, is here in New York and ready to do his part. Now that he is, I'll step in to see to it that he's put in contact with the people he needs to meet to ensure the success of his cause. What that means, my bumbling young friend, is that your services are no longer required."

"No longer required?" I sputtered. "Now see here, Cromwell, you can't just dismiss me like some incompetent clerk. I'm an army officer, by God. A regular too, do you hear me? Why, I'll—"

About that time Cromwell rang the bell and the door to his office swung open. There before me stood a neatly attired gentleman who eyed me quietly. I might have been inclined to continue to lambaste Cromwell had not this newcomer stood well over six and a half feet tall and weighed about two hundred fifty pounds. I took one look at the vast expanse of cloth stretched across his broad chest and fell silent. Cromwell, it seemed, had anticipated an unpleasant scene with me.

"Mr. Drummond, Captain Travers here was just leaving. Could you see to it that he finds his way to the street?"

Mr. Drummond did precisely that, and none too gently, either. As I was transported bodily from his presence, Cromwell called cheerily after me, "Good day, Captain Travers, and the very best of luck in all your future endeavors."

As soon as I had picked myself up from the gutter and brushed the dust from my backside, I began to walk. In a fog, I headed north, not quite knowing where I was going or why. Slowly, though, my reason reasserted itself. Although still distraught, I decided on my previously anticipated destination. I set a course for the Hoffman House.

My afternoon at the hotel's enormous teak bar was not quite the light-hearted occasion I had earlier envisioned. Instead, as I quaffed bourbon after bourbon, I turned over in my mind Cromwell's duplicity. He was able to play his trump card only because Amador had now emerged in the light of day, fully prepared to play the role of revolutionary. Since such was the case, what further need had he of me? My charter had been to stir up a revolt and to make sure it prospered. Since all the ingredients to attain that end were now apparently at hand, there was no need of old Fenny. I was expendable, by God, an oafish minion who could be tossed aside with impunity once he'd served his purpose. Damning myself for a fool, I ordered another double.

As I put the glass to my lips, though, an idea popped unbidden into my alcohol-shrouded mind. It was an idea so audacious that at first my reason fled before it in alarm. Then, however, I returned to it, timidly at first but then more brazenly. I turned the concept about and examined it from several different angles until finally I was convinced. I had found a solution that would serve nicely. Oh, it was a bit desperate, but these happened to be desperate times. I drained my drink and slammed down the glass.

"Bartender," I called. "Is there a telephone on the premises?"

He directed me to a telephone room off the lobby where I made arrangements to place a long-distance call to Washington.

"May I have the party you wish to call?" asked the Washington operator when she came on the line.

I hesitated only a second before I answered. "I wish to speak with Ambassador Tomas Herrán at the Colombian Legation."

I waited as she put me through. There was some difficulty getting Herrán on the line, but I insisted that I had a message of vital importance to the sovereignty of Colombia. I would speak to no one other than the ambassador. After some minutes a weak, scratchy voice came on the line; it was Herrán.

In Spanish, I told him to ask no questions but to only listen. Then I gave him an earful. Herrán heard me out, but when I was done he could contain himself no longer.

"Who is this?" he squawked. "I demand that you identify yourself."

He was still yelling when I rang off. Next, I strolled around the corner to a Western Union office. From there I dispatched a telegram to Gates that read:

BETRAYAL FROM THE LAWYER STOP CONTACT THE
DIRECTORS IMMEDIATELY STOP

SURVEYOR

21

New York City
25 September 1903

I was in the lobby of the Fifth Avenue Hotel when Dr. Amador hobbled down the staircase as quickly as his rheumatism would allow. Great tears were in his eyes, and he babbled forth a torrent of incoherent Spanish. It was only with difficulty that I got him off to a quiet corner.

"What's the matter?" I hissed, although in truth I already knew.

"It's that cur, Cromwell," Amador practically wailed. "I called upon him this morning because I had heard nothing since our arrival. He practically threw me out of his office. He swore he never wanted to see me again, and that as far as he was concerned I did not exist. What has happened? What has made this jackal abandon us?"

I feigned a look of astonished disbelief. "I have no idea, Doctor. Why, evidently something must have spooked our friend."

Indeed, something had. What I had told Señor Herrán was that Dr. Amador was in New York to gain American support for a revolution on the isthmus. What was more, Amador's key American agent in this regard was none other than Mr. Cromwell. After my telephone call, the wheels had quickly gone into motion. Herrán had apparently called Cromwell directly and blasted him with dire imprecations. I could well imagine what transpired between them, and I had no doubt that Herrán pointed out to Cromwell that Colombia could seize all the assets of the Panama Railroad, as well as the property rights of the New Panama Canal Company, if either of those entities involved itself in sedition against Bogotá.

That was all Cromwell needed to hear. If the railroad was forfeited, there went all his stock. Further, if the rights of the New Panama Canal Company were seized, there would be nothing with which to pay the fat fee he expected for his many labors over the past years to bring about the creation of a canal on the isthmus. Rattled to the core, Cromwell was heading for cover, ready to disavow Amador three times before the cock could crow. The thought gratified me immensely, for Cromwell, a master legal brawler, had finally tangled with someone who didn't play by his rules.

"Captain," said Amador, weeping, "it is all over before it even begins. My mission here is a failure. I want to go home immediately. We will make our peace with the Colombians, and if there is to be a canal in the future, it will be on whatever terms Bogotá dictates."

If there was to be a canal, I thought grimly, it would be on my terms and not on those of either Bogotá or Cromwell. "Doctor," I soothed, "let's not be rash. Remember, Cromwell does not speak for the American government. He is only a lawyer, whereas I am a soldier. I would not have been in Panama if my government were not interested in your success."

The old fellow interrupted his hysterics long enough to reply, "*Sí,* there is truth in what you say, Captain. What is it you suggest?"

"Return to your room. Sit tight and let me report to Washington. I'll tell 'em that now is the time to strike and that you and your friends in Panama are the right group to get the job done. I'll tell 'em you need guns and money, and pronto."

Amador produced a handkerchief and blew his nose noisily. When he had regained some measure of self-control, he asked timidly, "Will—will these contacts of yours listen to you?"

I leaned forward and fixed the good doctor with a fiercely earnest gaze. "Of course they will. Why do you think I was chosen to visit you? I was chosen because this administration and this president set a great deal of store by what I say."

Now Amador was smiling, although feebly. "I—I feel so foolish, Captain, for allowing that scoundrel Cromwell to plunge me into such despair. Of course you're right. There must be allies of my cause in Washington or you would never have been sent to Panama in the first place."

"That's the spirit," I told him, giving him a pat on his frail shoulder. "Now go back to your room and wait. And remember, have nothing more to do with Cromwell. You must promise me that."

"You have my word," promised Amador, and he shuffled off to do as I bid.

Then I went to the telephone in the hotel lobby and rang up 49 Wall Street. "Mr. Cromwell, please," I said to the female voice that answered.

The was a pause, and then the same voice came back on the line. "I'm sorry, Mr. Cromwell is not accepting any telephone calls today. He's ill."

"I'm so very sorry to hear that, ma'am. Give him this message for me then, would you?"

"Certainly, sir. What is it?" she chirped.

"Write it down so you don't miss a word."

"I'm ready," the woman assured me sweetly. "Go ahead."

"Okay, here it goes. Dear Mr. Cromwell, you left-handed, forked-tongued sidewinder," I dictated calmly. "You tried to cheat me, and your under-handed scheme blew up right in your face. Now get on this telephone line immediately, you damned four-flusher, or the trouble you think you have now will be only a pale shadow of the calamities I'll deposit at your door." I paused, then asked brightly, "That's it. Do you have it all, dear?"

Shaken, she gasped, "Yes, sir."

"Good. Now deliver it," I ordered. "I'll hold."

Ten seconds later Cromwell was on the line. "Yes?"

"Cromwell, I want a resolution drawn for the board of directors of the Panama Railroad. I want it to be legally binding and irrevocable."

"What—what kind of resolution?" he asked uncertainly.

"It will be a resolution prohibiting the addition of any stock or classes of stock for the next two years. Do you have that?"

There was silence, and then he said tightly, "Yes, I've got it, Travers."

"Have that resolution, complete with the corporate seal, delivered to Mr. Gates."

"John Gates?"

"The very same. Tell Gates that I expect him to direct his attorneys to ensure the documents are duly filed with the directors." Gates seemed the straightest shooter of the bunch, you see, so I had decided to put my trust in him. He was mighty rough and gruff, but I suspected that if I held up my part of the bargain, he'd do the same. Importantly, that meant that I had to do more than let events take their natural course; the task before me now involved nothing less than delivering a signed canal treaty.

"Anything else?" asked Cromwell, seething.

"Yes, two things. First, I expect that you, in your capacity as corpo-rate counsel, will give the resolution your unqualified support. And second, if you double-cross me one more time, Cromwell, I'll come looking for you with my Colt."

Before Cromwell could get a word in edgewise, I rang off the line. Then I was on my way to Washington. I was still wearing rough-looking surveying togs, covered by a sturdy tweed overcoat I'd purchased hurriedly at Brooks Brothers, but that couldn't be helped. Time was of the essence, and besides, my attire was irrelevant to what needed to be done. The only thing that mattered was that my message be delivered in person. I telegraphed ahead to the War Department before I left. Not wanting to put any substance into my open wire, my message stated:

SECTY WAR
WAR DEPARTMENT, WASHINGTON D.C.

DEPARTING NEW YORK THIS DATE STOP WILL MEET WITH SECRETARY ROOT UPON ARRIVAL STOP

TRAVERS

That was it. Root would know it was important, I figured.

I arrived at the Baltimore and Ohio Railroad Station in the capital six hours later. I hurried outside past the construction for the new Union Station, and then took an open-sided trolley to the Willard Hotel, on the corner of Pennsylvania Avenue and 14th Street Northwest. I checked in and then rang up the War Department from the lobby. I was put right through to Root's executive assistant, who urged me to present myself forthwith.

After a quick shave and a haircut, I strolled down Pennsylvania Avenue in the crisp September air. Ordinarily a day like this would feel mild to me, but after my stay in the tropics I was almost chilled to the bone. Upon reaching Lafayette Square and 17th Street, I crossed the avenue and entered the gray monolithic pile of stones called the State, War, and Navy Building. Directly across the street, the setting sun illuminated the White House with its dying rays.

To my surprise, Root met me in the hallway outside his office, his coat on and hat in hand. "Welcome back, Captain Travers. The president wants to see you right away."

"Oh? Will General Wood accompany us, sir? I rather thought he might have wanted to be on hand to receive my report."

"General Wood would have liked that very much, Captain Travers, but I'm afraid he's been called off to the Philippines," answered Root. "He's been appointed as the governor of Mindanao. A splendid opportunity for him, I rather think. If I recall your record correctly, Captain Travers, you've been in the islands yourself, haven't you?"

"You're quite right, sir, with a good bit of time spent right on Mindanao. I can't agree with you more that General Wood's new assignment will be a first-class opportunity for him."

To fight, that is, I added silently. As soon as Wood stepped ashore on that benighted island, he would be up to his ears in tribal wars, slave raids, and every manner of deviltry known to man. Prominent among the dangers he would face would be opium-crazed *juramentados,* Muslim fanatics who thought that killing a Christian—any Christian—was the highest attainment possible in this life. Next to the troubles heaped on Wood's new plate, the goings-on in Panama would seem as tame as a rhetoric exercise at a debating club.

Thanking my lucky stars at being where I was rather than out in the Pacific with Wood, I followed Root as he set off for the White House. We swept up the north portico with its massive marble columns and were immediately ushered in by a lackey. Root forged on into the entrance hall where, smack in the middle of the marble floor, a beautiful rendition of the presidential seal was embedded for all the world to tread upon. Now that, I thought, was surely a touch added by an artisan who either possessed a very wry sense of humor or else whose payment for services rendered to his government had been delayed overly long.

We mounted the stairway to the second floor, where the upstairs butler bowed us into the Green Room. This fellow assured Secretary Root, "The president will be but a moment, sir," and then he withdrew and left us to cool our heels.

As we waited I looked about. The Green Room was a rather sparsely appointed chamber, all done up in various shades of emerald. Upon the polished parquet floor lay an enormous polar bear rug, no doubt a victim of the quick-shooting Roosevelt. The arctic whiteness of the bear hide contrasted starkly with the green hues everywhere else in view. By the cold hearth was a matched set of jade-colored Chinese urns, one on either side like sentinels guarding some portal. The urns were huge things of glazed porcelain, not unlike the ones I'd seen spirited through the streets of Peking by the victorious allied army back in 1900.

It's been said that old habits die hard, and I suppose that's true, for I was gazing upon those urns with a decidedly mercantile frame of mind when the butler reappeared and informed us that, "President Roosevelt will see you now, gentlemen."

He led us down a hallway past oil paintings of grim-looking gents whom I reckoned to be deceased chief executives, then into the Treaty Room, which

Roosevelt had set up as a sort of study. He was at his desk when we entered but was instantly on his feet.

"Travers! Come in, my boy, come in."

He gave me a thunderous clap to the shoulder that reverberated through the room and rattled my teeth something awful. It was the sort of unexpectedly violent blow that made me want to immediately return the favor in spades, but I checked that impulse and instead smiled with all apparent sincerity. "Mr. President, it's a pleasure to see you again."

It was only then that I noticed a diminutive gentleman hovering a bit to the side so that I had not seen him upon my entrance. He sported an outsized beard for one so tiny, I thought. This hirsute display, shot through as it was with gray, coupled with the little fellow's grave demeanor, gave him rather the aspect of an elder of Zion.

"Captain Travers, this is Secretary of State Hay. He's been following your progress carefully," said Roosevelt as he planted himself back in his chair and motioned us to take seats around the desk.

"A pleasure to meet you, sir."

"The pleasure is all mine, Captain Travers," replied Hay with a tone of voice that had not a hint of pleasure about it.

Roosevelt took over from there. "We received a cipher message from Major Black. He told us about your disappearance, along with Captain Longbottom. I don't mind saying that the news gave us all a bit of a fright. But here you are, Captain Travers, all hale and hearty and, by gad, looking none the worse for wear than if you had been off on a fishing trip."

I let that one slide by as Roosevelt called for brandy, which Hay primly declined. When a glass had been placed in my ready hand, Roosevelt fixed me with his fiercest glare and demanded, "What's the situation down there, Travers?"

After twenty minutes and two brandies, I had related to Roosevelt the main points about what had transpired during my sojourn in Panama. As for the troubling events of the past two days, I doled out those facts charily indeed. I told Roosevelt and Hay about Cromwell's cold shoulder for Amador but of course omitted any reference to my bold, and what some might term treasonous, call to Señor Herrán, or my subsequent conversation with Cromwell.

When I was done, Secretary Hay shook his head in bewilderment. "Hmmm. That's a very odd attitude on the part of Mr. Cromwell. Why, he's been the most stalwart champion of the Panama route right from the very beginning."

I shrugged. "Who can say, Mr. Secretary? Perhaps Mr. Cromwell sensed that the time for words is done and the time for action is here. Being more facile with the former than the latter, maybe he decided that it was prudent to step back and let others finish what he started."

Roosevelt was not inclined to be so charitable. "This is no time for shrinking violets. If Mr. Cromwell no longer has any stomach for the fight, so be it. Mark my words though, gentlemen; nothing of any consequence will get done in Panama unless we do it ourselves."

"And that cannot be, sir," rejoined Secretary Hay, sounding surprisingly firm too, for I rather thought that not many people took exception to the bombastic Roosevelt to his face. "Whatever might occur in Panama, and I stress the word *might,* must be seen as a popular uprising," continued Hay. "For the sake of our future relations with our Latin neighbors, we must deport ourselves on the isthmus with strict neutrality. Why, Mexico is already a powder keg. I shudder to think of what would become of that country if we, through some indiscretion in Panama, gave credence to Mexico's barely suppressed fears of aggression from the north."

"Mexico be damned, Hay," spat Roosevelt. "I want that canal, but at the least cost in blood and treasure."

"And Dr. Amador wants a public commitment of support from the United States," I pointed out to both of them, adding as an aside, "that, and enough money to buy his own army and navy."

"Overt support for the Panamanian secessionists is out of the question until the revolution is a fait accompli," averred Hay, unshaken by Roosevelt's bellicose attitude.

I expected a Rooseveltian eruption at Hay's failure to roll over, but to my surprise it was the irascible Rough Rider who pulled in his reins. He sat back and with a weary shake of the head sighed, "That's the damnably hard part about all of this, gentlemen. We and the Panamanian secessionists are like two old maids dancing. Each wants the other to lead, and the result is a lot of bumping and jostling but damned little progress."

"Nor should there be, Mr. President," maintained Secretary Hay quietly, "until the Panamanians take the responsibility for their destiny in their own hands."

Hay was maddeningly cautious and insufferably proper, yet by the same token I had to admit that he had the grit to stare Roosevelt down, a thing I would daresay Roosevelt needed from time to time. Seeing that his secretary of state was making good sense, and not liking the fact at all, Roosevelt turned to a kindred spirit for support.

"Travers, you've gotten the lay of the land in Panama. What do you think about all of this?"

I swished the last of my brandy in my glass, swallowed it with an appreciative "Ahhh," and then held forth. "If you wait for the Panamanians to secure their own liberty, Mr. President, your great-grandchildren will still have to sail around the Horn to get to California. The Panamanians are so in dread of the hangman's noose that they jump at their own shadows. Nothing will happen of a constructive nature down there until Uncle Sam shows up with gunboats and troops."

"That is most unwelcome news," muttered Roosevelt.

"But not unexpected," added Secretary Hay.

Roosevelt rose and went to a window where he stood gazing into the fading light cast by the sun as it settled slowly beyond the placid Potomac. "The problem is, Captain Travers, that I happen to agree with Secretary Hay. If this revolution appears to be an exercise of raw North American power, the resulting government will never have any legitimacy. For form's sake, we'll have to go through Amador and his people."

"Then do so, but make it clear to them that you're prepared to fix the game to ensure that they win. Float a few navy ships down their way," I suggested. "Call it routine maneuvers, or call it a special drill. Call it whatever you want, but just have them off the coast when Amador's people stage their uprising. Would that be interference with Colombia's sovereignty? Oh, I suppose small minds might think so"—here Secretary Hay sucked in his breath sharply, but I plowed right on—"yet it's not unlike the sort of thing our British cousins do every day of the week in some corner of the globe or another. I say there's nothing illegal or underhanded about such persuasion. No, on the contrary, it's the sort of mailed fist in a velvet glove that small nations like Colombia rather expect to encounter when they cross paths with their moral superiors."

Roosevelt was listening raptly, and I could tell that although he had misgivings, I was preaching to the choir as far as he was concerned. "I say, Travers, do you think a display of naval power alone might do the trick? Perhaps we could have a small complement of marines on board too. They would be highly visible, but they would not be ordered ashore."

Roosevelt, as he had admitted, was looking for the lever that was the easiest and least costly in political terms to pull. Another officer might have humored his wishful thinking and opined that a military feint alone might suffice to launch the locals into a full-blown insurrection. I had cash on the line, though, and that meant I wanted to stack the deck.

"No, halfway measures won't do, Mr. President. What's required is both ships and a credible force of marines ashore. Several companies at least. Remember, the Colombians have a battalion of troops at Panama City and another company at Colón. We need to keep those troops from entering the fray to crush the revolt, and the only way to do that is to put them eyeball to eyeball with our boys. That means that the marines must land."

"That could get tricky," fretted Roosevelt, turning over my words in his mind. "There are ways, though. We could assert that we are exercising our right to keep the railroad line open in times of upheaval. There's a treaty on that very point too. Let's see, what was the name of the dratted thing? Named after some musty old Britisher. Don't tell me; it's right on the tip of my tongue."

Secretary Hay, though, did tell him. "You're referring to the Bidlack Treaty of 1846, Mr. President. Mr. Bidlack, by the way, was an American."

"Whatever," sniffed Roosevelt with a wave of the hand, for he was more a naval historian than a chronicler of long-forgotten compacts with third-rate nations.

"We've used the Bidlack Treaty in the past to good effect," observed Root. "It allows us to guarantee free passage along the railroad line, and to enforce that free passage by any means necessary."

"That's exactly my point, Elihu. Under the terms of the Bidlack Treaty, if the railroad were to be threatened, say by Colombian troops rushing about trying to suppress a revolt, we just might be able to set a force of marines ashore and be well within our rights to do so."

Roosevelt looked about beaming, as though he expected applause. I didn't start clapping, but I liked what I was hearing, so much so that I finished Roosevelt's inspiring vision for him. "With our navy blockading both coasts so that no reinforcements could come from Colombia, and marines on every street corner in Colón and Panama City, I'd say the stage would be perfectly set for the locals to do their part. Providing, of course, that between now and then you send rifles into the country secretly and make sure they get into the hands of the independence movement."

Roosevelt nodded his head at Root as I spoke these words. The secretary of war produced a beautiful tortoiseshell fountain pen, its clip and bands of pure gold, and scratched out a note to himself. I was certain those rifles would begin appearing on the docks of Colón forthwith.

"When all those pieces of the puzzle are in place," I continued, "I'd say we would be just about guaranteed the revolution we want."

Roosevelt gave Hay a satisfied grin at this, but the little secretary wasn't buying what I was selling. Instead he delivered a sharp reproof to us all. "Mr. President, I admire Captain Travers's martial spirit, and I understand that he has gone through great personal hardship to provide you with a firsthand account of the present situation in Panama. Yet because Captain Travers is a soldier and not a diplomat, he possesses a necessarily limited understanding of the terms of the Bidlack Treaty. Others in this room, though, are undoubtedly more aware of the hidden snares awaiting us should we act in consonance with Captain Travers's counsel." Here he shot a look of censure at Root before continuing. "Specifically, sir, you must recall that the Bidlack Treaty also binds the United States to support the sovereignty of Colombia on the isthmus. To employ the Bidlack Treaty as a ruse for destabilizing Panama would be a blatant treaty violation."

Perhaps I was feeling my brandy, or perhaps I was just concerned that Hay's unnatural fixation with legalities might get in the way of a tidy little payday for old Fenny. Whatever the reason, it was I rather than Roosevelt or Root who rose in opposition to this challenge.

"Mr. Secretary, perhaps the course of action I suggest isn't precisely proper. Maybe it does do some violence to a scrap of paper signed more than fifty years ago. The point is, though, that the people we're dealing with in Bogotá, and their military commanders on the isthmus, aren't a particularly likable set. They murder and rob as they see fit, and if we suffer them to do so they'll bump along merrily in the same fashion in perpetuity. Now I don't think that anyone in this room wants that, do they?" There was studied silence all around at this. Encouraged by not being immediately shouted down, I continued. "The best hope for Panama, and us, is a canal under American sovereignty. If that is our goal, and I think it is, then my plan or something close to it must be enacted. Let's just hold our noses and plunge in and get the job done. If that means sending in marines in violation of some dusty old treaty, then I say let's do it."

"I still don't like it," Hay insisted stubbornly.

Roosevelt, though, was studying his secretary of war, not Hay. Root, a trained barrister, was not one to disregard legalities lightly, and I realized that Roosevelt was using him as a sort of weather vane to gauge the effect of my proposal. Root considered my words in silence. After some minutes of contemplation, his political instincts gained the ascendancy over his forensic concerns.

"Captain Travers's advice has a certain elemental logic. After all, we're not talking about invading Denmark."

"I agree," snapped Roosevelt decisively, then immediately cautioned, "We need to communicate our intentions to Dr. Amador but in a manner that can't be traced directly back to this administration."

"Absolutely, sir," concurred Root. "We need a convincing cover."

I thought about this a minute. Cromwell was out; Herrán's communication had nearly driven him insane with fear. He wanted nothing further to do with either Amador or his revolution. That left only Bunau-Varilla. "What about the Frog?" I suggested.

Roosevelt laughed uproariously. "Bunau-Varilla? Why, I'd rather entrust the fate of a Panama canal to a banjo player from a minstrel show. Tell me, Travers, have you ever met Mr. Bunau-Varilla?"

My heart raced wildly; how could Roosevelt have guessed about my liaison with the Frenchman? Or did he know about my scheme with Gates, Cromwell, and Davis? Had I been smoked out by my own blundering words? In the instant it took me to think these thoughts, though, I glanced quickly about at the faces around me and saw no questioning looks, no hint of suspicion. Roosevelt's comment had been innocent.

Masking my sudden fear with the guile of a trained cardsharper, I gave a ready smile and said smoothly, "Met him? Why no. I know only what you've told me about him—that and what I've read in the papers. According to the press, though, he seems to be a remarkable enough fellow."

"Remarkable?" snorted Roosevelt. "Well, I suppose that Mr. Bunau-Varilla would agree with you, Travers. Elihu, you've met our French friend, have you not?"

"Yes, Mr. President. Last spring in Paris. It was an occasion I shall not quickly forget."

"I know what you mean," said Roosevelt, grinning. "A few years back I brushed elbows with Monsieur Bunau-Varilla in Dayton. It was during his whistle-stop tour of this country in support of his canal. I had no more than tipped my hat to the man before he launched into a thirty-minute harangue about Panama. It took the entire congressional delegation from Ohio to pry the little pest loose from my lapels. To say that Bunau-Varilla is brash is to understate the case. In comparison to him, William Jennings Bryan on the campaign trail would seem a shrinking violet, and we all know what a shameless self-promoter Bryan is. No, Bunau-Varilla's estimation of himself could be exceeded only by that of, of . . ."

Here, as Roosevelt flailed around for the name of an appropriately vain luminary, I was half inclined to venture, "You, Mr. President?"

Root, however, spoke first. "Napoleon, or perhaps Caesar, sir."

"Yes, exactly. Thank God the fellow's an engineer and not a general, or he would probably try to seize Panama with French troops, and then maybe snap up Mexico while he was in the neighborhood."

At this point Hay emerged from his sulk, seemingly intrigued at the mention of Bunau-Varilla. "You know, sir, Monsieur Bunau-Varilla does have the ear of both the French and the Panamanians."

"That's my point," I interjected. "I say that we call him in and feed him just enough of our plan to make him useful. We'll tell Bunau-Varilla in general terms that it's in the best interests of France and the United States for the canal to proceed under the auspices of a new government in Panama. Then we suggest that he contact Amador in New York and fill the good doctor with words of encouragement. Amador, armed with promises of succor, can then return to Panama to bolster his fellow conspirators. When all is in readiness, have a ship or two appear off the coast, wait for an opportune moment to send in the marines, and, well, that should be that. We get what we want and Monsieur Bunau-Varilla thinks it's all his doing. Your administration, Mr. President, will have a believable cover and, what's more important, an independent Panama to deal with."

Hay frowned at this manipulative scheme, for it didn't square with his concept that a great power should fashion its policies out in the open for all the world to see. After all, if we could cook up such tawdry schemes to defraud a sovereign state of its territory, where then was our vaunted moral superiority over the less enlightened races? Weren't we in truth little better than the brigands in Bogotá whom we decried at every turn? As all of this played across Hay's honest features, I glanced at Roosevelt to gauge his reaction. Happily, it was one of supreme satisfaction.

"Why, that's bully, Travers, simply bully. Yes, why not let Bunau-Varilla believe he's got the ball in this game? He's not remotely associated with this government—"

"Indeed, he's not even a citizen," I pointed out, drawing a further look of delight from Roosevelt.

"An excellent point, Travers," approved Root, his sharp lawyer's mind clicking. "If this plan comes off the track for some reason, Bogotá will direct its complaints to Paris, not Washington."

Now even Hay saw the merit of my ruse. "But what about the money, Travers?" he asked. "You said Amador wanted six million dollars."

"That's what he wants, all right," I said, "but that figure was based on him having to buy his own gunboats. If we provide them, then Amador needs funds sufficient only to bribe a few officials and buy arms." I did some quick calculations in my head. There was Colonel Huertas to pay off, as well as his officers and troops. Oh, and yes, Kingston Jack and his rabble. Summing it all up, I announced, "If Amador can get a hundred thousand American gold dollars, he'll be satisfied."

"But how can we give him those funds without implicating this government?" The question was from Root. Like the cagey trial lawyer he was, Root was probing for weaknesses in my scheme.

I smiled broadly, for I had already thought of a solution to this problem. "We don't."

A scowl swept across Roosevelt's face at this. "What? You mean just put these people up to a revolution and then leave 'em in the lurch?"

"No, that's not what I mean at all," I insisted. "You just call in Monsieur Bunau-Varilla for a little chat. If your words are sweet enough, the Frenchman and his backers will pony up the necessary grubstake. You may rely upon it."

Here I was thinking of Gates and his crowd, you see. A hundred thousand would be small change to them. If Bunau-Varilla returned from a meeting with Roosevelt convinced that the president was soliciting his active involvement in Panama, I was certain that the egomaniacal Frenchman would move heaven and earth to get into the game, even if that meant putting his own money on the table.

Root was leery, though, of having the president cast in the role of dispensing blandishments to the Frenchman. If the thing was not handled right, such a meeting could come back to haunt Roosevelt. "What sort of words from the president do you have in mind, Captain Travers?"

Here I addressed myself directly to Roosevelt. "You tell Bunau-Varilla that you wouldn't be surprised if American gunboats arrived off the coast of Panama on a certain date, and that if Amador's cash needs are also met in the meantime, well, it's entirely possible that a Panamanian revolution might occur. Don't tell Bunau-Varilla that we plan to find a pretext to send marines ashore to neutralize the Colombian troops before they can react. No, just leave that for him to figure out. From what I've heard, Bunau-Varilla seems to have a nimble enough mind. I rather think he'll surmise just what we intend, and from that he'll deduce what he has to do to help us."

Hay nodded at this, for the pieces of the puzzle seemed to be falling into place. If Amador returned home with the promised funds and visible assurances of American military support, the revolutionaries would become restive in Panama City and Colón. That would then provoke a reaction from Bogotá, which would in turn provide an arguably legitimate pretext for intervention. "I think, Captain Travers," he opined, "that with one certain refinement, your plan might have merit."

I cocked an ear at this. "Refinement? What do you mean, sir?"

"That we refrain from landing marines until after the trouble starts. If we can manage that, we will remain within the terms of the Bidlack Treaty."

I thought about this a minute. It wasn't as I wanted things. No, I wanted marines on shore well before the festivities commenced, to encourage the Panamanians. If I couldn't have that, though, then having marines just offshore was the next best thing.

"The problem your condition raises, sir, lies in the timing between the uprising and the landing of the marines. If, during that interval, Colonel Huertas or Comandante Reyes could crush the rebellion, well then, that would be that."

"I say it's a chance we need to take in order to retain some veneer of legality."

I could see that Hay intended to remain firm, and I reluctantly accepted his condition with one caveat. "Let it be as you say, sir, as long as the Colombians are on the ground before us. There exists, though, the possibility that our navy may be confronted by Colombian reinforcements at sea. If that happens prior to the declaration of a coup on the isthmus, then I think we should be agreed that our navy has the right to turn back any such reinforcements. Forbid them to land, I say."

"That's a remote possibility, Captain Travers," tut-tutted Hay. "There's no need for such a consensus until we actually cross that bridge."

Seeing that neither Roosevelt nor Root was inclined to side with me over what appeared to be an improbable scenario, I conceded the point. "As you say, sir, but be advised that when the trouble starts, we need to be ready to move like greased lightning."

"Then we're agreed," barked Roosevelt with a slap of his knee. "That leaves just one last detail to settle, gentlemen."

"And that is, Mr. President?" inquired Root.

"Why, we need to set the date for this revolution."

Hay pondered the question. "It should be soon. Amador and his supporters will not be able to maintain their resolve indefinitely."

"I agree wholeheartedly," I chimed in. "The only troops on the isthmus right now are Colonel Huertas's battalion in Panama City and Comandante

Reyes's forces in Colón. If Bogotá sends significant reinforcements into the area, all bets will be off."

Roosevelt nodded his understanding. "It should be a day when the attention of the American public is directed elsewhere. The less scrutiny on this affair, the better."

"Christmastime?" suggested Hay.

Roosevelt shook his head. "No, that's too far away. We need to act in weeks, not months."

"Why not Election Day?" I suggested. I glanced at the calendar on the president's desk. "That's the third of November."

The irony of it all immediately appealed to Roosevelt. "Yes, that's it, Travers!" he chortled. "What a supremely fitting touch, too. We'll break Panama loose on Election Day. Yes, by gad, that's it. That's when we'll show our hand and teach those bandits in Bogotá a lesson they'll never forget."

Root cleared his throat. "I'm afraid there is yet another detail to be cleared up. How shall we go about getting Monsieur Bunau-Varilla to see the president? It won't do, in my view, for such an invitation to issue from the State or War departments."

Roosevelt's head swiveled in my direction. "Can you handle that, Travers?"

Of course I could, but desiring to keep my relationship with the Frenchman a secret, I demurred. "I'm not certain, sir. Where is this fellow now?"

"In Paris," Hay answered. "I'm constantly apprised of Monsieur Bunau-Varilla's whereabouts by dint of the fact that he bombards me with wires offering unsolicited advice on the Panama situation. I'll provide the address to you, Captain Travers."

"Paris, eh? Well, allowing for an ocean passage, I'll have him in New York in about two weeks," I promised.

22

New York City
26 September 1903

I wired Bunau-Varilla as soon as Roosevelt dismissed me, and the next day I was back in New York. I rang up Amador at his hotel and told him that he was to sit tight. Things would soon clarify themselves, I assured him. Then I telephoned Richard Harding Davis and told him about Cromwell's sudden cold feet and, in the most general of terms, about my trip to Washington. I informed him that plans were being put in motion, plans that I was not at liberty to divulge. I confided that Amador was shaky, and God alone knew what sort of despairing ciphers he had been sending back to Colón and Panama City since Cromwell had turned tail. I also informed Davis in no uncertain terms that the time had come for Gates to lend a hand. He and his industrialist friends had to let Senator Arango and his coterie know that they were not alone, and that help was on the way. Davis promised to do his part and rang off.

He was true to his word, for that same day there was a knock on my door at the St. James. I opened the door and there stood a radiant Doctor Amador. "Captain Travers," he said excitedly, "your words of encouragement were true ones! Look, I received this not an hour ago."

He thrust a telegram at me, which I hastily read.

BE OF GOOD CHEER STOP FRIENDS ARE EVERYWHERE STOP REMAIN IN THE CITY AND THEY WILL CONTACT YOU STOP

LINDO

"Who the devil is Lindo?"

"He's a Panamanian banker with interests in New York City," replied Amador. "How Lindo knew I was here is beyond me, but it is evident that I have friends other than the cowardly Mr. Cromwell."

"So it seems," I agreed. "I think my visit to Washington paid off, my friend. Yes, indeed. I suggest we just sit back now and let events unfold at their own pace."

Amador agreed, and for the next two weeks I played nursemaid and companion to the old fellow, whose moods ranged from boisterous enthusiasm to glum despair and then back again. He was a handful all right, and I hoped Bunau-Varilla would arrive soon, since I knew that Amador could not tolerate the strain indefinitely.

That's why when I received Davis's call at the beginning of October, I was overjoyed. "Our French friend is in town," he said. "I've told him about the doctor's ailments. He wants an appointment straightaway."

"Where's he staying?" I asked.

"At the Waldorf-Astoria."

"I'm on my way with the doctor," I said and then hung up. I hurried uptown and collected an overjoyed Amador, then we traveled by hansom cab to the Waldorf. From the desk clerk we learned that Bunau-Varilla was in room 1162 and we went up in the elevator. When I knocked, Bunau-Varilla himself opened the door.

"Ah, *mon capitaine*," he said with a stiff little bow, and seeing Amador, he added, "*docteur*." Bunau-Varilla showed us to a settee, and when we were settled he ensconced himself in an armchair opposite Amador.

"Why are you here?" he began. His tone was curt, condescending.

I rolled my eyes in annoyance at his impertinent formality. "You know damned well why we're—" I began testily, only to be cut short with a sudden chop of a well-manicured hand.

"*Mon capitaine*, I address myself to Dr. Amador. It is he with whom I have business."

"Why, you snail-eating horned toad!" I sputtered in outrage. "Just who the devil do you think you're talking to? If it wasn't for me, Amador here would be back in Panama already, and your whole canal scheme would have died aborning."

Amador, though, having been pent up in his hotel room except for his conversations with me over the last two weeks, wanted to pour his heart out to Bunau-Varilla. Amador was so rattled by the responsibility that had been placed on his frail shoulders that he was prepared to flock to anyone who promised to lift that burden. Bunau-Varilla, moreover, was a former director general of the Compagnie Universelle, an eminent personage who, in Amador's eyes at least, was to be accorded the highest respect.

"Captain Travers, please," Amador implored me, "Monsieur Bunau-Varilla is a friend of the revolution. Let us treat him with the dignity he deserves."

Bunau-Varilla lapped up this servility, striking a regal pose in his armchair and looking for all the world like a British sahib accepting the submission of some wayward nabob. The Frenchman listened intently as Amador poured out his tale of woe, starting with the shocking intelligence from Longbottom that the Americans expected his countrymen to free themselves and then on to the inexplicable desertion of Cromwell. He shared his terror that he might return home with nothing to show for his efforts, and that the perfidious Colombians might take vengeance against his compatriots if they were ever unmasked. Money was what he needed, $6 million for gunboats and rifles to be exact, and assurances of American protection.

When Amador was done, Bunau-Varilla gave his waxed mustache a decisive tug and launched into a bombastic lecture. "Dr. Amador, you have been unforgivably naive in placing any trust in Mr. Cromwell. He is a lawyer, a mercenary, and now he has abandoned you in your hour of need. Only I have your true interests at heart, and only I am able to see into the fog of the future in order to guide your enterprise to a successful completion." Bunau-Varilla ignored the sarcastic smirk on my face as he mouthed this tripe, concentrating instead on Amador, who sat before him as though mesmerized. "I urge you now to put all your affairs in my hands, and to rest easy in your soul. If you will do this, I shall see that you are not disappointed."

I was amazed at Bunau-Varilla's megalomania. He truly believed that the sun and the stars revolved around him, and that only he could bring off the coup in Panama. To my further astonishment, moreover, Amador shared that opinion, for the old boy shook with great sobs of gratitude and wept, "Oh, *monsieur,* these old ears are grateful for your words. Everything shall be as you desire."

"Everything?" demanded Bunau-Varilla.

Amador, perhaps uncertain as to where the Frenchman was going, replied, *"Monsieur?"*

"The revolution, Doctor. Are your people ready to rise, and to do so at my command?"

Amador didn't like the sound of the word *command,* but he was a bit over a barrel at the moment and more than a little taken aback by Bunau-Varilla's bluntness. As for me, I was elated, for it was a French citizen posing the question. Bringing Bunau-Varilla onto this stage had been a stroke of pure genius on my part. "Of course, *monsieur,"* Amador stammered out. "At your command."

As nauseating as this scene was, my goal was partially accomplished. I had wanted first to get Amador to place his confidence in Bunau-Varilla, and I had succeeded beyond my wildest imaginings. The hard part, though, would be getting Bunau-Varilla pointed in the right direction—that is, due south—for a meeting with Roosevelt. It was with this objective in mind that I spoke up. "Nice-sounding words, Phil, but just how do you intend to solve the doctor's problems?"

Bunau-Varilla's eyebrows arched at this. He was a man accustomed to being received with deference by business magnates and powerful government officials. He was unaccustomed to being interrogated by a lowly captain, and certainly not one who impudently used his Christian name unbidden.

"Captain, may I have a private word with you?" He rose and gestured toward a closed door.

"There can be no secrets from me," protested Amador. "I must know everything."

"Doctor, did you not just promise to entrust your affairs to me for safekeeping?"

"Well yes, but—"

"Then I must have your trust. Do I have it or not?"

Amador fidgeted about in his chair, and for a moment I feared he would burst into tears once more. The poor old boy was being buffeted about on an unfriendly sea and had seen his cherished dream of a free Panama smashed to smithereens just days before. His old heart could not weather much more disappointment. "*Sí.* You have it, *monsieur,*" breathed Amador in a frail voice.

"*Bon.* Now, if you would be so kind, Captain." Bunau-Varilla strode through the door and I followed. When he closed it and lit the gas lamp, I found myself in his bedroom, a place I rather hoped never to find myself with a Frenchman.

Forcing my uneasiness from my mind, I repeated, "Just how do you intend to solve the doctor's problems?"

"That is my affair, Captain Travers," he sniffed.

I was not about to be put off, though. "That may be, but if you want a little friendly advice—"

Bunau-Varilla interrupted me with an astonished laugh. "Advice? From you? Captain Travers, please, don't waste my time. I am a man of great experience in the world. I certainly do not require your assistance in arranging Dr. Amador's affairs."

Getting him corralled was going to be a struggle, so I produced my ace in the hole. "Tell me, Phil, do you have any idea why Cromwell abandoned Dr. Amador?"

With a dismissive shrug, Bunau-Varilla replied, "No, and neither do I care."

"Well maybe you should, partner," I countered levelly. "What I heard is that the Colombians got wind of Dr. Amador's visit to New York. They told Cromwell that if he wasn't careful, they'd seize all the assets of the Panama Railroad and the New Panama Canal Company. He wouldn't make a penny from any revolution, and what's more he'd lose whatever he already owned in Panama."

All of this was conjecture on my part, but conjecture based on a good grasp of the facts as I understood them. My words struck a responsive chord, though, for now I had Bunau-Varilla's undivided attention. "Where did you hear this?" he demanded.

"Oh, come now, Phil," I snorted contemptuously. "You're a man of the world. You certainly realize that one never reveals one's sources of information. To do so would be naive, wouldn't you agree?"

I had him, and from the way he now twitched about, I could tell he was suddenly more amenable to sharing his plans with me.

"I repeat, what did you have in mind for helping Dr. Amador?"

"I would raise the money he needs to buy gunboats," he answered with a baleful glare. "Six million dollars. And then I would man them with mercenaries. Once they were in place, the revolution could proceed."

"That would take months, maybe years," I pointed out. "It's not workable."

"But the Panamanians need gunboats, n'est-ce pas? Otherwise Bogotá could reinforce the isthmus at will."

"I don't disagree, but can't you think of a quicker way to get the ships?"

I decided to employ the Socratic method with Bunau-Varilla, you see. He would never accept any idea of mine, so I'd just lead him about by the nose until he went down the path I desired.

"Well, certainly there's a quicker way, Captain Travers. I could ask your government to make them available." He spoke with a harsh laugh, as though such a thing was unimaginable. I saw my opening, though, and plunged in.

"Say, now there's an interesting idea. Do you think that would be possible?" I asked with a look of pure wonderment.

That brought Bunau-Varilla up short. Here was an American officer who did not instantly dismiss the notion of armed intervention in Panama as nothing more than a Turkish pipe dream. "I'm not sure, Captain Travers. I suppose that anything is possible, but seeking direct military support? That would be a very ticklish proposition. I could not possibly do so unless there was some circumstance that might incline the Americans to respond favorably to such a request."

"You mean like the presence of Dr. Amador in New York with his hat in hand?"

Bunau-Varilla silently mulled over my words. Finally, he began nodding his balding pate and said quietly, as though speaking to himself, "Why, of course. We should ask the Americans for naval support. After all, this is in their interest too. Hmmm, let me see. I count many members of Congress among my acquaintances."

"Congress doesn't have any gunboats," I said pointedly. "Only the navy has 'em. Who do you know in the administration?"

Bunau-Varilla thought a moment. "I correspond frequently with Secretary Hay. I count him as a close friend of mine, you know. Very close indeed." I suppressed a grin at this, and instead nodded gravely as Bunau-Varilla cogitated a while longer, then said, "It might not do, though, Captain Travers, for me to contact a cabinet officer directly. I think discretion should be my guide, *non*? There is, however, a certain Mr. Loomis whom I count among my acquaintances. Mr. Loomis happens to be Secretary Hay's deputy. I think he is the man I need to contact."

"Then send Mr. Loomis a wire. Tell him you desire an interview, and the sooner the better."

"Just like that?" mocked Bunau-Varilla. "Mr. Loomis will simply make himself available on a moment's notice? Let us be rational, Captain Travers. I have no portfolio, and I have no more claim on Mr. Loomis's time than any other private party."

Bunau-Varilla's sudden modesty, although refreshing, was particularly ill timed. He needed some further convincing, and I gave it to him. "I think Mr. Loomis might be receptive to your wire if you make sure to include one important fact."

"And that is?"

"Tell Loomis that you'll be accompanied by me."

23

Washington, D.C.
10 October, 1903

Bunau-Varilla and I debouched at the Baltimore and Ohio Railroad Station and hurried over to the Cosmos Club on Lafayette Square. We lounged about the reading room until a liveried lackey delivered a message announcing that Assistant Secretary of State Loomis was available to see us. We hurried over to the State Department, where we were ushered into Loomis's presence.

A tall, handsome fellow, elegantly mustached and coiffured, Loomis listened to Bunau-Varilla's pitch. The Frenchman waxed eloquent about destiny and the fate of nations and about honor and commitment. Intermingled with his rhetoric he managed to hint several times that Amador needed American gunboats or the revolution in Panama would be stillborn. Loomis nodded occasionally, did not interrupt with questions, and when

Bunau-Varilla was finished merely stood and announced: "Gentlemen, please follow me."

Perplexed, Bunau-Varilla inquired, "To where, *monsieur?*"

"To see President Roosevelt."

"*Mon dieu!*" gasped Bunau-Varilla. "Is it possible?"

I slapped him on the back. "Looks like you just got lucky, Phil."

Loomis led us across the way to the White House, through the now familiar north portico, and into the Treaty Room, where Roosevelt waited with Secretary Hay. Unknown to Bunau-Varilla, the big scam was on. Loomis did the introductions, and Roosevelt handled his part like a trained thespian. He greeted Bunau-Varilla effusively, telling him how very much he had treasured the memory of their last meeting.

Then he turned to me and said, "Ah, Captain Travers. I haven't seen you since, why let me see now. I think it was 1901, right after you returned from Peking in triumph. I trust all is well with you?"

"Just splendid, sir," I assured him.

"Good, my boy. Very good." Roosevelt begged us to be seated, whereupon Bunau-Varilla launched into the same oration he'd delivered to Loomis. He went on for a good ten minutes, with Roosevelt listening politely and with uncharacteristic passivity. Then, when Bunau-Varilla first uttered the word *revolution,* the president reacted. Displaying an unexpected acting ability, he gave a start of the head and blurted out in apparent amazement, "I say, sir, did you just say 'revolution'?"

When Bunau-Varilla nodded emphatically, Roosevelt leaned forward a bit in his chair and asked dramatically, "Do you think such a thing would be possible?"

"With the help of your great republic, sir, I would say *oui.*"

Roosevelt gave Hay a look of complete astonishment. "I can scarcely credit my ears, Mr. Hay," he proclaimed. "I had no idea that things had come to such a pass for the people of Panama."

"You have my word on it, Mr. President," insisted Bunau-Varilla. "Unimpeachable sources have informed me that the isthmus will rise if the United States guarantees the revolution with gunboats." Then it was his turn to lean forward in his chair. He fixed his gaze on Roosevelt and asked point-blank, "Can I tell the Panamanians, and a certain Dr. Amador in particular, that American gunboats will appear in the event of a revolt against Bogotá?"

Ever the politician, Roosevelt merely smiled beatifically and looked at Hay. The secretary of state fought to retain an appropriately grave expression, but Roosevelt's theatrics overbore his natural reserve. Despite his best efforts, a grudging grin poked through Hay's beard.

Bunau-Varilla looked from one to the other, realizing now that a charade was being played out for his benefit. Slyly, he observed, "Although you may have certain views on the matter, Mr. President, I must, er, assume you are not free to state them plainly."

"No, I don't suppose I am," concurred Roosevelt jovially, all but winking at Bunau-Varilla as he did so. Now I too was smiling openly, as was Hay, and with the three of us grinning like miners on payday, the Frenchman saw that although nobody in the room was prepared to put voice to their innermost thoughts, the answer to his question about American gunboats was as plain as day.

A broad smile creased Bunau-Varilla's pinched little face, and he murmured, "*Eh bien,* Mr. President. This has indeed been a most informative session. I wish to thank you profusely for seeing me on such short notice. Whatever course of events unfolds in Panama, I shall never be able to say that I ever heard you personally utter a word of encouragement or support for the revolution."

No sooner had those words passed Bunau-Varilla's lips than Roosevelt found his tongue once more. "Splendid meeting you, Monsieur Bunau-Varilla. Splendid."

He rose, signaling that the interview was at an end. "As for your venture, well, suffice it to say that whatever claims Bogotá ever had on this government for assistance were forfeited when the Hay-Herrán Treaty was rejected. Also, I want you to know that this country will be a true friend to any democracy anywhere in the world."

That caught Bunau-Varilla's ear, all right. He stood rooted to the spot waiting to see what other pearls might drop from Roosevelt's mouth. None, however, followed.

"Stop by whenever you're in town, *monsieur,*" Roosevelt continued genially as he escorted Bunau-Varilla across his threshold. "It's been a rare pleasure, a rare pleasure indeed."

Then Loomis took charge and ushered Bunau-Varilla and me away. In an hour we were back on a northbound train. Bunau-Varilla, brimming with self-satisfaction, could not remain silent. "Your president wants this revolution to succeed, Captain Travers."

"Oh?" I said. "I don't believe I heard him say any such thing."

"No words were needed. His very essence cried out that he would stand by the side of the Panamanian people in their struggle to be free."

"Well, you're entitled to your own opinion, I suppose."

Bunau-Varilla took this for agreement and smiled smugly. Suddenly his smile turned to a look of consternation. "*Sacré bleu,* I forgot to ask him!"

"Ask what?"

"What day to start the revolution! How will the United States Navy know when to arrive in Panamanian waters if there is no agreed date to start the revolution?"

Damn, he was right. In our glee at his quick grasp of Roosevelt's unspoken desires, we had completely forgotten to nail down that key detail. How could we have been so stupid? I gave the matter some hurried thought. Bunau-Varilla seemed the type who liked riddles, so I gave him one.

"No, I disagree. If you want to interpret the president's comments in the way you have, then I think you might find that he did indeed set a date."

"But how can that be?" demanded Bunau-Varilla. "All he said was that whatever claims Bogotá ever had on his government were forfeited when the Hay-Herrán Treaty was rejected."

"And what else?"

"Let me see. Ah, yes. He said also that your country would be a true friend to any democracy in the world."

"Exactly," I said pointedly. "Don't you see what he was driving at?"

That did the trick, for immediately the Frenchman's subtle mind went to work. He saw conspiracies everywhere, so it was only natural that he might believe that Roosevelt's words contained hidden meanings. Unfortunately, the message I wanted him to find, a date that had never been spoken, would require a little more illumination to uncover.

"Hmmm," he murmured. "Forfeited claims. Friend of democracy. No, I am sorry, Captain Travers. I find no date communicated in any of that. *C'est impossible.*"

He was right, but I was enjoying myself now and decided to tweak the insufferable little prig a bit before feeding him another bogus hint. "Oh, come now, Phil. It can't be as all-fired murky as you're making it."

"Murky?" he protested. "If there is a date buried in your president's words, it is more than murky. It is completely impenetrable."

"Think, man, think," I urged as he bristled at my presumption. "What happens in most democracies? What makes 'em special, eh?"

"Why, they vote," he spat, for he was tiring of my shenanigans.

The thought that I wore on him so quickly gratified me immensely, and I pressed on. "Now you're hot on the trail, Phil. And what else?"

"What else?" he cried in exasperation. "Nothing else, Travers. I see no connection to anything in this."

"Phil, Phil," I chided him remorselessly. "Is this the same fellow who told old Amador to leave everything in his hands? Why, don't tell me you can't unravel a simple little puzzle that's been dangled right before your eyes."

"Captain, I warn you, do not toy with me."

"I'm not toying with you. I'm trying to help, but you're not letting me. Now, you told me that folks in democracies vote, right? When precisely do they do that, Phil?"

"On election day, and don't you call me Phil again, you insolent swine!" he shrieked. He looked as though he was about to lay his hands on me when a jolting look of enlightenment came over him.

"Election Day," he repeated softly. "Yes, that must be it! November third. Travers, I've done it. I have deciphered the unfathomable."

"Absolutely remarkable," I sniggered, then I pulled down the brim of my hat to get some shut-eye as Bunau-Varilla sat there congratulating himself for a further ten minutes.

When we arrived at New York shortly after dawn, we met with Amador. Time was short, and we all agreed that Bunau-Varilla must make his funding arrangements as quickly as possible for all to be in readiness by Election Day. Bunau-Varilla made it clear to Amador, though, that the amount to be forthcoming would be considerably less than the $6 million the doctor had expected. Before Amador could protest, Bunau-Varilla hinted that whatever gunboats might be needed would be supplied by unnamed northern friends. When Amador pressed Bunau-Varilla for details, especially for an iron-clad guarantee of American support, the Frenchman rebuffed him with a curt, "I have been to Washington, have I not? I have sat in the presence of this nation's greatest men. The support you seek is at hand, but do not ask me how I know this. Let trust and discretion be your watchwords."

With his lofty rhetoric still ringing in the air, Bunau-Varilla swept off to see about fund-raising. Once the Frenchman was gone, I made arrangements to travel back to Colón with Amador. I hadn't mentioned this to Roosevelt or Root—both of whom, I was sure, assumed that, with Bunau-Varilla in the picture, my role in Panama was over. That, however, wasn't the way I saw things. Although I led Amador to believe that I had certain military surveying duties to attend to, the truth of the matter was that I planned to hover about unobtrusively to ensure that Amador played his part properly. That is, he was to deliver the message that help was on the way in as cheery a fashion as possible to encourage the maximum number of fools to rally to the banner of revolution.

Also, there was another reason why I had to return to Panama: if Amador's nerve failed, or that of Arango, I needed to be readily at hand to do something about it. Despite my assurances to Hay that the American footprint in Panama would be negligible, the fact of the matter was that I intended for there to be a revolution come hell or high water. I didn't care who I had to wheedle, bribe, or cajole to get the damned thing going—and if I implicated the American government in the process, then so be it. Let the Democrats crucify Roosevelt in the newspapers, and let the army cashier me for my rashness. In the end I'd have $80,000 to console me, and with that tidy sum in my coffers I could weather any amount of disgrace.

With our travel arrangements made, I set out alone to settle one last piece of business. I hailed a hansom and told the driver to take me to Fifth Avenue and 71st Street. In fifteen minutes I arrived at the curb before George Duncan's sprawling mansion. I eyed the massive front door, framed by twin columns of matching gray limestone.

"Go up to the corner and pull around the curb. Then wait," I ordered the cabdriver.

There I sat for the better part of two hours, positioned so that I could see the front of Duncan's place. The flow of city traffic passed me by— wagons and carriages of all descriptions. I took no notice of any of them until a sky blue landau trimmed in gold appeared. I recognized it at once; it was Duncan's personal coach, the one he had swept me away in when I returned from Peking as the conquering hero. The landau slowed to a halt, and on cue Duncan appeared at his door, walked briskly out to his carriage, and then was off.

I paid off the cabbie with a generous handful of Agent McAllister's greenbacks, then hurried around the corner, bounded up the granite steps two at a time, and pulled the bell cord. The door swung open to reveal Duncan's dour butler, whose name I still didn't know after all these years.

"I'm here to see Miss Brenoble," I announced.

The fellow's eyes flew wide at the sight of me. "Why, Captain Travers. I had no idea you were in town. We heard nothing after the wedding was . . ." Here his voice trailed off awkwardly.

"Yes, well, that's why I'm here. I need to see Alice, and at once. Announce me, won't you, er," I paused and decided to take stab at his name, "Gus?"

He shook his head, but only partly because I had gotten his name wrong. "I'm afraid that's not possible, sir. When Mr. Duncan returned from Saratoga, he gave strict orders that if you were to appear, on no account were you to be allowed to see Miss Alice until after he had settled certain matters with you. So you see, Captain Travers, I'm afraid I cannot grant you admittance under the current circumstances." He started to close the door, paused, and then turned back to me. "Oh, and my name is Gilbert, not Gus."

"Surely you're mistaken, my man," I cried hotly.

"No, I'm certain," he maintained stoutly. "My name really is Gilbert."

"Not about that, damn you!" I roared. "I mean about Alice. She and I are engaged to be married. There must be some mistake here. You must have misunderstood Mr. Duncan's intent."

"There is no mistake, sir. Good day." With that he withdrew and closed the door in my face.

"Damn you, Gus!" I ranted. "Open this door before I beat it down."

I pounded on the solid mahogany until my hands began to swell. Stymied, I stomped off, cursing and swearing with each step. By God, I was humbugged, and there could be no mistaking the reason why. Duncan was determined to move Alice's trust beyond my grasp, and he had hit upon a scheme for doing so; he would keep her far from my reach until I signed his damnable documents.

I knew I could thwart Duncan if only I could get to Alice, but how to accomplish that feat escaped me at the moment. Unfortunately, Duncan's mansion was as sturdy as a fortress, and short of blowing my way in with explosives, I knew of no way to breach that bastion.

I was still damning Duncan and his butler when I happened to look up and see a familiar metropolitan sight. It was a dray, drawn by two swaybacked nags that were only steps away from the glue factory. Up on the driver's seat sat an enormously fat German calling out to two black bucks who followed behind with shovels. These three, I saw, were street sweepers under contract to the city. They made their living by shoveling horse droppings from the thoroughfares of New York.

As soon as I spotted them, I saw the solution to my rebuff. I let loose with a piercing whistle and called, "Hey, Dutch. I need a word with you!"

"*Nein*," came the churlish reply. "I'm on der job."

I fished into my pocket and withdrew a thick roll of greenbacks. At the sight of my money, the German reined in, a hard glint of greed in his little eyes. "Talk away, mister."

In ten minutes all was in readiness. I was back at Duncan's front door, crouched to one side. I pulled the bell cord once more and then scuttled for shelter on the far side of one of the columns. In a few minutes I heard the door swing open, followed by a sharp intake of breath.

"Good God, man, have you lost your mind?" cried Gilbert, aghast at the spectacle that greeted his disbelieving eyes.

"Here is der goods vot Mister Duncan ordered," said the German stolidly, leaning on his shovel.

"What? Nobody ordered a load of manure, you fool!" exploded the butler as he flew down the steps to where the big German stood beside a steaming pile the height of a small boy. The Blacks were just as cheery, for I had also crossed their palms with a day's salary, and all for just a few minutes of work.

"Remove this—this cargo at once!" demanded Gilbert, his face a mixture of revulsion and outrage in equal parts.

"We need to talk price, mister," replied the German roughly, for I had planted the idea in his thick skull that the occupants were likely to pay as handsomely for removal as I had for delivery.

"Price? Don't tell me you intend to charge me for this travesty," yelled Gilbert. Then, losing his poise completely, the butler commenced to fire off a string of particularly inartful maledictions, only to be met with guttural curses from the game German. With the battle fully joined now, I slipped inside undetected.

I had been in Duncan's abode before, under more hospitable conditions to be sure, and so I knew my way around. I crept up the spiral staircase and down the hall to Alice's bedroom. When I opened the door, though, it was empty. Then I heard soft humming coming from somewhere farther down the hallway. I made my way in that direction until I came upon a doorway that led into a large sunroom. I peered carefully inside the room and saw a trim figure busily scratching away at a writing tablet.

I took one look at those luxuriant auburn tresses and cried, "Alice!"

Alice turned, disbelief on her face, and then joy. She was up and in my arms in an instant, and we kissed and then kissed some more.

"Fenny, my love," she cried. "I had no word from you, not a single line. I can't tell you the anguish I suffered from not knowing where you were."

She drew back and eyed me carefully. "You've been on some campaign or another. You've got that same lean, hard look you had out in the Philippines when you went into the hills in search of those awful Moros."

She had me dead to rights, but I smiled disarmingly and said, "I've simply been away on business, Alice. Government business, like the agents said on that night back in Saratoga. I can't tell you too much, other than to say that I must leave town again soon, but I couldn't depart without seeing you once more."

Tears were in her eyes now, and she begged, "Oh, Fenny, please don't go. It will kill me if you leave me again not knowing where you are or what might become of you."

"I must, dear, but you mustn't worry. I'll be perfectly safe, and if things work out as I expect they will, I'll be home again before you know it."

"When exactly will that be?" she sniffed.

Not desiring to being pinned down like a butterfly on display, I equivocated, "Soon, my love. I can say no more. You understand, don't you?"

The look in her eyes told me that she didn't, but she was too well bred to make a scene. "All I can say, Fenny, is that I love you, and because I do, I shall try to understand."

"That's my girl," I said, giving her another smack on her full lips, before I asked, "What's all this nonsense with your butler not admitting me? He insisted that Uncle George has banned me from the premises. Is the man daft?"

Alice looked down. "No, he's not, Fenny. Uncle George has been acting strangely ever since the two of you spoke at Sycamore. He's insisted that there are matters that must be resolved between the two of you before the wedding can go forward."

"Has Uncle George, er, laid out what those matters might be?"

"No. Oh, I've asked, Fenny, but he insists that it's between the two of you and no one else. No matter how I try to make him see that what concerns you concerns me as well, it's been no good. He's shut me out completely."

I considered this. Uncle George was by nature secretive and noncommunicative, and he would be especially so about his plans to cut me out of Alice's fortune. He rightly believed that Alice, who by nature was generous to a fault, would be appalled at his miserly scheme. No, he couldn't confide to her his plans for me, and for once the very stealth that had served him so well in the rough-and-tumble of New York's business world would prove to be his undoing.

I drew Alice to me with an arm around her slender waist and felt her heaving bosom against my chest. "Dearest," I said warmly, "I've done a great deal of thinking about the two of us."

Alice gave me a hopeful smile in reply, for my words were sweet music to her ears. "And?" she prompted with a coquettish tilt of her pretty head.

"Well, I wonder if I couldn't coax you to get your bonnet and take your gallant officer's arm. Time is short, my dearest, and there's someplace I'd like to bring you."

"Where?"

"It's a secret, my love. You must trust me."

"You know I'd go anywhere with you, Fenny. Give me a few moments and I'll be at your complete disposal."

When she was ready, Alice promenaded with me right past the startled Gilbert, who could only sputter in bewilderment as we hurried down Fifth Avenue, around a corner, and disappeared from view.

24

Colón, Panama
27 October, 1903

"What? You bring us a scrap of cloth and a vague promise of money from a Frenchman?" bellowed Arango to a cowed Amador. "By the saints, you were in New York for more than a month! We expected you to return with millions of Yankee dollars and an absolute guarantee from the Americans that they would side with us against the Colombians!"

"But, but El Maestro. I beg you to hear me out. Those are the very things that I bring to you," quailed Amador miserably.

"You bring no such things!" raged Arango. "Show me the money, Manuel. Show me a declaration of solidarity from a high American official. Where are they? Place them on the table before me."

I was at Amador's side as he endured this broadside, and take my word for it, it was not at all pleasant. We had arrived in Colón earlier in the day. As soon as our ship docked at Pier 2, Amador and I had hurried ashore. Our landfall had been a low-key affair. That was my doing, for I had insisted that Amador wire ahead from New York to warn Shaler to ensure that nobody greet Amador at the wharf. The less attention his return attracted, I figured, the better.

Prescott, though, alerted by Shaler, was expecting us. He hustled us unnoticed into a nearly deserted railroad car, and in two hours' time we arrived at the station in Panama City. There Senator Arango had a carriage waiting, and before long we were in the parlor of Fredrico Boyd. Present with Arango and Boyd were Arosemena and the others. Amador, exhausted from his travels, made his report in a deliberate, matter-of-fact fashion. When he was done, he looked about at his comrades as if expecting their heartfelt thanks for his efforts on their behalf. What he received instead was stunned silence, followed quickly by a nasty showdown with Senator Arango.

"El Maestro, as God is my judge, I have done all that you asked."

"Bah, you have failed, Manuel. You have returned nearly penniless and with only the word of the Frenchman, nothing else. You are a gullible fool, and I see now that I sent a feeble old man to do a job that required vigor and purpose."

I thought this last blast was a bit harsh, but Arango was absolutely right about one thing: Amador had returned with no cash. Oh, following our meeting with Roosevelt, Bunau-Varilla had been a flurry of action, all right. As promised he had arranged for funding with his bankers, and, as expected, just before Amador and I sailed, he summoned us back to the Waldorf-Astoria. I thought he would simply hand Amador the grubstake and then the two of us would be on our merry way back to Panama. With Bunau-Varilla, however, nothing was ever simple.

The Frenchman, it seemed, had been unwilling to release any funds to Amador without certain collateral. He seated us back on the same settee and pulled up his chair to face us. In his clipped, almost brutal way, he got right to the heart of the matter. "There is one condition I must place on my aid to your nation, Dr. Amador."

"Condition?" I had demanded narrowly, for I sensed that Bunau-Varilla had something up his sleeve.

"Yes, what condition might that be, Monsieur Bunau-Varilla?" Amador had squeaked at my side. "You never mentioned a condition before this moment. It was my firm understanding that you would aid us willingly because of your financial interests in Panama."

"That and, of course, because I am a friend to liberty. Yet despite my heartfelt wishes for the success of your enterprise, *Docteur,* upon reflection I have decided that I must place a condition on my support."

Amador had sighed; to him Bunau-Varilla was the rainmaker, and without the Frenchman there could be no revolution. I knew better, of course, and so I listened with care to the little pip-squeak's last-minute proviso. If it was inimical to my interests, I had planned to haul him up short.

"I must be appointed to draw up any resulting canal treaty with Secretary Hay," Bunau-Varilla had demanded. "Before I provide a sou, I must receive written confirmation of that fact from both you and Senator Arango."

For a second Amador hadn't been able to grasp the import of Bunau-Varilla's words. He shook his head in bewilderment and asked with a pained grin, "You can't mean that you are demanding an appointment to represent Panama, can you, *monsieur?*"

The answer, though, had struck Amador like a thunderclap. "That is exactly what I am saying, Dr. Amador. The moment the revolution is announced, this telegram must be dispatched to me here in New York. When I receive it, I shall release all the promised funds."

He had handed a draft message to Amador, who took it with benumbed hands. The old boy adjusted his spectacles feebly and read the thing. When he was finished he looked up and sat completely motionless. Whatever was on that sheet of paper had shaken Amador to the core, and so I snatched the draft from him and did my own perusing. When I was done, I knew why Amador had been shocked. Bunau-Varilla's missive was a bombshell fabricated of sheer Gallic brass. It stated:

> The government has just been formed by popular acclamation. Its authority extends from Colón to Panama City inclusive. I request you accept the mission of minister plenipotentiary in order to obtain the recognition of the republic and signature of canal treaty. You have full powers to appoint a banker for the republic at New York, and to open credit for immediate urgent expenses.

When Amador was able to speak again, he had stammered out in disbelief, "But certainly this is some sort of levity on your part, Monsieur Bunau-Varilla. I mean, how would such a thing be possible? How can a Frenchman become Panama's first foreign representative?"

Bunau-Varilla's eyes had flashed, and he countered firmly, "I assure you, Dr. Amador, I am completely serious."

"But your request, *monsieur,* is preposterous!"

Preposterous or not, it was what Bunau-Varilla wanted, and after an hour of moaning and objecting, wheedling and cajoling, Amador had finally capitulated. As for me, I thought the matter over as they argued, and I decided not to intervene on Amador's behalf. In my book, you see, Bunau-Varilla was first and foremost a businessman, his manifold protestations of lofty idealism notwithstanding. That meant he wanted to make money from this deal, which in turn meant abiding by the gentleman's agreement he had with Roosevelt. One thing that could upset the applecart would be for a bunch of swell-headed Panamanians, upon securing their independence, to up the ante with Uncle Sam. It was plain that Roosevelt expected to get from the new republic the same terms that had been offered to Bogotá in the Hay-Herrán Treaty. If Arango and his coterie successfully seized the reins of power, they might question those terms, especially the part about the New Panama Canal Company receiving $40 million. Bunau-Varilla could prevent such last-minute renegotiations only if he held signatory authority for the new republic. I knew where my interests lay: I got paid when Uncle Sam got his canal. That meant that I was naturally disinclined to interfere with Bunau-Varilla's little ploy.

No sooner had Bunau-Varilla beaten down Amador on that issue, though, than he raised a second one. He went to his rolltop desk, unlocked it, and produced a plainly wrapped bundle, which he transferred to Amador with the greatest solemnity.

Still in shock from Bunau-Varilla's demand for ministerial powers, and acutely aware now that the Frenchman was hardly the Father Christmas type, Amador had asked with trepidation, "What is this, *monsieur*?"

"Open it and see," was all Bunau-Varilla would say.

Amador had complied and unwrapped a small package containing what appeared to be a bolt of bright cloth. He held it up to the sunlight and studied it curiously. "Ah, you have brought me a shawl for Señora Amador, no?"

"*Mais, non.* What you hold is the flag of Panama, our new nation," Bunau-Varilla had announced proudly.

I looked at the thing and winced. It was a garish rag with yellow suns and stripes all set on a white background in a pattern that vaguely suggested Old Glory. Perhaps the gauche symbols held special meaning for Bunau-Varilla, but I could sense that Amador was unimpressed. Although he hid it well, I had no doubt that Amador was more than a little affronted by the impertinence of the Frenchman at daring to dictate to the Panamanians what their banner would be. At that moment, though, Bunau-Varilla held all the cards. Amador could do little more than choke back his outrage and mouth through clenched teeth, "I thank you, *monsieur,* on behalf of my companions for this, um, honor."

Thankfully, Bunau-Varilla had had no more surprises, and a subdued Dr. Amador and I had taken our leave. Amador had confided to me as we made our way to the docks that Bunau-Varilla's terms, while stiff, were probably a necessary cost for securing the freedom of Panama. Senator Arango and the others, Amador had assured me, would understand this.

As things turned out, Amador was dead wrong. When, safe in the parlor of Fredrico Boyd, he pulled the comical flag from its package, the hideous thing was uniformly derided by all present as an obscene joke. Then, when he disclosed Bunau-Varilla's insistence on being named the plenipotentiary of the new republic, groans and curses filled the chamber. In the end, El Maestro had heard all he cared to from the thoroughly shaken Amador. He cast his angry gaze in my direction.

"What about you, Captain Travers?" he demanded. "Can you tell us what guarantees the American government is prepared to make to vouchsafe our revolution?"

I hemmed and hawed at this, thinking all the while that Hay would have fainted dead away at such a question. All I could think to say was, "Well, I can state that Monsieur Bunau-Varilla was in Washington and that he had a personal meeting with President Roosevelt."

This assuaged nobody, of course, and the meeting degenerated into angry factions bickering and snarling at each other and at the now thoroughly miserable Amador. The elderly physician had hoped to be welcomed home as a hero; instead, he was branded as a fumbling nincompoop and cast aside as younger, more aggressive men clamored around him. Finally Arango held up his hand for silence.

"This is my decision on the matter. The United States must be forced to commit itself. There will be no revolution until we see American warships off our shores." Turning to Amador, Arango ordered, "Cable Bunau-Varilla. Tell him to have the United States dispatch ships to our waters in two days or the revolution is off. We will all reaffirm our allegiance to Bogotá and then the Yankees can go back to negotiating with Bogotá for their canal."

I did some quick calculations. Two days from now was October 29. There would be no ships until November 3, or late on the second at the earliest. Somehow I had to maneuver Amador into convincing Arango to roll back his sudden deadline. Amador gave me the opening for doing just that when he looked to me imploringly and begged, "Please, Captain Travers, make them see that the future of Panama depends on cooperating with Monsieur Bunau-Varilla."

I was up and talking at once. "Be reasonable, Señor Arango," I urged. "If such a wire were to be sent this very instant to Monsieur Bunau-Varilla, it would take a full day just to arrange matters with the United States Navy. Even then, there would be a decision to be made as to just what ships are available to answer the summons. No, two days is an absurdly short time for such a complex operation."

Fredrico Boyd, the newspaperman, unfortunately proved to be knowledgeable on this point. "We've been following the notices in the American newspapers regarding the movements of warships, Captain Travers. The *Dixie* is currently en route to Guantánamo, Cuba, and the *Nashville* is at Kingston, Jamaica."

"Then the ship that the Americans would send is the *Nashville*," concluded Arango. "Kingston is two days away by fast steamer. Allowing the day you say it would take for the Frenchman to arrange our demand in Washington, Captain Travers, the total time required to bring the *Nashville* to Colón is no more than three days. Dr. Amador," he repeated, "send the message to Bunau-Varilla as directed. Tell him that the Americans must have a gunboat off Colón in three days."

Three days was only October 30, I realized. That was still too soon, and I racked my brain for a way to squeeze out a few more days. "Wait," I pleaded. "What if it's not the *Nashville* that's sent? We know nothing of her supplies or a thousand other details that could render her unsuitable for this mission. The *Dixie*'s just arriving on station. She might be the one to come."

This was all a ploy, of course, for I fully agreed with Arango that the *Nashville* would in all likelihood be the ship that came. Arango, though, failed to rely on his own common sense and instead considered my words. "When could the *Dixie* be here?" he asked Boyd.

"Three days," Boyd replied, "plus another day for recoaling at Guantánamo. Adding to that the extra day that Captain Travers says would be needed makes five days in all."

That would be the first of November. It was the best I could hope for, I told myself.

Arango nodded. "Then five days it is. Dr. Amador, send the message to the Frenchman. We shall see whether we have friends in the north or not."

"What about Monsieur Bunau-Varilla's condition?" asked Amador. "He insisted that there would be no money from him until you and I agreed that he would be first representative of the republic in Washington."

Arango considered this. "We need the money. If a scrap of paper is the Frenchman's price, then let him have it and be damned. As soon as the revolution is declared, wire Bunau-Varilla that he is appointed as our minister to Washington."

With that, the gloomy meeting concluded. Amador and I sought out Shaler to give him Arango's dictate. We found him in his office at the Panama City railroad station. Together the three of us crafted the message for Bunau-Varilla. This was all a charade to me, of course, for I knew that whether a wire went forth or not, gunboats would appear over the horizon by November 3.

Amador didn't know that, though, and he set to work with a will. Bunau-Varilla, as things turned out, had given Amador something more valuable than his ludicrous flag. He had also provided Amador with a list of code words to be used should emergency communications be necessary once Amador returned to Panama. The doctor now dug these out and laid them upon the table before us.

"Let me see. Yes, here's the first word," decided Amador, inspecting the list. "Fate. That means this message is for Bunau-Varilla."

"Okay, Fate it is," I said, writing the word on a slip of paper.

"Next is Bad," continued Amador. "Bad means Atlantic."

"Okay, Bad," I wrote.

"Powerful," said Amador next. "Powerful means five days."

"Right," I said, writing down Powerful. "Okay, that's Fate Bad Powerful. Now what's the code word for gunboat?"

Amador scanned his list. "There isn't one."

I hastily reviewed the list. The word wasn't there, by God.

"How about steamer?" suggested Shaler.

I was aghast. "No, no, we can't use steamer. That's too obvious. Why, if this message is intercepted, that word could hang us." I saw no reason to rile the Colombians, you see, until help was on hand.

"Okay, you're right," agreed Shaler. "Steamer won't do. Hmmm, let me think. Steamer kind of suggests smoke."

"Or vapor," suggested Amador.

"That's it. Use vapor instead," I urged. "Bunau-Varilla's a bright boy; he'll get our meaning."

"How do we tell him to send the ship to Colón?" asked Shaler sensibly enough. "After all, there are other ports in Panama."

He was right, and the code again didn't allow for this.

"That point is too important to leave to chance," decided Amador. "No, we'll have to be very precise. I think we should say Urge Vapor Colón."

"Urge Vapor Colón," repeated Shaler, looking to me. "What do you think, Captain Travers?"

"Well, I would prefer to not be so damned obvious, but the doctor's right. We need to make sure the ship goes where we need it. Colón it is, I suppose."

I jotted all this down and handed the result to Shaler. The superintendent was about to carry the message to the telegraph office for transmission when suddenly came the sound of horses whinnying and a carriage halting just outside. All eyes turned to the door. We tensed as it swung open. My hand dropped toward my Colt, for betrayal was heavy in the dank air. Had the Colombians decided to come for us? Was the crazy dream of a Panama canal dead at last, and me along with it? All of this flashed through my mind when who should step into view but Señora Amador.

"Maria!" cried the doctor at the sight of his wife. "Whatever has possessed you to come here? There is danger everywhere in the streets."

"More than you know, Manuel."

"What do you mean?"

"A message for you was slipped under our door."

Amador, confused, could only ask, "What did it say?"

"You are in the gravest danger," Señora Amador replied. "A battalion of *tiradores*"—sharpshooters—"is en route from Barranquilla by sea to Colón. They are led by General Tobar."

Amador gasped, and I squeaked in alarm, "When will they arrive?"

"The message said four days, maybe five. Certainly no longer."

"Madonna," moaned Amador, and I was feeling none too chipper myself.

Shaler, though, kept his head enough to do some cogitating. "With all due respect, Señora Amador, how do we know that your news is reliable?"

"He's right," I seconded. "After all, the Colombians have every reason to plant false rumors to distract and divide us."

"I had the same thought, Captain Travers," said Señora Amador. "That is why I sought out Major Black at the American consulate before I came here. He confirmed that he had been hearing similar rumors through his operatives in Bogotá."

Black, I knew, was a particularly accurate source of bad news. "Damn," I muttered, "a fresh battalion in Colón will certainly muddy the waters."

"To say the least, Captain," agreed Shaler. "Yet still, none of this came over the wires, Señora. That causes me to discount what you're telling us."

Señora Amador was not at all taken aback by Shaler's caution. Instead, she told him, "Within the past few hours, the gunboat *Bogotá* sailed into the bay off Panama City. I believe she brought the word of these reinforcements."

Shaler's face clouded. "That would fit. After all, if the Colombians wanted to ensure secrecy, it would stand to reason that they would send this sort of news by courier. I suppose you may be right after all, Señora." Then he brightened a bit and observed, "Your intelligence, although grave, may nonetheless be cause for guarded optimism."

This surprised Señora Amador, who challenged, "How so, Señor Shaler?"

"I'm not sure I'm following you either, Superintendent," I put in. Where, I wondered, was the silver lining in a message that said a band of trained killers was heading our way?

"Well, if this information is accurate, then I suspect that the source must be someone within the Colombian military. Someone," he added pointedly, "who doesn't want us to be caught completely by surprise."

"Do you mean Colonel Huertas?"

"That would be my guess. He's straddling the fence, I think, appearing to be loyal to Bogotá, but also positioning himself in case some attractive opportunity suddenly presents itself."

"Like an American intervention?" suggested Señora Amador.

"Precisely."

Maybe Shaler was right, I mused. After all, the Panamanians were certainly addicted to intrigue and double-dealing. Huertas was blood of their blood, and that meant he was as slippery as they came. Yet even if Huertas was secretly on our side, the arrival of heavy Colombian reinforcements before November 3 was unnerving. It was as though some unseen watcher had discerned our plan at the eleventh hour and was now moving to block it.

Where I was merely shaken, though, old Amador was cast into deep melancholy. His wife's ill tidings had completely snapped his already frayed nerves. "All is now lost," he despaired. "With General Tobar comes the end of our dream. The Colombians will arrest us all."

Shaler went to a map on the wall and did some quick calculating. "Captain Travers, do you believe that our navy can arrive here by November second?"

Deciding there was nothing to lose by being honest, at least partly, I replied, "Not really, Superintendent. The second was Senator Arango's date, not mine. I think that if we send a wire right now, the navy will arrive by the third." I saw no advantage in sharing with Shaler the fact that November 3 was the navy's prearranged arrival date.

Eyeing the map, Shaler spoke. "If the Colombians arrive from Barranquilla in four days, they will win the race. But if they take five days, they'll arrive in Colón at the same time as the United States Navy."

None of this cheered Amador in the slightest. "If the Colombians get ashore first, Señor Shaler, there is nothing the Americans can do to help us," he fretted. "I say the timing is all wrong for us. It is clear that Bogotá knows what we are up to, and the *tiradores* are being sent to smother us. I will go to El Maestro and tell him that we must put aside our plans and try as best we can to heal our rift with Bogotá while there is still time."

"Now see here, Manuel," remonstrated Shaler. "We can't lose our heads about this. Sure, things look grim, but we need to stay with our plan and send this wire." Shaler went on for another five minutes, pleading and cajoling with Amador not to break ranks. Amador for his part stubbornly deflected

Shaler's exhortations, insisting that the dream was dead and that it was time to face facts. It was clear to me that no amount of argument was going to revive Amador's flagging spirits. With this dismal scene unfolding before me, I was certain that things couldn't get much worse. I was wrong, for Señora Amador had further news to impart.

"There is something else I must tell you, Manuel," she announced, sadness in her voice. Her barely controlled emotion, coupled with the sudden tears that welled up in her eyes, caused both Shaler and Amador to fall silent.

"Maria, what is it?" asked Amador, ashen-faced.

"Serafina is missing," Señora Amador almost sobbed.

Amador staggered back, as if physically hit. "Missing? What do you mean?"

"She went for a ride toward the hills this afternoon. A vaquero found her horse but no trace of Serafina."

"Perhaps her horse became spooked and threw her," suggested Shaler. "Maybe she's afoot this very moment."

Señora Amador shook her head. "Serafina is too good a horsewoman to be thrown, Señor Shaler. No, she did not have a riding accident. She has been kidnapped by someone. I feel that in my bones."

I had seen Serafina handle a horse and I knew that she rode like a Comanche. She would never have been thrown. That meant that Señora Amador was right; Serafina was in danger.

Old Amador cried out, "How can this be? Could bandits have taken her?"

"I don't know what to think, Manuel," replied Señora Amador.

"We'll organize search parties, ma'am," promised Shaler. "If she's been taken by bandits, we'll get her back, I swear it."

Now I spoke up, for there could be but one explanation for Serafina's disappearance. "We're not dealing with bandits, Superintendent."

"Eh, what that's you say, Travers? Not bandits? Who else would do such a thing?"

"Comandante Reyes."

Now all eyes were on me. "Comandante Reyes?" echoed Shaler with disbelief in his voice. "Surely not even he would risk the ire of every gentleman in Panama by such a dirty, low-down act."

"Under normal circumstances, perhaps not," I conceded, "but these are not normal times. What's more, we know that Reyes lusts after Serafina."

"Your words are true, Captain," affirmed Señora Amador. "It is no secret that Reyes has vowed to have Serafina."

"The way I see it, Superintendent," I explained, "Reyes realizes that if the *tiradores* arrive before our navy can thwart their landing, they will be the real power in Panama. If Huertas is truly a fence sitter as you think, he'll watch quietly as the *tiradores* suppress the revolution. All of this means that Comandante Reyes has no fear of retaliation from any quarter. Indeed, it may be his intention to personally hang Dr. Amador and Senator Arango, as well as anyone else who might protest his taking of Serafina."

The ensuing silence told me that the others agreed with my words. There was no other explanation for Reyes's sudden boldness, you see. He expected a bloodbath to erupt soon in this land, and when it was over, he planned to be in the ascendancy. At length the silence was broken by Señora Amador. The galling thought of living beneath Reyes's heel had steeled her nerves for action.

"If we are to die anyway," she announced dramatically, "then let us at least die fighting."

"Maria," protested her husband, "do not talk foolishness. Now is the time for caution, not rashness."

Señora Amador ignored his entreaties. "Send your telegram to the Americans, Señor Shaler. Tell them about the Colombian reinforcements, and tell them to hurry to our aid. As for Senator Arango and the others, they know nothing of what I have told you. Let it be our secret, I say, for if word of the reinforcements gets to them, their resolve will melt." This indirect reproof of her husband stung, for old Amador stiffened under the lash of her words. Undaunted, Señora Amador plowed on. "We must continue to mobilize whatever forces we can muster. We can arm them with the rifles that have begun to arrive on our docks." These arms, I knew, were Root's doing. "With these we must prepare as best we can, and pray the *norte americano* ships arrive before it is too late."

Amador, shaken and pale, at first seemed speechless in the face of his wife's fiery defiance. Then, slowly nodding, he said, "It takes a woman to show us our duty as men. Let us do as Maria says. Let us fight for our freedom; if we fail, at least we die fighting in the cause of liberty."

With Amador back in the fold, I turned my attention to revising the coded message in light of the news Señora Amador had brought us. I hastily studied Bunau-Varilla's list of code words and cobbled together a new missive using the limited selection of terms. One of these was News, which meant Colombian troops arriving. Another was Tiger, which meant more than 200. Yes, they would do, I decided. Bunau-Varilla would get the point. Sitting down with Amador's first draft, I edited it to read instead, "Fate News Bad Powerful Tiger. Urge Vapor Colón."

Shaler read the message, nodded his approval, and then hurried off to find his telegraph operator.

25

The following days were ones of watchful uncertainty and frenzied activity. Unaware of the danger approaching from Barranquilla, Arango issued a call to arms. Supporters of independence were ordered to gather at Panama City and hold themselves in readiness for the arrival of the Americans. I saw them as they gathered near Parque Catedral, perhaps four hundred ill-disciplined men and boys. Shopkeepers and clerks they were, with a smattering of plowboys and hod carriers thrown in for good measure, but not a soldier among them. A few carried rifles, but most were armed with fowling pieces, swords, pikes, and even clubs. As they scattered into the alleys and garrets of the town to hide until summoned forth by Arango, I felt a deep despair. This rabble would be no match for the *tiradores,* nor for Huertas's battalion should the inscrutable colonel decide to throw his support to Bogotá at the last minute. The uneven quality of Arango's loyalists convinced me more than ever that Colonel Huertas would have to be bought.

Shaler agreed and took it upon himself to see to that vital detail. Through Senator Arango an approach to Colonel Huertas was made, and with me at Shaler's side, negotiations commenced. The little martinet bargained like a fishmonger's wife and more than once threatened to walk out on Shaler. Shaler, though, was a shrewd bargainer himself and landed a telling blow when he pointed out that Tobar was a general whereas Huertas was a mere colonel. It was clear that Bogotá planned to subordinate him to Tobar, and when that happened Huertas would never again be a power broker on the isthmus. Put another way, Shaler explained, the price Huertas could command in the marketplace of bribes and gratuities would dwindle significantly as soon as General Tobar splashed ashore. Huertas, Shaler suggested, needed to strike while the iron was hot.

Huertas dickered for a while longer, but the wind was out of his sails and in the end a deal was struck. The colonel would get $65,000, a princely sum. No cash could change hands, of course, since the $100,000 promised by Bunau-Varilla had not arrived, nor would it until the Frenchman had the appointment he demanded. Huertas was told nothing of this, though. Instead he was assured that the necessary funds would be released immediately upon the outbreak of the revolution and that he would be among the first to receive any disbursements. As for his men, each soldier would receive $50, but only after affairs had been settled and the United States made its agreed-upon payment to the new republic. With these terms arranged, hands were shook and affirmations of undying affection were passed all around. Both Shaler and I knew, though, that the loyalty of the wily Huertas was an ethereal thing. Would he turn upon us when the chips were down? Only time could answer that key question.

As for General Varon—the skipper of the gunboat *Padilla,* which lay at anchor off Panama City—things were even more questionable. Varon had been augmented by the *Bogotá,* and his little flotilla had to be neutralized. Arango offered Varon $35,000 for his support—that is, to guarantee the neutrality of both the *Padilla* and the *Bogotá*—a figure that represented the balance left of the $100,000 after Huertas got his cut. Varon, perhaps insulted by the paltry amount when compared to that offered to Huertas, and undoubtedly miffed that he might have to share some of his take with the skipper of the *Bogotá,* was noncommittal. Yet Varon didn't immediately shoot Arango's emissary, which was taken by all the conspirators as a hopeful sign. In the end, though, I had no idea whether Varon had been bought and intended to stay that way, or whether he planned to shell the bejesus out of Panama City as soon as the fireworks started.

Meanwhile, I had other fish to fry as well. Through Prescott, I sent messages to Kingston Jack and Henry in Colón to muster with the Antillean's followers near the stockyards in Colón on November 2. They were to stay out of sight but be ready to help in a pinch. Also, I told Kingston Jack to search high and low on the Caribbean side of the isthmus for Serafina. If Reyes had her, I figured, he would have spirited her away to somewhere near Colón, since he controlled the place.

While all of this was going on, Bunau-Varilla on November 1 wired a reply from New York to Amador's telegram, stating, "ALL RIGHT WILL REACH TWO DAYS AND HALF."

I read and reread the wire. What the blazes did "reach two days and half" mean? And, more importantly, where would this undefined reaching occur? It was vintage Bunau-Varilla, exquisitely obscure and subject to multiple interpretations. Arango, though, saw no ambiguity in Bunau-Varilla's message. No, he was much buoyed by the thing, choosing to read in the cryptic words an ironclad guarantee that American ships would arrive in Colón in two and a half days. Amador remained subdued, for he knew that even with Bunau-Varilla's latest wire, the conspiracy would collapse in an instant if El Maestro and the others caught a whiff of the danger en route from Colombia.

It was this threat that absorbed most of my attention, for even with the preordained arrival of the American navy on November 3, the Colombian reinforcements could seal the fate of Panama. Shaler shared my fears, and together we traveled over to Colón, where in the company of the stalwart Prescott we surveyed the environs of the station and the stone freight house.

"If the *tiradores* get ashore, it may come down to a fight," I told them. "And if that happens, we must do all in our power to hold the Colombian reinforcements on this side of the isthmus. That will give Amador time to coax Huertas into openly affirming his support and taking steps to deny General Tobar access to Panama City. Then, with the American navy at anchor off Colón, and with the active support of Huertas, maybe we can convince Tobar to sail for home."

"Is there any chance of simply bottling them up on their ship?" asked Prescott. "After all, if they can't get ashore, they can't do any mischief."

"The answer to that question depends on when our navy arrives," I replied. "If we have a warship here when the Colombians sail into the harbor, then maybe so. At the moment, though, I'd say we have to plan for the eventuality that the Colombians may win the race to Colón."

"If the *tiradores* do get ashore and reinforce Comandante Reyes's men, we'll be hard pressed to keep them in Colón," opined Shaler. "Kingston Jack's men will be no match for that combined force, and I doubt that Colonel Huertas has the stomach to fight his own kind."

This was a sobering assessment, and the sense of gloom it brought to me was only darkened when Prescott suggested, "Perhaps, sir, Captain Travers here could be persuaded to lead the volunteers Senator Arango has raised. With their numbers, maybe we could prevent a Colombian landing. I could pile the volunteers onto a special train and have them over here in no time."

That seemed reasonable to Shaler, so he asked, "How about it, Captain?"

My heart skipped a beat, for the last thing I intended to do was to place myself in the line of fire. No, I had come down here to instigate others into doing that, thank you. I would have a damned hard time spending my expected windfall, you see, if I was lying dead in some filthy Colón alleyway. Shaler was looking at me expectantly, but I could share none of this with him, of course. Instead, with a stern look in my eyes I growled, "It's a hard thing to ask a soldier to stand to the side when the guns begin to roar, Superintendent, yet that is what I must do. I have strict orders, I'm afraid, to avoid directly involving the United States in any fighting."

That was a fair enough interpretation of what Hay had said, and for once I was actually staying within the letter of my orders. I could be damned obedient, you see, when it suited my purposes.

"Well, I suppose that's wise, Captain Travers," Prescott allowed, thankfully dropping his foolish notion.

His comment about the train, though, had started me thinking. I looked about at the rolling stock all around me, and then to the edge of town where the track began to ascend the wild cordillera of the interior. I remembered something Senator Arango had said back on the first day I set foot in Panama. It was right after he announced that Amador was to be the interim president. Longbottom had demanded to know how the plotters would deal with the Colombian army, and in response Arango had spoken of the railroad. I recalled Arango's words, and as I did a plan formed in my mind.

"The railroad's the key," I said, half to myself.

"Eh? What's that you're saying, Travers?" queried Shaler.

"Simply this. Nobody can move across the isthmus except on your railcars, isn't that so, Superintendent?"

"Yes, but what of it? The Colombians will just seize whatever stock they need when they come ashore and roll over to Panama City in high style."

"That's just my point. You need to clear all the rolling stock out of Colón."

Now Prescott spoke up, for he saw my plan. "Why, he's right, Superintendent. We should move all the rolling stock to the Pacific coast and hold it there. Then, if the Colombians do land ahead of our navy, they'll be stranded here in Colón."

"Exactly," I affirmed. "If we manage to hold them here until the navy arrives, there'll be American marines on board who can take matters in hand from that point on."

Shaler wasn't so certain. "But can't the Colombians simply land from the Pacific side and seize the rolling stock in Panama City?"

I shook my head, for Black had given me a fair understanding of the Colombian order of battle. "Other than Huertas's battalion, there are no Colombian garrisons on the Pacific coast. What's more, the crews of General Varon's gunboats off Panama City are too weak to muster a credible shore party. The rolling stock will be secure on the Pacific side of the isthmus."

That did it for Shaler. "Then I agree. It's the only hope we have, Captain Travers." He hurriedly gave the necessary orders, and soon long lines of cars were leaving the yards, climbing Monkey Hill, and disappearing into the distance en route to Panama City.

All this activity did not escape the notice of Comandante Reyes. He promptly stormed up to the station office at the head of a squad of soldiers. I stifled an impulse to throw myself on the little tyrant and pummel him until he told me what he'd done with poor Serafina. The rifles of his escort, however, convinced me to bide my time, so I hurriedly concealed myself in a closet just as Reyes entered.

"What is the meaning of these rail movements?" he demanded as he entered. "Under whose orders are they occurring?"

"Why, mine, Comandante," replied Shaler.

Reyes glowered at him for he knew that by treaty he had no authority over the railroad. Deciding to shock Shaler into submission to his will, he snarled, "I have been notified that a battalion of *tiradores* is en route from Colombia, Señor Shaler. Your trains will be needed to transport those troops. Have them returned this instant."

Shaler was steady in the face of Reyes's dictate, playing his hand as coolly as you could have pleased. "I've also been notified of their arrival, Comandante," he retorted.

"What?" exploded Reyes. "That is not possible."

"Why, of course it is. Colonel Huertas himself told me about the *tiradores* and then asked me to send my cars to the yards in Panama City for complete maintenance. He said that the general's mission is too important for there to be any chance of a train breaking down because of its poor condition. I've ordered the repair work to proceed at all speed, and for the trains to be back here on November second."

All of this came from Shaler with the calm tone of sweet reason. He laid it out before Reyes so convincingly that it seemed the height of good sense. Indeed, the *comandante* even seemed a bit chagrined that he had questioned Shaler's actions. He drew himself erect and said coldly, "I accept your explanation. From this time forward, however, you are to make no movements of rail stock without my prior approval."

"Well now, Comandante," countered Shaler, "aren't you stepping outside your jurisdiction just a bit? The movements of this railroad are governed by treaty. Your order sounds to me a little like unlawful interference."

God, I thought as I eavesdropped on all of this, Shaler was more than just holding his own with Reyes. The flinty old Yankee was actually beating him back.

Reyes, recognizing the validity of Shaler's position, hissed in anger, "Your treaty be damned, Señor Shaler. I think the day of *yanqui* interference in the internal affairs of Panama is fast approaching an end." Then he strode angrily from the office with his squad on his heels.

"We'll have to be extra careful of him," warned Shaler when I emerged from my hiding place. "He's dangerous under the best of circumstances, but now with the arrival of General Tobar and what promises to be the commencement of a reign of terror, Reyes will be uncontrollable. Colón is a tinderbox, and our friend Reyes is likely to be the spark that sets the whole place ablaze."

When the last railcar was gone, we cleared for action. Sacks of meal were stacked in windows at the freight house, turning it into a makeshift fort. Arms were rounded up from private homes and stockpiled inside the freight house for ready use, and all railroad employees and able-bodied American citizens were notified by word of mouth to rally there at a moment's notice. When all was in readiness, I took my post in the freight house and, together with Prescott and Shaler, kept a weather eye peeled on the open roadstead of Limón Bay.

I must have dozed on my watch, for I was awakened by a sudden cry, "Smoke, ho! On the horizon! Smoke, ho!"

I was on my feet in an instant, with Shaler and Prescott at my elbow. We stared fixedly at the distant smudge in the otherwise clear air. Was it the American navy or the Colombians? We watched with bated breath as a shape appeared, took substance through the shimmering haze of the heat, and then grew near.

Shaler had a spyglass to his eye, and it was he who announced calmly, "That's the U.S.S. *Nashville,* boys."

By God, it was the navy! They were a day earlier than I had expected them, and were they ever a sight for sore eyes. Prescott whooped and I did a little jig of joy, and all in all we were in a state of exultation as the *Nashville* dropped anchor about a half mile off the end of Pier 2.

She was a two-stacked gunboat, white and gleaming against the placid harbor waters. White-clad tars swarmed about her deck, securing equipment and generally standing down from their ocean passage. My attention went to the *Nashville*'s eight 4-inch guns. These, I knew, would likely be the final arbiters of Panamanian independence.

"A boat's coming ashore," observed Prescott. As I watched, one of the *Nashville*'s whaleboats was lowered from its davits. A party filled the distant boat and soon it was pulling for Pier 2.

"Gentlemen," said Shaler, snapping closed his glass with undisguised satisfaction, "please accompany me to greet our guests."

We arrived at the end of the pier just as the boat was laying alongside. A lieutenant commander in starched tropical whites made his way up to the pier and touched his cap in salute. "Superintendent Shaler, I presume?" he asked.

"Yes, I'm Shaler. And you, sir, are?"

"Commander Hubbard, United States Navy."

Shaler quickly made introductions all around, then told Hubbard about the planned insurrection and of the imminent arrival of General Tobar. He also informed Hubbard about his decision to move the rolling stock to Panama City. With that background all laid out before Hubbard, Shaler inquired, "Commander, if I may be so bold to ask, what are the particulars of your instructions? Are you empowered to take a direct hand against General Tobar's troops?"

"Unfortunately, the answer is no, Mr. Shaler," replied Hubbard. "I'm to report to the American consul in Colón and await further orders. I have no authority to intercept the Colombians nor am I authorized to prevent them from landing. I can only take action to maintain freedom of movement on the railroad."

"Then you have no orders to support the independence movement?"

Hubbard, sensitive to Shaler's plight, confessed, "None at all, sir."

Shaler was flabbergasted, having assumed that the arrival of the *Nashville* would lift from his shoulders the responsibility for ensuring the success of the revolution. I too was taken aback, for I had been clear with Roosevelt on this very point; the navy had to intercept any Colombian reinforcements bound for the isthmus. Why, Hubbard's orders amounted to little more than showing the flag and hoping that the revolutionaries would take the lead in this business. That was precisely what I had told Hay and Roosevelt would never work. I saw now what Roosevelt had meant back in Sagamore Hill when he likened Hay to an old woman. The secretary of state was so blasted worried about maintaining the fiction that the United States was not usurping Colombia's sovereignty that he had eviscerated the eminently feasible plan that I had cooked up and that Roosevelt had approved. How Root could have let such a thing happen was beyond me, but I damned both him and Hay. Oh, it was all fine and good for them to set policy from on high, and to discount the warnings from a fellow who had firsthand knowledge of the Colombians and their ways. Neither of them, of course, would be on hand to deal with the imminent arrival of General Tobar.

"Excuse me, Commander," I asked, my guts churning as I considered the drastically altered situation before me, "but could you tell me the strength of your complement of marines?"

Hubbard hesitated before he replied, for he was uncomfortable being the bearer of so much bad news. "I have two marines on board, Captain Travers—an armorer and a corporal."

I couldn't have been more stunned than if Hubbard had slammed a board across my head. "What? Two marines? But I don't understand how that could be possible."

You see, I had some experience with marines from my days back on Samar during the desperate fighting against the *pulajans*. I had listened as Major Waller and Captain Bearss and the other marines of my acquaintance described their shipboard exploits around the Caribbean and the Orient. I had come to believe that every navy warship carried a powerful complement of marines, rather like fleas on a dog. Never in my wildest imaginings had it occurred to me that the Navy Department might send a cruiser to Colón with only two leathernecks on board. Yet, by God, that was exactly what Hubbard was saying.

"The only sizable marine force available for deployment to the Caribbean was the battalion at the Philadelphia Navy Yard," explained Commander Hubbard. "That battalion is currently on board the *Dixie,* which is due to arrive in Guantánamo, Cuba, today."

"Good Lord, that puts the marines two days away!" I exclaimed, unable to contain the dread that swept over me at this intelligence.

"I'm afraid that's correct, Captain Travers," confirmed Hubbard, feeling a bit awkward as he eyed the crestfallen faces around him.

Damn, I thought, Hay would have his way after all. Other than Henry, the shadowy Major Black, and poor old Fenny, not one American fighting man would be on hand for the start of the revolution. There was Longbottom too, of course, but he was still confined in the French hospital.

On that sour note, our little conclave concluded. Shaler promised to inform the American consul of Commander Hubbard's arrival and, with his message delivered, Hubbard repaired to the *Nashville*. Shaler immediately dispatched Prescott to Panama City, for he wanted his deputy on the Pacific end of the line to coordinate what promised to be a desperate minuet with the Colombians.

That was where matters stood when, well after dark, a light appeared far out at sea. The light drew closer, and I could see it was a large ship heading straight for the harbor. It was the gunboat *Cartagena* bearing General Tobar and the five hundred men of the Tiradore Battalion. The *Cartagena* dropped anchor not too far from the *Nashville* and remained quiet throughout the long night. At dawn, though, just as the first squawks of the parrots reached my ears from the nearby jungles, the *tiradores* began landing in force.

26

The news of General Tobar's arrival flashed back to Panama City by wire. The reaction there was not unexpected; I was in the telegraph office at the station with Shaler when the reply message came in from Amador. Shaler read it and said, "Everything's in chaos. The conspiracy is unraveling, and many supporters are heading for the hills. Amador, however, has vowed to stick to his guns, probably because Señora Amador insists. Arango, thankfully, is still with him."

"Great," I said glumly. "That's three against five hundred."

A freight agent hurried over to the station office from the direction of Pier 1. "Colombian officers coming ashore, sir," he called to Shaler.

"That's probably General Tobar," sighed Shaler. "I'll go greet him. Captain Travers, you stay out of sight in the freight building. You can see and hear most everything from there. I don't want you with me because I expect our friend Comandante Reyes will also be on hand to greet the general."

"As you wish," I agreed, taking up a position near an open window facing Pier 1.

Shaler hurried out into the already oppressive sun just as General Tobar and his entourage stepped ashore from their launch. Tobar, a squat, ugly fellow, was resplendent in his immaculate white uniform, red kepi, and glittering sword. As he lumbered toward Shaler, he seemed to glow and glisten with every step, so festooned was he with gold braid and epaulets. Hanging from his chest was a veritable bazaar of military decorations, stars and crosses mostly, the whole riot of baubles all crisscrossed with colorful cords. Oh, he was a wonder to behold, and if sheer martial splendor was the measure of a military man, General Tobar would certainly have been a conquering hero—on a par with Tamerlane, or maybe even Genghis Khan.

As Shaler neared, Tobar received the elderly superintendent like a potentate might some trembling burgher from a conquered town. It was clear from his strut and bluster that he had but one aim; he meant to smother the rebellion in its infancy.

"General, I welcome you to Colón," hailed Shaler. "I wish to assure you that the Panama Railroad will provide you with any assistance you may require."

"Excellent," grunted Tobar. He motioned to a tough-looking colonel just behind him. Unlike Huertas, this fellow seemed to be an hombre who had seen lead fly in anger. His uniform was devoid of Tobar's showy gewgaws, and the leather of his pistol belt looked as though it had seen hard service. Bogotá, I noticed, had sent forth at least one soldier cast from the same mold as Reyes. "This is Colonel Eliseo Torres, the commander of the Tiradore Battalion. You will immediately make cars available to transport his men to Panama City."

"Colonel, your request gives me the greatest pleasure," began Shaler with a slight bob of the head at Torres, "but—"

Before he completed his sentence, Reyes appeared. The *comandante* shouldered past Shaler and saluted. "General Tobar, I beg to report that the situation in Colón is quiet. My troops are in control of all the key points."

"Very good, Comandante Reyes," said Tobar with a smile. These two must know each other from back in Colombia, I concluded. Turning to Colonel Torres, Tobar added, "You must be very proud of your nephew, Colonel. He seems to be the epitome of military efficiency."

"*Sí, mi* general," agreed Colonel Torres.

Ah-ha, I thought, the light coming on at last. Colonel Torres was Reyes's uncle. That would explain why Reyes felt bold enough to seize Serafina. With his uncle on the isthmus at the head of a battalion of crack troops, Reyes's word would be the law in these parts.

General Tobar turned his attention back to Shaler. "Señor, as I said, please make the necessary arrangements for rail transport."

Shaler gave him the smile of a practiced gamesman. "I am yours to command, sir, and I understand that there is not a moment to waste. I have wired to Panama City to have the necessary railcars sent over at once—"

"The trains are not here?" interrupted Tobar, shooting Reyes a peeved look.

"No, *mi* general, they are not," explained Reyes. "Supervisor Shaler had them all moved to Panama City. This was done at the order of Colonel Huertas."

"Is this true?" demanded Tobar, anger starting to show in his face.

Shaler didn't blink an eye at the impending eruption. "What Comandante Reyes says is absolutely correct. The cars were due for maintenance, and as I've already explained to the *comandante,* Colonel Huertas's purpose was to ensure that you had at your disposal rail transport that would be in proper working order. The repairs have been completed and the required cars are moving to Colón even as we speak."

That calmed General Tobar somewhat. "I see. Well then, when will the cars be here?"

"Within hours, *mi* general. Please be assured that my employees are doing their utmost to hasten your men on their way. In the meantime, may I suggest that you and your immediate staff avail yourselves of the single car and locomotive that I have set aside for your use?"

He gestured in the direction of the station where a locomotive stood waiting, steam escaping quietly from its big smokestack. Attached to it was a coal tender and a single car. "Colonel Huertas personally asked me to expedite the passage of you and your staff to Panama City."

This had been my brainstorm, you see. As the railcars had left for Colón, it had suddenly occurred to me that if we could separate Tobar from his troops, there was a chance to decapitate the counterstroke from Bogotá. What needed to be done, I had explained to Shaler, was to lure the general into a single car with his key officers and then whisk them off to Panama City while the *tiradores* were left behind to cool their heels in Colón.

As I watched, General Tobar considered Shaler's proposal. The delay in transporting the Tiradore Battalion bothered him, but he was clearly anxious to hurry over to Panama City to confer with Colonel Huertas. The earlier he had firsthand information about the state of affairs on that side of the isthmus, the better. Besides, where was the harm? There was no organized resistance in Colón, and hadn't Reyes reported that his troops held all the vital points?

His mind made up, he announced, "I accept your offer, Señor Shaler." Turning to Colonel Torres, he ordered, "Colonel, you will be in overall command in my absence. Move the troops ashore and secure Colón. As soon as the necessary rolling stock arrives, transport the battalion to Panama City."

"*Sí, mi* general," responded Torres. He gave no snappy click of his heels nor a flashy salute but merely touched a beefy hand to the brim of his kepi.

"Keep Reyes with you to assist as needed," General Tobar added and then marched off toward the waiting train. His staff, a bit puzzled by this turn of events, followed their chief.

From my vantage point overlooking this scene, I considered the situation a moment. Tobar had taken the bait and appeared to be cooperating nicely with my plan to separate him from his troops. That meant that the key thing now was to ensure that Colonel Huertas kept his part of the bargain and backed up Amador and Arango as agreed. Since the neutralization of General Tobar was vital for success, I decided to place myself so as to ensure that it happened.

I slipped quietly from my perch and crept out the freight house door nearest the station. As inconspicuously as I could, I moseyed over to Tobar's train and climbed aboard. I drew a few stares from Tobar's staff, but those officers, apparently concluding I was a railroad employee of some sort or the other, quickly looked away. Shaler's eyes went wide at the sight of me, all right, but he clamped his jaws together and kept silent.

With the Colombians all settled, the train began gathering steam. It had not yet moved, though, for the engineer was awaiting the signal from Shaler to depart the station. Before Shaler could do so, however, a Colombian major suddenly became fidgety. He rose from his seat and approached General Tobar, mouthing something about wanting to stay with Colonel Torres and cautioning Tobar that it was imprudent to take so many staff officers with him in this manner. These were all reasonable concerns, and damn his eyes if Tobar didn't appear to be giving them due consideration.

Shaler, who had stepped down and was waving his hat in farewell, wore a look of consternation as more of the Colombians turned in their seats and seconded the major's concerns to Tobar. Suddenly, a wholesale flight from the car seemed imminent. If that happened the game was up.

Realizing there was not an instant to lose, I reached up and seized a signal cord hanging by the door. I tugged it twice, hard, and heard twin shrieking *wheets* as steam blasted from the whistle on the car's roof. Immediately, the locomotive lurched forward, for the engineer assumed the signal came from Shaler. The sudden movement knocked those on their feet into the nearest seats, and then we were away from the station.

By the time the most vocal of the Colombians recovered their equilibrium, the train was hurtling out of Colón. What followed next was what I took to be the Colombian version of a military staff meeting. The nervous major screamed out that Tobar was an idiot and a son of an idiot. This caused a captain to rally to his chief's support, calling the major's slanders against Tobar treason and suggesting that the major's father was guilty of carnal knowledge with canines. The major, livid with rage, went for his pistol, and there might have been gunplay right then and there had not other officers pulled the two apart. There was more shouting and bickering from other quarters, but by then Tobar had heard enough. With a roar like a shell burst, he ordered silence. What was done was done, he thundered, and, by Jesus, he didn't want to hear anything more about it.

Their feathers badly ruffled, his staff reluctantly subsided and took their seats once more for the trip to Panama City. With no other traffic on the line to delay us, in a mere two hours we were chugging into the station on the far end of the line. On the station platform was a welcoming committee of dignitaries. Governor Obaldia was there, identifiable by his sash of office, his demeanor giving no hint of where his ultimate loyalty in this matter lay. Around Obaldia was gathered a collection of aldermen, customs officials, businessmen, and clerics, all of them beaming widely and seemingly ecstatic at the arrival of Tobar. Arango, Amador, and the others, I noted with alarm, were not among them.

There too was the Colombia Battalion, drawn up for review in serried ranks with Mausers held at the "present" position in salute to General Tobar. At the head of his troops, saber drawn and ribbons dangling from his scrawny chest, was the diminutive figure of Colonel Huertas. Behind the battalion stood a row of elegant carriages ready to whisk away Tobar and his entourage.

No sooner had the train pulled in than a military band struck up a lively Spanish march and the front rank of troops fired a volley in welcome. The argumentative major started visibly at this blast but recovered himself when he realized that the discharge had not been in anger. With the smoke of the volley still whirling overhead, Governor Obaldia stepped forward and delivered a twenty-minute oration of welcome. Tobar took all this in graciously enough, casting a wary eye at Huertas's battalion all the while. Tobar, however, was becoming more reassured by the minute. Conditions on the isthmus were not as chaotic as he had been led to believe. His entourage too relaxed visibly, and soon smiles wreathed all their faces as they were led to their carriages for a fete at the Presidencia, the governor's official residence.

As Tobar left, I hurried to the station office. There I found Prescott standing anxiously over the shoulder of a telegraph operator as another message clattered in. "It's the latest from Shaler," he explained as I entered. "It seems Commander Hubbard has received further instructions from Washington. They're secret, but he shared them with Shaler, who feels you need to see them as well." Prescott handed the message to me and I quickly read it:

NASHVILLE, CARE AMERICAN CONSUL, COLÓN:

SECRET AND CONFIDENTIAL, MAINTAIN FREE AND UNINTERRUPTED TRANSIT. IF INTERRUPTION THREATENED BY ARMED FORCE, OCCUPY THE LINE OF THE RAILROAD.

PREVENT LANDING OF ANY ARMED FORCE WITH HOSTILE INTENT, EITHER GOVERNMENT OR INSURGENT, EITHER AT COLÓN, PORTOBELO, OR OTHER POINT. SEND COPY OF INSTRUCTIONS TO THE SENIOR OFFICER PRESENT UPON ARRIVAL OF *BOSTON*. HAVE SENT COPY OF INSTRUCTIONS AND HAVE TELEGRAPHED *DIXIE* TO PROCEED WITH ALL POSSIBLE DISPATCH FROM KINGSTON TO COLÓN. GOVERN-MENT FORCE REPORTED APPROACHING COLÓN IN VESSELS. PREVENT THEIR LANDING IF IN YOUR JUDGMENT THIS WOULD PRECIPITATE A CONFLICT. ACKNOWLEDGMENT IS REQUIRED.

DARLING, ACTING

"Well, talk about closing the barn door after the horse is gone," I muttered in disgust. "What's more, about all Hubbard could muster would be a shore party of bluejackets."

Reading between the lines, I could see that Roosevelt had gotten jittery in his traces. With the destiny of nations at stake, he now apparently had decided to jettison Hay's evenhanded approach for a more active policy. Unfortunately, his turnabout had come a little too late. The Colombians were ashore in force and Roosevelt would just have to play the cards already on the table.

There was good news in Prescott's message, though, particularly the part about the arrival of more ships. The *Boston* I recognized as a vessel assigned to the Pacific fleet, which meant she would be heading for Panama City. The great imponderable, of course, was the exact time of their arrival, and what actions General Tobar might take between now and then.

"Destroy this message," I ordered, "and mention it to no one else. Then wait here for any further messages from Shaler. I'm going into the city with Governor Obaldia and General Tobar. We've got to figure out some way to snag Tobar, or our little revolution could turn into a bloodbath."

With the welcoming ceremony concluded, the troops were marching back to the Chiriqui Barracks, the place in town where they were quartered. Chiriqui Barracks was down by the seawall, at the point where the battlements of Panama City jutted farthest into the Pacific. The battalion would remain there unless it could be rallied to Amador's cause. Not quite certain about what to do next, I decided to stick close to Tobar and climbed into the last coach to depart. I squeezed roughly between two skinny

sublieutenants, who squeaked a bit but ultimately put up with my effron-
tery. When the convoy of carriages reached the Presidencia, Tobar went
into the place willingly, his lackeys following.

Guessing that a hearty repast would fix Tobar in place for a while, I
hurried off to the *cuartel,* the military headquarters adjoining Chiriqui Barracks.
There a sentry challenged me, but Captain Salazar, Huertas's tall aide, was
the officer of the day. He ordered the sentry to let me pass, and I waited
impatiently for Huertas to return from the station at the head of his battalion. He found me pacing the floor of his office when he entered. There
was no time for niceties; I came straight to the point.

"I come from Superintendent Shaler. Is all in readiness?"

Ominously, Huertas didn't respond to my question. Instead, he loos-
ened his sword belt and seated himself behind his desk. He fished a cigarillo
from the humidor and, without offering one to me, slipped it between his
lips. He snapped his fingers, and Salazar, who had followed on Huertas's
heels like a trained spaniel, sprang forward with a match. It was only when
he had sent several rings of smoke wafting up to the rafters that Huertas
deigned to reply.

"I suppose," he said languidly. "I will tour the defenses with General Tobar
after his luncheon. Then, when he has been assured as to the state of our
military readiness, Captain Salazar here will place the general under arrest."

That all sounded more or less as agreed, but there was a note in Huertas's
voice that told me there was something else on his mind. Eyeing him narrowly,
I asked, "Is there some problem I should know about, Colonel?"

Huertas's smooth face became an impenetrable mask, and I knew that
beneath his dandified exterior lurked a mind as devious as any I had ever
encountered. His eyes narrowed into almost feline slits before he half
murmured, "The money."

"The money?" I demanded with alarm. "What about it? I mean, that's
all been agreed to, hasn't it? You've been promised sixty-five thousand
dollars, right? Each of your men, moreover, will get his back pay and a
ten-dollar bonus, fifty dollars each. Now all of that seems clear enough
to me."

"It's not enough, señor," announced Huertas flatly.

"Not enough?" I fairly screamed. "By Christ, Huertas, now is not the
time to be reopening negotiations!" I knew now the anger Roosevelt had
felt when dealing with the gang in Bogotá. Nothing was ever enough for
these people, even after a deal had been struck. "The money Shaler promised
you is more than you've ever seen in your life, Colonel," I raged on, "and

it's certainly more than you'll ever see if you remain loyal to Bogotá. What's more, if you drag your feet now and General Tobar escapes our snare, money will be the least of your problems. If Bogotá learns of your palavering with Shaler and Arango, I wouldn't be surprised if you end up swinging from a rope looped over a lamppost on Parque Catedral."

For a second, fear flashed in Huertas's dark eyes, but his avaricious instincts were now aroused and he struck right back in his attempt to squeeze more lucre from me. "Don't think I don't know that, *yanqui*," he spat. "But if I'm jailed, I'll take all the plotters, including Shaler, with me. And if that happens, well, I would not be too surprised if the junta in Bogotá decides that the time has now come to nationalize your precious railroad."

The danger to all involved bothered me not a whit. Oh, Shaler was a nice old fellow, and I wished him no harm, but he was fully aware that he was in a desperate enterprise that could go wildly astray. As for Amador and the others, they too knew the rules of Latin revolutions: the losers truly lost everything. So the fate of my collaborators was unimportant to me. What *was* critical to me, though, was my railroad stock; its value would plummet if this little peacock welshed on our deal and Bogotá seized the line. If I had more money to promise him, by God, I would have laid it before him then and there. Unfortunately, between his bribe and the pay-off for Varon, the money promised by Bunau-Varilla was exhausted, and at the moment I couldn't think of where to turn for more.

As I stood there deliberating on how to respond to this blatant extortion, fate took a hand in things. A sergeant hurried into the office and saluted. "Colonel, General Tobar is in the plaza outside the *caserne*."

Damn the luck, I thought. Either the luncheon ended earlier than expected, or Tobar had become reagitated about the delay in the arrival of the Tiradore Battalion from Colón. As the sergeant and Captain Salazar stood by expectantly, I turned to face Huertas. "Okay, Colonel, here's my final offer. Eighty thousand dollars for you. One thousand for each of your officers, plus the agreed-upon fifty dollars per soldier." A tight half smile appeared on Huertas's face at this, and, encouraged, I added with an easy lie, "The money's already in the Ehrman Bank right here in Panama City." Conscious of sudden heavy breathing behind me, and since I was already giving away money I didn't have and had no idea how to secure, I continued on munificently, "As for Captain Salazar, since he's obviously the one who will actually take General Tobar, I pledge ten thousand dollars American. Accept my terms this minute, or I'll walk out of here and you are all on your own."

I was bluffing, pure and simple, and I stood there waiting for the wily Huertas to call. If he did, the house of cards so painfully erected by Arango and the others would come fluttering down in an instant.

"We'll take it," wheezed Captain Salazar, intoxicated by visions of this unimaginable wealth.

Huertas shot him an angry look, but I could tell from the calculating expression on the colonel's face that I was pretty near his price. I decided that one final incentive might be in order.

"Don't forget, Colonel Huertas, that if the revolution succeeds, you will be the commander of the only armed force on the isthmus. Senator Arango and Dr. Amador expect that they'll head the new government, of course, but who knows? There might be an opportunity for a plucky fellow with a few rifles at his back to work his way to the top of the heap. If you think eighty thousand dollars is a lot of money, why, it pales in comparison to the riches that might be available to an hombre who held the keys to the coffers of a free Panama. Especially if those coffers were just recently filled to overflowing with ten million dollars in Yankee gold paid out for rights to the canal."

That did it. Lights came on in Huertas's eyes, and he stiffened with sudden resolve as visions of a future that he had never before dared to imagine danced in his head. "Shall we go outside and greet the general?" he asked, a slightly dazed expression on his face.

"By all means," I seconded.

On the plaza, General Tobar was taking a report from the sergeant of the guard, who stepped back at the approach of Colonel Huertas and Captain Salazar. I hung back, carefully watching the scene before me.

"*Mi* general," Colonel Huertas greeted his superior affably, "I trust your meal was excellent?"

"It was, Colonel, but I did not come to Panama City to eat. I came to ensure that any potential insurrection has no possible chance of success. Governor Obaldia has assured me that the situation here is under control, as have all the other officials I spoke to. Yet in the Presidencia a member of my staff was approached by a young man—a campesino, judging from his appearance. The young man handed my officer a note that claimed there are plans afoot for a revolution. The note says that armed bands are gathered secretly in the city, ready to rise at a moment's notice."

Who might that messenger have been? I wondered. Whoever he was, he was absolutely dead-on right, for Arango's irregulars were everywhere, awaiting the signal to sally forth in the name of liberty.

"Rumors always fly on the isthmus, *mi* general," Huertas said with a forced chuckle. "If I paid attention to them all, my men would be on alert every day of the year. I have made inquiries about this matter before you arrived, sir, and I am convinced that the citizens of Panama City are loyal to a man."

General Tobar was skittish, though, and remained unconvinced. "Nonetheless, Colonel, I want your battalion deployed about the city to suppress any unrest until I can bring Colonel Torres's battalion across from Colón. Assemble one company of soldiers immediately. I'll personally post them in Parque Catedral at all key points."

Huertas seemed agreeable enough, for he nodded at Captain Salazar. "Assemble your company, Captain."

Salazar saluted, turned, and bawled out the necessary orders. A hundred riflemen tumbled out of the barracks, formed into two ranks, and waited, their fixed bayonets gleaming wickedly in the tropical sun.

Salazar stationed himself at the head of the company, and Colonel Huertas sidled off to the side. When all was in readiness, General Tobar stepped smartly before the troops, his boot heels clicking on the flagstones as he did. His intent, I saw, was to inform the men of their mission and then march them off posthaste. He was no more than two feet from Salazar, with his staff watching idly some twenty feet distant.

Do it, Salazar! I raged silently to myself. Arrest him now, damn you, for you'll never have a better chance. Yet, to my complete consternation, nothing happened. Salazar, overborne by the enormity of the treason he was about to commit and spooked by the looming presence of General Tobar before him, simply froze. He stared blankly past General Tobar and quivered miserably in his boots. I realized instantly that Salazar was completely out of his depth. Despite the promise of riches that I had dangled before him, Salazar was but an instant away from swooning where he stood.

Everything teetered on a fulcrum of fear and uncertainty, for unless this moment was seized, all would be lost. Was I destined to remain impoverished? Was Cromwell fated to have the last laugh at my expense? These thoughts and others flashed through my brain in an instant, jolting me into action before I could stop myself. I found myself moving before I quite realized it, and stepping out damned lively, too. I sailed right past Huertas—who gawked at me in gap-jawed astonishment—and then around the flank of Salazar's company. I stopped only when I drew near to where Tobar and Salazar stood. Tobar's staff eyed me curiously as I came on but made no move to stop me, for they recognized me from the train ride across the isthmus. Perhaps I had come to deliver some message from Shaler, or perhaps to belatedly punch the general's ticket.

In a way, the latter was exactly what I aimed to do. "Take him," I snapped at Salazar.

"Eh? What is the meaning of this?" demanded General Tobar, confused by the sudden aura of authority emanating from a fellow he had assumed to be a lowly minion of the railroad.

"Shut up," I ordered Tobar. "Take him, Salazar," I repeated, opening my coat enough to show him the butt of the Colt jammed into my belt, "Seize him at once, or by God, I'll shoot him where he stands."

What Secretary of State Hay might have said had he seen my rough-and-tumble brand of American foreign policy, I shall never know. I can, however, vouch for General Tobar's reaction. At the sight of my Colt, he gasped and took a step back. He tried to call for help but could only stutter helplessly in bug-eyed fear.

As he did, Salazar at last shook himself free of the trance that possessed him. Trembling like a calf in a thunderstorm, he drew his pistol and trained it unsteadily on Tobar. "General," he stammered out, "you are my prisoner."

With the business end of Salazar's pistol waving in his face, Tobar's fear turned into defiance. "This is absurd. I protest!" he bellowed, but to no avail.

Half mad with fear, Salazar cried over his shoulder to his men, "Seize the general and all his aides. Do it for the sake of a free Panama!"

Not a single man moved. At that instant it seemed to me as though time stood still. I saw the soldiers look at each other, and here and there a bayonet wavered, but the ranks held steady. Their fear of Salazar was outweighed by their dread of Tobar, and exhortations grounded on vague notions of freedom were totally incomprehensible to them. Only one thing could goad these cattle into obedience, and I knew what it was.

"Obey Salazar, damn you," I cried out, "and you'll each have more gold than you can use. I'm talking about your back pay, *comprende?* Do as you're told and you'll have the money that you and your families are owed before the sun sets tonight."

A hundred pairs of black eyes were fixed on me now. Yet still the soldiers did not obey, for they had heard similar promises from their officers before. Always their pay would be forthcoming, and always their hopes were dashed at the last moment. The excuses offered to them were myriad, but the simple truth seemed to be that the paymasters in Colombia had simply forgotten about them. I sensed all this, you see, and that's why I then uttered the words that followed: "Superintendent Shaler will pay you himself using railroad funds."

A roar filled the air at this pronouncement, and as one the company lunged forward behind lowered bayonets. In an instant, the troops engulfed Tobar and his staff. As his officers were being borne away, Tobar demanded angrily, "By whose orders is this foul deed done?"

Salazar, self-possessed now that the climactic moment had passed, answered boldly, "By order of General Huertas."

General Huertas? I thought. The promotion suited Huertas just fine, though, for the ex-colonel grinned giddily, certain now that the daring coup would succeed. "General Tobar," pronounced Huertas grandly, "you are the guest of the new Republic of Panama. Please be at ease, and rest assured that you will be returned to Colombia as soon as the safety of the revolution has been secured."

"Revolution? What revolution?"

By way of answer, a signal cannon boomed from the seawall, and then the bells in all the churches in Panama City began to ring as one. From every corner of the city came cheers, and the streets began filling with delirious citizens hastening to join the soldiers of the garrison.

"Why, the revolution scheduled to coincide with your capture," answered Huertas genially. "Now, however, I must insist that you step into the *cuartel*."

Remonstrating against the coup, and roundly damning both Huertas and his troops, General Tobar was led away. It was only then that Amador and Arango, lurking just out of sight while this high drama was unfolding, burst into view.

"*Viva el Istmo Libre!*" bellowed Arango while Amador kicked up his heels and shouted with joy as he ran. They both embraced me, and it was only after some effort that I managed to break free of their grasp. The church bells continued to ring madly, and from the direction of Parque Catedral came a great roar from a thousand throats as a proclamation announcing the new republic was read. From all appearances, the first day of the revolution had been a resounding success.

With Tobar gone, I turned to Huertas. "General, you must secure this city against any reactionaries who might be lurking. Remember what Tobar said. A messenger at the Presidencia warned him of the uprising. That means you must be on your guard. Work with Amador and Arango to see that all remains peaceful here."

"*Sí*," promised Huertas, giving Arango and Amador measuring glances all the while. The little Napoleon was already sizing up the competition,

I could see. As far as I was concerned, of course, they could all have a go at each other as soon as the Colombians were run off the isthmus. At the moment, though, I had no time for their political machinations; the only thing that mattered was the consolidation of the revolution and the liberation of Colón.

"Senator Arango, have a wire sent to Washington immediately. Advise the State Department of the success of the coup here."

"I will at once, Captain Travers."

Amador, at his side, added, "And do not forget, El Maestro, we must send Bunau-Varilla his message too. Only then will he release the funds to pay General Huertas and the others."

Huertas gave me a look of astonishment at this. Withering under his glare, I explained lamely, "It's really just a technical matter, General. You know, to satisfy the bankers. Just a formality, nothing more."

Huertas was still eyeing me coldly when Arango snapped, "Let it be done."

I turned to go, but Senator Arango put a hand on my arm. "Captain Travers, where will you be, should I have need of you?"

"I'm heading back to Colón. The *tiradores* still remain to be dealt with. They have to be sent packing or there could yet be some serious fighting. Wire Shaler that the surveyor will be arriving soon."

Arango saw the wisdom of this. Fighting in Colón, if uncontained, would inevitably draw in the Colombia Battalion, the only force available to protect the new republic. "Then go, my friend," Arango agreed, and I was off like a shot, anxious to be away from Huertas. At the station I found Prescott and asked that the same train that had transported Tobar be put at my disposal. Prescott agreed and soon I was rolling back over the cordillera to Colón.

27

It was early morning when I arrived back in Colón. My passage had been delayed by stops at every station as irregulars searched me and the train and wired to Panama City for instructions. I found Colón quiet but tense. Colonel Torres's *tiradores* were everywhere in evidence, although Reyes's men were conspicuously absent. Commander Hubbard, pursuant to his secret orders, had issued a directive to Shaler prohibiting the transport of any troops by rail. That meant that Torres was bottled up in Colón, just as Shaler and I had planned.

At the station a railroad employee met me with a message. "Excuse me, sir, but I'm Tom Wardlaw, one of Superintendent Shaler's cashiers. He sent me to tell you that he's waiting for you at the Astor Hotel. I'm to take you there."

"Well then, lead on, Wardlaw," I said. He took me to a private room off the lobby. There I found Shaler, and with him were Henry, Kingston Jack, and Commander Hubbard.

"Have you found the girl?" I asked Kingston Jack.

The big Antillean nodded. "She's being held in a hacienda on the far side of Monkey Hill, Captain. Comandante Reyes is there too. I think he plans to hustle her aboard the *Cartagena* and carry her back to Bogotá."

"But why?" I wondered aloud. "Surely he can't expect the church to sanction such a match."

Here Shaler spoke up. "Knowing Reyes, I don't think marriage is in the picture. The señora is lovely but not wealthy. She lives on the charity of the Viscaya family since the death of her husband. She has no lands that she can call her own and, frankly, no real prospects. In light of that, I'd say Reyes intends to press her into service as his concubine until her beauty fades, and then discard her."

Now I'm no knight in shining armor, and ordinarily I don't inquire too closely into other people's peccadilloes. However, I was prepared to make an exception in the case of Reyes. He had tried to send me to hell, and now I aimed to return the favor. Kingston Jack and his band of hearties were just the fellows to do the job I had in mind. The kidnapping and probable rape of Serafina, moreover, gave me the excuse I needed to get started. I would have been quite happy to arrange the dispatch of Reyes with no thought of compensation, of course, but the prospect of savoring the delectable favors of a grateful Serafina was an admittedly compelling incentive.

There was a second good reason for settling accounts with Reyes. Other than General Tobar, he was the one man in Panama who could spur Colonel Torres into putting Colón to the sword. If the isthmus went up in flames, my investment in the Panama Railroad would go right along with it. All of this meant that Reyes needed to be corralled—and the sooner the better.

"Well, in view of what you're saying, Superintendent," I declared, "there seems to be no choice in the matter. It's our plain Christian duty to get back poor Serafina. If Kingston Jack and Henry would be so kind as to accompany me, I'll be on my way."

Superintendent Shaler gently laid a hand on my arm. I thought he was going to remind me that I had foresworn direct combat once before when

Prescott had suggested exactly that. Shaler, though, had other matters on his mind. "Before you go, I have still more troubling news, Captain Travers. It seems that Captain Longbottom has disappeared."

I started to ask him how that could possibly be troubling news, but instead I screwed up my face into an impromptu look of dismay. "Disappeared? Oh, Lord, tell me it isn't so. Why, I thought Joshua was chained safely to the wall of a French asylum here in town."

"He was, until a few hours ago. A squad of Colombians burst into the hospital and dragged him away."

"Do you have any idea where they might have taken him?"

Shaler shook his head. "No. I'm not even certain that he's still alive."

It was a mystery I certainly was not overly keen on solving. Besides, I already had a rather full plate at the moment. I brushed away the matter with a bluff, "Damn those bandits from Bogotá. If I get my hands on them, I'll make them rue the day they kidnapped a helpless American officer. My revenge will have to wait, though, until Serafina has been rescued."

Shaler nodded approvingly. "I know this is all dreadfully hard on you, Travers, what with Longbottom being a boon companion and all. Your choice, though, is the one any red-blooded man would have made. The woman should come first. I wish you Godspeed, son."

"We must be careful, Fenny," cautioned Henry. "There are five hundred troops in town, and if they move to reinforce Reyes, we'll never get the girl back."

I turned to Kingston Jack. "How many men do you have available?"

"About ten with rifles, another twenty with machetes."

"That's all? Why, I thought you had a small army of men at your beck and call."

"No longer, Captain. Comandante Reyes drove away most of my men right after you and Henry saved me from being lynched."

This was damned unwelcome information. "Okay," I said, "gather whatever men remain and assemble near the crest of Monkey Hill. We'll just have to pray that they'll suffice to do the job."

Wardlaw, Shaler's agent, the one who had brought me to the Astor, reappeared just then. "Sir," he said to Shaler, "Colonel Torres is at the railroad office. He wants to speak to you."

"Does Torres know the situation in Panama City?" I asked anxiously.

"Not yet, Captain Travers," Shaler answered, "but maybe it's time he did."

"How's that?" I asked, puzzled.

"If Torres knows that Panama City has risen, and that General Tobar has been made a prisoner, he may decide to give up his mission and return to Colombia."

"He just might at that," agreed Commander Hubbard.

"Hold on, Superintendent," I cautioned him. "What you're saying could be true—if we're dealing with a rational man. The problem is, however, that Torres is Reyes's uncle, and we all know that Reyes is as crazy as a bedbug. Torres might just be a mite touched in the head too."

"Meaning what, Captain Travers?" asked Commander Hubbard, not getting my point at all.

"Meaning that if you tell Torres about the situation in Panama City, he just might explode and go on a rampage here in Colón."

Commander Hubbard weighed this. "It's possible, I grant you, but not very likely. After all, Torres has to consider the presence of the *Nashville*. No, I'd say he'd probably decide to withdraw with as much dignity as the situation allows."

Shaler mulled all this over and then decided. "I agree with Commander Hubbard. It's time to send Colonel Torres packing."

Henry and Kingston Jack went off to gather Kingston Jack's men while I followed along behind Shaler and Commander Hubbard. As we emerged from the Astor Hotel, we could see a platoon of Colombian soldiers posted in the street outside the railroad ticket office. The glares they shot our way set my knees to knocking, and as we approached, the barrel-chested figure of Colonel Torres emerged from the station to confront us.

"*Buenos días,* Colonel," Shaler greeted him.

The bull-like Torres was grim-faced. "Señor Shaler, I have been unable to get messages through to General Tobar in Panama City. Also, I have not been able to learn from your employees exactly when my troops will be transported to Panama City as the general ordered. I must demand some answers from you on these matters."

When Shaler spoke there was a steely glint in his eyes. "Colonel, it does seem I owe you a bit of an explanation. The reason for all the delay and confusion is that there's been a coup in Panama City."

Colonel Torres gave a visible start as though Shaler had suddenly brandished a hissing fer-de-lance in the air over his head. "*Madre de Dios!* Did you say a coup?"

"*Sí,*" Shaler assured him firmly. "A good old-fashioned, down-home, Latin-style coup. General Tobar, it seems, is in good health but under house arrest, as is his entire staff. Colonel Huertas and the Colombia Battalion have declared for the new government of free Panama. So, as you can see, Colonel Torres, you and your troops won't be going to Panama City any-time soon. Are there any other questions I can answer for you?" Torres appeared numb with stupefaction, so Shaler continued along blithely. "The only possible course open to you now, sir, is to withdraw. Commander Hubbard is willing to allow your battalion to reembark on the—"

Shaler never finished his sentence. Torres's ashen features suddenly flashed a dangerous scarlet as his temporarily frozen brain suddenly sprang back to life. "Rebels in Panama City, you say?" he bellowed. "By the blood of the Savior, I will hang them all! And before I go, I will burn Colón to the ground!"

"Colonel, you don't understand—" Shaler began to remonstrate with him, only to be savagely cut off.

"Oh, but I do, Señor Shaler. I understand that you are in this sedition up to your skinny neck. When I have finished with the traitors in Panama City, I will return for you. I will also see to it that all rights of the Panama Railroad on the isthmus are forfeited." Then, pointing menacingly at Hubbard, he vowed, "And do not think that my government will ignore the role of your meddlesome president in this treachery. Mark my words, there will never be an American flag flown over this soil."

Shaler, seeing that things were spiraling hopelessly out of control, began backing away from Torres as one might from a mad dog.

"Don't argue with the man," I whispered urgently, seizing Shaler by the elbow and guiding him back across the street to the stone freight house.

Fortunately, Torres was so preoccupied in roaring out his orders to his troops that we were able to withdraw unmolested. Once I had Shaler and Commander Hubbard inside the freight house, I summed up the situation.

"Well, it seems your little speech didn't go over quite as you expected, Superintendent," I observed mildly.

Shaler could only hang his head, abashed at having so misjudged Torres's reaction. Commander Hubbard intervened on his behalf. "Captain Travers, please. Recriminations will get us nowhere. The only question left is what do we do now?"

"We get ready for the worst," I answered. "Commander, how many men do you have available for a shore party?"

"Forty at the most. I can spare an ensign to lead them."

"They will have to do. Signal your ship to have them landed at once. Also, have them bring along as much ammunition and as many spare rifles as you've got." To Shaler I added, "Send out the word through your railroad employees. Have all Americans gather here now, and tell them to attract as little attention as possible. Have them bring their women and children too. If Torres acts on his threat, there'll be a massacre in Colón."

Shaler, drawing himself together with his customary force of will, nodded. "There's a German steamer in the roadstead. I'll send a signal to her captain to take all the noncombatants aboard until this madness subsides."

Shaler and Hubbard both hurried off to do as I bid. Meanwhile, I ordered the railroad workers in the vicinity of the dock to set to, and soon a gang was at work strengthening the freight house's defenses. Barrels of cargo from the dock were manhandled into doorways to serve as parapets, while buckets of sand were gathered to smother any incendiaries that might be tossed our way by the Colombians.

As we feverishly prepared for battle, the Colombians were in plain sight on Pier 1 not a hundred yards away, hurriedly drawing rations and ammunition. About the time I was satisfied with the arrangements in the freight house, I saw whaleboats approaching Pier 2 from the *Nashville*. Shortly thereafter Shaler returned, having made his rounds to herd the innocents to safety. With him were the last of his employees and their dependents.

"The message has been spread," he assured me. "Almost every American in Colón is here. We'll use the *Nashville*'s boats to carry the women and children to safety."

"Good," I said. "When the landing party arrives, post the sailors at all the doors and windows. They should be able to hold off the Colombians indefinitely, especially if we're covered by the *Nashville*'s guns. As for me, I'm going after Reyes before the Colombians throw an impenetrable ring around this place."

"Can't Reyes wait, man?" queried Shaler worriedly. "After all, he and his men are the least of our troubles at the moment."

I shook my head. "No. You'll be safe here with Hubbard's reinforcements. Besides, I can't forget that Reyes has Serafina. God knows what he'd do to her if he finds out about the revolt. I'm sorry, but I've got to track down Reyes right now. Besides, I've thought of a use for his mangy hide."

"A use for Reyes? Whatever can you mean?" demanded Shaler.

To his irritation, though, he got no answer from me. Instead I drew my Colt and spun the cylinder to check that each chamber held a cartridge. Then I pushed the gun back into my belt and darted into the streets. Hugging the side of the freight house, I reached an alley that snaked through the warren of warehouses lining the waterfront. Using the alley I was able to slip through the still-mustering Colombians and away from the freight house.

When I thought the coast was clear, I sprinted across a deserted section of Front Street and into another alleyway on the far side.

I stopped and listened for some sound of pursuit. The only noise was that of soldiers in the distance calling out orders as they took up their positions around the freight house. From the sudden upsurge of volume in the shouted commands, it was clear that Torres's men were finally on the move in earnest. I had escaped entrapment by mere seconds. Turning, I crept up the alleyway to the next street over from the waterfront—Bolívar Street—and crossed it. Hearing no suggestion of danger, I concluded that I'd slipped clean past the Colombians. Accordingly, I turned right and followed the street in the direction of Monkey Hill.

I sacrificed stealth for speed, certain that every second meant the difference between life and death for Serafina. It was my haste that made me step before the gaping doors of a livery stable without first peering into the gloom within. That, as things turned out, was a big mistake.

"Halt!" cried a voice in Spanish.

Instantly I froze. Turning slowly, I found myself staring down the barrel of a loaded Mauser held by a Colombian soldier. It wasn't one of Torres's *tiradores,* however. It was Sergeant Gómez, Comandante Reyes's henchman, the one who had tried to lynch Kingston Jack and who had nearly sent Henry, Longbottom, and me to our deaths by tumbling us into a raging mountain river. The evil grin that spread across Gómez's scarred face told me that he recognized me. With Gómez was a pock-faced private who was covering a cowering couple with his Mauser. At first I had to squint to see them, but then my eyes adjusted to the darkness. "Tom? Tom Wardlaw?"

"Yes, it's me, Captain Travers," came the reply. Beside Wardlaw was a terrified woman whom I took to be his wife.

"Where are you going, gringo?" demanded Sergeant Gómez with a yellow-toothed grin. "Have you not heard that Colonel Torres has put Colón under martial law? Any person on the street now can be shot as a rebel."

I could smell the wine on his breath and saw the bloodshot whites of his eyes. No doubt he had gotten a hint that Torres might order the town to be razed, and decided to get a head start on the expected orgy of murder and mayhem. Wardlaw and the missus, unfortunately, appeared to be on the verge of becoming his first victims.

"Martial law?" I asked with a slow smile. "Why, I've heard no such thing." Even as I spoke, I edged away from the doorway, slowly backing in the direction whence I'd come.

"You look like a *haciendo*—a rich man," sneered the ugly private at the sergeant's side. "You have money on you, *sí*? *Yanqui* dollars?"

That gave me my opening, and I seized on it immediately. "Is it only money you want? Why yes, I believe I do have some, *amigo*." So saying, I commenced to slap about my person as if searching for my bankroll. "It's only a few thousand or so, but I suppose you can put it to better use than I, right?" Then I gave a guileless grin, reached into my coat, and announced grandly, "Ah, yes, here it is."

The private and his sergeant waited expectantly for me to produce my grubstake, after which, of course, they would gun me down in cold blood. When my hand emerged, though, it clutched a .45 Colt rather than a roll of greenbacks. My tormentors' eyes flew wide with fear. The private fired but not before I threw myself violently to the side, loosing a slug as I did. My bullet smashed straight into the private's Mauser, spinning the rifle from his hands and knocking him sprawling to the straw-covered ground with a yelp of surprise.

Immediately, Sergeant Gómez drew a bead on me and might have ventilated me had not Wardlaw lashed out with a booted foot and caught him in the kneecap. Gómez shrieked just as he squeezed the trigger, jerking his barrel up as he did. His shot sailed over my head and into the street beyond. Before he could work the bolt of his Mauser to chamber a second round, I squeezed the trigger of my Colt. Gómez grunted and then collapsed in a heap. A circle of bright red formed on his forehead where I'd drilled him dead center. I swung my barrel back to the private, who raised his hands in surrender.

"Thank God you came, Captain!" exclaimed Wardlaw. "I was sure I was a dead man, and as for my wife, well . . ." His voice trailed off and he gave an involuntary shudder.

The danger to Mrs. Wardlaw reminded me once more of Serafina. "Get your wife to the German steamer, Wardlaw. Superintendent Shaler has arranged for it to take all the women and children on board. Then hurry over to the freight house if you can. All the men are gathered there to hold off Torres if he decides to attack."

"I'm on my way," Wardlaw assured me, helping his wife to her feet. "What should we do with him?" he asked, indicating the private.

"Well, by all rights we should send him straight to hell. That's what he would have done to us."

As I cocked the hammer on my Colt, though, Mrs. Wardlaw uttered a great cry of revulsion. "Captain, you mustn't. Oh, Tom, please don't let him."

Wardlaw, just as distressed as his wife, said, "Captain Travers, please don't do this. It would be murder."

"Oh, all right," I muttered. I looked about and saw a length of rope hung over a nearby peg in the wall. "Tom, give me a hand, will you?"

"You aren't going to hang him, are you, Captain?" asked Mrs. Wardlaw fretfully, not quite certain that I had abandoned my homicidal intentions.

"No, not at all, ma'am," I assured her, and in a few minutes we had the Colombian gagged and tied up tighter than a miser's purse. Just then the sound of hooves pounding on the dirt street caught my ear, and I hauled the private deep into the dark recesses of the stable. A single rider flashed by, a mounted *tiradore*. I cautiously peeked outside in time to see him disappear at the end of the street, headed in the direction of Monkey Hill.

"The coast is clear," I told Wardlaw. "Get going."

The two of them hurried off down the deserted street as I resumed my trek. Once clear of the city, I followed the railroad tracks across the narrow neck of land that joined Punta Manzanillo to the rest of the isthmus. From there the land rose sharply to Monkey Hill, and when I gained that height I stopped to look for some sign of Kingston Jack or Henry. I saw no one except an old black codger squatting under a stately *cuipo* tree as his burro grazed on nearby grass.

I thought the fellow was asleep, until he raised his head and let out a piercing whistle. At his trill, a young black man emerged from the brush, machete in hand. With a West Indian lilt he asked, "Be you Captain Travers?"

I nodded and he gestured for me to follow him. Together we lit out along a dirt track that cut through the jungle canopy. After a few miles, the jungle opened onto cleared fields where herds of grazing cattle lolled. Up ahead was a hacienda with a roof of red Spanish tiles. My guide left the track well before the house and entered a thicket. Deep in the bushes a group of men waited. Among them were Henry and Kingston Jack.

"Is Serafina in there?"

Henry nodded. "In one of the upstairs bedrooms. Nothing has happened since we took up our watch, that is until about an hour ago when a rider went by."

"Yes, I saw him. He came from Colón. I think he's a messenger from Colonel Torres." As quickly as I could, I told them about the tense situation in Colón. "I expect that Torres has summoned Reyes for the hoedown he has in mind. And if I know Reyes, this is one invitation he won't be able to refuse. Torching Colón would suit him just fine."

"If Reyes is going on the warpath," cautioned Henry, "he might start with the lady."

"That's why we have to go in there and get her. How many men does Reyes have?"

Kingston Jack answered. "I've seen maybe fifteen." He pointed toward the hacienda. "Behind the main house are some outbuildings—cooking sheds and such. Also, there's a bunkhouse that was probably used by field hands. That's where Reyes quartered his men. He keeps two guards at each entrance to the main house, and a small roving patrol circles the place at all times. There's a barn farther apart from those buildings, but it seems to be deserted."

In the open field before the hacienda I could see two bored soldiers dutifully slogging across the cleared field between the grazing cows. Then I studied the hacienda, in particular the upstairs bedroom window that Henry had pointed out. It was distinguishable from the others by a metal balcony in the Spanish fashion. Immediately below the balcony was a wooden trellis festooned with climbing vines that reached up from the ground below.

"That's six men under arms at all times," I calculated. "We can overpower the guards on watch and then corner the rest in the bunkhouse. With the guards penned up, we can get into the house and take care of Reyes."

Kingston Jack nodded and quickly worked up a plan of attack. The scheme was explained to his men, who then slipped off in small groups to position themselves as Kingston Jack directed. First, the roving guards would be taken. When that was done, a shot would be fired to signal the fact. At the sound of the shot, small groups would simultaneously rush the guards at the front and rear entrances to the hacienda. At the same time another group would fire into the bunkhouse, pinning the remaining Colombians in place.

Henry and I joined the group stealing forward to attack the front door, while Kingston Jack led the group that was to seize the rear entrance. We crept carefully forward, using drainage ditches and hedges to shield us from the eyes of the none-too-vigilant guards. The two Colombians guarding the front door chatted and joked with each other as we advanced, never suspecting that their doom was at hand. Silently my group crossed a gravel drive, crept through a verdant garden, and halted. We were no more than twenty yards from the guards now, and I could plainly see the bolts on their Mausers and the bayonets hanging at their waists. Around me Antilleans spread out and silently readied their machetes for the sudden rush to come.

As expected, to our ears came the sharp report of a rifle. The two Colombians came alert at the sound and looked out uncertainly toward the fields whence it had come. Instantly, my companions and I were on our feet, a phalanx of howling demons hurling ourselves upon the petrified guards. One Colombian ran, and the other raised his hands in surrender. The runner was instantly taken from behind by a brawny fellow who brought his wicked machete blade down on the Colombian's exposed neck. The steel flashed and then the severed head was rolling in the dust. The other guard was immediately overpowered, trussed up with his own leather belt, and left under the watch of two Antilleans.

Henry, I, and one of Kingston Jack's men cautiously approached the great door at the main entrance. I tried to open it, but the thing refused to budge.

"It's locked!"

Henry pushed past me and put his shoulder to the door, but to no avail. "It's barred from the inside," he said.

"What'll we do now?"

"We wait here," Henry decided. "The bar can be lifted only from the inside, so Kingston Jack and his group will have to batter down the back door to let us in."

"Damnit," I raged, furious at myself for not having thought of this possibility. The galling part of it all was that Reyes might hear our fumbling about and decide to murder Serafina before we could intervene. The thought of such exquisite femininity being wantonly extinguished by a madman like Reyes temporarily blinded me, I guess. Whatever the reason, I put out of my mind the lessons learned from a lifetime of steadfastly seeing to the safety of old Fenny no matter what the costs. What happened next was something completely out of character for me; I volunteered to take the lead in a desperate assault.

I looked about hurriedly and spotted a hitching post consisting of a heavy teak log supported on each end by a wooden stake. I pointed at it. "Tear that thing loose from its mooring and use it as a battering ram. Break down the door and then hustle upstairs. I'm going up the trellis to the second-floor balcony. I'll try to slip in and hold off Reyes until you get inside to help me."

As I spoke, I heard the sound of a ferocious struggle close at hand. It was Kingston Jack's group at the rear entrance in close combat with the sentries there. Then shots rang out, but it was unclear whether they were fired toward the bunkhouse, or whether the Colombians had somehow rallied and were holding their own. Whatever the case, it was evident that only seconds remained to get upstairs and confront Reyes.

Henry was off and running at once and, together with the Antilleans, he set to. In seconds they had secured the makeshift battering ram and were pounding a steady tattoo on the door. I took advantage of the racket they were raising to scramble up the trellis, shaking leaves and insects loose as I went. I hauled myself up to the narrow balcony, scrambled over the railing, and paused just outside a glass door.

Peering inside, I saw that the door opened upon what appeared to be a master bedchamber. Ever so carefully, I tried the latch. The door opened at my touch. I listened a second, but heard nothing. Drawing back the hammer of my Colt, I entered the darkened room.

It was only then that I heard it. It was a soft murmur coming from the bed. Under the covers was a form, a motionless bundle. I crossed the room and drew back the covers. By thunder, it was Serafina! She was clad in a long shift and was gagged and bound so securely that it seemed that she was all but immobile.

Hurriedly, I tried to loosen her bonds, whispering as I did, "Where is Reyes?"

Before I had the chance to work loose Serafina's gag, though, Comandante Reyes answered my question for me. "Right behind you, Captain Travers." I whirled to see Reyes emerge from behind a dressing screen. He held a pistol, and it was aimed right at my heart. "Your weapon," he demanded, holding out his hand.

From below came the sound of intensified firing, and I could hear timbers splinter as Henry and the others demolished the front door. They were in at last, but they would not be here in time to help me.

"Quickly, Captain Travers," demanded Reyes, "or I'll put a bullet in you and one in the señora too."

His cold, hard eyes told me that, if pressed, he would do exactly as he said. Slowly, I handed him my Colt and raised my hands.

"An excellent decision, Captain," he sneered. "Now I will not be forced to kill you with unseemly haste."

I desperately needed more time for Henry and Kingston Jack to fight their way up to the second floor, so I retorted hotly, "You'll never get away with this, Reyes. American marines are in Colón right now. They'll track you down, I swear it."

Reyes laughed. "Track me down? I hardly think so, Captain Travers. No, your marines are not in Colón. What's more, when they finally do arrive, they'll find a revolution that's all but extinguished. My uncle has sent me a message saying that he is about to see to that. Without you to stir the pot, my dear captain, your marines will be unsure and hesitant. They'll wire Washington for instructions, and as they wait, I'll see to it that the traitors in this land are exterminated."

"Oh?" I blustered. "Well, you're dead wrong, Reyes. Shaler is fortifying the freight house as we speak, and the *Nashville*'s got her guns trained on Colonel Torres's men. All that remains to be done is to ferry General Huertas's troops over from Panama City, and your side is finished."

I was putting the best possible gloss on the facts, of course, yet I knew there were a thousand uncertainties, and any one of them could spell disaster. What if Torres rushed the freight house and flushed out Hubbard's shore party? What if General Varon shelled Panama City with his gunboats and Huertas decided to become unbought? I thrust these possibilities to the back of my mind, though, as I sparred with Reyes, yet even my best case didn't impress him.

"Even if all your words are true, Travers, your fate is nonetheless sealed. You have been a thorn in my side since you arrived in Colón, and now it is time to pluck out that thorn."

Reyes aimed, and I was certain that I was on my way to eternity. At that very instant, though, a tremendous crash came against the bedroom door, accompanied by the cries of men. Startled, Reyes took his eyes from me for a fraction of a second.

It was all the time I needed, for instantly I was on him. With my left hand I seized the barrel of his pistol, and with my right I delivered a roundhouse punch to his temple. Reyes's knees buckled, but he managed to pull the trigger as he fell. The shot pulverized the plaster ceiling above, showering us both with a fine white powder. I fell on top of Reyes, pummeling him with a flurry of blows while I held his shooting iron immobile. As I beat him savagely, I heard Henry and Kingston Jack at work on the bedroom door with their battering ram. In seconds they would be in and Reyes would be in the bag.

Or so I thought until I felt something cold and hard thrust against my ear and a sultry voice say, "Make one more move, my dear Captain Travers, and I will blow your handsome head from your shoulders."

I turned my head, amazed to see Serafina freed miraculously from her bonds. Strangely, she was standing over me with a double-barreled shotgun trained on my head. "Serafina, dearest," I sputtered in astonishment. "I—I don't understand. I came to—"

"To rescue me?" she prompted sweetly.

I nodded dumbly.

Her high-pitched laugh told me what a complete fool I'd been. "Oh, my poor Fenny. You are hopelessly naive, aren't you? You accepted everything I told you about myself without question, deluded by your animal passions and your male smugness."

"Serafina, please," I protested. "This is crazy. How on earth can you take the side of the man who killed your husband?"

A shriek of merriment greeted this outburst. "Oh, you are so dense, my darling Fenny. Did it ever occur to you that my affections for Oscar were not quite as deep as you have been led to believe?"

A look of horror swept across my face. "Do you mean that you—are you saying that you abetted Reyes in the murder of your husband?"

"You still don't understand, do you? No, I didn't abet Emilio in murdering Oscar. Quite to the contrary, Fenny. I killed Oscar and Emilio assisted me. You see, Emilio and I are more than merely lovers. We are both loyal servants of Bogotá. I am the regional intelligence officer, Captain Travers. Emilio takes orders from me."

I tried to speak, but at first words would not come. I was rooted there, gasping like a fish out of water. "Then—then you are the one they call the Raven," I finally managed to croak. "You're the one Major Black warned me about."

"Excellent," said Serafina with approval. "Finally you're showing a glimmer of cleverness. A pity it's coming too late to save you, though. Nonetheless, before you go, you may as well know the truth. Yes, I am the Raven. After I killed Oscar and directed Emilio to accept all the blame, I convinced that old fool Amador to take me in. That was no problem at all, really. I just made a claim of kinship on Señora Amador. It was a stroke of genius, don't you think?"

The evil brilliance of her bold move was readily apparent. "Why, you were able to tell the Colombians everything."

"You would think so," she agreed. "After all, I was under the roof of one of the archconspirators. I was, of course, aware of Amador's trip to New York, the one occasioned by your visit. Also, I was one of the first to learn of his homecoming from New York in your company. How else do you think Bogotá was informed to hurry the Tiradore Battalion to Panama at precisely this time? If Amador had returned alone from New York, I would have concluded that his mission had failed. Because you accompanied him, however, I suspected that his pitiful dream was still alive. When your cable arrived directing that there was to be no reception upon Amador's arrival, though, I was absolutely certain that the time was at hand. Why else would you have tried to suppress the fact of Amador's return?"

She was right, and as I lay there I damned myself for being such a transparent fool. Serafina, heedless of my chagrin, prattled right along. "What I didn't know, however, was the name of every one of Arango's supporters. They are infernally timid creatures, you know. I realized, though, that when Arango ordered them to assemble, all the rats would creep from their holes. When that happened, Colonel Torres would appear and cut off their heads. Now, thanks to you, that is very near to happening. The Amadors will die, of course, as will Arango and his coterie. Huertas and all his officers will also be sent before firing squads, as will General Varon if he falters in his duty."

"But why, Serafina?" I demanded, my voice quivering with shock at the extent of her duplicity. "Why would you betray your husband and everything he stood for?"

Her lovely face turned brutally hard, and a light of pure malice seemed to glow forth from her eyes. "I see I have whetted your curiosity, Fenny. Very well, then. I'll tell you what you want to know. In truth, Oscar, despite his exalted lineage, was unable to satisfy his wife as a man should. He was an intellectual who spurned the pleasures of the flesh. I needed them, though, and I tried to make Oscar understand my desires. I sought understanding, but instead he spurned me and called me a harlot. It was only after Oscar made it clear he would not be a true husband to me that I turned to Pedro."

"Pedro? The fellow you sent to fetch me? The one with the burro?"

"Yes. Pedro was a simple campesino, but at least he was a man. He became my lover, that is until Oscar learned of our liaison. He beat me, and confined me to the hacienda. He would have divorced me, but divorce is impossible in this Catholic land. Instead, he turned me into a nun without vows. It was on Pedro, though, that Oscar vented his true rage. He personally cut out Pedro's tongue so that he could never tell the tale of having cuckolded a grandee. Then, to ensure there could be no repeat of my transgressions, he relieved Pedro of his manhood."

I wasn't sure I was following Serafina. "Good God, you're not saying that your husband castrated Pedro?"

"That is exactly what I mean, Captain Travers," she assured me grimly. Then, despite the mighty pounding reverberating on the bedroom door, Serafina fell silent, a strange, wistful expression on her face as if she was off somewhere in a world of her own. She recovered quickly, though, and her savage mask slipped back in place. "All of this explains, my dear Fenny, why when the civil war erupted, I saw it as a way to escape my hell. Oscar was a liberal, for the Viscayas have a long liberal tradition. Oscar's party regularly gathered at his hacienda. I made good use of my ears on those occasions, and I sent the information I gleaned through Pedro to the conservative side."

"To Reyes," I said, the light finally dawning on me.

"Yes, to Emilio Reyes. We became confederates, and eventually lovers, and have been ever since those days. I became Bogota's most trusted agent on the isthmus and remain so to this day. What is more, when the feeble revolution you are championing is crushed, Captain Travers, the junta in Bogotá has made it clear that it will show its gratitude for my loyal support in a most tangible way. All the lands that Oscar held will be forfeited by the Viscaya family and deeded to me. I will be the only woman on the isthmus to hold clear title to her own lands, and when that happens I will never be beholden to any man again. I shall finally have the life of freedom, power, and property that I crave."

She was mad, I saw. Perhaps she had been deranged by the horrors of the civil war, or perhaps she had been unbalanced from the start and everything she had told me was nothing but the wild ravings of a lunatic. Whatever the truth of the matter, I had no doubt that Serafina was willing to annihilate anyone who got in her way, and my immediate goal was to avoid becoming another of her victims.

"Serafina, that's one of the most touching stories I have ever heard. Why, it's clear to me that your husband got precisely what he deserved. Yes, I daresay you let him off lightly by allowing him to live so long. And as for poor Emilio here," I said, absently patting the inert form beneath me, "well, I have to confess, I thoroughly misjudged him. It's apparent now that he's a prince of a fellow once you get to know him. That's exactly what I intend to do, too, just as soon as all of this unpleasantness subsides. For the present, though, I think what I ought to do is to mosey along. I'll just leave you to the serious business you have at hand, dearest. Yes, indeed, I wish you all the best, and I'm certain that by the time the dust settles you'll have title to half of Panama."

I made a move to rise, but a prod from the shotgun barrels stopped me. "Not so quick, sweet Fenny."

"Now Serafina," I protested, "be sensible, won't you? I thought that you and I had something, well, special together. What about that evening we spent at your hacienda? Doesn't that mean anything to you?"

"My poor darling. You are indeed a child. Don't you know why I had Pedro bring you to me?"

"Because you loved me madly and wanted me always by your side?" I asked hopefully.

Serafina laughed outright at my foolishness. "I must admit I was impressed by the power of your loins, Fenny, but no, that was not the reason. I summoned you to get the information I needed."

"Information? Whatever are you talking about?"

"I wanted to know whether your fellow officer, Captain Longbottom, had spoken truly when he said that the United States was not prepared to fight the traitors' battles for them. You assured me that such was the case, and I quickly passed on your answer to Bogotá. What that meant, of course, was that if the junta reacted firmly at the first sign of rebellion, there would be no repercussions from your Mr. Roosevelt. So you see, Captain Travers, you have largely yourself to thank for the presence of the Tiradore Battalion in Colón today."

I damned myself once more for being such a buffoon, for I recalled now that she had indeed posed that very question to me. Self-recrimination, though, was a luxury I could ill afford at the moment; my immediate concern was to get out of this room with a whole skin.

"Well, I'm pleased as punch that I was of service, my dear," I said with a nervous little chuckle. "What do you say we let one hand wash the other, eh? I mean I helped you out, and now it's time for you to return the favor. How about moving your shotgun away from my noggin and letting me slip out that window? That sounds fair, now, doesn't it?"

"It is not my habit to discard sources of information when I am through with them, Fenny, especially when they might still be dangerous to me. No, I kill such people, just as I tried to kill you after our night of passion."

A cold bolt of fear and horror shot through me at this. "What? It was you who set those swordsmen on Longbottom and me?"

"Of course, silly. Who else would have done such a thing? Not Huertas. No, he's afraid of his shadow and would never dare to antagonize the colossus of the North. Unfortunately, though, my men failed, and I sent an encoded wire stating that fact to Colón. That was why Emilio was able to intercept you along the rail line, Fenny. Unfortunately you escaped him too, and so the task remains to be accomplished."

"Dear God, Serafina, you must be joking. You can't be serious about killing me in cold blood. Not after all we've been through together."

"Yes, poor Fenny, I'm afraid so. That's why I lured you here, don't you see? I wasn't completely sure that you would come to my rescue, though. That's why I took the added precaution of seizing your companion, Captain Longbottom."

"What? Longbottom's here? But where?"

"Oh, don't worry so, Fenny. Your friend is safe enough, at least for the time being. But don't tell me you didn't know I had taken him to this place." My look of utter amazement gave her the answer to her question, and Serafina laughed almost girlishly. "Well, well, dear Emilio was for once much too stealthy for his own good. I had wanted to leave a trail that would draw you to Captain Longbottom. I knew that you would come after him at all costs, and when you did, I would be waiting. It's really a pity, you know, since I would much rather have kept you as a lover. Unfortunately, you are determined to see Arango's revolution succeed, and that makes you a very dangerous man. With you gone, though, the *norte americanos* will step back from their Panamanian lackeys and force them to act for themselves. When that happens, the traitors will lose their nerve. Yes, they will falter because they are weaklings. I must admit, though, that Arango has done surprisingly well in Panama City. I sent a note to General Tobar warning him about Huertas, but I have since learned that the general was not wary enough to avoid capture."

"That was your note?" I asked with wonderment. "Why, that means that the campesino who delivered it was—"

"Pedro. Yes, poor, dear Pedro. Even now, though, Fenny, my operatives are busily plying Colonel Huertas's officers with bribes. I feel certain that General Tobar will escape his bonds, and when that happens, Colonel Huertas's life will be forfeit."

"Huertas and the others will never allow that, Serafina. No, Panama City will remain firmly in the camp of the revolutionaries."

"Oh, but you are wrong, Fenny. As soon as I am finished with you, I will travel there myself. Believe me when I say that I will undo all the damage that you have wrought. Your friends Arango and Amador will quail before me. Oh, yes, they will. They will lose their hold on Panama City, and when they do, Colonel Torres will strike in Colón. Emilio will be at his uncle's side, and then the killing will start in earnest."

She cocked the hammers on the twin barrels, and I knew that it would be but seconds before my brains were splattered on the far wall. There was no question of her faltering, for I had seen Serafina finish off the terrifying El Diablo with all the sangfroid of a professional assassin. I took what I thought was my last breath when suddenly the entire bedroom door flew off its hinges.

Henry, seeing my imminent demise through the cracks in the wood, had driven the battering ram forward with demonic fury. Serafina whirled and fired from the hip. The blast shredded the leading Antillean and peppered Henry from head to foot. Instantly, Henry turned tail, and Kingston Jack was right behind him. Serafina's second blast emptied the hallway where my rescuers had been standing just an instant before.

Without pausing, Serafina threw open the shotgun's breech and slapped in two more shells. I needed no prompting about what would happen when she snapped the breech closed again. No, she would finish me off without an ounce of remorse in her heart.

I was not about to become another notch on her gun, thank you. In a flash I was up, gained the glass door to the balcony with two quick steps, and dove headlong over the railing. Serafina threw the shotgun to her shoulder as I ran, and aimed as I sailed through the air. In that awful moment, as I hung suspended in space before her, I realized that I had become a clay pigeon in a sort of bizarre skeet shoot. I felt the blast as she fired, and an unearthly whirring noise as hundreds of buckshot pellets passed over my back. Enough of them made contact, though, to hurt like the dickens, and I knew that had Serafina aimed just a cat's whisker lower, I would have been completely skinned when I hit the ground.

It was a damned rough landing nonetheless, hard enough to knock me temporarily senseless. For an instant I lay there stunned, and it took a titanic effort for me to rise groggily to my feet. Finding nothing was broken, I started to stagger off toward the woods whence I had come, expecting Serafina to appear at the balcony above me at any moment and pepper me anew. Henry and Kingston Jack, I decided, could deal with the crazy harridan, for I had had a bellyful of her.

Yet even in my dazed condition, something that Serafina had said stuck in my mind. She claimed she had lured me to this place. That just didn't make sense, you see, for there were so few Colombians here that it was a foregone conclusion that Kingston Jack's men would overwhelm them. Unless, that is . . .

I never completed my thought, for at that moment Henry and all the Antilleans came scampering around the corner of the hacienda in disarray. With them they dragged along Longbottom, bruised and battered and looking very much the worse for wear.

The sight of them in retreat sent me into a fury. It was all well and good for me to make a tactical withdrawal, but I expected these boys to stand firm and fight it out no matter how much hot lead was flying about. "Get back in there and get that loco bitch!" I railed at them. "She's alone on the top floor with her damned scattergun. You can take her easily."

Henry shook his head. "She's a dead shot, Fenny. She got two men, and we barely had time to grab the captain before she was on us. What's more, Captain Longbottom says she ain't alone."

"Not alone? What the devil is that supposed to mean?"

Henry turned to Longbottom now. From his lolling head and vacant stare, I could see that Longbottom was on his last legs. "They're everywhere!" he raved. "They'll kill us all. It's an ambush, by God. They'll kill us all."

The French cure evidently hadn't taken with him, and I made a note to march him straight back to the sanatorium as soon as the shooting was over. "He's as crazy as a loon," I said to Henry. "You just leave him with me, and then you and Kingston Jack get back in there and finish off that wild woman. You have her outgunned ten to one—"

That's as far as I got, for the doors of the "deserted" barn suddenly flew open and a solid phalanx of infantrymen burst into view. "Run, Fenny!" cried Henry. "We've been bushwhacked!"

"Lordy, lordy," gasped Kingston Jack as he took to his heels.

The tide had changed in the twinkling of an eye, and the hunter had suddenly become the hunted. For a second I could only stand there and stammer, "But—but we're the ones who are supposed to be doing the ambushing here. This isn't fair, damnit."

It was Henry who snapped me back to reality. "So long, Fenny," he called as he lit out after Kingston Jack. "Those Colombians were just laying for us."

Blast it, Serafina had told the truth for once! With a full platoon of soldiers in hot pursuit, the trauma of my fall was instantly forgotten. I flashed past both Henry and Kingston Jack, slowed as they were by the pellets in their hides, and set a course for the shelter of the jungle. With the Antilleans and Henry hard on my heels, and Longbottom being borne along as well, we bounded between startled cows and leaped ditches as we went.

The Colombians stayed with us, though, and as I sped across the open country, I ventured a hasty glance over my shoulder. Our pursuers easily outnumbered us two to one, and, more ominously, they were much better armed. Comandante Reyes was with them, his bloodied face contorted in rage. Taking up the rear was Serafina, her skirts hitched high and her lovely legs flying as she came on. I had no doubt she intended to be right in the thick of things when the killing started. There could be no question of standing against the foe; the only sane option was to flee for our lives.

"Get into the bushes!" cried Kingston Jack to his men as he ran. "Break into small groups and make your way back to Colón. I'll find you there."

It was as good a plan as any, and might have worked had not the Colombians been thinking a step ahead of us. "Look there!" cried one of Kingston Jack's men. "They're waiting for us!"

I followed where he was pointing and, by the blazes, he was right. Reyes had secreted a squad along our likely escape route. These soldiers now rose from their hiding places and took aim.

"Hold up here, men!" cried Kingston Jack. "Fight back as best you can, and make every shot count!"

"This looks like the end, Fenny," gasped Henry.

I was too petrified to respond. Bullets where whistling among us from every direction, and it seemed that they all had my name on them. Longbottom, dazed, staggered uncomprehendingly about our little pocket of death. I seized him by the shoulders, threw him to the ground, and then cowered down behind him. I used him as a human breastwork, you see, figuring that if I had to die I would at least have the satisfaction of having him lead the way. Men screamed out their life's breath all around me as hot metal smashed through flesh. Not three feet from me a youth thrashed about in his death agonies, half his face shot away and gore spraying everywhere. Oh, it was horrible, and I knew that obliteration for me could come at any instant. I braced myself for what promised to be a painful end to a sordid and dissipated life.

Death, however, did not come. Instead, the most amazing thing happened. From the brush behind Reyes something slender flew into the air and plunged into the neck of a soldier who was just in the act of firing. The soldier yelped once, then shuddered and sank to the ground, his eyes rolling back in his head as though he were in some sort of paroxysm.

What the dickens was going on? I wondered, when a second shaft followed the first. By God, they were arrows, I realized as a second Colombian fell. The air was suddenly filled with the lethal shafts, all of them raining down on the foe. Then to my ears came savage shouts and whoops, sounds that were both bloodcurdling yet oddly familiar.

Where had I heard them before? I wondered. Then I remembered; it had been among the moss-covered stones of the deserted Spanish fort. By God, those were Cuna battle cries, and at that moment they sounded like the sweetest music imaginable. Around me, soldiers were throwing down their arms and running, unnerved by the destruction that seemed to come from nowhere. Through the foliage I caught sight of copper limbs and black hair, and I counted more than a hundred Cunas converging on this one spot. They had the Colombians surrounded and were butchering them like sheep in an abattoir. Screams of terror filled the air, and I realized that the cunning Indians had turned their golden frog arrows into instruments of war. Any Colombian who was so much as nicked by a Cuna shaft was marked for instant death.

It was over in minutes. A knot of Cunas in feathered headdresses approached and I raised a hand in greeting. I recognized their leader at once, for it was none other than my adoptive father, Tiger.

"Tiger, Moon Child thanks you for his life."

The *sahila* grunted his acknowledgment. "I told you, Moon Child, that I would not forget the Spanish. I decided to make war on them when they were at their weakest. That is why I followed them to this place. Now it is done. Never again will the Tule have to fear Spanish guns coming from the sea."

I nodded. "*Sí*. It is over. May Tiger long be honored for this victory."

Tiger, though, was not prepared to celebrate just yet. "Besides the soldiers, Moon Child, there is another prisoner." He turned and shouted out a command in Tule. Two brawny warriors led forward a struggling figure. It was Serafina. She stood defiantly before her captors, her eyes blazing with an insane fury. When she saw me, she spat, "I curse you, *yanqui*. You have been a bane since the first day you appeared. May you burn in hell."

"She has the tongue of a witch," observed Tiger with impressive astuteness. In the straightforward manner of his kind, he slipped a war club from the thong about his waist and seized Serafina by her luxuriant tresses. "The witch must die."

"Hold, Tiger," I pleaded, laying a hand on his upraised arm. "The woman is not a witch. She's just, well"—I didn't want to say loco, for that was as good as being a witch as far as Tiger was concerned—"upset. The Spanish you killed were her friends. Her harsh words are those of a grieving woman, not a witch."

"Speak plainly, Moon Child. What is it you would have me do with the woman?"

I was in a bit of a quandary on that point. After all, just minutes before, Serafina had been doing her damnedest to exterminate me, and had I been able to get my hands on my Colt, I would have gladly repaid her in kind. Now, however, the heat of battle had passed, and watching a beautiful gal being bludgeoned to death struck me as, well, wasteful. No, I decided, there was a more appropriate fate in store for the willful Serafina.

"Tell me, Tiger, has Fish Hawk yet accepted Harvest Wife back into his family? Has he put behind him the accusations against her of being a witch?"

"No, Moon Child. She was released from the flames because of you, but there still lingers around her a cloud. Fish Hawk has kept his distance from her ever since."

"Then give Fish Hawk a new daughter, one who is not tainted. Take this woman to him. Let her be adopted into the Jaguar Clan, and let her be given as a bride to a warrior. She will secure for Fish Hawk a new son-in-law to serve him in his dotage."

Tiger considered this. Female prisoners were rare among the Cunas, for they never waged wars of aggression. My words were compelling, though, since Harvest Wife was Fish Hawk's only daughter. Because of her unwise liaison with me, there was virtually no hope of her landing another husband.

"It shall be as you ask, Moon Child," he decided. "I will spare the life of the woman because you saved the life of The One Who Watches." He grasped me by the wrist, and I did the same to him. I knew what the gesture meant; his obligation to me was discharged, and henceforth I had no claim upon him. "I will go now to the land of my people and never come this way again," he said. "May the spirits of the Jaguar Clan be with you always, Moon Child."

"And with you, Tiger."

Serafina was led away, her tongue wagging with each step. "Travers, stop them. You can't do this! I demand you order them to release me. I am a gentlewoman, with a pedigree that you can only envy. I am no filthy campesina to be bought and sold like a milk cow!"

"Now, now, my dear," I soothed her merrily as she was hauled off. "You said that you wanted to hold your own property, didn't you? Well, cheer up then. The Cunas are remarkably progressive in that regard. Not only will they allow you to be a businesswoman, by George, but they'll insist upon it. I'm sure you'll enjoy yourself no end. Yes, my love, you'll soon be the proud owner of your own lobster baskets. True, since you're a *waker* gal, you may have to spend a few years in the cassava fields having the daylights beaten out of you by cranky old hags. Soon enough, though, that will all be behind you and you can settle down among your new kinsmen."

"Cassava fields?" wailed Serafina. "Fenny, I beg of you! Do not let me be taken away to slavery!"

"No, don't thank me, my love. I'm certain you would have done the same for me. Oh, and whatever you do out on the Cuna islands, for God's sake don't covet thy neighbor's husband. The Cuna are death on that sort of thing, I'll have you know."

A piercing shriek of protest was her only reply, and then she and the Cunas were gone, swallowed up by the jungle. Serafina was on her way to a life that she could never have imagined when she set her snare for me, and the thought gave me nothing but the sweetest pleasure.

"Ah, well, dear me," I sniffed contentedly. "Let's see now. Has anyone found our old friend Reyes?"

"Kingston Jack's men have him, I suppose. They were trying to save as many Colombians as possible from the Cunas. But why do you ask about Reyes? What do you have in mind, Fenny?"

"Oh, I just thought I'd bring him along when I go to meet his uncle, that's all."

28

An hour later we were back in Colón. Careful to stay in the back alleys, we made our way to the freight house. The town was still—a hopeful sign; had Torres already launched an assault on Shaler, we would have heard gunplay. As we neared the railroad station, I was able to see the deployment of Torres's forces. The Colombians had thrown up fortifications on three sides of the freight house, hemming Shaler's men inside their bastion. Their only escape would be to the sea. Snipers lurked on nearby roofs, their sights trained on the windows of the freight house.

Out on the roadstead, I saw that the *Nashville* had moved closer to shore, her 4-inch guns trained on the encircling *tiradores*. Puzzlingly, the *Cartagena* was nowhere in sight. Since the capture of General Tobar, the aim of Shaler and the others had been to convince Colonel Torres to reembark his troops and sail for home. Now, with the *Cartagena* gone, how the dickens would we get rid of these unwelcome guests? I wondered.

The situation was clearly a powder keg waiting to blow sky-high at the slightest spark. The only surprise was that Colonel Torres had not already started shooting. The reason for that, I suspected, was his concern about Reyes and his uncertainty about the fate of General Tobar. Those two points were Torres's weaknesses, and I realized that I had to find some way to exploit them—and to do so in a hurry.

To my surprise, I found the railroad station unoccupied. Perhaps, I surmised, Colonel Torres was afraid that such a flagrant violation of the Bidlack Treaty would provoke Washington unnecessarily. Whatever the reason, I was not going to look a gift horse in the mouth. Henry, the Antilleans, and I slipped in a back door and padded quietly to Shaler's office.

"The telephone may still work," I said, figuring that the Colombians, not used to things like telephones, might have neglected to cut the wire. I tried to ring up the freight house across the street. To my delight, a voice answered.

"Shaler here."

"Superintendent, it's Travers. I'm right across the street."

"What news do you have of the girl, Travers?"

"Serafina's safe. I've placed her where the Colombians will never find her."

"Excellent work," Shaler congratulated me. "But what about Reyes? Did you get him too?"

"Oh, I got him, all right," I assured him. "But what happened to the *Cartagena*? Where did she go?"

"She put out to sea right after you set out for the Viscaya woman," answered Shaler. "The *Nashville* steamed closer to shore to get better fields of fire for her guns. When she did, the Colombian captain panicked and weighed anchor. He was gone before anyone could stop him."

"Now how do we ship Torres's men home?"

There was silence for a moment and, for the first time since the revolution began, I heard a note of discouragement in Shaler's voice. "I don't know, son. That's just a bridge we'll have to cross after we somehow convince Torres that he should leave."

"Speaking of Torres, I can see *tiradores* all over the streets," I said. "They've got you boxed in. Have you had any contact with either Colonel Torres or Panama City?"

"Yes, on both counts. I wired Prescott about the standoff here. He consulted with Amador and Arango, and the three of them decided the best thing to do would be to send General Tobar back here to talk to Colonel Torres. Once Torres realizes that the Pacific coast is firmly in the hands of the new republic, he might be persuaded to leave Colón."

I didn't like the sound of that at all and told Shaler exactly that. "I'm not so sure that's wise, Superintendent. After all, didn't we move heaven and earth to separate Tobar from the *tiradores* in the first place? Bringing him back again seems plain foolish, don't you think?"

"Sure there's a risk, Travers, but what other options do we have?"

I didn't know, but I still didn't cotton to the notion of bringing the general back to his troops. "Has General Tobar said point-blank that he would order Colonel Torres to leave Panama?"

"Well, not in so many words," began Shaler.

"Then I say we keep the general right where he is. If you bring back Tobar, I think he'll order Torres to fight."

"Captain Travers, please be reasonable. You see the situation around you. Torres is determined to fight anyway. How could bringing back General Tobar make matters any worse?"

Since he asked, I told him. "If Colonel Torres was really raring to fight, Superintendent, he would be firing away right now, orders or no. The truth of the matter is, he's confused. He hasn't heard from General Tobar for more than a day, and that has him rattled. What's more, he sent a dispatch rider to Comandante Reyes in the past few hours, and he's probably staying his hand until he receives a reply from that quarter. He's uncertain, you see, but all that will change if you send General Tobar to him. Tobar will order the colonel to fight, and when he does, all of Torres's doubts and hesitations will evaporate. He'll simply salute and start shooting. You'll have the very conflagration you've tried so hard to avoid."

Shaler listened in silence. I had been right about Torres before, and now I seemed to be talking sense once again. "Blast it," muttered Shaler, "I'm afraid you're correct, Travers."

"There's no harm done as long as we keep General Tobar in our clutches. Where is he now?"

"On a special train being sent over from Panama City. He'll be here in an hour or so."

"Can you wire or telephone over to Prescott to stop it?"

"No," replied Shaler. "Those lines went down a short while ago. In fact, about the only one left standing is the one you and I are using."

"Damn the luck." The Colombians were clearly more aware of the importance of our communications than I had thought. "Then an hour is all the time we have left to convince Torres to leave."

"How will we do that, Travers?"

I thought for a moment. "Does Torres know that Tobar is on his way?"

"Not yet," answered Shaler. "I didn't see any advantage to telling him."

"Good. That still leaves Torres thinking that he's isolated, which means it's at least possible that he might make a decision on his own rather than waiting for directions from Tobar." I thought for a moment and then asked, "What about the *Dixie*? Where is she?"

"All I know is that she left Jamaica two days ago. She could be one hour from Colón or ten hours. It all depends on how much steam she lays on along the way."

I peered through a window and gave the sky an appraising look. Dark thunderheads were gathering, and it appeared that we would soon be in for a tropical cloudburst. The only security for Colón and ultimately for the fledgling Republic of Panama would be the *Dixie*'s marines, but it was clear that things were too volatile to sit back and await their arrival. I had to act now, before Tobar arrived and gave some backbone to the wavering Colonel Torres. At length, I made my decision.

"Okay, here's what we do. Call a parley with Torres. Tell him we have some news that we want to share with him, but don't give him any specifics. Tell him to meet you in front of the freight house in thirty minutes."

"What will I tell him when he arrives?" asked Shaler anxiously.

"Nothing. I'll be there to do the talking."

Shaler did as he was told. As we huddled in the deserted station office, we heard shouts from the freight house across the street. It was Shaler, calling out to the *tiradore* pickets that he wanted to meet with their colonel. In thirty minutes Colonel Torres, accompanied by an adjutant bearing a white flag of truce, marched down Front Street and halted outside the freight house. The heavily barricaded door opened just enough to let Shaler slip outside. He walked toward Colonel Torres, halted about five yards away, and waited.

It was then I stepped out of the station office behind Torres. The colonel turned in surprise, and I could see *tiradores* on the roofs hurriedly shifting their aim to cover me. I stopped a minute to allay any fears Torres might have of an ambush, and then with a measured tread stepped across the street.

"Good afternoon, Colonel," I said.

Torres looked from Shaler to me and back again. "Who is this man?" he demanded of Shaler.

I answered for Shaler. "Captain Travers, United States Army."

"So, the *yanquis* are involved everywhere in this little farce," sneered Torres. "It is as I suspected."

"That's not true, Colonel—" Shaler began to remonstrate, but I held up a hand to silence him. You see, I had decided that the time had come to lay some cards on the table for the benefit of Colonel Torres.

"That's right, Colonel, we are," I assured him brashly. "How else do you think Tobar and his staff were taken? You're not just fighting a few bumbling rustics in some backwater province, friend. You're taking on Uncle Sam."

The looming guns of the *Nashville* underscored every word I said, but Torres was tough and refused to allow himself to be intimidated. He snarled angrily in reply, "If all you say is true, Captain Travers, where are the *norte americano* troops? I see only you, and that means I hold dominion in Colón."

"True enough, Colonel," I said, smiling, then added somberly, "for now." I pointed to the horizon beyond the harbor. "Just out of sight is a troop transport carrying United States Marines—hundreds of them, with field guns and machine guns. They'll be here in an hour." Shaler started at my boldness, but I ignored him and plunged on. "What's more, they know you're here. They have orders to secure Colón, no matter what the cost."

Torres bridled at the threat. "Then I will order my men to fight. We will not surrender to the invaders."

"Oh? Who are the invaders, Colonel? You have been told that Panama City is in the hands of the revolutionaries. General Huertas stands with them. You are isolated here in Colón. There can be no reinforcements from Colombia as long as the *Nashville* guards the harbor. Her guns will also ensure that our marines will be able to get ashore and close with your troops. Once you are defeated—and believe me, you will be—you have only two choices. You can surrender and thereby gain the everlasting ridicule of your countrymen, or you can retreat south, into the Darien. Have you ever been in the Darien, Colonel?"

The worried look on Torres's face told me he had. Retreat through the Darien, he knew, was impossible. No military force had ever successfully traversed that howling wilderness. And as for taking on American marines, Torres was well aware of the disaster that had befallen the once mighty Spanish in Cuba. He had no illusion about his prospects of winning such a contest. Yet still he was unwilling to be cowed.

"If that's all true, Captain Travers, why should I not choose a soldier's death right here? I can order my men to fight and we will be remembered in the history of my country as martyrs."

"I suppose you could do that," I allowed carefully, "but then you would also be remembered by your family as something else as well."

This non sequitur brought Torres up short. "My family? What has my family got to do with this, gringo?" he demanded, for he was in no mood for riddles. Even Shaler was uncertain about where I was going now, for he gave me a look of concern.

"I'm referring to your nephew, Colonel. He's in my power. If there's shooting, Comandante Reyes will be the first to go, and your relatives will blame it all on you."

"Emilio? You have my nephew? But how?" asked Torres, suddenly perplexed and fearful, for indeed Reyes had failed to join him in Colón as ordered.

"Never mind how. All that matters is that he's my prisoner."

Torres, suspicious that I might be bluffing, demanded, "Prove what you say, Captain Travers."

"Certainly," I said, smiling pleasantly. I turned and nodded toward the railroad office. At my signal Reyes dutifully appeared at a window, standing between Henry and Kingston Jack. He looked grim, his kepi pulled low down on his brow. He neither spoke nor gestured but merely stared silently at his uncle.

"How white he is," murmured Torres.

"No doubt he is still angry at having been taken unawares with all of his men," I opined. At another signal from me, Henry and Kingston Jack took away Reyes. "There you have it, Colonel," I said, turning back to Torres. "At the first hostile sign from you, we kill Reyes."

"That would be murder," spat Torres. "If you are truly an American officer as you claim, Captain Travers, you would do no such thing."

"Oh? If you don't think I would execute your nephew, then you obviously don't know me or your nephew. Reyes, you see, is a cold-blooded killer. He's a slaver and a murderer. Yes, he's pure scum, Colonel, and although I may be an officer, I'll gladly blow his brains out this very instant. If you don't believe me, just call my bluff, *amigo,* and you'll have the unenviable task of explaining your actions to dear Emilio's family back in Bogotá."

As hardened a soldier as Torres was, the thought of watching his nephew being put to death before his eyes made him cringe. I could see him thinking as he stood there, searching for some way to avert my wrath while avoiding the ignominy of being run out of Colón. Ultimately, though, he could think of none.

"I want Emilio back," he said, the braggadocio gone from his voice. "I also want gold to pay my troops. When I have all that, I'll leave."

"No. You and your troops leave first, then I'll deliver Reyes and the gold."

"Hold on just a darned minute," interrupted Shaler. "How much gold are we talking about here?"

Torres answered. "Twenty thousand American dollars."

I looked at Shaler. "Does the railroad have a vault in town?"

"Yes, but I have no authority to hand over funds on your say-so, Travers. Why, the directors would have my scalp if I did any such thing."

"They'll have it anyway if Colón goes up in flames."

Shaler looked from me to Torres. "The money's inside the freight house," he said, "but there's only eight thousand dollars in there."

"Then that's all you get, Colonel," I announced. "Eight thousand dollars."

"But—" Torres started to protest. I cut him off with a chop of my hand.

"There's no time to get more, and that's all Shaler has. If you're not gone by the time the American marines arrive, you won't collect a cent."

Torres's jaws tightened in fury, but he was over a barrel and he knew it. Then he remembered another problem. "How can I leave? My ship is gone."

I had thought of that too. I pointed down the waterfront to the pier belonging to the Royal Mail Steamship Company, a British line. "The *Orinoco*," I said, indicating a packet ship moored to the dock. "We'll send you on that."

"But that's a British ship, Travers," objected Shaler. "We can't just order the British to do our bidding."

"We have no choice," I countered. "Make it worth their while. Promise them a bonus for returning the colonel's battalion to Colombia, or offer them a concession on railroad fares."

Shaler considered this. There was really no other choice, and he knew it. "I'll see to it," he agreed finally.

"Good." Turning to Torres once more, I directed, "Colonel, get your troops on the *Orinoco*. Once they're aboard, we'll send along the gold and Reyes."

"Can I have your word that there will be no tricks, Captain Travers?"

"You have my word as an American officer." We shook on the deal and he marched off to assemble his battalion.

As Torres withdrew, Shaler asked with admiration, "Captain Travers, however did you get that wild man Reyes to behave himself? With just a few screams, he could have roused his uncle to a fighting frenzy."

"Oh, nothing could have been easier. You see, Reyes is the very model of decorum because he's as dead as a doornail."

"Dead?" cried Shaler, aghast.

"Yep, a Cuna arrow laid him low not two hours ago."

"But, for God's sake, Travers, you just gave your word as an officer that there would be no tricks!"

"Superintendent Shaler, please," I snapped in reply. "A lecture on professional ethics is the last thing I need at the moment. If I told Torres the truth, he'd never leave Colón as long as he had a soldier capable of firing a rifle. A little white lie is a small price to pay for saving hundreds of lives, don't you think?"

Shaler was beyond thinking at this point. He merely stood there gazing numbly at me.

"Now, now, pull yourself together, Superintendent. Why don't you just run along and see about hiring the *Orinoco*, eh?"

With a visible effort, Shaler drew himself erect and headed for the Royal Mail offices. In a matter of minutes, the *tiradores* were forming into columns on Front Street and marching off in Shaler's wake. After a heated discussion with the agent for the British company, terms were arranged for the passage of Torres's troops. The gangplank of the *Orinoco* was lowered and the *tiradores* began streaming aboard, Colonel Torres in the lead to supervise the loading operation from the bridge.

Shaler was at my side on the dock when a stevedore called out, "Smoke on the horizon."

Then bells began ringing on the *Nashville* and semaphore flags began waving on her bridge. I didn't need to wait for the translation. "It's the *Dixie*," I said. "Torres just barely made it out."

When the last *tiradore* had gone aboard, two railroad employees appeared, each bearing a heavy canvas sack. One of them was Wardlaw, the cashier. Shaler cupped his hands and shouted up to Torres on the bridge. "There's four thousand dollars in each bag, Colonel. American twenty-dollar gold pieces."

Torres waved his acknowledgment and two stevedores took the bags from the railroad men and hurried them aboard. Then Henry and Kingston Jack appeared, bearing between them a heavy steamer trunk. Water trickled from the bottom of the trunk.

"What in the name of heaven is that?" whispered Shaler in alarm.

"It's Reyes, on ice. I promised to deliver him, didn't I?"

"Oh, my God," moaned Shaler. "What's Torres going to do when he finds out you're sending his nephew to him like that?"

"Nothing, as long as he makes that discovery at sea. What I want you to do right now, however, is to tell Torres that the trunk contains champagne. You know, a little bon voyage gift from you to him on behalf of the Panama Railroad."

"Champagne?" echoed Shaler, appalled.

I nodded firmly. "Tell him."

Shaler cupped his hands and shouted up to Torres, who shouted down his acceptance of this gift. Stevedores took the trunk from Henry and Kingston Jack and hefted it up the gangplank in the wake of the gold.

"What now?" hissed Shaler, panic rising in his voice. "Torres expects Reyes to walk up that gangplank, and that isn't going to happen. What's to keep him from ordering his men to gun us down where we stand?"

As he spoke, the *Dixie* steamed into the harbor and headed straight for the pier next to the *Orinoco*. As she docked, the threatening clouds finally opened and a deluge pelted the quay. The *tiradores* on the deck of the *Orinoco* pressed back from the rails to get under whatever cover they could find. I saw Colonel Torres cast a worried glance in the direction of the *Dixie* as hundreds of khaki-clad figures lined her rails in preparation for landing. He had never seen American marines up close before, and the sight of so many rough-and-ready fellows staring boldly back at him was an unsettling thing to behold.

"My nephew!" called Torres from the bridge. "Send him aboard!"

Shaler eyed me in desperation. "Travers, what in heaven's name do we do now?"

I was on my own, and I knew it. What happened in the next few seconds would determine whether the occupation of Colón was a quiet footnote in history or the biggest bloodbath since Custer's last stand. I turned and signaled down the waterfront to where Henry and Kingston Jack stood. Henry called out an order and a group of Kingston Jack's men appeared from a side street, marching a solitary figure toward the *Orinoco*. The figure wore the uniform of a Colombian *comandante,* the visor of his kepi shielding his face from Torres on the bridge of the *Orinoco*. "Let's go," I prompted Shaler quietly, and together we moved off in the direction of the approaching men. As we neared them, the escort of Antilleans halted, allowing the solitary Colombian to continue alone. I saw beneath the brim of the kepi the pockmarked face of a terrified private, the one I had captured back in the barn when I rescued the Wardlaws.

"Walk straight up the gangplank without a word or you're a dead man," I warned him as we passed.

The private nodded fearfully and kept walking. As he went, the sheets of rain redoubled in volume, nearly obliterating Torres's view of the scene. With Henry and Kingston Jack, I turned to watch the *Dixie*. Long files of marines were ashore now, some heading into the town to secure the streets and others marching in our direction behind an officer.

The Colombian private gained the slippery gangplank of the *Orinoco* and shakily made his way up to the deck. The gathered *tiradores,* who knew neither Reyes nor the private, snapped to and rendered salutes. Then the ship's whistle gave a great blast, the gangplank was raised, and the hawsers were cast off. The *Orinoco* swung into the rain-swept current and sailed away.

As the *Orinoco* receded in the distance, the commander of the marines splashed up to Shaler and rendered a snappy salute. "Major John Lejeune reporting, sir. My orders are to secure the city."

"Am I ever glad to see you, Major," said Shaler grinning with delight. "Very glad indeed. Thanks to Captain Travers here, though, I think your task is well in hand."

I extended a hand to Lejeune. "Welcome to Colón, Major."

Behind us the Antilleans and Americans were beginning to celebrate the victory, and cheering could be heard from all quarters as fearful residents emerged to learn that the nightmare was over.

"Captain Travers, eh?" said Lejeune. "I've heard a great deal about your exploits on Samar with Major Waller. The pleasure is all mine, sir."

I smiled at the compliment and said to Shaler, "Superintendent, I see that you're in good hands. Now, if you'll excuse me, I intend to duck out of this rain and get some rest. In the meantime, I would greatly appreciate it if you could book passage for Captain Longbottom and me back to the States. Now that Colonel Torres is gone, the real battle is about to begin."

"I'm sorry, Captain Travers, but I don't follow you. What battle are you referring to?" asked Lejeune, perplexed.

Shaler, however, knew exactly what I meant. "I'll arrange your passage on the first ship heading north, Captain Travers," promised Shaler. "I expect that a lot of people from Panama City will be wanting to go along with you."

"Stall them," I urged. "I need at least a day's head start."

"I'll try," Shaler promised, "but it'll be like wrestling with wildcats."

29

Washington, D.C.
18 November, 1903

Shaler was as good as his word. He arranged passage for me on a United
Fruit Company banana boat out of Bocas del Toro. The vessel's destination was the port of Baltimore, where she put in on November 12. From
Baltimore I telegraphed Alice with the news of my return and then caught
a train south to Washington. There Secretary Root arranged accommodations for me at the Willard. Also installed in the Willard, I learned, was
the envoy extraordinary and minister plenipotentiary from the new Republic
of Panama, namely Monsieur Bunau-Varilla.

As soon as Root was closeted with me in his office, he made it clear
that the Panamanians had no intention of allowing Bunau-Varilla to remain a minister very long. "A special commission departed Colón immediately after you left, Captain Travers. It consists of Dr. Amador, Fredrico
Boyd, and Carlos Arosemena. They sailed on the *City of Washington,* which
docked in New York earlier today."

"Then there isn't much time," I replied. "Does Bunau-Varilla know he
has visitors on the way?"

"Oh, yes. That's why he's holed up in his lodgings at this very moment
putting the final touches on a proposed canal treaty. If it's acceptable to
Hay, it will be signed and immediately submitted to the Senate for a vote."

"Securing passage may be a bit of a trick," I said. "If I recall correctly,
President Roosevelt said that the southern senators were dead set against
Panama and wanted a canal through Nicaragua instead. Bunau-Varilla will
have to pen a complete giveaway to appease them."

Here a sly look came over Root. "Yes, I suppose you're right on that
score, Captain Travers. That's why I planned to pay a little visit on Monsieur Bunau-Varilla. Now that you're here, though, I would be delighted
if you would accompany me."

On the short walk to the Willard, Root inquired about Longbottom. "Oh,
he was resting comfortably when I departed Colón, sir." I didn't bother

to add that when Longbottom had caught sight of the French hospital upon his return to town, he had thrown such a fit that it had been a cinch to convince Lejeune to clap him in irons once more. "I've been informed that he is to be moved to the military hospital at Charleston, South Carolina, to be near his family. Thankfully, his prognosis is good."

"I certainly hope so," replied Root. "He's such a promising young officer. I suppose, though, that the strains on him out in the jungle were simply unimaginable."

"It was a trial, all right," I assured him.

"I've been informed, Captain Travers, that Captain Longbottom owes you a large debt of gratitude for his very survival. I've had a wire from Major Black telling me how you led a party that rescued poor Longbottom from the Colombian army."

"Whatever I did for Captain Longbottom, sir, I did because of the type of fellow he is. I'm certain he would have served me the same had our roles been reversed."

Root gave me a look of stern admiration, for it was clear I was very much his sort of fellow. "Well said, Travers. Well said."

By then we had reached the Willard, and the hotel manager immediately took us in hand. He showed us to a suite of rooms directly down the hall from where Bunau-Varilla was at work. We waited there for perhaps a half hour when there came a knock on the door. When I opened it, the envoy extraordinary himself strode in.

"Ah, Captain Travers," Bunau-Varilla greeted me happily. "Please accept my congratulations on a very difficult job well done. The revolution could not have proceeded better had I been in Panama myself."

Bunau-Varilla was his usual humble self, I could see, but all I said in reply was, "I'm so very glad you see things that way," adding meaningfully, "and I hope you'll tell all your friends."

"Of course, *mon capitaine*," he assured me with a Gallic twirl of his mustache. "I shall sing your praises to one and all."

If Root caught anything in this exchange, he gave no hint of it. Instead he asked, "Do you have a draft of the treaty ready, *monsieur*?"

"*Oui*," replied Bunau-Varilla. "It is right here." He handed several carefully penned sheaves to Root. "I trust you will find everything to be satisfactory."

Root quickly scanned the document, with me peering over his shoulder. What I saw boggled my mind. Bunau-Varilla's proposed treaty, you see, would confer upon the United States a canal zone across the isthmus that was ten miles wide. I knew from my conversations with Amador and

Arango that they had been prepared to grant rights to a zone only six miles wide. Furthermore, Bunau-Varilla's treaty ceded virtual sovereignty to the United States within the canal zone, something that Amador would never have agreed to. Most importantly, however, was the fact that the lease to be conferred by Bunau-Varilla's draft was for a period of one hundred years, renewable at the option of the United States in perpetuity!

It was everything Roosevelt could have wanted and more. That this treaty as written would pass Congress was a dead certainty. I carefully cleared my throat and said as casually as my pounding heart would allow me, "Well, you seem to have hit all the major items of concern, Monsieur Bunau-Varilla."

"That is my opinion as well, Captain Travers," seconded Root jovially.

"Has Secretary Hay been kept apprised of any of this?" I asked Root.

He nodded. "Yes. An earlier draft was sent over to the State Department yesterday. It was returned to Monsieur Bunau-Varilla this morning with all of Secretary Hay's recommended changes. Isn't that so, sir?"

"It is exactly as you say, excellency," affirmed Bunau-Varilla. "The document you now hold may be considered final. It represents perfectly the understanding between my republic and the United States." Here the little bantam lost me for a second, for it took me a moment to realize that the republic to which he was referring was Panama, not France. "The treaty as you see it is ready to be signed."

"And the sooner the better," I said, when at that moment there came a knock on the door and a fellow in a silk hat and morning coat appeared. "Gentlemen, Secretary Root, please excuse the interruption," he said.

"Ah, Mr. Loomis." Nodding toward Bunau-Varilla and me, Root said, "I believe you've met my two companions before, isn't that so?"

"Yes, indeed. Monsieur Bunau-Varilla, Captain Travers, it's a pleasure as always."

When we had shook hands all around, Mr. Loomis announced, "Sir, Secretary Hay has instructed me to escort the honored minister from Panama to meet with him at his private residence. Both you and Captain Travers are invited as well."

"Splendid," replied Root with the buoyant air of a lawyer on the verge of settling a troublesome estate. "Gentlemen, shall we?"

With Bunau-Varilla clutching his handiwork, we followed Loomis out of the Willard and down Pennsylvania Avenue to Lafayette Square. We crossed the square to Hay's residence, a modest brick affair, where Loomis pulled the bell cord. He stepped aside to admit us when Hay's butler opened the portal, and the lot of us were ushered into a cluttered little study. Secretary Hay rose as we entered.

"Monsieur Bunau-Varilla," said Hay with a stiff bow, then gestured to a chair beside his desk. Root and I slipped in and took chairs that were arranged against a far wall. When everyone had been settled, Bunau-Varilla presented the proposed treaty to Hay, who studied it intently.

When Hay raised his head once more, Bunau-Varilla inquired tentatively, "Is everything in order, sir?"

"Yes, completely. I've already discussed these terms with President Roosevelt. He has informed me that this treaty in every respect meets his expectations. The president, Monsieur Bunau-Varilla, is extremely confident that it will be acceptable to Congress in its present form. He has instructed me to sign it on behalf of the United States."

Bunau-Varilla was quivering like a bird dog in a chicken coop and twirling his mustache wildly. Oh, he was delirious with joy for this moment represented the culmination of years of effort on his part to package Panama and sell her off to the highest bidder. I could see he was near to wetting his britches in exultation, and at Hay's pronouncement he croaked hoarsely, "Then shall we sign?"

Hay, though by nature a taciturn fellow, could barely suppress his own glee at the coup he was about to bring off. He all but winked at the preening Frenchman, and allowed with a smug little smile, "Why, I'd be delighted to, sir."

Quills were produced for the signing, but Root fished into his jacket and produced his elegant pen, the same one he had used when he made a note to send rifles to Panama. "John," he said to Hay, "if you would be so kind, I would like a memento of this historic occasion for my children."

Hay obliged him good-naturedly, signing his name with Root's pen and then handed it back. When he finished, he gave a quill to Bunau-Varilla, who immediately executed his signature with a grand flourish. Hay blew the ink dry, rose, and took Bunau-Varilla's hand. "On behalf of the United States, sir, I extend my best wishes to the Republic of Panama."

"On behalf of Panama, excellency, I thank you," replied Bunau-Varilla rapturously.

I took all this in with tongue in cheek, of course, but nonetheless I did have to give the devil his due. Bunau-Varilla was about the slickest snake-oil peddler I'd ever seen. Why, he had just bound Panama to an eternal treaty with Uncle Sam, and he wasn't even a citizen of the place!

Struggling with his emotions now that the great moment was upon him, Hay became expansive. "Let us not forget about the contributions of others to this supreme achievement," he said. "I think we would all agree that we might not be standing here at all but for the valiant efforts of Captain Travers."

I gave a little bob of the head at this and fixed a bluff expression on my face, the sort that I imagined might be appropriate for a certified snatcher of small states. "It was nothing, sir," I assured Hay gravely. "It was my great honor to be of service to my country in its hour of need."

"Then, gentlemen," announced Hay, "this business is done. If you'll excuse me, I must step across to the executive mansion to confer with the president."

"I'll be going with Secretary Hay, Captain Travers," Root said. "I trust you can find your way back to the Willard."

At the moment, however, the Willard wasn't where I wanted to be, and I told Root so. "Sir, if I may. I've been on extended service for some months now, and if you recall, my wedding was interrupted by this business back in the summer. If I may be so bold, sir, I request that I be allowed a few weeks' leave. I'd like to go to New York to be with my fiancée."

Root looked to Hay, who nodded. "Very well, Captain," agreed Root. "Telegraph when you arrive in New York. Hold yourself available there should I need to contact you."

Now Bunau-Varilla spoke up. "Allow me to be of assistance, Captain Travers. After all, I am in your debt for the great service you have rendered Panama. It would be my great privilege to make my carriage available to take you to the station."

"Why, that would be most kind of you, sir," I readily agreed. In no time we had walked back to the Willard for my things and then gone to the station, where Bunau-Varilla took my arm and escorted me to the ticket office. There I learned that the next train to New York would depart in just a few minutes.

"Let me see you to your train," Bunau-Varilla insisted.

"By all means, Phil."

Bunau-Varilla loosed a proper little titter at this, proclaiming himself an ardent admirer of my Yankee informality. I laughed right along with him, and off we went, seemingly the best of friends content to enjoy each other's company. In truth, I rapidly discovered that it was exceedingly difficult to tolerate Bunau-Varilla for any length of time. He went on and on about his canal achievement, and what a swell fellow he was and so forth until I concluded that he was composing his memoirs in his head and trying them out on me to gauge the effect. The effect, to be blunt, was wearisome, and the only thing that kept a civil tongue in my head was the knowledge that this whole business was behind me. I had upheld my part of the bargain, by God, and now the Panama Railroad stock was mine to enjoy. Given the wild inflation in value it had undergone since word of the revolution flashed back to the States, there was no question that in a very short time I'd be damned near financially independent.

All this meant that I was still smiling as Bunau-Varilla guided me to my train. I pretended to pay his ramblings the closest attention, and was doing such a good job of it that I barely noticed when the arriving train from New York rolled to a stop a short distance away and began disgorging its passengers. Then, however, I froze in horror. Glaring directly at us were Amador, Fredrico Boyd, and Arosemena!

"Holy Moses!"

Bunau-Varilla followed my shocked gaze. "*Merde!*" he gasped just as the furious trio caught sight of us and stormed over.

"Señor Bunau-Varilla," Amador shrieked as he came on. "Why have you not answered our many cables? You were instructed to sign nothing and to wait in New York until our arrival. Why are you here? Have you disobeyed our orders?"

"Cables? Orders? I know of no such things. The last communication I received from Panama was your cable wisely appointing me minister."

"You lie, you French dog!" sputtered Boyd.

Bunau-Varilla drew himself up to his full height, which was somewhere around my elbow. "You call me a liar, sir? I beg to remind you that at all times I have conducted myself with the strictest regard for the interests of the Republic of Panama."

Amador's eyes narrowed, for he knew enough about Bunau-Varilla to realize he'd have to pry the facts from the wily Frenchman. "Then tell us precisely how you have conducted yourself. Have you had any meetings with the American government?"

Bunau-Varilla's reply was imperious, condescending. "Of course, *Docteur.* Such is a necessary duty of an envoy, *non*?"

"Documents," demanded Boyd. "Have you signed any documents with the Americans?"

"Well . . ." began Bunau-Varilla, struggling for just the right way to lay his fait accompli before the Panamanians. "The Republic of Panama is henceforth under the protection of the United States. I have just signed the Canal Treaty."

Now Amador was shaking with rage. "The terms," he managed to spit out. "What are the terms?"

Bunau-Varilla faltered in the face of Amador's wrath, and for the first time since I had made his acquaintance I saw the Frenchman actually at a loss for words. The best he could manage was a lame, "The terms? Why, er, hmmm. The terms, you say? Let me think, *monsieur,* let me think."

I couldn't suppress a grin as I watched him twist in the wind before me. He knew perfectly well that the truth would not go over well with the already exercised Panamanians. Seeing Bunau-Varilla standing there as if suddenly stricken dumb, Amador turned to me.

"Captain Travers, you are a military man, a man of honor. You and I have stood shoulder to shoulder in the cause of freedom. I call upon you, sir, to disclose here and now the terms of any treaty executed by Monsieur Bunau-Varilla with your country."

Since my take from this escapade was now secure, I no longer needed Bunau-Varilla or the Panamanians. That meant I could indulge in some uncharacteristic candor, and I took full advantage of the opportunity. "Boys, your esteemed minister here is just too modest to announce all the good news himself. Since you asked me, though, I'll lay it right out for you. On behalf of the great nation of Panama, Monsieur Bunau-Varilla has just signed over a canal zone ten miles wide to the United States of America."

Arosemena's eyes flew wide in astonishment. "Ten miles wide? *¡Dios mío!*"

Amador, too, blanched at Bunau-Varilla's largesse. "My God, what have you done, señor? Have you sold us out? We are the ones who took all the risks and faced all the danger while you sat in New York safe and sound."

Bunau-Varilla was a schemer and a manipulator, all right, but he could be a scrapper if he thought his honor was being impugned. "I did not flinch from my duty!" he shrilled in his own defense. "I would have gladly shed my blood for my adopted country if only I wasn't needed elsewhere to assure the success of the revolution."

"What about sovereignty?" demanded Boyd angrily, monumentally unimpressed with Bunau-Varilla's histrionics. "What does the treaty say about sovereignty?"

Bunau-Varilla's uneasiness was rapidly yielding to rising panic; his great show of indignation had failed to quell in the slightest the emotions of the Panamanians. Their anger was manifest, and what he had to say about sovereignty could be the thing that pushed them completely over the edge.

"Well, you all must appreciate, *mes amis,* that the issue of sovereignty had to be addressed," Bunau-Varilla hedged uncomfortably. "Sovereignty was and remains the premier concern of the Americans. In all fairness, it is only their gunboats that will save you from a vengeful Bogotá."

"Bogotá is a hag with dry tits," spat Boyd. "What we fear now are the *yanquis* and you. Now, answer the question, *monsieur*."

Bunau-Varilla, however, was reduced to bug-eyed silence. A straight answer to Boyd's question, he was certain, would virtually guarantee violence. In all his years of chicanery and questionable dealing, he had never had to endure a physical assault. At the moment, though, he had one staring him full in the face, and the thought unmanned him.

As for me, a little set-to meant nothing. Besides, these fellows didn't appear to be packing any shooting irons. What was more, I relished the opportunity to take Bunau-Varilla down a peg or two, and so I reared back and gave the Panamanians the information they hungered for. "He handed over everything, boys. Sovereignty in the canal zone will reside exclusively with Uncle Sam. Yep, the place will be as American as Ohio, and if that's not okay with you, well, too bad."

Amador gasped and sagged against Arosemena, clutching at his heart. Boyd sprang straight for Bunau-Varilla's throat, causing the Frenchman to loose a shriek of pure bloody murder. I stepped back as Bunau-Varilla and Boyd tussled wildly on the platform. Down they went, with Arosemena piling on top, when a conductor bellowed, "All aboard to New York!"

I deftly made my way clear of the struggle and doffed my hat in farewell. "Gentlemen, I must be off. It's been such a joy to meet each of you again."

I hurried to the nearest car and took a seat just as the train pulled away from the station. My last glimpse of Panama's first official delegation to America was a spectacle I shall long remember. As I watched, Boyd hauled back and delivered a huge openhanded smack to the nose of the extraordinary envoy and minister plenipotentiary.

"Take that, you little cockroach!" he screamed.

The blow bloodied Bunau-Varilla and he cried out in pain and terror. "Police! *Au secours!* Police!"

The red torrent that gushed forth from Bunau-Varilla's snout told me that the little upstart had at last attained the honor he insisted he so fervently desired. That is, he finally had the opportunity to shed his blood for Panama.

30

"Fenny, I'm simply thrilled," sighed Alice. "I had no idea when, or even if, you would return."

"There, there, my love," I soothed her, patting her soft shoulder and giving her a little peck on her red lips, which she hungrily returned. "All that matters is that I'm back now, and here I'll remain for a good long time."

"I'm so glad," she beamed contentedly. "As for the wedding ceremony, well, all my plans went out the window last August, but I haven't given up. No, I aim to get you before an altar yet, Fenwick Travers."

"Then I'm surely lost," I said with a look of feigned resignation.

"Yes you are, and I warn you, don't try to slip away on me again. This time I mean business. Why, I've already started looking for a suitable church. Uncle George is helping me, too, but he says it will take at least a month."

That was fine with me. In fact, sweet Alice could take two months or two years if she needed them. All that mattered was that I had her once more and I was safely out of the line of fire. Beyond that, if Alice demanded a church wedding as her price for her eternal availability, by God, marriage vows before a preacher she would have. Her announcement, though, seemed to demand some sort of encouraging response from me, so I murmured obligingly, "Every moment will be sweet bliss as I await that blessed day."

That did the trick, for she melted into my arms at once. "Oh, Fenny, I do love you so," she sighed and offered up her lips for yet another kiss.

I took it, of course, and several more, for we were quite alone, and no interruption was at all likely. We were on the divan in my suite just upstairs from Sherry's at Fifth Avenue and 44th Street. The digs had been arranged by Bet-a-Million Gates as a little welcome home gift. It was a cozy nest for my trysts with dear Alice, which I squeezed in with regularity between my bouts at the gambling tables at Canfield's Clubhouse just a few doors away on 44th Street. The New York club was Canfield's winter base of operations when Saratoga was abandoned by the summer crowd.

Life was indeed delightful since my return from Washington. As for money, well, I had convinced Gates to let me borrow against the expected appreciation of my railroad stock. In addition, I had been holding my own at Canfield's tables. All in all, I was as comfortable as I ever had been in this life, and I looked forward to whiling away the winter nights in Alice's company.

When she at last came up for air, Alice continued on without missing a beat. "As for the honeymoon, Newport is really not appropriate in December, Fenny. I think we should go south instead, don't you agree?"

"Just as long as we don't go back to Panama," I said laughing. Alice giggled too, which quickly led to another round of bussing and fond groping. We were making a merry old time of it when Alice suddenly remembered something.

Holding me at arm's length, she said, "I received a letter from Uncle George today. He's still out in Arizona, you know, checking on his mines or some such thing. Anyway, he heard that you had returned from Panama, and he dashed off a note to you. He enclosed it in a letter to me but instructed that I was not to read it. It's just for your eyes, but he hinted that it had to do with whatever the two of you were discussing back in Sycamore last summer."

She handed over a small envelope, which I quickly tore open. Duncan had laboriously typed out his message on the tiniest sheets of paper imaginable, really no more than note cards. I was certain that their size was related somehow to saving a few pennies, and I laughed at the thought as I began reading. I hadn't gotten far, though, before the smile was gone from my face.

My Dear Captain Travers,

My felicitations on your surviving the wilds of Panama. Knowing you as I do, I expect that your first order of business will be to collect your prize, my darling Alice. I realize that I cannot stop her from marrying you, and I won't try. Instead, I will make your victory a hollow one. I want you to know that upon the advice of my attorney, Mr. Cromwell of Sullivan and Cromwell, I have taken all necessary steps to disestablish Alice's trust, effective the 11th of

Here the first page ended. As I reached for the next one, I felt a surge of concern mixed with triumph. Concern, of course, because I had no idea that Duncan's lawyer was Cromwell. Why triumph, though, you might ask? The reason was simple; I had seen Duncan's move coming and I had already acted to forestall it. Back in October when I had returned from Washington with Bunau-Varilla and slipped away to see Alice, I convinced her to marry me before a justice of the peace, secretly, of course. I told her that we could have a proper ceremony when I returned, but in the interim we would be man and wife. Alice, the dear, sweet puss, had agreed at once, and a marriage license with our names on it had been duly issued. Since her trust existed at the time of the marriage, it was Alice's now and there was not a damned thing Duncan could do about it. I had beaten him at his own game, I crowed silently! Or at least so I thought until I read the second page of Duncan's missive.

> October 1903. You may wonder at the date. It happens to be the day that my butler, Gilbert, informed me of the events leading to the deposition of a load of manure on my walkway. I directed Mr. Cromwell to do a bit of investigating immediately. He found your marriage license at City Hall, unfiled at the time, and advised me to void the trust, which I did that very day. The question of whether or not I acted in time could keep legions of lawyers employed should the matter be litigated. Do you care to try my hand?

> > Regards,
> > George Duncan

I must have paled noticeably, for Alice became concerned. "Fenny, what is it? Is everything all right with Uncle George?"

"Oh, yes, just fine," I managed to reply, crumpling the note and dropping it into my pocket. "Your uncle just wanted to, er, send me his regards, and to let me know that I had been very much on his mind."

"Oh, that is so like dear Uncle George. It has been one of the greatest joys of my life that the two of you have gotten along as well as you have."

"Well," I smiled wanly, "we certainly are birds of a feather."

Alice, though, was curious about what else Uncle George had to say and was just in the act of asking me precisely that when a knock came on the door.

"Captain Travers, open up. It's Secretary Root."

I was on my feet at once. Root? What the devil was he doing here? All my instincts cried that here was trouble, but just what sort I couldn't imagine. Warily, I opened the door.

Root was in with the sort of nimble hop that even a veteran brush salesman could not have bettered. Seeing Alice, he gave a courtly bow and said, "Charmed, ma'am."

"Sir, this is Alice Brenoble, my wi—er, my fiancée." I added pointedly, "We were just discussing our wedding plans, sir, the ones that were interrupted so abruptly last summer."

Root look pained at this but didn't offer to leave. Instead he asked, "Captain Travers, is there someplace we could talk?"

"Whatever you have to say to me, sir, you can say in front of Alice," I insisted.

Root was adamant. "No, I can't do that, Captain."

Alice, though, was not to be easily shunted aside. "You must tell me, Mr. Root, are you here to send Fenny away again?"

Root saw that there was no use in lying to her, since she seemed to sense the truth anyway. "Yes, I'm afraid so, Miss Brenoble. Captain Travers must leave the country at once. He will be gone for some time."

"Out of the country?" I shouted. "But why? And more importantly, where am I going?"

"The where I can answer," replied Root. "You are to report to our military mission in Tokyo in the Empire of Japan. You will proceed as soon as transport can be arranged. As for the why, I'm afraid I'm not at liberty to divulge that in the present company. It can be discussed only between you and me."

"Japan?" gasped Alice. "Why, that's all the way around the world."

Root nodded grimly.

Alice made up her mind at once. "Then I shall go with him. I don't care if I have to be shipped in a steamer trunk. I won't allow us to be separated again. That's my final word on the matter."

She rose and headed for the door. "Fenny, you stay where I can find you. You're not escaping me again," she vowed, and planting her bonnet firmly on her head, she strode purposefully from the suite.

When the door closed, I turned to Root. "Just what's going on here?" I demanded. "I'm not due to go overseas; after all, I just got back from Panama."

"That's exactly the point," retorted Root. "This Panama business has taken a nasty turn in the press. The major dailies were quiet after the revolution because they were too distracted with election results from across the nation. That was the reason Teddy seconded that date in the first place. He thought he could manage the press after the fact, you see. His plan was to explain the thing to the American public in terms that would mollify his critics and hold embarrassing questions to a minimum. Unfortunately, the situation has started to get out of hand."

"But what has any of this got to do with me?" I asked uncertainly.

"The dailies are having a field day with what they call Roosevelt's 'big stick' imperialism, Travers. They don't buy his story that the United States had nothing to do with the revolution. They insist there are too many trails that lead back to the White House. One of those trails, unfortunately, is you."

"Me? Why, the president needn't worry on that score. I'll never talk."

"Perhaps," said Root dubiously, "but even if you don't, your whereabouts over the past several months are enough to raise questions about the army's involvement in Panama. The president has decided it would be in the best interests of the country if you were not, er, available for the foreseeable future."

"Best interests of the country? Why, that's hogwash and you know it," I railed, adding only grudgingly, "sir. What you mean is that my presence is inconvenient to Roosevelt for political reasons. That's why I'm to be hied off to the wilds of Asia, isn't it?"

Root, a veteran of a dozen bruising political battles, was unapologetic in the face of my accusation. "Yes, that's it in a nutshell, Captain. You're going to Japan and I'll brook no argument on the point."

I had but one ace in the hole, and I played it shamelessly. "But what about my wedding?" I implored. "Poor Alice has been stymied once before on that score, and now it looks like the same thing is about to happen again. Doesn't the president care about a young girl's tender heart?"

"Marry her before a justice of the peace, and then be on your way. As soon as you're settled, I'll arrange for her to join you in Japan."

Since I had already done exactly that, there seemed to be nothing further to say. From the stern look in Root's calculating eyes, I knew there would be no appealing his decision. "I'll, er, need a few days to get my affairs in order. There are, well, various papers I need to attend to."

Root saw right through me. "Captain Travers, I know all about the railroad stock."

I started involuntarily at this revelation and immediately began to take evasive action. "Stock? Whatever are you talking about, sir? I have no knowledge of any—"

Root held up his hand to stop me. "Captain, please. I have as many contacts within the Panama Railroad as does Mr. Cromwell. Don't forget, I was a New York lawyer long before I became the secretary of war. Now, I want to make myself perfectly clear on this point. I don't object to your arrangement with Cromwell and his associates. Oh, I would have appreciated knowing about your little deal before I advised that Monsieur Bunau-Varilla be brought to the White House, but that's all water under the bridge. Besides, when I was your age, I invested quite briskly, and I found that the greatest rewards came with the greatest risks. I'm certain that your railroad stock will net you a tidy return in time, and I don't begrudge you your profit. All I'm saying, Captain Travers, is that for the near future, there can be no connection whatsoever between you and that stock."

"No connection? What exactly are you saying?"

"I'm arranging to have your holdings put in a trust that will shield its true ownership from public scrutiny for a period of time. In fact, the certificates have already been transferred from your bank."

"But how did you even know where they were?" I asked, dumbfounded at the extent of Root's knowledge.

"When Agent McAllister dropped you by the Nassau Bank before your initial trip to Panama, that fact was reported to me. When I later heard rumblings about the stock deal, I was able to make an educated guess about where the certificates might be located. Yesterday, at the request of the attorney general of the United States, certain court documents were handed down here in New York. Those papers authorized agents of the War Department to search your safety-deposit box."

Damn—I was cleaned out, and all nice and legal too from the sound of it. Something Root had said, however, gave me hope. "You mentioned that I was to have no connection with the stock for the near future. Might I ask, sir, exactly how long a period of time are you thinking about holding onto my property?"

Root shrugged. "That depends on too many political imponderables for me to even hazard a guess. I'd say at least five years, maybe as long as ten."

Five years! Why, the stock was as good as gone for all practical purposes, I thought bitterly. I'd done my duty in Panama, and for what? Only Cromwell, Bunau-Varilla, and of course Roosevelt had come out ahead in the game.

Root drew out his timepiece and glanced at it. "Ready for lunch?" he asked. "I've arranged for a table downstairs in Sherry's. Won't you join me?"

"I hope the tab is on you," I said sourly. "I'm a little short at the moment."

"Come now, Captain. Don't be so glum. This is but a minor setback in what I would venture to say will prove to be a career filled with many opportunities for remuneration. But, er, do me a favor and change into civilian clothing, won't you? I want you to start being as inconspicuous as possible. If anyone asks who you are, tell them you're a clerk from the War Department."

In a foul mood, I did as Root bid and followed him down to the dining room. At the sight of him, the maître d' fluttered to our side and showed us to a table with an excellent view of the entire room. It was the noon hour, and Sherry's was well on its way to becoming packed as usual. Many of the most famous and infamous figures in town were arriving to enjoy the fare and, more importantly, to be seen.

Among these were lawyers and judges who quickly started an impromptu parade to our table to shake Root's hand and put in a plug for a client or some project or another. The parade became a stampede, and I was all but forgotten as Root was engulfed in a sea of fawning supplicants. Some wanted federal judgeships, others wanted contracts with the War Department, and, oh, wouldn't the secretary please secure an appointment to West Point for a deserving nephew? Their needs were endless, but none of them concerned me in the least. I was bored and angry at the same time, and as I sipped listlessly at a colorless broth placed before me by a waiter, I damned both Duncan and Root in equal measure.

A sudden sheen of light from across the room caught my eye. I looked up to see Diamond Jim Brady at a table in the company of two lovelies. Seeing that he had my attention, Jim made his way ponderously over to my table. "Welcome back, Fenny," he hailed me. "I've been reading the papers. They're mighty interesting nowadays." He gave me a big wink and handed me a huge Havana. The jurists besieging Root looked curiously at the "clerk" to whom Diamond Jim was paying court, but they said nothing. "I wanted to thank you for what you did for Chickamauga," Brady continued. "That horse meant the world to me, and I just wanted to say I'm much obliged, pal."

"You're more than welcome, Jim," I replied. "I'm just sorry the colt is gone."

"Oh, but he's not entirely gone," Jim corrected me.

"Not gone? But I was there, Jim," I insisted. "I saw the whole thing."

"Oh, sure he's dead, Fenny, but he's not gone. You see, I decided to go Marcus Daly one better."

What the devil was he talking about? I wondered. "I'm not sure I'm with you, Jim."

Brady roared with hilarity at my bewilderment. "Why, I had him stuffed, Fenny! Chickamauga is smack-dab in the middle of the foyer of my town house. I see him every day of the week."

I laughed despite my troubles. "Well, well. Good for you, Jim. Good for you."

Brady, though, had other news for me. He leaned down and whispered into my ear, "There's someone else here whom you know, Fenny." He nodded off into a corner where a sinister face was looking my way. It was Rothstein and a crowd of his cronies. They were all staring nervously in my direction. "Rothstein had no idea you'd be here today, Fenny," explained Brady. "He was having lunch when you walked in, and there was no way for him to escape without your noticing. He's been like a scalded cat since that night up in Saratoga."

"Good," I grunted. "My only regret is that I didn't finish the rodent while I had the chance."

"Be that as it may, Fenny, there's more I have to tell you." Here Brady paused to make sure he wasn't being overheard before continuing in a hushed voice. "Rothstein has gotten into boxing in a big way since Saratoga. He arranges fights all over the East Coast now. In fact, there's a barge fight tonight on the East River. The favorite is getting three-to-one odds."

I looked searchingly at Jim. "But he's going to lose, isn't he?"

Almost imperceptibly, Brady nodded. "That was the plan, Fenny, until you showed up. You see, Rothstein doesn't want to be around if you lose money to one of his schemes."

"What are you saying, Jim?"

"Expect him to ask your permission to put in the fix—and when he does, make him cut you in."

I laid a finger alongside my nose. "Thanks, Jim," I said gratefully.

Brady gave me a clap on the shoulder and waddled back to his table. As if on cue, one of Rothstein's retainers—a thin, weedy fellow in a chalk-striped suit—rose and approached me.

"Er, Captain Travers?" he inquired diffidently.

Root eyed the fellow casually but then turned to hear a probate judge make a pitch for finding a berth for his son somewhere in the bowels of the War Department.

"Yes?" I answered.

"Well, Mr. Rothstein was wondering if—"

"I know all about it," I said, cutting him off.

"And what do you say, Captain?"

He had been sent to get an answer, and I saw he was prepared to stand there until he received one. As he waited, Rothstein looked on anxiously, and I found myself relishing the bastard's discomfiture. Here he was, the uncrowned king of the New York underworld, reduced to seeking my permission to run a scam—and all because I turned into a wild man when I got a Colt in my hand. I could have said no and rubbed Rothstein's nose in the dirt, I suppose. I didn't, though, for here was an opportunity to make some easy money, a scarce commodity at the moment. After all, hadn't Brady said the odds on the favorite were three to one? That meant, of course, a tidy profit for whoever wagered on the underdog. The only problem was that I had no money to put on anyone.

"Here's my answer," I decided at length. "The event can proceed, but on one condition."

"Which is?" asked the messenger, suspicion in his voice.

"That Rothstein take my personal check and place a bet for me on the underdog."

Rothstein's man didn't blink an eye at my demand. He knew that I was asking for free money, but then Rothstein expected to make plenty of lucre tonight. "How much?" was all he said.

I leaned forward and whispered, "Five thousand dollars." That represented nearly three years' salary for me. If I got my payoff in cash and somehow slipped it past Root's confiscatory minions, I just might land on my feet after all.

"Done."

I took out my checkbook and prepared to write a draft. My Nassau Bank holdings were gone, all my army pay had long ago been spent, and the borrowings on my stock were about depleted. Any check of mine wouldn't be worth the paper it was written on. None of this slowed me a whit; turning to Root, I asked, "Excuse me, Mr. Secretary, but might I borrow your pen?"

Root, now in the middle of a discussion on the legal intricacies of trust-busting with a very overweight barrister, nodded distractedly and produced the same pen used to sign the Hay-Bunau-Varilla Treaty. I took it and merrily wrote out my worthless draft. I handed it over to the flunky, who made a beeline back to his master. Rothstein took a look at the check and then nodded at me. We had a deal.

I capped Root's pen and discreetly dropped it into my pocket. "Oh, waiter," I called, snapping my fingers. "Wine please. Pommard 1884, and be quick about it."